LITERARY CHARLESTON:
A LOWCOUNTRY READER

LITERARY CHARLESTON:
A LOWCOUNTRY READER

Edited and with an Introduction by
Curtis Worthington

Foreword by
Louis D. Rubin, Jr.

Wyrick & Company

Published by
Wyrick & Company
Post Office Box 89
Charleston, S.C. 29402

Printed in the United States of America

Library of Congress Cataloging-in-Publication Data

Literary Charleston : a lowcountry reader / edited with an
  introduction by Curtis Worthington ; foreword by Louis D.
  Rubin, Jr.
        p.   cm.
  Includes bibliographical references and index.
  ISBN 0-941711-17-X (alk. paper)
  1. American literature--South Carolina--Charleston.
  2. American literature--South Carolina--Charleston Region.
  3. Charleston Region (S.C.)--Literary collections.
  4. Charleston (S.C.)--Literary collections. I.Worthington,
  Curtis, 1951-   .
  PS559.C5L58 1996
  810.8'032757915--dc20   96-13696

Cover: *Charleston—The Celebrated Southern Port
Over the Rooftops in 1870* by John Stobart.
Reproduced by permission of the artist.

For Suzanne and Cecelia
Southern Sisters

CONTENTS

Foreword   xi

Acknowledgements   xv

Introduction   xix

Prologue

William Bartram
    from *The Travels of William Bartram*   3

The Charleston School

Paul Hamilton Hayne
    Aspects of the Pines   7
    Laocoon   8
    Magnolia Gardens   8

William Gilmore Simms
    The Edge of the Swamp   9
    Ephraim Bartlett, the Edisto Raftsman   12

Henry Timrod
    Charleston   27
    The Cotton Boll   28
    Ode. Sung on the Occasion of Decorating
        the Graves of the Confederate Dead, at
        Magnolia Cemetery, Charleston, S.C.,
        1867.   33

Sea Island Lore

William Elliott
    A Day at Chee-ha   37

Edgar Allan Poe
    The Gold Bug   44

Early Twentieth Century Influences

Henry James
    from *The American Scene*   85

Amy Lowell
    Charleston. South Carolina   92
    The Middleton Place   93
    Epitaph In A Churchyard In Charleston,
       South Carolina   94

Owen Wister
    from *Lady Baltimore*   95

The Poetry Society of South Carolina in the 1920s

Hervey Allen
    Alchemy   105

John Bennett
    The Wandering Minstrel's Song   106

DuBose Heyward
    Dusk   107
    Buzzard Island   108

Josephine Pinckney
    Sea-Drinking Cities   109
    Hag   110

Beatrice Witte Ravenel
    Tidewater   111
    The Pirates   113
    The Yemassee Lands   120

"Renaissance" Charleston and Beyond

John Bennett
    Madame Margot   125

John Galsworthy
A Hedonist 142

DuBose Heyward
from *Porgy* 150

Ludwig Lewisohn
from *The Case of Mr. Crump* 166

Rafael Sabatini
from *The Carolinian* 175

Herbert Ravenel Sass
Carolina Marshes 191

Contemporary Poetry

James Dickey
The Salt Marsh 203
Slave Quarters 204

August Kleinzahler
Longitude Lane 210

Nick Lindsay
Pilot Boat 211
Poem 212

Wendy Salinger
Seasmoke 214
Charleston, South Carolina, 7 P.M. 216

Contemporary Prose

Pat Conroy
from *The Prince of Tides* 221

Shelby Foote
from *The Civil War: A Narrative* 239

William Price Fox
Coley Moke 251
Monck's Corner 259

Harlan Greene
    from *Why We Never Danced
        the Charleston*   262

Josephine Humphreys
    from *Rich in Love*   276

Nick Lindsay
    from *An Oral History of Edisto Island:
        Sam Gadsden Tells the Story*   293
    from *An Oral History of Edisto Island:
        The Life and Times of Bubberson Brown*   313

Walker Percy
    from *The Last Gentleman*   315

Padgett Powell
    from *Edisto*   323

Louis D. Rubin, Jr.
    Finisterre   330

Epilogue

Andy Warhol
    Love (Prime)   363

Selected Bibliography   369

Index   379

FOREWORD

What is there to the city of Charleston, South Carolina, that makes so many people write about it? By any ratio of *per capita* population to total number of words on the printed page, Charleston must surely be among the more intensely chronicled cities in the United States.

To attempt to collect everything that has been written about Charleston, or even merely those writings of a literary nature, as distinct from journalism, sociology, political analysis or whatever, would be a formidable assignment. For better or for worse, prose and poetry that takes Charleston for its inspiration has been produced with the regularity of those Clyde-Mallory liners that for generations provided thrice-weekly service between the city and other Atlantic seaboard ports. The coastal passenger ships have long since disappeared, but the application of literary craft to the city not only continues but has gained both in quantity and—with the advent of Josephine Humphreys on the local literary scene—in excellence as well.

Curtis Worthington set out in this book to assemble, from among the formidable trove of eligible literary work, representative writings that importantly involve Charleston and the Carolina Lowcountry. Dating from the late eighteenth century to our own juncture at the close of the twentieth, the selections are essentially of two kinds: those written by noted visitors to the city, and those by resident authors.

The former, whose ranks include Edgar Allan Poe, Henry James, Amy Lowell, Owen Wister, John Galsworthy, and Walker Percy, were sufficiently impressed with the locale itself to wish to recreate it in its own right. Charleston, Amy Lowell declared, "has more poetic appeal than almost any city in America"—this from a resident of

Boston! Even Poe, who habitually set his fiction in imaginary places "out of SPACE—out of TIME," was so taken with the tangible reality of harbor and land that the onetime U.S. Army sergeant, stationed for a time at Fort Moultrie, did what otherwise he almost never did: he set "The Gold Bug" specifically and identifiably in a known American place. So much so, indeed, that it is quite possible, from the description of the treasure hunters' route, to trace their approximate path across the harbor to Sullivans Island, through the marsh and up the creek, and onto the mainland to the east of Mount Pleasant.

As for the numerous local authors, Charlestonians whether by birth or by adoption, their topography is not only geographical but of the spirit as well. From William Gilmore Simms and Henry Timrod of antebellum and Confederate days, to DuBose Heyward and Beatrice Ravenel in the 1920s, and nowadays Josephine Humphreys, the urge to write has involved the need to explore one's identity in and through the relationship to the community. Heyward even went so far as to declare lyrically that "these my songs, my all, belong to" his native city. For Simms and Humphreys (and very likely for Heyward as well) the motivation would appear to be rather more complicated. But whoever the Charleston writer may be and whatever the nature of his or her formal linkage to the city, the literary evocation of the place is almost taken for granted, never a mere convenience of plausible setting. Inevitably it is made to matter profoundly.

I do not envy Curtis Worthington the task of selecting which writings, from among so many possible choices, should be contained in this book. There was so much there, with strong claims for inclusion. One's own choices might in some instances have been different. But beyond doubt he has assembled a remarkably interesting book, offering a Lowcountry literary harvest of generous and striking dimensions. There can be no question about it: the place has a way of seizing the imagination, compelling a response to its pervasive immanence. It can be loved, it can be hated;

there can be some of both in one's reaction; but it cannot be ignored.

Visitors to Charleston—and nowadays they arrive in throngs not only during the garden season but all year around—will enjoy matching up what others have made of the place with their own responses. Residents and ex-residents will experience the thrill of watching what is local and familiar take on the intensity and strangeness of the artistic image. An intelligent, informative introduction by the editor sets the stage historically for this fascinating literary visit to a unique American city.

LOUIS D. RUBIN, JR.

ACKNOWLEDGEMENTS

For their contributions to the production of this volume, grateful acknowledgement is made by the editor to the following: John Bennett, Jane Brown, Suzanne Crews, Jennie Fant, Gene Furchgott, Anne Hanahan, Nona Hastie, Amy Worthington Hauslohner, Teri Lynn Herbert, Steve Hoffius, Buddy Jenrette, Teddy Lesesne, Nick Lindsay, Cheri Lovell, Betty Newsom, Dee Rhodes, Michael C. Robertson, Louis D. Rubin, Jr., Jane Shealy, Lamar Smith, W.C. Worthington, Jr., Pete Wyrick, John Ziegler, and especially Jane Tyler, my loving wife, who supported me and patiently tolerated the complaints as it unfolded. Without their help, this book would not have been possible. Any errors of omission or commission, however, are the editor's alone.

For permission to use the following, the editor is grateful:
The Travels of William Bartram, Naturalist's Edition. Edited with commentary and an annotated index by Francis Harper. New Haven: Yale University Press, 1958.
"Aspects of the Pines" by Paul Hamilton Hayne and "The Edge of the Swamp" by William Gilmore Simms from *Southern Writing 1585-1920* Edited by Richard Beale Davis, C. Hugh Holman, Louis D. Rubin, Jr. New York: The Odyssey Press, 1970.
"Laocoon" and "Magnolia Gardens" from *Poems of Paul Hamilton Hayne.* Boston: D. Lothrop and Company, 1882.
"Ephraim Bartlett, The Edisto Raftsman" from *The Writings of William Gilmore Simms: Centennial Edition, Volume V, Stories and Tales.* Columbia: University of South Carolina Press, 1974.
Poems of Henry Timrod with Memoir and Portrait. Boston and New York: Houghton, Mifflin Company, 1899.
"A Day at Chee-Ha" from *Carolina Sports by Land and*

INTRODUCTION

Consider the relationship between a real place and the representation of that place in fiction. Fiction, indeed all creative writing, subverts geographic realities to its own purpose, creating a particular relationship between the literal place of experience and the experience of that place through imaginative language. The literal place, present in the created world of the imaginative work, is a place transfigured: the mundane face of reality transposed to another plane.

How does one transpose the reality of Charleston and the Lowcountry—of the unique place that has served as a source of inspiration to the generations of writers and artists who have experienced it?

One describes the smell of the salt air and the "pluff" mud, the wisteria and Confederate jasmine; the languorous atmosphere of sea breeze and humidity; the landscape of moss-covered oaks, magnolia, palmetto, oleander and cypress.

One draws a picture of a school of bottle-nosed dolphins playing alongside the departing shrimp boat, or the deep-sea fishing boat returning with its catch of king mackerel, tuna and wahoo; the appearance at dawn of an alligator, a snowy egret or great blue heron in a tidal creek; the creekman in his johnboat seeking shrimp, crabs or oysters.

One records the voice of the "crabman" (sadly, now silent) pulling his cart through narrow streets past single houses south of Broad; the song of musicians (happily, still here) practicing or performing in the same streets during the Spoleto Festival; the night music of the cicadas and whippoorwills; the Gullah language and the quaint mispronunciations of French Huguenot names.

One captures the beauty of St. Michael's spire, the formal gardens and piazzas, the sailing regattas in the harbor, the dark swamps of Berkeley County and the white sand of the barrier island beaches.

All play a part in the imagery, in a geography that is lush, sensuous and tropical—full of brooding mystery and inescapable romance.

The literary heritage of Charleston and the South Carolina Lowcountry was born in the earliest days of the city. Founded in 1670, Charleston quickly became the leading center of politics, commerce and culture in the colonial South. From its inception, the city was marked by a great cultural diversity which included Europeans of Spanish, French and English descent, native Americans indigenous to the region, and black Africans imported as slaves. Diverse religious traditions further colored the colony: Anglican, Huguenot, Jewish, Baptist, Presbyterian, Catholic. Merchants, planters and pirates all had a hand in shaping society as it evolved through the eighteenth and nineteenth centuries. Charleston became a city which "was civilized and hedonistic in a balance that created a culture of exquisitely refined grace in which incomparable luxury was tempered by a demanding discipline of intellect and education." (Ripley, 151-152)*

The attentive and successful preservation of gardens, homes and historic places in modern Charleston provides a physical setting which enhances an appreciation for early cultural influences. The society which produced such elegant architecture and landscaping was also concerned with other forms of aesthetic pursuit.

Perhaps the earliest literary genre in which Charleston established its reputation was drama. The first theater in North America opened at the corner of Church and Dock (now Queen) Streets on February 12, 1736, with a production of George Farquhar's "The Recruiting Officer." The present Dock Street Theater, built in the early part of the nineteenth century as the Planters' Hotel, was renovated in 1937 on the design of an eighteenth century theater, and each spring provides a performance site for Spoleto Festival USA. Thus, as in many other unique elements of Charleston, an important manifestation of contemporary

* For works cited, see "Selected Bibliography" on page 369.

artistic and literary achievement remains connected to the earliest cultural pursuits of the city. The long-standing municipal appreciation for creativity and the ambiance of this "sea-drinking city" has for centuries attracted an ever-growing artistic community.

Blessed with ground fertile for agriculture, forests abundant with game, and waters rich with the fruits of the sea, the Lowcountry harbored the development of a social system—plantation society—which exerted a wide-ranging influence on local culture. As the plantations thrived, an aristocratic class grew which "built Barbadian-influenced single houses, Georgian mansions with walled gardens and piazzas, stately public buildings and dignified churches." (Saunders and McAden, 18) As trading and shipping developed, luxuries were imported, and the sons of planters were sent to Europe for their education. The society flourished, and, with it, music, dance and literary pursuits.

The plantation system, with its attendant slavery, also yielded the rich folklore and musical traditions of Africa. As Harlan Greene has said, "the delicate interplay of black and white that would write Charleston's history began quite early. Their overlapping chronicles are as connected and fretted as the coils in the sweetgrass Gullah baskets sold in the city market." (Greene, *Charleston,* 11)

The cultural melange that is Charleston has evolved and developed from colonial times through Revolutionary, antebellum, Confederate War and Reconstruction eras, into the twentieth century. Through these changing times, Charleston has nurtured a share of literary activity—a share not obvious on cursory consideration. The present collection of fiction, poetry and essay attempts to reflect something of the spirit of Charleston and its environs through imaginative language. It includes the writings of local residents, as well as those of well-known literary visitors.

The prologue of this book, taken from the opening chapter of William Bartram's *Travels Through North and South Carolina* (1791), presents Charleston as a well-ordered haven, a symbol of humankind's innocence at the beginning of life. Bartram (1739-1823), from Philadelphia, failed in his early career as a planter in the Caribbean. From a young age, he had shown talent in drawing and painting, and in later life distinguished himself as a botanist, explorer and writer. The descriptions of flora and fauna in his *Travels* provided source material for English romantic poets, including Coleridge and Wordsworth. In *Travels*, Bartram describes his voyage on the open sea, where he encounters a terrible storm. He presents the image of nature's fury unleashed, the chaos of a disordered universe, but also of the primordial sea which is the wellspring of life. From chaos, Bartram sails into Charleston harbor, likening what he sees to earthly paradise at the beginning of time: life before the fall into sin and death. Bartram's narrative, then, is placed at the beginning of this collective vision of the Charleston of the imagination.

In contrast, the collection closes with an ironic reversal of this position. Andy Warhol's (1928-1987) story of a Charleston debutante who joins the demimonde of New York and sinks into a life of debauchery and depravity, describes the violation of a sense of an ordered world. The woman of manners and breeding, brought up according to the rigid social standards of Charleston, rejects her past. Warhol, as several of the lowcountry writers, presents New York as the foil of Charleston: the dark side of the urban face, the city of lower consciousness against the city of upper consciousness. This idea reflects, and perhaps extends, the antebellum philosophy that all that is northern is bad and all that is southern is good.

Charleston fostered two "literary schools" or movements: the first in the nineteenth century, prior to the War Between the States; the second, the so-called "Charleston Renaissance," in the early part of the twentieth century.

The Charleston School

Stephen Vincent Benet has described Paul Hamilton

Hayne, William Gilmore Simms and Henry Timrod as "men of letters who supported the Southern cause." In the 1850s, Hayne, Simms and Timrod formed a group which included other writers and individuals of status and influence in Charleston. They met in a bookstore, owned by John Russell, on the east side of King Street between Wentworth and Hasell Streets. For two years prior to the war (1857-1859), they published *Russell's Magazine*, a literary magazine named for the group's venue.

Paul Hamilton Hayne (1838-1886)

Hayne and Timrod had been friends since boyhood. Both were primarily interested in poetry and poetics, and were principally influenced by English romantic poets of the day. Hayne, unique among the writers in his group, came from an aristocratic Charleston family of some means. His father died when Hayne was a child, and the boy was brought up by his uncle, Robert L. Hayne, who became a U. S. Senator.

Hayne had set out to read law, but his devotion to literature grew stronger. He became a contributor to the *Southern Literary Messenger*, served as editor of *Russell's Magazine*, and, along with his colleagues, became an apologist for the Southern cause. When the war began, Hayne was unable to enlist in the Confederate army because of health problems. Sherman's army burned his family's plantation home and after the war the financially ruined Hayne settled in Augusta, Georgia. He lived modestly, but was able to support his family through his writing. He remained devoted to his friend Timrod and edited Timrod's collected poems, which were published posthumously in 1873.

Attention to Hayne's work has largely centered on poetry of the war, including "The Battle of Charleston Harbor" and "Charleston." Of the poetry not related to war, "Magnolia Gardens" has been included in this collection, along with "Aspects of the Pines" and a lesser-known but interesting poem, "Laocoon." The latter is an Italian sonnet in which the poet describes the local image of a burning oak log, through which he sees a vision of the mythological figure of the title. Laocoon, a Trojan priest, incurred the wrath of the goddess Athena by warning his people not to accept the misbegotten horse, and by tossing a spear at the foot of Athena's statue. In retribution, Athena had Laocoon and his sons strangled by a sea serpent at the water's edge as they made sacrifices to the god Poseidon. Hayne interweaves local images—contrasting a death by water with the poetic image of consumption by fire—into the retelling of a somewhat obscure classical myth.

William Gilmore Simms (1806-1870)

William Gilmore Simms, today the best known of the antebellum Charleston School, is principally remembered for his prose and for the volume of his work, which far exceeds that of his compatriots. Simms was born in Charleston, but, unlike Hayne, was not of a prominent family. His mother died when he was very young and Simms was raised by his grandmother. When his father emigrated to Mississippi to work on a plantation and attempted to take the boy with him by force, Simms caused such a riot in the street that police were summoned and prevented his abduction.

Older than his literary colleagues and never well accepted by the Charleston establishment, Simms became quite prominent in Europe and received frequent visitors to Charleston. No one in Charleston understood the interest in Simms by these intellectual outsiders until the publication of *The Charleston Book* in 1845, edited by Simms, a volume that included work by some of the better-known authors of the time, as well as writing by prominent members of the local establishment.

As a young adult, Simms effected a reconciliation with his father and spent a lengthy period with him in Mississippi. Their frequent travels by horseback through what was then the western frontier gave Simms the source material for his so-called "border romances." After his return to Charleston, Simms married Chevelette Roche, heiress to Woodlands plantation, and adopted the role of "lord of the manor" as a southern planter. Louis D. Rubin, Jr., argues that Simms, essentially a romantic and estranged from the aristocratic class by birth, created for himself a mythos which was compatible with the emerging southern philosophy that ultimately resulted in secession and the formation of the Confederate States. (Rubin, *Edge*, 54-102) This mythos presumed southern society to be a feudal system, similar in some ways to medieval European agrarian society, composed of many large plantations presided over by enlightened families of noble origin. The work on the plantation was performed by people of a lesser class who, in return for their work, received provision for all their needs, and the entire system was protected by a code of chivalry. This philosophy bore little relationship to reality: relatively few members of society lived on large plantations and the majority of citizens owned few or no slaves. Simms, however, subscribed fully to this romantic notion. He attempted to live the life himself, and his writing as a southern apologist was largely influenced by this philosophy.

Simms's best writings are not his essays and treatises, however, but his novels. These include the "border romances," such as *The Yemassee* (1835), a fictional treatment of the Indians in 1715 South Carolina; the "Revolutionary War romances," such as *The Partisan* (1835), in which he creates a Falstaff-like character whom he names, interestingly, Captain Porgy; and his last and possibly best known novel, *The Cassique of the Kiawah* (1859). Simms's "Ephraim Bartlett, the Edisto Raftsman" (1852), included here, was first published in *Literary World* as an installment in "Home Sketches or Life Along Highways and Byways of the South."

In the two decades preceding the Civil War, Simms served in the South Carolina legislature. He contributed to numerous literary journals, including *Russell's Magazine*, and edited, for a time, the *Southern Quarterly Review*. He was prolific with his writing during the period. He also carried on a then little-noticed feud with another major Southern writer with Charleston connections, Edgar Allan Poe. At the time, Simms was the better known of the two. During the war, Simms' home at Woodlands was burned, and shortly thereafter, his wife and four of his children died. Like Hayne, he continued to make a living through his writing until his own death.

Although Simms has been compared to James Fenimore Cooper and Sir Walter Scott, he does not enjoy the literary status of either of those writers. Rubin has argued that in the case of Simms, as well as Timrod and Hayne, this failure is based upon the fact that the milieu in which he wrote—the southern cause and southern philosophy, tied as they were to the system of slavery—barred any kind of searching inquiry into the tension between man in nature and in society. Alternatively, Simms' lack of acclaim may well have resulted from the subversion of his imaginative vision to a social or political goal.

Henry Timrod (1828-1867)

Born in Charleston to relatively humble circumstances, Henry Timrod was raised by his mother after his father's death in 1838. Because Timrod lacked means and spent much of his life in ill health, his education was sporadic. He became friends with Hayne at an early age, and enjoyed a friendship that lasted a lifetime.

Timrod became known as "the poet laureate of the Confederacy" for his patriotic lyrics glorifying the southern cause in the War Between the States. "What makes Timrod's best war poetry superior in kind to the now forgotten verses of all his Southern contemporaries," points out Louis Rubin, "is just [his] ability to go beyond the patriotic assertion of loyalty and defiance into a deeper evocation of the historical occasion." (Rubin, *Edge*, 210) The public social and political concerns which served as the source material for Timrod's work are fully identified with the private vision of the poet. His literary colleagues were the English romantic poets of the nineteenth century, including Byron, Wordsworth and Tennyson, though, unlike them, he failed to look beyond his own particular circumstances. His literary principles were recorded in the 1859 essay entitled "Literature in the South," in which he argues that form and beauty constitute the true material of poetry, rather than philosophical truth.

Timrod contributed to *Russell's Magazine* and *Southern Literary Messenger* before the war. This collection includes three of his better-known war poems, including "Charleston," "The Cotton Boll" and perhaps, most interesting of all, "Ode. Sung on the Occasion of Decorating the Graves of the Confederate Dead, at Magnolia Cemetery, Charleston, S.C., 1867.," a poem first published in the Charleston *News and Courier* on June 18, 1867. After being discharged from the Confederate army in 1864, he settled in Columbia, where he died destitute.

Sea Island Lore

Two other nineteenth century writers who were not members of the Charleston School are represented in this collection. William Elliott (1788-1863) was a southern planter of the type Simms so admired and aspired to become. He descended from a landed Beaufort County family of social distinction and significant assets. Following his education at Harvard, Elliott returned home in 1808 to take over the administration of the family plantation after the death of his father. He married a young woman of equally important social and financial standing in Charleston. Elliott served in the South Carolina legislature, but in 1832 stood down from his seat because of his opposition to nullification. From that time until the outbreak of the Civil War, his writing career developed. He also traveled extensively and lectured frequently on agricultural topics, representing South Carolina at the 1855 Paris Exposition. Elliott vehemently opposed secession, but sided with the Confederacy once the war began. Like so many southern planters, he lost virtually everything as the Confederacy crumbled. He died before the war ended.

The tale included in this volume comes from Elliott's *Carolina Sports by Land and Water; Including Incidents of Devilfishing, Wildcat, Deer, and Bear Hunting, Etc.*, a collection of hunting and fishing tales that gives an excellent picture of country life in the Lowcountry in the early part of the nineteenth century. Derived from the style of James Boswell's eighteenth century English essay, these pieces, remarkably, reflect similarities to the approach of today's sportsman to his game.

Edgar Allan Poe (1809-1849) surely had no recollection of his first visit to Charleston as the infant child of traveling actors. It is uncertain what became of Poe's father; but upon his mother's death in 1811, the three-year-old Poe was adopted (though not legally) by John Allan, a merchant of Scottish birth. Poe attended schools in England and Richmond and later entered the University of Virginia at Charlottesville for a short sojourn. Although he performed well academically, especially in the realm of English and foreign languages, Poe apparently spent a good deal of his time engaged in hard drinking and gambling. His vices yielded enormous debts, with which his stepfather refused to help.

In May of 1827, Poe enlisted in the United States Army under the name of Edgar Perry. The regiment to which he belonged was dispatched to Fort Moultrie on Sullivan's Island, from which General William Moultrie had repulsed the British attack on Charleston Harbor in 1776. During the time that Poe was billeted to the fort, he wrote the poems "Al Aaraaf" and "To Science." Clearly, his year-and-a-half on Sullivan's Island provided images which remained with him throughout his life, as is evident in "The Oblong Box" (1844) and "The Gold Bug" (1843), included in this collection, in which the romantic landscape of the Lowcountry serves as a setting. According to Daniel Hoffman, this is the only case in the entire Poe canon where an existing folk tale (that of Captain Kidd) serves as the basis for a story. (Hoffman, 125) A pleasant but unfounded tradition among some Charlestonians holds that Annabel Lee was a girl Poe had loved while resident on Sullivan's Island, the "Kingdom by the Sea."

The Poetry Society of South Carolina and the "Charleston Renaissance"

The second school of writing in Charleston's literary history was established in the early 1920s, when the American South, generally, was ascendant in literature. The main centers of poetic activity were the Fugitive group in Nashville—which included John Crowe Ransom, Allen Tate and Robert Penn Warren—and a similarly active group in Charleston. The Poetry Society of South Carolina, which became a focal point of the local literary community, was founded in 1921 by John Bennett, Hervey Allen, DuBose Heyward, Beatrice Ravenel and Josephine Pinckney. The group communicated with the Nashville poets, and in April of 1922, edited the first southern issue of *Poetry Magazine* under the sponsorship and direction of editor Harriet Monroe.

John Bennett (1865-1956)

If anyone can be said to be the father of the "Charleston Renaissance" of the 1920s, it is John Bennett. Born in Chillicothe, Ohio, in 1865, Bennett came to Charleston from New York in 1898 and married Susan Adger Smythe of Charleston in 1902. He remained in the Lowcountry for the rest of his life. Bennett's book, *Master Skylark* (1897), is still considered a classic of children's literature, while *The Treasure of Peyre Gaillard* (1906), set in the Lowcountry, was his first attempt at writing fiction for adults. He contributed frequently to *Harper's Magazine* and *The Atlantic Monthly*.

Bennett served as DuBose Heyward's confidante and confessor in the creation of the character of Porgy, and the subsequent novel, play and opera. His influence upon the development of *Porgy*, in all its manifestations, continued until well into the 1930s. When the first director of the opera *Porgy and Bess*, Rouben Mamoulian, visited Charleston and the sea islands to get an impression of the local scene, John Bennett introduced him to the city.

In 1946 Bennett published *Doctor to the Dead*, a

collection of eerie and macabre tales with local settings, many well known in local folklore, which included "Madame Margot." Perhaps Bennett's best-known short story, published in a longer version as a novella, "Madame Margot" is essentially the retelling of the legend of Faust, a legend with a long literary history. Bennett's tale, with its particular Charleston flavor and characteristic change of gender, includes some of the frequently examined themes in local literature, including an interest in the occult and supernatural, the connection between Lowcountry and Caribbean cultures, and the complex relationships between black and white societies in Charleston.

Hervey Allen (1889-1949)

Hervey Allen, a native of Philadelphia who settled in Charleston and taught English at the Porter Military Academy, was included in the Yale Series of Younger Poets, still a prestigious recognition. His novel *Anthony Adverse,* also proved highly successful. As a co-founder of the Poetry Society, he too was dedicated to a rejuvenation of the cultural life of the South through a remaking or transformation of the old traditions. Allen introduced Bennett to DuBose Heyward, with whom Allen published a collection of poems, *Carolina Chansons* (1924), from which some of the entries in this collection are taken. Allen went on to become an authority on Edgar Allan Poe, editing an anthology of Poe's writing, as well as writing a biography of Poe entitled *Israfel* after Poe's poem of that name. His fascination with Poe and his interest in Poe's connection to Charleston are reflected in the poem "Alchemy," with its central concept of Poe's sojourn on Sullivans Island.

Josephine Pinckney (1895-1957)

While Bennett, Allen and Heyward made their literary mark through their prose, the most remarkable of the poetry created at that time was produced by two women, Josephine Pinckney and Beatrice Ravenel. Pinckney was a member of a literary discussion group consisting of a number of women under the leadership of Laura Bragg, the director of The Charleston Museum. This group ultimately amalgamated with Bennett's, to the great benefit of The Poetry Society. Pinckney's book of poetry entitled *Sea-Drinking Cities* was published by Harper and Brothers in 1927, from which the selections in this collection are taken. Pinckney went on to write several novels which were well received in their day, but have now largely fallen into oblivion. *Three O'Clock Dinner* (1945), examines the complex relationship between a proper South-of-Broad family and a local family of more humble origin. *Great Mischief* (1948), an occult tale, examines a post-Civil War pharmacist who delves into the occult and establishes a romantic and sexual relationship with a beautiful young witch or "hag." The climax of the novel is apocalyptic, a vision of the end of time, reflected through the imagery of the Charleston earthquake of 1886. The nature of the "hag," as seen in local folklore, is previewed in the poem of the same name, included in this collection.

Many believe that Pinckney and Beatrice Ravenel would have flourished as poets on a national scale if they had not been so influenced, indeed stifled, by stringent upbringing in Charleston society with its rigid value system, especially where women were concerned. Pinckney nevertheless made her mark and maintained a high profile in the literary scene of the time, both locally and nationally. Her close personal connections were sufficiently wide-ranging to include such prominent persons of the time as Henry Luce.

The issue of the relationship between Charleston writers and Charleston society is problematic. Not only the women, but all of the local writers of the '20s and '30s were thought by many critics to suffer from the rigid social standards of the local community. Michael O'Brien has considered this problem in some detail in his essay "'The South Considers Her Most Peculiar': Charleston and Modern Southern Thought." He alludes to Allen Tate's theory regarding the best southern literature, a theory which calls for a balance between the dictates of a set of standards, social, cultural and artistic, and alienation from such standards. Charleston writers, in the scheme of both Tate and Rubin, have adhered too much to social convention. Indeed, Heyward's novel, *Peter Ashley*, "is a meditation on alienation and belonging," in which the protagonist, a scion of the pre-war South comes down squarely on the camp of belonging. But as O'Brien points out: ". . . the critical standards that have marginalized Charleston are not immortal. It is becoming fair to hazard that the neoagrarian interpretation of southern literature is in decline, perhaps moribund. The canon of southern literature begins to change, to take previously marginal voices more seriously, most obviously the female and the black. To put it politely, the relevance of Nashville to these themes is modest. But the relevance of Charleston in the 1920s and 1930s, oddly enough for so elite a white culture, is much greater. For one thing, its interest in landscape and preservation is likely to seem less quaint to a younger generation reared in the environmental movement. For another, an unusual number of Charlestonian writers were women, and one of the great ventures of the city's literature was representing black culture." (O'Brien, 133)

Beatrice Witte Ravenel (1870-1956)

Beatrice Witte, the third daughter of a well-to-do Charleston banker, lived for many years in a home at 112 Rutledge Avenue (now Ashley Hall). All of the Witte daughters distinguished themselves by their accomplishments and by their marriages to local men. Beatrice was educated at Radcliffe and, during her Cambridge, Massachusetts years, became well acquainted with the intelligentsia there. She began writing poetry during this time, but did not begin writing in earnest until after the death of her first husband, Francis Ravenel, in 1920. Interestingly, Francis Ravenel's mother was Harriott Horry Ravenel, who wrote the social history, *Charleston: The Place and the People* (1906) and who also wrote a biography of Eliza Lucas. *The Arrow of Lightning*, by Beatrice Witte Ravenel, was published in 1925, and the poems included in this collection are taken from it. Instrumental in the early activities of The Poetry Society of South Carolina, Beatrice Ravenel became friends with Amy Lowell during the Massachusetts poet's visit to Charleston on behalf of the Society. The two carried on an active correspondence, and Lowell's progressive ideas on poetry and poetics influenced Ravenel. Ravenel's poetry is increasingly regarded as the very best produced during the "Charleston Renaissance."

DuBose Heyward (1885-1940)

Of the Charleston writers of the 1920s, DuBose Heyward remains today the best known outside Charleston, principally because of the international success of the opera *Porgy and Bess*. Born to an old Charleston family, Heyward was the great-great-grandson of Thomas Heyward, a signer of the Declaration of Independence.

In his youth, Heyward worked on the Charleston waterfront, an experience which gave him some of the source material for the life of the stevedores portrayed in *Porgy* (1925). He suffered from polio at 18, and during his recuperation began to write. In 1922, he married Dorothy Kuhn, a playwright he had met at the Edward McDowell Writing Colony in New Hampshire. Heyward became an insurance salesman, but left that vocation in 1924 to write full time. Dorothy Kuhn Heyward, with her great wealth of knowledge of the theater, became his major collaborator and confidante, the influence of John Bennett notwithstanding.

The elements of reality that were transfigured in Heyward's fictional world are well known. Heyward lived at 76 Church Street near the double tenement known as Cabbage Row. In the fictional world of his *Porgy*, he changed the name to Catfish Row and relocated it to Vanderhorst Wharf at the waterfront. Kiawah Island, the Mosquito Fleet, the Jenkins Orphanage Band, the 1911 hurricane and the dockside experience of Heyward's youth came to life in his tale.

Likewise, the figure of "Goat" Sammy Smalls; unable to walk, Smalls traveled in his handmade cart pulled by a goat. In 1924 an article appeared in the Charleston *News and Courier* reporting an aggravated assault charge against Smalls for his alleged attempt to shoot a local woman. The intensity of this crippled beggar appealed to Heyward and the imaginative seed of Porgy was planted.

Heyward's long-standing interest in the way of life of the local black population was clearly reflected in his most notable writing, *Porgy* (and its descendants) and *Mamba's Daughters* (1929). Although it has been pointed out that Heyward was no social reformer, he was able to observe and render black culture in a way never before achieved or even attempted, depicting it with objectivity and affection, without the pity or cant of the time. He was fascinated by the juxtaposition of the two cultures existing in Charleston and the Lowcountry, and saw each, it can be argued, especially after reading *Mamba's Daughters,* as an ironic reflection of the other—"upstairs, downstairs" in a Charleston setting.

Indeed, the social fabric of Charleston figures prominently in local literature. White society, governed by rigid standards in a long tradition, appears to hold sway— the upper consciousness, it is constantly impinged upon by forces from below or within: a dark side, the under-consciousness, a central core of unbridled creative energy and will within, primitive and unrelenting. These two positions are paradoxically ever present in the social framework of Charleston, and in the writing not only of Heyward, but of many of the writers represented in this collection.

In 1926, Dubose and Dorothy Heyward turned the novel *Porgy* into the play of the same name, which was produced in New York by the Theater Guild. Shortly after *Porgy* went to Broadway, Heyward began a collaboration with composer George Gershwin that was destined to produce perhaps the most famous American opera, *Porgy and Bess.*

Gershwin came to South Carolina in the summer of 1934

to immerse himself in the culture of the sea islands: to experience the folk music of the Lowcountry blacks, to capture the rhythms and the cadences of local songs for use in his "classical" operatic treatment of the story of Porgy. A letter to his mother is revealing: "The place down here looks like a battered, old South Sea Island. There was a storm 2 weeks ago which tore down a few houses along the beach & the place is so primitive they just let them stay that way. Imagine, there is not one telephone on the whole island—public or private. The nearest phone is about 10 miles away.

"Our first three days here were cool, the place being swept by an ocean breeze. Yesterday was the first hot day (it must have been 95° in town) & it brought out the flys [sic], the knats [sic], mosquitoes. There are so many swamps in the district that when the breeze comes in from the land there is nothing to do but scratch. We wear nothing but bathing suits all day long & certainly enjoy that part of it.

"DuBose Heyward is coming down tomorrow to spend two weeks & I hope to get some work done on the opera." (Kimball and Simm, 174)

Gershwin apparently created quite a sensation in both black and white society during his short two months in the Lowcountry. He often visited black churches on James Island and during a "shout" (the singing of spirituals accompanied by loud clapping of hands and stamping of feet to the rhythm), Gershwin not only joined in, but apparently became the most prominent "shouter" in the congregation. By contrast, one evening at the home of Mr. and Mrs. James Hagood at 46 South Battery, his jazz performance on the piano not only delighted his hosts, but caused neighbors to come out on their porches in order to hear better. Gershwin hosted Mrs. Joseph I. Waring and her mother one evening at his Folly Beach cottage. Apparently, Mrs. Waring's mother found Gershwin's ego a bit hard to take. However, he and Mrs. Waring became very good friends for the remainder of his stay in Charleston.

The tremendous popularity and success of the opera *Porgy and Bess* has assured that DuBose Heyward will be remembered. Much of the attention that is paid presently to all of the writers of the "Charleston Renaissance" can be credited to the notoriety that Heyward received on account of *Porgy*. His other writings, especially *Mamba's Daughters*, are well worth lengthy consideration. Heyward, who died in 1940, is buried in St. Philip's churchyard, not far from the grave of John C. Calhoun.

Early Twentieth Century Influences

Three writers of national prominence visited and wrote about Charleston in the early part of the twentieth century: Henry James, Amy Lowell and Owen Wister. Henry James (1843-1916) largely set the standard for literary tastes in the early part of the century. He is well known for his short stories and novels (*The European, Daisy Miller, Washington Square, Portrait of a Lady, The Bostonians, The Aspern Papers, The Turn of the Screw, The Ambassadors*), as well as his essays. James, an expatriate most of his life, came back to the United States in 1904, after a 20-year sojourn in Europe, and traveled throughout the country, writing lengthy essays on his travels. The resulting *The American Scene* contains the essay on "Charleston," from which an excerpt has been included in this collection. James's encounter with Charleston is important, and yet, after reading his observations, one feels that he largely missed the point. He apparently had very little intercourse with the general population and describes a beautiful but sadly decayed physical setting. No true "society" seems to exist for him and he appears to find no men, only a matriarchy which copes, at best. James's perception may have been somewhat valid in postwar Charleston, but a reading of Wister's *Lady Baltimore* is enough to convince one that there was, at this time, a very complex, active and proud social structure in the city, based solidly on old traditions that had never wavered. Likewise, James's vision of black society seems to suggest that he regarded the local black as no more than a former slave, with no supporting socioeconomic structure remaining. For James, the black person is "a man without a country." James entirely misses the rich and ancient cultural heritage inherent in black society from the beginning of life in America, a heritage reaching back to its African origins. He does not touch the "humanness" of any of the local citizens, such as is seen later in Heyward or in other social contexts in James's own novels.

Amy Lowell (1874-1925) was a member of the celebrated New England family which included many distinguished poets, including James Russell Lowell and Robert Lowell. She embraced the "imagist" movement in poetry, as did the earliest and most famous member of that school, Ezra Pound, and promoted a rebirth of interest in poetry, poetics, and especially new forms in this country. She paid several visits to Charleston and was invited as a guest reader by The Poetry Society of South Carolina, an organization which she encouraged and supported over many years. The 1921 *Yearbook of The Poetry Society of South Carolina* includes this greeting from her: "Charleston ought to have a Poetry Society, and a poetry society which cares more for poetry than the politics thereof. For why?

"Because Charleston has more poetic appeal than almost any city in America. Some fifteen years ago I passed a few weeks there and those weeks have left an indelible impression upon me. It was in the spring, the azaleas in the Middleton Place in full bloom, with the sea cool, stretched blue, with the houses as lovely and fresh as their own gardens. It is a place for poets, indeed. History touches legend in Charleston; art has harnessed nature, and nature has ramped away and transcended art, the town is beautiful with the past, and glorious with the present; its wealth of folklore has been very little touched upon in poetry. What a mine for someone, what an atmosphere!" (*Yearbook*, 17)

She remained a lifelong friend, confidante and correspondent to Beatrice Witte Ravenel.

Owen Wister (1860-1938) is known mainly for his novel

The Virginian. He visited Charleston frequently, was well known to Charleston society and was a keen observer of the unique aspects of the downtown social order. His observations became the source material for the romantic novel *Lady Baltimore*, set in the thinly-disguised Charleston known as "King's Port." A close friend of President Teddy Roosevelt, Wister at one time stayed at the Villa Margherita on the Battery with President Roosevelt's party.

Several other writers active during the period of the "Charleston Renaissance," some not formally associated with the movement, have been included in this collection. In Charleston, Herbert Ravenel Sass (1881-1958) and Samuel Gaillard Stoney (1892-1968) became well known as local men of letters. Sass was the author of the novels *The Emperor Brims* and *Look Back to Glory*. Samuel Gaillard Stoney established his reputation as an essayist and wrote, among other things, *Plantations of the Lowcountry* and *Charleston: Azaleas and Old Bricks*.

John Galsworthy (1867-1933), the British playwright, novelist and Nobel prize winner, known for his depiction of the English upper classes, visited Charleston in 1919. From the Villa Margherita on South Battery, he wrote to a friend in England: ". . . This carries our dear love to you from a wonderful place so strangely unAmerican, as America is in the north. A place too of wonderful subtle colourings, and scents (not to say sometimes smells), and old time houses, and families, and dreaminess about time. To-day we went by car to the Magnolia Gardens eleven miles away—a dream of a place, really a dream. The Southern voices are very soft and pretty and the owners thereof are awfully nice." (Marrot, 473)

Charleston was ripe fruit for Galsworthy's social commentary. "A Hedonist," reprinted here, appeared in *Century Magazine* in 1921.

Ludwig Lewisohn (1833-1955) was born in Germany of Orthodox Jewish parents who immigrated to St. Matthews, South Carolina, when Lewisohn was an infant. From there they moved to Charleston in 1892 and Lewisohn spent the remainder of his youth in the city, graduating from the High School of Charleston and the College of Charleston. He was most widely admired for his autobiography, *Up Stream and Mid-Channel*, and especially successful as an editor and critic. His field of expertise was German literature, particularly the poet Rilke. He wrote a number of works in which Charleston figures as a major setting (*The Case of Mr. Crump*, was published by Farrar, Straus and Company in 1947).

Raphael Sabatini (1875-1950), born in Italy, did not learn English until later in life, yet he wrote exclusively in English. Closely associated with Joseph Conrad, Sabatini wrote historical romances which served as material for a number of early motion pictures (*Scaramouche*, 1921; *Captain Blood*, 1922). *The Carolinian*, written in 1924, reflects Sabatini's research into local history and geography.

Contemporary Poetry and Prose

The final sections of this anthology contain the prose and poetry of contemporary writers. While the two "schools" of Charleston literature represent the periods of greatest intensity in the literary life of Charleston, each was considered eccentric when judged by the critical standards of its own day. The two schools of Charleston writing fare little better when judged by most modern literary standards, and the writers in each have achieved little in the way of status in the larger context of literature as a whole. In the latter half of the twentieth century, however, Charleston has progressively attained greater attention and influence in the artistic and literary worlds. Writers of national prominence have become interested in the city. At the same time, the Lowcountry has recently inspired writers from the region who have attained distinguished reputations on a national scale. In the world of poetry, there is James Dickey; in fiction, Pat Conroy and Josephine Humphreys; and in letters, Louis D. Rubin, Jr.

In considering contemporary poetry for inclusion in this collection, it seemed essential to include James Dickey.

Georgian by birth, he is probably the most distinguished Southern poet of the last 30 years, and presently serves as professor of English and Poet-in-Residence at the University of South Carolina. His best selling 1970 novel, *Deliverance*, was made into a popular motion picture. Inducted into the South Carolina Academy of Authors in 1986, Dickey effected the posthumous induction of Henry Timrod into that body in 1992.

Among other poets included in the contemporary section is Wendy Salinger, originally from North Carolina, who now lives in New York. Salinger spent a period of time on Folly Beach, South Carolina, and from that sojourn created *Folly River*, from which the present entries are taken. *Folly River* won the National Poetry Series open competition in 1980, and Salinger's poetry has appeared in *The New Yorker* and other major periodicals.

August Kleinzahler, who has Charleston cousins, was born in Jersey City and educated at the Horace Mann School—alma mater of William Carlos Williams and Jack Kerouac. He attended the University of Wisconsin and the University of Victoria (British Columbia). He has published several volumes of poetry, including *Earthquake Weather* (1989) which was nominated for the National Book Critics Circle Award. In 1990, he was the recipient of a Guggenheim Fellowship in poetry. He resides in San Francisco.

Also in this collection are both narrative and poetic contributions from Nick Lindsay. Lindsay has lived most of his life on Edisto Island, where he has involved himself intimately in the local community. A poet, novelist and historian, Lindsay spent a number of years as a professor at Goshen College in Indiana where he continues to give lectures and courses on a regular basis. He is well known for his readings of the poetry of his father, Vachel Lindsay. Lindsay brought to fruition the two volumes of *An Oral History of Edisto Island*, transcribing from the words of Sam Gadsden and Bubberson Brown. Sam Gadsden, a social historian, was principally concerned with an accurate rendition of the facts concerning the origins and development of Edisto. Bubberson Brown, on the other hand, a true storyteller, was concerned with myth making, the creation of fiction. The two works considered together are remarkable. Much of Bubberson Brown's narrative actually takes on the dimensions of James Joyce: prose so dense that it approaches poetry. In particular, the end, included here, is "apocalyptic," looking forward and backward to the beginning and end of time.

Contemporary prose is represented by a number of prominent writers, among them Pat Conroy, Josephine Humphreys and Shelby Foote. Conroy, a native of Beaufort, South Carolina, grew up in a military family and attended The Citadel. He lived for a time in Atlanta and California and now resides on Fripp Island. Several of his novels have been highly successful. A recent work, *The Prince of Tides*, includes some of the most beautiful descriptions ever written of the tidal marshlands of the Lowcountry. The passage chosen for this excerpt, the story of the albino porpoise, is firmly based on fact and is practically a short story unto itself. There was indeed an albino porpoise named Carolina Snowball (in fact, a bottle-nose dolphin), that was frequently sighted in the waters of St. Helena Sound in the late 1950s and early 1960s. The porpoise was eventually captured by officials from the Miami Seaquarium, against the wishes of the local populace. Unlike the fate of the porpoise in Conroy's story, the real Carolina Snowball died shortly afterwards, in captivity. In this work, the "whiteness" of the porpoise is a symbol of the innocence of nature unbridled—nature in its purest form, as it was created in the world before evil entered it in the form of humankind. In Conroy's story, people are the aggressors, designing to harness nature and destroy innocence, and consequently controlling the natural individual within (compare this to the previous comments on the structure of Charleston society). To free the white porpoise is to free the purity of the natural individual within ourselves.

Josephine Humphreys grew up in Charleston and

attended Ashley Hall and Duke University. The recipient of
a Guggenheim Fellowship in 1986, she has published three
novels: *Dreams of Sleep*, for which she received the Ernest
Hemingway Foundation Award for first fiction in 1985;
Rich in Love, which was later filmed in Mt. Pleasant and
Charleston; and *The Fireman's Fair*. Humphreys continues
to live in the Charleston area. An intensely personal essay,
accompanied by family photographs of the author and her
sisters, appears in *A World Unsuspected: Portraits of
Southern Childhood*, which also contains an essay by
Padgett Powell.

Powell, born in Gainesville, Florida, returned to the place
of his birth to teach at the University of Florida. He lived
for a time in and around Charleston. His first novel, *Edisto*,
was published in 1983 and bespeaks a unique appreciation
of the culture and nuances of the Lowcountry. Powell's
second novel, *A Woman Named Drown*, was published in
1987.

Harlan Greene also grew up in Charleston and, for
several years, served as archivist for the South Carolina
Historical Society. He presently lives in North Carolina, and
is the author of two novels, including *Why We Never
Danced the Charleston*, which comments on lower
consciousness impinging on upper consciousness in
Charleston society in the image of spontaneous "fast
dancing" at the St. Cecelia Ball, and the quick and
unmitigated response of the representatives of the local
society to suppress it. Josephine Humphreys, Padgett Powell
and Harlan Greene were all associated with the College of
Charleston in 1984-1985, the academic year in which all
three published their first novels.

William Price Fox lives in Columbia, South Carolina,
where he is a writer-in-residence at The University of South
Carolina. Well known for his essays and short stories on life
in his native state, he is the author of *Doctor Golf*; *Light
Moonshine Bright*; *Dixiana Moon*, and *Ruby Red*. "Coley
Moke" and "Monck's Corner," included in this collection,
are from his *Southern Fried Plus Six*.

Shelby Foote, a native of Mississippi, was educated at the University of North Carolina at Chapel Hill. He is well known for his novels and narrative histories, including *Shiloh*, a melodramatic account of the events surrounding the pivotal "western" battle. Foote recently figured prominently in Ken Burns' *The Civil War* on Public Broadcasting System. The excerpt in this collection is from *The Civil War: A Narrative*.

Walker Percy was born in Birmingham, Alabama, attended the University of North Carolina, and received the degree of Doctor of Medicine from Columbia University. He left medicine early, turning to writing, and was successful in having his work accepted in *The Partisan Review, Sewanee Review* and other major literary magazines. He won the 1962 National Book Award for his first novel, *The Moviegoer*. His other books include *Love in the Ruins, Message in the Bottle*, and *The Last Gentleman*, from which the present excerpt is taken.

Louis D. Rubin, Jr. is University Distinguished Professor of English emeritus at the University of North Carolina, Chapel Hill. The founder of Algonquin Books of Chapel Hill, Rubin was born and raised in Charleston and is the author of many critical essays on Southern literature. One of the most distinguished living men of letters in the South, he has also written a number of works of fiction.

Many will be disappointed by certain omissions in this anthology. Limitations of time and space dictated selectivity, but the selection of works that were finally chosen attempts to reflect the totality of the imaginative Charleston in all its facets. Many writers have lived in, written about, performed, directed, and otherwise been associated with Charleston and the Lowcountry: John James Audubon, Benjamin Brawley, Clyde Bresee, William Cullen Bryant, Mary Boykin Chestnut, Donald Davidson, Ralph Waldo Emerson, Robert Frost, Edward King, Susan Pettigru King, Allen Ginsberg, Francis Griswold, Hugh Swinton Legare, James Matthewes Legare, Carson McCullers, Isaac Jenkins

Mikell, Edna St. Vincent Millay (who is said to have scandalized the servants at Magnolia Gardens by wandering through the grounds naked), Arthur Miller, Chalmers Murray, V. S. Naipaul, Julia Peterkin, Elizabeth Allston Pringle, Josiah Quincy, Theodore Rosengarten, Carl Sandburg, George Herbert Sass, Valerie Sayers, Gertrude Stein, William Styron, William Makepeace Thackeray, John Townsend Trowbridge, Oscar Wilde and Tennessee Williams.

The Charleston of the imagination has appealed to many more writers than may be evident at first glance. Sinclair Lewis has Carol Kennicott in *Main Street* stay in the Villa Margherita "by the palms of the Charleston battery and the metallic harbor." Likewise, Vladimir Nabokov has his protagonist travel to Magnolia Gardens to entertain "grim" Lolita, in the novel of the same name. What is it about Charleston and the Lowcountry that appeals specifically to writers? For John James Audubon, it was the lifestyle enjoyed by his host, the Reverend John Bachman: "out shooting every Day—Skinning, Drawing, Talking Ornithology, the Whole Evening, Noon and Morning—in a word . . ., I certainly would be as happy a mortal as Mr. Bachman himself is at this present moment, when he has returned from his congregation—congratulated me on my day's work and now sets amid his family in a room above me enjoying the results. . ." (Durant and Harwood, 330-331)

Carl Sandburg admired the city's physical proportions: "the skylines, gables, porches, harbor lights and silhouettes, streets full of life, grace of speech and custom, in Charleston, a wide range of tangible and intangible presences, pull at one's heart and memory after having been in that town and felt its heartbeats." (*Yearbook*, 23)

Thomas Wolfe's motivation for writing about Charleston was more basic: "'You can still git beer in Charleston,'" he wrote in the 1929 *Look Homeward, Angel*. "'You can go swimmin' in the ocean at the Isle of Palms,' . . . then, reverent, he added, 'you can go the Navy Yard and see the ships.'" (Wolfe, 295)

The abiding sense of the past interests V. S. Naipaul: "Charleston was claimed by the large events of a continental history, and its small time beginnings are now indescribably romantic, when it was on a par with slave colonies like Antigua or Barbados or Jamaica, and looked to them for trade and support." (Naipaul, 89)

Charlestonians themselves constitute Harlan Greene's source of inspiration: "Charleston residents still eat rice and she-crab soup and hoppin' john on New Year's. They sit on piazzas and paint their shutters 'Charleston green'. They dislike difference and encourage eccentricity. They go to oyster roasts at Rockville and to St. Cecilia balls where the guest list is determined by inheritance and geography. They live in a city that demands good manners, yet smiles tolerantly on many things as anyone must who has seen for so long the vanity and nobility of the human species. She just may be that combination of Mediterranean manners and Caribbean ways suggested by John Bennett." (Greene, *Charleston*, 45)

It is perhaps because of all these things that writers are attracted to Charleston and the Lowcountry: the architecture, the pleasure-seeking style, the vegetation, the decadence, the climate, the sense of history, the tradition. The writers' Charleston possesses an honorable heritage. May it continue to shine as a literary gem of the new South.

PROLOGUE

William Bartram

from *The Travels of William Bartram*

At the request of Dr. Fothergill, of London, to search the Floridas, and the western parts of Carolina and Georgia, for the discovery of rare and useful productions of nature, chiefly in the vegetable kingdom; in April, 1773, I embarked for Charleston, South-Carolina, on board the brigantine Charleston Packet, Captain Wright, the brig —— —, Captain Mason, being in company with us, and bound to the same port. We had a pleasant run down the Delaware, 150 miles to Cape Henlopen, the two vessels entering the Atlantic together. For the first twenty-four hours, we had a prosperous gale, and were cheerful and happy in the prospect of a quick and pleasant voyage; but, alas! how vain and uncertain are human expectations! how quickly is the flattering scene changed! The powerful winds, now rushing forth from their secret abodes, suddenly spread terror and devastation; and the wide ocean, which, a few moments past, was gentle and placid, is now thrown into disorder, and heaped into mountains, whose white curling crests seem to sweep the skies!

This furious gale continued near two days and nights, and not a little damaged our sails, cabin furniture, and state-rooms, besides retarding our passage. The storm having abated, a lively gale from N.W. continued four or five days, when shifting to N. and lastly to N.E. on the tenth of our departure from Cape Henlopen, early in the morning, we descried a sail astern, and in a short time discovered it to be Capt. Mason, who soon came up with us. We hailed each other, being joyful to meet again, after so many dangers. He suffered greatly by the gale, but providentially made a good harbour within Cape Hatteras. As he ran by us, he threw on board ten or a dozen bass, a large and delicious fish, having caught a great number of them whilst he was detained in harbour. He got into Charleston that evening, and we the next morning, about eleven o'clock.

There are few objects out at sea to attract the notice of the traveller, but what are sublime, awful, and majestic: the seas themselves, in a tempest, exhibit a tremendous scene, where the winds assert their power, and, in furious conflict, seem to set the ocean on fire. On the other hand, nothing can be more sublime than the view of the encircling horizon, after the turbulent winds have taken their flight, and the lately agitated bosom of the deep has again become calm and pacific; the gentle moon rising in dignity from the east, attended by millions of glittering orbs; the luminous appearance of the seas at night, when all the waters seem transmuted into liquid silver; the prodigious bands of porpoises foreboding tempest, that appear to cover the ocean; the mighty whale, sovereign of the watery realms, who cleaves the seas in his course; the sudden appearance of land from the sea, the strand stretching each way, beyond the utmost reach of sight; the alternate appearance and recess of the coast, whilst the far distant blue hills slowly retreat and disappear; or, as we approach the coast, the capes and promontories first strike our sight, emerging from the watery expanse, and, like mighty giants, elevating their crests towards the skies; the water suddenly alive with its scaly inhabitants; squadrons of sea-fowl sweeping through the air, impregnated with the breath of fragrant aromatic trees and flowers; the amplitude and magnificence of these scenes are great indeed, and may present to the imagination, an idea of the first appearance of the earth to man at the creation.

On my arrival at Charleston, I waited on Doctor Chalmer, a gentleman of eminence in his profession and public employments, to whom I was recommended by my worthy patron, and to whom I was to apply for counsel and assistance, for carrying into effect my intended travels: the Doctor received me with perfect politeness, and, on every occasion, treated me with friendship; and by means of the countenance with which he gave me, and the marks of esteem with which he honoured me, I became acquainted with many of the worthy families . . .

THE CHARLESTON SCHOOL

THE CIRCULAR STAIRCASE

Paul Hamilton Hayne

ASPECTS OF THE PINES

Tall, sombre, grim, against the morning sky
    They rise, scarce touched by melancholy airs,
Which stir the fadeless foliage dreamfully,
    As if from realms of mystical despairs.

Tall, sombre, grim, they stand with dusky gleams
    Brightening to gold within the woodland's core,
Beneath the gracious noontide's tranquil beams—
    But the weird winds of morning sigh no more,

A stillness, strange divine, ineffable,
    Broods round and o'er them in the wind's surcease,
And on each tinted copse and shimmering dell
    Rests the mute rapture of deep hearted peace.

Last, sunset comes—the solemn joy and might
    Borne from the West when cloudless day declines—
Low, flutelike breezes sweep the waves of light,
    And lifting dark green tresses of the pines,

Till every lock is luminous—gently float,
    Fraught with hale odors up the heavens afar
To faint when twilight on her virginal throat
    Wears for a gem the tremulous vesper star.

LAOCOON

A gnarled and massive oak log, shapeless, old,
Hewed down of late from yonder hillside gray,
Grotesquely curved, across our hearthstone lay;
About it, serpent-wise, the red flames rolled
In writhing convolutions; fold on fold
They crept and clung with slow portentous sway
Of deadly coils; or in malignant play,
Keen tongues outflashed, ´twixt vaporous gloom and gold.
Lo! as I gazed, from out that flaming gyre
There loomed a wild, weird image, all astrain
With strangled limbs, hot brow, and eyeballs dire,
Big with the anguish of the bursting brain:
Laocoon's form, Laocoon's fateful pain.
A frescoed dream on flickering walls of fire!

MAGNOLIA GARDENS

Yes, found at last, —the earthly paradise!
Here by slow currents of the silvery stream
It smiles, a shining wonder, a fair dream,
A matchless miracle to mortal eyes:
What whorls of dazzling color flash and rise
From rich azalean flowers, whose petals teem
With such harmonious tints as brightly gleam
In sunset rainbows arched o'er perfect skies!
But see! beyond those blended blooms of fire,
Vast tier on tier the lordly foliage tower
Which crowns the centuried oaks' broad crested calm:
Thus on bold beauty falls the shade of power;
Yet beauty still unquelled, fulfils desire,
Unfolds her blossoms, and outbreathes her balm!

William Gilmore Simms

THE EDGE OF THE SWAMP

'Tis a wild spot, and even in summer hours,
With wondrous wealth of beauty and a charm
For the sad fancy, hath the gloomiest look,
That awes with strange repulsion. There, the bird
Sings never merrily in the sombre trees,
That seem to have never known a term of youth,
Their young leaves all being blighted. A rank growth
Spreads venomously round, with power to taint;
And blistering dews await the thoughtless hand
That rudely parts the thicket. Cypresses,
Each a great ghastly giant, eld and gray,
Stride o'er the dusk, dank tract, —with buttresses
Spread round, apart, not seeming to sustain,
Yet link'd by secret twines, that underneath,
Blend with each arching trunk. Fantastic vines,
That swing like monstrous serpents in the sun,
Bind top to top, until the encircling trees
Group all in close embrace. Vast skeletons
Of forests, that have perish'd ages gone,
Moulder, in mighty masses, on the plain;
Now buried in some dark and mystic tarn,
Or sprawl'd above it, resting on great arms,
And making, for the opossum and the fox,
Bridges, that help them as they roam by night.
Alternate stream and lake, between the banks,
Glimmer in doubtful light: smooth, silent, dark,
They tell not what they harbor; but, beware!
Lest, rising to the tree on which you stand,
You sudden see the moccasin snake heave up
His yellow shining belly and flat head
Of burnish'd copper. Stretch'd at length, behold
Where yonder Cayman, in his natural home,
The mammoth lizard, all his armor on,
Slumbers half-buried in the sedgy grass,

Beside the green ooze where he shelters him.
The place, so like the gloomiest realm of death,
Is yet the abode of thousand forms of life, —
The terrible, the beautiful, the strange, —
Wingéd and creeping creatures, such as make
The instinctive flesh with apprehension crawl,
When sudden we behold. Hark! at our voice
The whooping crane, gaunt fisher in these realms,
Erects his skeleton form and shrieks in flight,
On great white wings. A pair of summer ducks,
Most princely in their plumage, as they hear
His cry, with senses quickening all to fear,
Dash up from the lagoon with marvellous haste,
Following his guidance. See! aroused by these,
And startled by our progress o'er the stream,
The steel-jaw'd Cayman, from his grassy slope,
Slides silent to the slimy green abode,
Which is his province. You behold him now,
His bristling back uprising as he speeds
To safety, in the centre of the lake,
Whence his head peers alone, —a shapeless knot,
That shows no sign of life; the hooded eye,
Nathless, being ever vigilant and sharp,
Measuring the victim. See! a butterfly,
That, travelling all the day, has counted climes
Only by flowers, to rest himself a while,
And, as a wanderer in a foreign land,
To pause and look around him ere he goes,
Lights on the monster's brow. The surly mute
Straightway goes down; so suddenly, that he,
The dandy of the summer flowers and woods,
Dips his light wings, and soils his golden coat,
With the rank waters of the turbid lake.
Wondering and vex'd, the pluméd citizen
Flies with an eager terror to the banks,
Seeking more genial natures, —but in vain.
Here are no gardens such as he desires,
No innocent flowers of beauty, no delights

Of sweetness free from taint. The genial growth
He loves, finds here no harbor. Fetid shrubs,
That scent the gloomy atmosphere, offend
His pure patrician fancies. On the trees,
That look like felon spectres, he beholds
No blossoming beauties; and for smiling heavens,
That flutter his wings with breezes of pure balm,
He nothing sees but sadness —aspects dread,
That gather frowning, cloud and fiend in one,
As if in combat, fiercely to defend
Their empire from the intrusive wing and beam.
The example of the butterfly be ours.
He spreads his lacquer'd wings above the trees,
And speeds with free flight, warning us to seek
For a more genial home, and couch more sweet
Than these drear borders offer us tonight.

EPHRAIM BARTLETT,

THE EDISTO RAFTSMAN

I resume my narrative. In my last, we had just hurried across the common road, once greatly travelled, leading along the Ashley, to the ancient village of Dorchester. Something was said of the fine old plantations along this river. It was the aristocratic region during the Revolution; and when the Virginians and Marylanders, at the close of the war, who had come to the succor of Carolina against the British, drew nigh to Charleston, their hearts were won and their eyes ravished, by the hospitalities and sweets of this neighborhood. Many brave fellows found their wives along this river, which was bordered by flourishing farms and plantations, and crowned by equal luxury and refinement. Here, too, dwelt many of those high-spirited and noble dames whose courage and patriotism contributed so largely to furnish that glorious chapter in Revolutionary history, which has been given to the women of that period. The scene is sadly changed at this season. The plantations along the Ashley are no longer flourishing as then. The land has fallen in value, not exhausted, but no longer fertile and populous. The health of the country is alleged to be no longer what it was. This I regard as all absurdity. The truth is that the cultivation was always inferior; and the first fertile freshness of the soil being exhausted, the opening of new lands in other regions naturally diverted a restless people from their old abodes. The river is still a broad and beautiful one, navigable for steamers and schooners up to Dorchester, which, by land, is twenty-one miles from Charleston. There is abundant means for restoring its fertility. Vast beds of marl, of the best quality, skirt the river all along the route, and there is still a forest growth sufficiently dense to afford the vegetable material necessary to the preparation of compost. As for the health of the neighborhood, I have no sort of question, that, with a dense population, addressed to farming, and adequate to a proper drainage, it would prove quite as salubrious as any portion of the country. Staple culture has been always the curse of Carolina. It has prevented thorough tillage, without which no country can ever ascertain its own resources, or be sure of its health at any time.

Cooper river, on the right, is at a greater distance from us. This, too, was a prosperous and well cultivated region in the Revolution. In a considerable degree it still remains so, and is distinguished by flourishing country seats, which their owners only occupy during spring and winter. The cultivation is chiefly rice, and the rice plantation is notoriously and fatally sickly, except among the negroes. They flourish in a climate which is death to the European. But of this river hereafter. I may persuade you, in future pages, to a special journey in this quarter, when our details and descriptions may be more specific. Between the two rivers the country is full of interest and full of game, to those who can delay to hunt for it. He who runs over the railroad only, sees nothing and can form no conception of it. A few miles further, on the right, there is a stately relic of the old British parochial establishment, a church edifice dedicated to St. James, which modern veneration has lately restored with becoming art, and re-awakened with proper rituals. Built of brick, with a richly painted interior and tesselated aisles, surrounded by patriarchal oaks, and a numerous tenantry of dead in solemn tomb and ivy-mantled monument, you almost fancy yourself in the midst of an antiquity which mocks the finger of the historian. In this neighborhood flourished a goodly population. Large estates and great wealth were associated with equally large refinement and a liberal hospitality, and the land was marked by peculiar fertility. The fertility is not wanting now, but the population is gone—influenced by similar considerations with those which stripped the sister river of its thousands.

Until late years, the game was abundant in this region. The swamps which girdled the rivers afforded a sure refuge, and the deer stole forth to the ridges between, to browse at midnight, seeking refuge in the swamps by day. We have just darted through an extensive tract named Izard's camp, which used to be famous hunting-ground for the city sportsmen. Twenty years ago I have cracked away at a group of deer, myself, in these forest pastures, and even now you may rouse the hunt profitably in the ancient ranges. There are a few sportsmen who still know where to seek with certainty for the buck at the proper season. The woods, though mostly pine, have large tracts of oak and hickory. The scrubby oak denotes a light sandy soil, of small tenacity, and, most usually, old fields which have been abandoned. Along the smaller water-courses, the creeks and branches, long strips of fertile territory may be had; and the higher swamp lands only need drainage to afford tracts of inexhaustible fertility, equal to any Mississippi bottom. The introduction of farming culture will find these and reclaim them, and restore the poorer regions.

A thousand stories of the Revolution, peculiar to this country, would reward the seeker. Nor is it wanting in other sources of interest. Traditions are abundant which belong more to the spiritual nature of the people than their national history. The poorer classes in the low country of the South were full of superstition. Poverty, for that matter, usually is so, but more particularly when it dwells in a region which is distinguished by any natural peculiarities. Thus the highlands of Scotland cherish a faith in spectral forms that rise in the mist and vapor of the mountain; and the Brownie is but the grim accompaniment of a life, that, lacking somewhat in human association, must seek its companions among the spiritual; and these must derive their aspects from the gloomy fortunes of the seeker. The Banshee of Ireland is but the finally speaking monitor of a fate that has always more or less threatened the fortunes of the declining family; and the Norwegian hunting demons are such as are equally evoked by the sports which he pursues and the necessities by which he is pursued himself. In the wild, deep, dark, and tangled masses of a Carolina swamp region, where, even by daylight, mystic shadows harbor and walk capriciously with every change of the always doubtful sunlight, the mind sees and seeks a spiritual presence, which, though it may sometimes oppress, always affords company. Here, solitude, which is the source of the spiritual and contemplative, is always to be found; and forces herself—certainly at one season of the year—upon the scattered forester and farmer. The man who lives by pursuit of the game, the deer or turkey, will be apt to conjure up, in the silent, dim avenues through which he wanders, some companion for his thought, which will, in time, become a presence to his eye; and, in the secluded toils of the farmer, on the borders of swamp and forest, he will occasionally find himself disturbed by a visitor or spectator which his own loneliness of life has extorted from his imagination, which has shaped it to a becoming aspect with the scene and climate under which he dwells. Many of these wild walkers of the wood are supposed to have been gods and spirits of the Indian tribes, who have also left startling memories behind them; and though reluctant to confess his superstitions—for the white hunter and forester dread ridicule more than anything beside—yet a proper investigation might find treasures of superstition and grim tradition among our people of this region, such as would not discredit any of the inventions of imagination.

One of these traditions occurs to me at this moment, the scene of which is at hand but a short distance from us, but not visible from the railroad. Here is not only a haunted house, but a haunted tract of forest. The tale was told me many years ago, as derived from the narrative of a raftsman of the Edisto. The Edisto, of which we may speak hereafter, is the great *lumber* river of South Carolina. Its extent is considerable, penetrating several district divisions of the State, and upon its two great arms or arteries, and its tributary creeks or branches, it owns perhaps no less than one hundred and fifty mills for sawing lumber. It supplies Charleston, by a sinuous route, almost wholly; and large shipments of its timber are made to the island of Cuba, to Virginia, and recently to New York, and other places. Its navigation is difficult, and, as it approaches the sea, somewhat perilous. Many of its rafts have been driven out to sea and lost, with all on board. It requires, accordingly, an experienced pilot to thread its intricacies, and such an one was Ephraim Bartlett, a worthy fellow, who has passed pretty much out of the memories of the present generation.

Ephraim was a good pilot of the Edisto, one of the best; but he had an unfortunate faith in whiskey, which greatly impaired his standing in society. It did not injure his reputation, however, as a pilot; since it was well known that Ephraim never drank on the voyage, but only on the return; and as this was invariably by land, no evil could accrue from his bad habit to anybody but himself. He rewarded himself for his abstinence on the river, by free indulgence when on shore. His intervals of leisure were given up wholly to his potations; and between the sale of one fleet of rafts, and the preparation for the market of another, Ephraim, I am sorry to say, was a case which would have staggered the temperance societies. But the signal once given by his employers, he would shake himself free from the evil spirit, by a plunge into the river. Purification followed—his head was soon as clear for business as ever; and, wound about with a bandanna handkerchief of flaming spot in place of a hat, it would be seen conspicuous on the raft, making for the city. With cheerful song and cry he made his way down, pole in hand, to ward off the overhanging branches of the trees, or to force aside the obstructions. Accompanied by a single negro, still remembered by many as old 'Bram Geiger, his course was usually prosperous. His lumber usually found the best market, and Ephraim and Bram, laying in their little supplies in Charleston, with a sack over their shoulders, and staff or gun in hand, would set out from the city on their return to Lexington, the district of country from which they descended. On these occasions, Ephraim never forgot his jug. This was taken with him empty on the raft, but returned filled, upon his or Bram's shoulders. They took turns in carrying it, concealing it from too officious observers by securing it in one end of the sack. In the other might be found a few clothes, and a fair supply of tobacco.

On the particular occasion when Ephraim discovered for himself that the ancient house and tract were haunted, it happened that he left the city about mid-day. It was Saturday, at twelve or one o'clock, according to his account, when they set out, laden as usual. They reached the house, which was probably twelve or thirteen miles from town, long before sundown; and might have stretched away a few miles farther, but for a cramp in the stomach, which seized upon Old 'Bram. Ephraim at once had resort to his jug, and a strong noggin was prepared for the relief of the suffering negro. At the same time, as Bram swore that he must die, that nothing could possibly save him under such sufferings as he experienced, Ephraim concluded to take lodgings temporarily in the old house, which happened to be within a few hundred yards of the spot, and to lie by for the rest of the day. The building was of brick, two stories in height, but utterly out of repair—doors and windows gone, floors destroyed, and the entire fabric within quite dismantled. It was a long time before Bram was relieved from his suffering and fright. Repeated doses of the potent beverage were necessary to a cure; and, by the time this was effected, the old fellow was asleep. In the meantime, Ephraim had built a rousing fire in the old chimney: and gathered *lightwood* (resinous pine) sufficient to keep up the fire all night; had covered the old negro with his own blanket, which he bore strapped beneath the sack upon his shoulders; and had opened his wallet of dried meat and city bread for his supper. Meanwhile the fumes of the whiskey had ascended gratefully to his own nostrils; and it seemed only reasonable that he should indulge himself with a dram, having bestowed no less than three upon his companion. He drank accordingly, and as he had no coffee to his supper, he employed the whiskey, which he thought by no means a bad substitute. He may have swallowed three several doses in emulation of Bram, and in anticipation of a similar attack, before he had quite finished supper. He admits that he certainly drank again when his meal was ended, by way of washing down the fragments. Bram, meanwhile, with the blazing fire at his feet, continued to sleep on very comfortably. When Ephraim got to sleep is not so certain. He admits that he was kept awake till a late hour by the fumes of the whiskey, and by strange noises that reached him from the forest. He recalled to memory the bad character of the dwelling and neighborhood as haunted; and is not so sure, but thinks it possible that this recollection prompted him to take another draught, a stirrup cup, as it were, before yielding himself to sleep. But he denies that he was in any way affected by the whiskey. To use his own language, he had none of the "how-come-you-so" sensation upon him, but insists that he said his prayers, rationally, like any other Christian, put several fresh brands upon the fire, and sank into the most sober of all mortal slumbers.

I am the more particular in stating these details, since a question has been made in regard to them. Bram had his story also. He admits that he was sick, and physicked as described—that Ephraim had gathered the fuel, made the fire, and covered him with his blanket, while he slept—but he alleges that he awoke at midnight, when Ephraim himself was asleep, and being still a little distressed in the abdominal region, he proceeded to help himself out of the jug, without disturbing the repose of his comrade; and he affirms, on his honesty, that he then found the jug fully half emptied, which had been quite full when he left the city; and he insisted that, in giving him several doses, Ephraim had always been very careful not to make them over strong. Bram admits that, when he had occasion to help himself, as the attack was still threatening, he preferred to take an over dose rather than peril his safety by mincing the matter. It is very certain, from the united testimonies of the two, the whiskey had, one half of it, most unaccountably disappeared before the night was half over. I must suffer Ephraim to tell the rest of the story for himself, and assert his own argument.

"Well, now, you see, my friends," telling his story to a

group, "as I said afore, it was mighty late that night afore I shut my eyes. I reckon twarn't far from day-peep when I slipped off into a hearty sleep, and then I slept like a cat after a supper. Don't you be thinking now 'twas owing to the whiskey that I was wakeful, or that I slept so sound at last. 'Bram's troubles in the stomach made me oneasy, and them strange noises in the woods helped the matter."

"But what were the noises like, Ephraim?"

"Oh! like a'most anything and every thing. Horns-a-blowing, horses a-snorting, cats a-crying, and then sich a rushing and a trampling of four-footed beasts, that I could ´a-swore it was a fox hunt for all the world. But it warn't that! No! 'Twas a hunt agin natur'. The hounds, and horses, and horns that made that racket, warn't belonging to this world. I felt suspicious about it then, and I reckon I knows it now, if such a matter ever is to be made known. Well, as I was a-saying, I got to sleep at last near upon day-light. How long I did sleep there's no telling. 'Twas mighty late when I waked, and then the noise was in my ears again. I raised myself on end, and sat up in my blanket. The fire was gone out clean, and I was a little coldish. 'Bram, the nigger, had scruged himself into the very ashes, and had quite kivered up his head in the blanket. How he drawed his breath there's no telling, since the tip of his nose warn't to be seen nowhere. Says I, ''Bram, do you hear them noises?' But never a word did he answer. Says I, to myself, 'the nigger's smothered.' So I onwrapt him mighty quick, and heard him grunt. Then I know'd there was no harm done. The nigger was only drunk."

"Nebber been drunk dat time," was the usual interruption of 'Bram, whenever he was present at the narration.

"'Bram, you was most certainly drunk, sense I tried my best to waken you, and couldn't get you up."

"Ha! da's 'cause I bin want for sleep, so I nebber consent for ye'r (hear). I bin ye'r berry well all de time; but a man wha's bin trouble wid 'fliction in the stomach all night, mus' hab he sleep out in de morning. I bin ye'r well enough, I tell you."

"You old rascal, if I had thought so, I'd ha' chunk'd you with a lightwood knot!—but the nigger *was* asleep, my friends, in a regular drunk sleep, if ever he was; for when I hearn the noises coming nigh—the hounds and the horses—I drawed him away from the ashes by the legs, and laid him close up agin' the wall t'other side of the fire-place, and pretty much out of sight. I kivered him snug with the blanket, and let him take his sleep out, though I was beginning to be more and more jub'ous about them noises. You see, 'twas the regular noises of a deer-hunt. I could hear the drivers beating about in the thick; then the shout; then the dogs, yelping out whenever they struck upon the trail; I know'd when they nosed the cold trail, and when the scent got warm; and then I heerd the regular rush, when the deer was started, all the dogs in full blast, and making the merriest music. Then I heerd the crack of the gun—first one gun, then another, then another, and another, a matter of four shots—and I felt sure they must ha' got the meat. The horns sounded; the dogs were stopped, and, for a little while, nothing but silence. Oh! I felt awful all over, and monstrous jub'ous of something strange!"

"But why should you feel awful and what should there be so strange about a deer-hunt near Izard's Camp—a place where you may start deer even at this day?"

"Why, 'twas Sunday, you see, and nobody now, in our times, hunts deer, or anything, a-Sundays; and it 'twan't till after midnight on Saturday that I heer'd the noises. That was enough to make me jub'ous. But when I remember'd how they used to tell me of the rich English gentleman, named Lumley, that once lived in the neighborhood, long afore the old Revolution; what a wicked man he was, and how he used to hunt a-Sundays; and how a judgment came upon him; and how he was lost, in one of his huntings, for a matter of six months or more; and when he was found, 'twas only his skeleton. Well I reckon, to think of all that, was enough to give me a bad scare—and it did. People reckoned he must have been snake-bit, for there were the bones of the snake beside him, with the rattles on, eleven and the button; he must have killed the snake after he was struck. But it didn't help him. He never got away from the spot till they found his skileton, and they know'd him by the ring upon his finger, and his knife, and horn, and gun; but all the iron was ruined, eaten up by the rust. Well, when I heer'd the horns a-Sunday, I recollected all about Squire Lumley, and his wickedness; and, before I seed anything, I was all over in a shiver. Well, presently I heerd the horns blowing merrily again, and the sounds come fresher than ever to my ears. I was oneasy enough, and I made another trial to wake up 'Bram, but 'twas of no use. He was sounder than ever."

"I 'speck I bin asleep den, for true," was the modest interruption of 'Bram, at this stage of the narrative. With a grave shake of the head, Ephraim continued—

"I went out then in front of the house, and the horns were coming nigher from behind it. I was a-thinking to run and hide in the bushes, but I was so beflustered that I was afeer'd I should run right into the jaws of the danger. Though, when I thought of the matter agin', I got a little bolder, and I said to myself, 'what's the danger, I wonder. I'm in a free country. I'm troubling no man's property. I've let down no man's fence. I've left no man's gate open to let in the cattle. This old house nobody lives in, and I wouldn't ha' troubled it, ef so be Bram hadn't been taken sick in his bowels. What's the danger?' When I thought, in this way, to myself, I went in and took a sup of whiskey—a small sup— only a taste—by way of keeping my courage up. I tried to waken Bram again, for I said, 'two's always better than one, though one's a nigger,' but 'twas no use; Bram's sleep was sounder than ever. It was pretty cl'ar that he had soak'd the whiskey mighty deep that night!"

"Ki! Mass Ephraim! How you talk! Ef you nebber been drink more than me, dat night, you nebber been scare wid de hunters dat blessed Sunday morning."

"The nigger will talk!" said Ephraim, contemptuously, as he continued his narrative.

"Well, I felt stronger after I had taken that little sup, and

21

went out again. Just then there came a blast of the horns almost in my very ears, and in the next minute I hear'd the trampling of horses. Soon a matter of twenty dogs burst out of the woods, and pushed directly for the house as if they knowed it; and then came the riders—five in all—four white men and one nigger. Ef I was scared at the sounds afore, the sight of these people didn't make me feel any easier. They were well enough to look at in the face, but, lord bless you, they were dressed in sich an outlandish fashion! Why, even the nigger had on short breeches, reaching only to his knees, and then stockings blue and red streaked, fitting close to his legs;—and sich a leg, all the calf turned in front, and the long part of his foot pretty much where the heel ought to be. Then he had buckles at his knees, and buckles on his shoes, jest for all the world like his master. And he wore a cap like his master, though not quite so handsome, and a great coat of bright indigo blue, with the cuffs and collar trimmed with yellow. His breeches were of a coarse buff, the same color with the gentlemen, only theirs were made with a finer article—the raal buff, I reckon. They had on red coats that were mighty pretty, and all their horns were silver mounted. Our Governor and his officers, nowadays, never had on prettier regimentals. Well, up they rode, never taking any more notice of me than ef I was a dog; and I saw the nigger throw down a fine buck from his saddle. There was only one, but he had a most powerful head of horns. While they were all getting off their horses, and the nigger was taking 'em, I turned quietly into the house ag'in to try if a kick or two could get Bram out of his blankets. But, lord have mercy, when I look in, what should I see but another nigger there spreading a table with a cloth as white as the driven snow, and a-setting plates, and knives, and forks, and spoons, and bottles, and salt, and pepper, and mustard, and horse-radish, all as ef he had a cupboard somewhere at his hand. I was amazed, and worse than amazed, when I seed my own jug among the other things. But I hadn't the heart to touch it. For that matter, the nigger that was setting out the things kept as sharp an eye upon me as ef I was a thief. But soon the dishes began to show upon the table. There were the pots upon the fire, the gridiron, the Dutch oven, and everything, and the most rousing fire, and Bram still asleep in the corner, and knowing nothing about it. I was all over in a sweat. Soon, the gentlemen began to come in, but they took no sort of notice of me; and I slipped out and looked at their horses; but as the nigger was standing by 'em, and looking so strange, I didn't go too nigh. But the deer was still a-lying where he first threw it, and I thought I'd turn the head over and see the critter fairly, when, as I'm a living man, the antlers slipped through my fingers jest as fast as I tried to take 'em, —like so much water or smoke. There was a feel to me as ef I had touched something, but I couldn't take hold no how, and while I was a-trying, the nigger holla'd, in a gruff voice, from the horses—'Don't you touch Maussa's meat!' I was getting desp'rate mighty fast, and I thought I'd push back, and try what good another sup of whiskey would do. Well, when I went into the house, the gentlemen were all a-setting round the table, and busy with knife and fork, jest as ef they were the commonest people. There was a mighty smart chance for feeding at the table. Ham and turkey, a pair of as fine wild ducks, English, as you ever seed; a beef tongue, potetters (potatoes), cabbage, eggs, and other matters, and all for jest five men and their servants. Jest then, one of the gentlemen set his eyes on me, and p'inted to one of the bottles— says he, jest as if I had been his own servant —

"'Hand the bottle.'

"And somehow, I felt as ef I couldn't help myself, but must hand it, sure enough. When he had poured out the liquor, which was a mighty deep red, yet clear as the sunshine, he gin me back the bottle, and I thought I'd take a taste of the stuff, jest to see what it was. I got a chance, and poured out a tolerable dram—supposing it was a sort of red bald face (whiskey)—into a cup and tossed it off in a twinkle. But it warn't bald face, nor brandy, nor wine, nor any liquor that I ever know'd before. It hadn't a strong taste, but was something like a cordial, with a flavor like fruit and essence. 'Twarn't strong, I say; so I tried it ag'in an' ag'in, whenever I could git a chance; for I rather liked the flavor; and I warn't mealy-mouthed at helping myself, as they had enough of the critter, and, by this time, they had begun upon my own old bald-face. They seemed to like it well enough. They tried it several times, as if 'twas something new to them, and they didn't find it hard to make the acquaintance. I didn't quarrel with them, you may be sure, for I never was begrudgeful of my liquor; and, besides, wasn't I trying their'n? Well, I can't tell you how long this lasted. 'Twas a good while; and they kept me busy; one after the other on 'em calling out to me to hand 'em this, and hand 'em that, and even the nigger motioning me to help him with this thing and the other. He didn't say much, and always spoke in a whisper. But, it so happened, that, when I was stretching out for one of the bottles, to try another taste of the cordial, one of the cursed dogs would come always in my way. At last, I gin the beast a kick; and, would you believe it, my foot went clean through him—through skin, and ribs, and body, jest the same as if I had kicked the wind or the water. I did not feel him with my foot. I was all over in a trimble; and the dog yelped, jest as if I had hurt him. Sure enough, at this, the great dark-favored man that sot at the head of the table, he fastened his eye upon me and said in a big threatening voice:

"'Who kick'd my dog?'

"By this time, my blood was up a little. What with the scare I had, and the stuff I'd been a-drinking, I felt a little desperate; and my eye was sot upon the man pretty bold as I said:

"'I was just reaching for my own liquor,'—(now that warn't exactly true, I confess, for I was reaching for one of their own bottles)—'when the dog came in my way, and I just brushed him with my foot.'

"'Nobody shall kick my dog but myself,' said he, more fierce than ever; and looking as if he meant kicking! That made me a sort o'wolfish, and, just then, something put the old story of Lumley and the rattlesnake fresh into my head; and, I couldn't help myself—but I gin him for answer as nice an imitation of a snake's rattle—you know how well I kin do it, my friends—as ever he heerd in his born days.

"Lord! you should have seen the stir and heard the racket. Every fellow was on his feet in a minnit, and before I could dodge, the great dark-featured man, he rose up, and seized my jug by the handle, and whirled it furious about his head, and then he sent it at me, with such a curse, and such a cry, that I thought all the house a-tumbling to pieces. Like a great wind, they all rushed by me, men and dogs, and nigger, throwing me down in the door-way, and going over me as ef I was nothing in the way. Whether it was the jug that hit me, or them rushing over, and trampling me down, I can't say; but there I lay, pretty much stunned and stupefied; not knowing anything for a long time;—and when I opened my eyes, and could look around me, there I was with Bram stooping over me and trying to raise me from the ground."

"*Dat's* true!" said Bram, laying special emphasis on *dat's* (that's) and shaking his head significantly. Ephraim continued:

"The strangers were all gone in the twinkling of an eye, —they had swept the platters, —carried off every thing clean, —carried off tables and chairs, bottles and cups, plates and dishes, dinner and drink, pots and ovens, and had even put out the fire; sence, when Bram waked up, there was not a sign of it to be seen. My jug was broke all to pieces, and lying beside me at the door, and not a drop of liquor to be had. What they didn't drink, they wasted, the spiteful divels, when they broke the jug over my head."

Such was Ephraim's story, grown into a faith with many, of the Haunted Forest and House near Izard's Camp. In Ephraim's presence, Bram does not venture to deny a syllable of the story. He only professes to have seen nothing of it, except the full jug when they arrived at the house, and the broken and empty vessel when he awoke from his sleep. In Ephraim's absence, however, he does not scruple to express his doubts wholly of the ghostly visitors and the strange liquor. His notion is, that Ephraim got drunk upon the *"bald-face"* (whiskey) and dreamed the rest. His only subject of difficulty is that the jug should have been broken. He denies, for himself, that he took a drop too much—considering the state of his stomach. —We must resume our journey hereafter.

Henry Timrod

CHARLESTON

Calm as that second summer which precedes
    The first fall of the snow,
In the broad sunlight of heroic deeds,
    The city bides the foe.

As yet, behind their ramparts stern and proud,
    Her bolted thunders sleep—
Dark Sumter, like a battlemented cloud,
    Looms o'er the solemn deep.

No Calpe frowns from lofty cliff or scar
    To guard the holy strand;
But Moultrie holds in leash her dogs of war
    Above the level sand.

And down the dunes a thousand guns lie couched,
    Unseen, beside the flood—
Like tigers in some Oriental jungle crouched
    That wait and watch for blood.

Meanwhile, through streets still echoing with trade,
    Walk grave and thoughtful men,
Whose hands may one day wield the patriot's blade
    As lightly as the pen.

And maidens, with such eyes as would grow dim
    Over a bleeding hound,
Seem each one to have caught the strength of him
    Whose sword she sadly bound.

Thus girt without and garrisoned at home,
    Day patient following day,
Old Charleston looks from roof, and spire, and dome,
    Across her tranquil bay.

Ships, through a hundred foes, from Saxon lands
    And spicy Indian ports,
Bring Saxon steel and iron to her hands,
    And summer to her courts.

But still, along yon dim Atlantic line,
    The only hostile smoke
Creeps like a harmless mist above the brine,
    From some frail, floating oak.

Shall the Spring dawn, and she still clad in smiles,
    And with an unscathed brow,
Rest in the strong arms of her palm-crowned isles,
    As fair and free as now?

We know not; in the temple of the Fates
    God has inscribed her doom;
And, all untroubled in her faith, she waits
    The triumph or the tomb.

THE COTTON BOLL

While I recline
At ease beneath
This immemorial pine,
Small sphere!
(By dusky fingers brought this morning here
And shown with boastful smiles),
I turn thy cloven sheath,
Through which the soft white fibres peer,
That, with their gossamer bands,
Unite, like love, the sea-divided lands,
And slowly, thread by thread,
Draw forth the folded strands.
Than which the trembling line,
By whose frail help yon startled spider fled
Down the tall spear-grass from his swinging bed,

28

Is scarce more fine;
And as the tangled skein
Unravels in my hands,
Betwixt me and the noonday light,
A veil seems lifted, and for miles and miles
The landscape broadens on my sight,
As, in the little boll, there lurked a spell
Like that which, in the ocean shell,
With mystic sound,
Breaks down the narrow walls that hem us round,
And turns some city lane
Into the restless main,
With all his capes and isles!
Yonder bird,
Which floats, as if at rest,
In those blue tracts above the thunder, where
No vapors cloud the stainless air,
And never sound is heard,
Unless at such rare time
When, from the City of the Blest,
Rings down some golden chime,
Sees not from his high place
So vast a cirque of summer space
As widens round me in one mighty field,
Which, rimmed by seas and sands,
Doth hail its earliest daylight in the beams
Of gray Atlantic dawns;
And, broad as realms made up of many lands,
Is lost afar
Behind the crimson hills and purple lawns
Of sunset, among plains which roll their streams
Against the Evening Star!
And lo!
To the remotest point of sight,
Although I gaze upon no waste of snow,
The endless field is white;
And the whole landscape glows,
For many a shining league away,

With such accumulated light
As Polar lands would flash beneath a tropic day!
Nor lack there (for the vision grows,
And the small charm within my hands—
More potent even than the fabled one,
Which oped whatever golden mystery
Lay hid in fairy wood or magic vale,
The curious ointment of the Arabian tale—
Beyond all mortal sense
Doth stretch my sight's horizon, and I see,
Beneath its simple influence,
As if with Uriel's crown,
I stood in some great temple of the Sun,
And looked, as Uriel, down!)
Nor lack there pastures rich and fields all green
With all the common gifts of God,
For temperate airs and torrid sheen
Weave Edens of the sod;
Through lands which look one sea of billowy gold
Broad rivers wind their devious ways;
A hundred isles in their embraces fold
A hundred luminous bays;
And through yon purple haze
Vast mountains lift their plumed peaks cloud-crowned;
And, save where up their sides the ploughman creeps,
An unhewn forest girds them grandly round,
In whose dark shades a future navy sleeps!
Ye Stars, which, though unseen, yet with me gaze
Upon this loveliest fragment of the earth!
Thou Sun, that kindlest all thy gentlest rays
Above it, as to light a favorite hearth!
Ye Clouds, that in your temples in the West
See nothing brighter than its humblest flowers!
And you, ye Winds, that on the ocean's breast
Are kissed to coolness ere ye reach its bowers!
Bear witness with me in my song of praise,
And tell the world that, since the world began,
No fairer land hath fired a poet's lays,

Or given a home to man!
But these are charms already widely blown!
His be the meed whose pencil's trace
Hath touched our very swamps with grace,
And round whose tuneful way
All Southern laurels bloom;
The Poet of "The Woodlands," unto whom
Alike are known
The flute's low breathing and the trumpet's tone,
And the soft west wind's sighs;
But who shall utter all the debt,
O Land wherein all powers are met
That bind a people's heart,
The world doth owe thee at this day,
And which it never can repay,
Yet scarcely deigns to own!
Where sleeps the poet who shall fitly sing
The source wherefrom doth spring
That mighty commerce which, confined
To the mean channels of no selfish mart,
Goes out to every shore
Of this broad earth, and throngs the sea with ships
That bear no thunders; hushes hungry lips
In alien lands;
Joins with a delicate web remotest strands;
And gladdening rich and poor,
Doth gild Parisian domes,
Or feed the cottage-smoke of English homes,
And only bounds its blessings by mankind!
In offices like these, thy mission lies,
My Country! and it shall not end
As long as rain shall fall and Heaven bend
In blue above thee; though thy foes be hard
And cruel as their weapons, it shall guard
Thy hearth-stones as a bulwark; make thee great
In white and bloodless state;
And haply, as the years increase—
Still working through its humbler reach

With that large wisdom which the ages teach—
Revive the half-dead dream of universal peace!
As men who labor in that mine
Of Cornwall, hollowed out beneath the bed
Of ocean, when a storm rolls overhead,
Hear the dull booming of the world of brine
Above them, and a mighty muffled roar
Of winds and waters, yet toil calmly on,
And split the rock, and pile the massive ore,
Or carve a niche, or shape the arched roof;
So I, as calmly, weave my woof
Of song, chanting the days to come,
Unsilenced, though the quiet summer air
Stirs with the bruit of battles, and each dawn
Wakes from its starry silence to the hum
Of many gathering armies. Still,
In that we sometimes hear,
Upon the Northern winds, the voice of woe
Not wholly drowned in triumph, though I know
The end must crown us, and a few brief years
Dry all our tears,
I may not sing too gladly. To Thy will
Resigned, O Lord! we cannot all forget
That there is much even Victory must regret.
And, therefore, not too long
From the great burthen of our country's wrong
Delay our just release!
And, if it may be, save
These sacred fields of peace
From stain of patriot or of hostile blood!
Oh, help us, Lord! to roll the crimson flood
Back on its course, and, while our banners wing
Northward, strike with us! till the Goth shall cling
To his own blasted altar-stones, and crave
Mercy; and we shall grant it, and dictate
The lenient future of his fate
There, where some rotting ships and crumbling quays
Shall one day mark the Port which ruled the Western seas.

ODE

SUNG ON THE OCCASION
OF DECORATING THE GRAVES
OF THE CONFEDERATE DEAD,
AT MAGNOLIA CEMETERY,
CHARLESTON, S.C., 1867.

I.

Sleep sweetly in your humble graves,
    Sleep, martyrs of a fallen cause;
Though yet no marble column craves
    The pilgrim here to pause.

II.

In seeds of laurel in the earth
    The blossom of your fame is blown,
And somewhere, waiting for its birth,
    The shaft is in the stone!

III.

Meanwhile, behalf the tardy years
    Which keep in trust your storied tombs,
Behold! your sisters bring their tears,
    And these memorial blooms.

IV.

Small tributes! but your shades will smile
    More proudly on these wreaths to-day,
Than when some cannon-moulded pile
    Shall overlook this bay.

V.

Stoop, angels, hither from the skies!
    There is no holier spot of ground
Than where defeated valor lies,
    By mourning beauty crowned!

SEA ISLAND LORE

William Elliott

A DAY AT CHEE-HA

The traveller in South Carolina, who passes along the road between the Ashepoo and Combahee rivers will be struck by the appearance of two lofty white columns, rising among the pines that skirt the road. They are the only survivors of eight, which supported, in times anterior to our revolutionary war, a sylvan temple, erected by a gentleman, who, to the higher qualities of a devoted patriot, united the taste and liberality of the sportsman. The spot was admirably chosen, being on the brow of a piney ridge, which slopes away at a long gun-shot's length into a thick swamp; and many a deer has, we doubt not, in times past, been shot from the temple when it stood in its pride—as we ourselves have struck them from its ruins. From this ruin, stretching eastwardly some twelve or fourteen miles, is a neck of land, known from the Indian name of the small river that waters and almost bisects it, as Chee-ha—or, as it is incorrectly written, Chy-haw! It is now the best hunting-ground in Carolina —for which the following reasons may be given. The lands are distributed in large tracts; there are therefore few proprietors. The rich land is confined to the belt of the rivers, and there remains a wide expanse of barrens, traversed by deep swamps, always difficult and sometimes impassable, in which the deer find a secure retreat.

At a small hunting-lodge located in this region, it has often been my good fortune to meet a select body of hunting friends, and enjoy in their company the pleasures of the chase.

I give you one of my "days"—not that the success was unusual, it was by no means so; but that it was somewhat more marked by incident than most of its fellows. We turned, out, *after breakfast*, on a fine day in February, with a pack of twelve hounds, and two whippers in, or drivers, as we call them. The field consisted of one old shot besides myself, and two sportsmen who had not yet "fleshed their maiden swords." When we reached the ground, we had to experience the fate which all tardy sportsmen deserve, and must often undergo: the fresh print of dogs' feet, and the deep impression of horses' hoofs, showed us that another party had anticipated us in the drive, and that the game had been started and was off. Two expedients suggested themselves—we must either leave our ground, and in that case incur the risk of sharing the same fate in our next drive; or, we must beat up the ground now before us in a way which our predecessors in the field had probably neglected to do. We chose the latter part: and finding that the drive embraced two descriptions of ground—first, the main wood, which we inferred had already been taken, and next, the briery thickets that skirted a contiguous old field—into these thickets we pushed. Nor had we entered far, before the long, deep, querulous note of "Ruler," as he challenged on a trail, told us to expect the game. A few minutes later, and the whole pack announced the still more exciting fact—"the game is up." The first move of the deer was into a back-water, which he crossed, while the pack, half swimming, half wading, came yelping at his heels. He next dashed across an old field and made for a thicket, which he entered; it was a piece of briery and tangled ground, which the dogs could not traverse without infinite toil. By these two moves, he gained a great start of the hounds: if he kept on, we were thrown out, and our dogs lost for the day—if he doubled, and the nature of the ground favored that supposition, there were two points whereat he would be most likely to be intercepted. I consulted the wind, and made my choice. I was wrong. It proved to be a young deer, who did not need the wind, and he made for the pass I had *not selected*. The pack now turned; we found from their cry, that the deer had doubled, and our hearts beat high with expectation, as mounted on our respective hunters, we stretched ourselves across the old field which he must necessarily traverse, before he could regain the shelter of the wood. And now I saw my veteran comrade stretch his neck as if he spied something in the thicket; then with a sudden fling he brought his double barrel to his shoulder and fired. His horse, admonished by the spur, then fetched a caracole; from the new position, a new glimpse of the deer is gained—and crack! goes the second barrel. In a few moments, I saw one of our recruits dismount and fire. Soon after, the deer made his appearance and approached the second, who descended from his horse and fired. The deer kept on seemingly untouched, and had gained the crown of the hill when his second barrel brought him to the ground in sight of the whole field. We all rode to the spot, to congratulate our novice on his first exploit in sylvan warfare—when, as he stooped to examine the direction of his shot, our friend Loveleap slipped his knife into the throat of the deer, and before his purpose could be guessed at, bathed his face with the blood of his victim. (This, you must know, *is hunter's law* with us, on the killing a first deer). As our young sportsman started up from the ablution—his face glaring like an Indian chief's in all the splendor of war-paint—Robin the hunter touched his cap and thus accosted him:

"Maussa Tickle, if you wash off dat blood dis day—you neber hab luck again so long as you hunt."

"Wash it off!" cried we all, with one accord; "who ever heard of such a folly. He can be no true sportsman, who is ashamed of such a livery."

Thus beset, and moved thereunto, by other sage advices showered upon him by his companions in sport, he wore his bloody mask to the close of that long day's sport, and sooth to say, returned to receive the congratulations of his young and lovely wife, his face still adorned with the stains of victory. Whether he was received, as victors are wont to be, returning from other fields of blood, is a point whereon I shall refuse to satisfy the impertinent curiosity of my reader; but I am bound, in deference to historic truth, to add—that the claims of our novice, to the merit and penalties of this day's hunt, were equally incomplete, for it appeared on after inspection, that Loveleap had given the mortal wound, and that Tickle had merely given the "coup de grâce" to a deer, that, if unfired on, would have fallen of itself, in a run of a hundred yards. It must be believed, however, that we were quite too generous to divulge this unpleasant discovery to our novice, in the first pride of his triumph!

And now we tried other grounds, which our precursors in the field had already beaten; so that the prime of the day was wasted before we made another start. At last, in the afternoon, a splendid burst from the whole pack made us aware that a second deer had suddenly been roused. I was riding to reach a pass (or *stand* as we term it), when I saw a buck dashing along before the hounds at the top of his speed; the distance was seventy-five yards—but I reined in my horse and let slip at him. To my surprise, he fell; but before I could reach the spot, from which I was separated by a thick underwood, he had shuffled off and disappeared. The hounds came roaring on, and showed me by their course that he had made for a marsh that lay hard by. For that we all pushed in hopes of anticipating him. He was before us, we saw him plunge into the canal, and mount the opposite bank, though evidently in distress and crippled in one of his hind legs. The dogs rush furiously on (the scent of blood in their nostrils), plunge into the canal, sweep over the bank, and soon pursuers and pursued are shut out from sight, as they wind among the thick covers that lie scattered over the face of the marsh.

"What use of horse now!" said Robin, as (sliding from his saddle where his horse instinctively made a dead halt at the edge of the impracticable Serbonian bog that lay before him) he began to climb a tree that overlooked the field of action—"what use of horse now?"

From this "vantage ground," however, he looked in vain to catch a glimpse of the deer. The eye of a lynx could not penetrate the thick mass of grass, that stretched upward six feet from the surface of the marsh. The cry of the hounds now grew faint from distance, and now again came swelling on the breeze; when suddenly our ears were saluted by a full burst from the whole pack, in that loud, open note, which tells a practised ear that the cry comes from the water.

"Zounds, Robin!" cried I, in the excitement of the moment, "they have him at bay there—there in the canal. Down from your perch, my lad, or they'll eat him, horns and all, before you reach him."

Robin apparently did not partake of this enthusiasm, for he maintained his perch on the tree, and coolly observed—"What use, maussa? fore I git dere, dem dog polish ebery bone."

"You are afraid, you rascal! you have only to swim the canal and then" —

"Got maussa," said Robin, as he looked ruefully over the field of his proposed missionary labors; "if he be water, I swim 'um—if he be bog, I bog 'um—if he be brier, I kratch tru um—but who de debble, but otter, no so alligator, go tru all tree one time!"

The thought was just stealing its way into my mind, that under the excitement of my feelings, I was giving an order that I might have hesitated personally to execute, when the cry of the hounds, lately so clamorous, totally ceased. "There," cried I, in the disappointed tone of a sportsman who had lost a fine buck, "save your skin, you loitering rascal! You may sleep where you sit, for by this time they have eaten him sure enough." This conclusion was soon overset by the solitary cry of Ruler, which was now heard, half a mile to the left of the scene of the late uproar.

"Again! What is this? *It is* the cry of Ruler! ho! I understand it—the deer is not eaten, but has taken the canal—and the nose of that prince of hounds, has scented him down the running stream.—Aye, aye, he makes for the wood—and now to cut him off." No sooner said than done. I gave the spur to my horse, and shot off accordingly; but not in time to prevent the success of the masterly manœuver by which the buck, baffling his pursuers, was now seen straining every nerve to regain the shelter of the wood. I made a desperate effort to cut him off, but reached the wood only in time to note the direction he had taken. It was now sunset, and the white, oustpread tail of the deer was my only guide in the pursuit, as he glided among the trees. "Now for it, Boxer—show your speed, my gallant nag." The horse, as if he entered fully into the purpose of his rider, stretched himself to the utmost, obedient to the slightest touch of the reins, as he threaded the intricacies of the forest; and was gaining rapidly on the deer, when plash! he came to a dead halt—his fore legs plunged in a quagmire, over which the buck with his split hoofs had bounded in security. What a baulk! "but here goes"—and the gun was brought instantly to the shoulder, and the left-hand barrel fired. The distance was eighty yards, and the shot ineffectual. Making a slight circuit to avoid the bog, I again push at the deer and again approach. "Ah, if I had but reserved the charge, I had so idly wasted!" But no matter, I must run him down—and gaining a position on his flank, I spurred my horse full upon his broadside, to bear him to the ground. The noble animal (he *was* a noble animal, for he traced, with some baser admixture indeed, through Boxer, Medley, Gimcrack, to the Godolphin Arabian) refused to trample on his fellow quadruped; and, in spite of the goading spur, ranged up close along side of the buck, as if his only pride lay in surpassing him in speed. This brought me in close contact with the buck. Detaching my right foot from the stirrup, I struck the armed heel of my boot full against his head; he reeled from the blow and plunged into a neighboring thicket—too close for horse to enter. I fling myself from my horse, and pursue on foot—he gains on me: I dash down my now useless gun, and, freed from all encumbrance, press after the panting animal. A large, fallen oak lies across his path; he gathers himself up for the leap, and falls exhausted directly across it. Before he could recover his legs, and while he lay thus poised on the tree, I fling myself at full length upon the body of the struggling deer—my left hand clasps his neck, while my right detaches the knife; whose fatal blade, in another moment, is buried in his throat. There he lay in his blood, and I remained sole occupant of the field. I seize my horn, but am utterly breathless, and incapable of sounding it: I strive to shout, but my voice is extinct from fatigue and exhaustion. I retrace my steps, while the waning light yet sufficed to show me the track of the deer—recover my horse and gun, and return to the tree where my victim lay. But how apprise my comrades of my position? My last shot, however, had not been unnoted—and soon their voices are heard cheering on "Ruler," while far in the advance of the yet baffled pack, he follows unerringly on the tracks of the deer. They came at last: but found me still so exhausted from fatigue, that to wave my blood knife, and point to the victim where he lay at my feet, were all the history I could then give of the spirit-stirring incidents I have just recorded. Other hunting matches have I been engaged in, wherein double the number of deer have been killed; but never have I engaged in one of deeper and more absorbing interest, than that which marked this "day at Chee-ha."

VENATOR.

Edgar Allan Poe

THE GOLD-BUG

What ho! what ho! this fellow is dancing mad!
He hath been bitten by the Tarantula.

- All in the Wrong

Many years ago, I contracted an intimacy with a Mr. William Legrand. He was of an ancient Huguenot family, and had once been wealthy; but a series of misfortunes had reduced him to want. To avoid the mortification consequent upon his disasters, he left New Orleans, the city of his forefathers, and took up his residence at Sullivan's Island, near Charleston, South Carolina.

This Island is a very singular one. It consists of little else than the sea sand, and is about three miles long. Its breadth at no point exceeds a quarter of a mile. It is separated from the main land by a scarcely perceptible creek, oozing its way through a wilderness of reeds and slime, a favorite resort of the marsh-hen. The vegetation, as might be supposed, is scant, or at least dwarfish. No trees of any magnitude are to be seen. Near the western extremity, where Fort Moultrie stands, and where are some miserable frame buildings, tenanted, during summer, by the fugitives from Charleston dust and fever, may be found, indeed, the bristly palmetto; but the whole island, with the exception of this western point, and a line of hard, white beach on the seacoast, is covered with a dense undergrowth of the sweet myrtle, so much prized by the horticulturists of England. The shrub here often attains the height of fifteen or twenty feet, and forms an almost impenetrable coppice, burthening the air with its fragrance.

In the inmost recesses of this coppice, not far from the eastern or more remote end of the island, Legrand had built himself a small hut, which he occupied when I first, by mere accident, made his acquaintance. This soon ripened into friendship—for there was much in the recluse to excite interest and esteem. I found him well educated, with unusual powers of mind, but infected with misanthropy, and subject to perverse moods of alternate enthusiasm and melancholy. He had with him many books, but rarely employed them. His chief amusements were gunning and fishing, or sauntering along the bank and through the myrtles, in quest of shells or entomological specimens;—his collection of the latter might have been envied by a Swammerdamm. In these excursions he was usually accompanied by an old negro, called Jupiter, who had been manumitted before the reverses of the family, but who could be induced, neither by threats nor by promises, to abandon what he considered his right of attendance upon the footsteps of his young "Massa Will." It is not improbable that the relatives of Legrand, conceiving him to be somewhat unsettled in intellect, had contrived to instil this obstinacy into Jupiter, with a view to the supervision and guardianship of the wanderer.

The winters in the latitude of Sullivan's Island are seldom very severe, and in the fall of the year it is a rare event indeed when a fire is considered necessary. About the middle of October, 18—, there occurred, however, a day of remarkable chilliness. Just before sunset I scrambled my way through the evergreens to the hut of my friend, whom I had not visited for several weeks—my residence being, at the time, in Charleston, a distance of nine miles from the island, while the facilities of passage and re-passage were very far behind those of the present day. Upon reaching the hut I rapped, as was my custom, and getting no reply, sought for the key where I knew it was secreted, unlocked the door and went in. A fine fire was blazing upon the hearth. It was a novelty, and by no means an unwelcome one. I threw off an overcoat, took an armchair by the crackling logs, and waited patiently the arrival of my hosts.

Soon after dark they arrived, and gave me a most cordial welcome. Jupiter, grinning from ear to ear, bustled about to prepare some marsh-hens for supper. Legrand was in one of his fits—how else shall I term them?—of enthusiasm. He had found an unknown bivalve, forming a new genus, and, more than this, he had hunted down and secured, with Jupiter's assistance, a *scarabæus* which he believed to be totally new, but in respect to which he wished to have my opinion on the morrow.

"And why not to-night?" I asked, rubbing my hands over the blaze, and wishing the whole tribe of *scarabæi* at the devil.

"Ah, if I had only known you were here!" said Legrand, "but it's so long since I saw you; and how could I foresee that you would pay me a visit this very night of all others? As I was coming home I met Lieutenant G — —, from the fort, and, very foolishly, I lent him the bug; so it will be impossible for you to see it until the morning. Stay here to-night, and I will send Jup down for it at sunrise. It is the loveliest thing in creation!"

"What? —sunrise?"

"Nonsense! no! —the bug. It is of a brilliant gold color—about the size of a large hickory-nut—with two jet black spots near one extremity of the back, and another, somewhat longer, at the other. The *antennæ* are —"

"Day aint *no* tin in him, Massa Will, I keep a tellin on you," here interrupted Jupiter; "de bug is a goole bug, solid, ebery bit of him, inside and all, sep him wing—neber feel half so hebby a bug in my life."

"Well, suppose it is, Jup," replied Legrand, somewhat more earnestly, it seemed to me, than the occasion demanded, "is that any reason for your letting the birds burn? The color"—here he turned to me—"is really almost enough to warrant Jupiter's idea. You never saw a more brilliant metallic lustre than the scales emit—but of this you cannot judge till to-morrow. In the mean time I can give you some idea of the shape." Saying this, he seated himself at a small table, on which were a pen and ink, but no paper. He looked for some in a drawer, but found none.

"Never mind," said he at length, "this will answer;" and he drew from his waistcoat pocket a scrap of what I took to be very dirty foolscap, and made upon it a rough drawing with the pen. While he did this, I retained my seat by the fire, for I was still chilly. When the design was complete, he handed it to me without rising. As I received it, a loud growl was heard, succeeded by a scratching at the door. Jupiter opened it, and a large Newfoundland, belonging to Legrand, rushed in, leaped upon my shoulders, and loaded me with caresses; for I had shown him much attention during previous visits. When his gambols were over, I looked at the paper, and, to speak the truth, found myself not a little puzzled at what my friend had depicted.

"Well!" I said, after contemplating it for some minutes, "this is a strange *scarabæus,* I must confess: new to me: never saw anything like it before—unless it was a skull, or a death's-head—which it more nearly resembles than anything else that has come under *my* observation."

"A death's-head!" echoed Legrand—"Oh—yes—well, it has something of that appearance upon paper, no doubt! The two upper black spots look like eyes, eh? and the longer one at the bottom like a mouth—and then the shape of the whole is oval."

"Perhaps so," said I; "but, Legrand, I fear you are no artist. I must wait until I see the beetle itself, if I am to form any idea of its personal appearance."

"Well, I don't know," said he, a little nettled, "I draw tolerably—*should* do it at least—have had good masters, and flatter myself that I am not quite a blockhead."

"But, my dear fellow, you are joking then," said I, "this is a very passable *skull*—indeed, I may say that it is a very *excellent* skull, according to the vulgar notions about such specimens of physiology—and your *scarabæus* must be the queerest *scarabæus* in the world if it resembles it. Why, we may get up a very thrilling bit of superstition upon this hint. I presume you will call the bug *scarabæus caput hominis* [head-of-a-man beetle], or something of that kind—there are many similar titles in the Natural Histories. But where are the *antennæ* you spoke of?"

"The *antennæ!*" said Legrand, who seemed to be getting unaccountably warm upon the subject; "I am sure you must see the *antennæ*. I made them as distinct as they are in the original insect, and I presume that is sufficient."

"Well, well," I said, "perhaps you have—still I don't see them;" and I handed him the paper without additional remark, not wishing to ruffle his temper; but I was much surprised at the turn affairs had taken; his ill humor puzzled me—and, as for the drawing of the beetle, there were positively *no antennæ* visible, and the whole *did* bear a very close resemblance to the ordinary cut of a death's-head.

He received the paper very peevishly, and was about to crumple it, apparently to throw it in the fire, when a casual glance at the design seemed suddenly to rivet his attention. In an instant his face grew violently red—in another as excessively pale. For some minutes he continued to scrutinize the drawing minutely where he sat. At length he arose, took a candle from the table, and proceeded to seat himself upon a sea-chest in the farthest corner of the room. Here again he made an anxious examination of the paper; turning it in all directions. He said nothing, however, and his conduct greatly astonished me; yet I thought it prudent not to exacerbate the growing moodiness of his temper by any comment. Presently he took from his coat pocket a wallet, placed the paper carefully in it, and deposited both in a writing-desk, which he locked. He now grew more composed in his demeanor; but his original air of enthusiasm had quite disappeared. Yet he seemed not so much sulky as abstracted. As the evening wore away he became more and more absorbed in reverie, from which no sallies of mine could arouse him. It had been my intention to pass the night at the hut, as I had frequently done before, but, seeing my host in this mood, I deemed it proper to take leave. He did not press me to remain, but, as I departed, he shook my hand with even more than his usual cordiality.

It was about a month after this (and during the interval I had seen nothing of Legrand) when I received a visit, at Charleston, from his man, Jupiter. I had never seen the good old negro look so dispirited, and I feared that some serious disaster had befallen my friend.

"Well, Jup," said I, "what is the matter now?—how is your master?"

"Why, to speak de troof, massa, him not so berry well as mought be."

"Not well! I am truly sorry to hear it. What does he complain of?"

"Dar! dat's it!—him neber plain ob notin—but him berry sick for all dat."

"*Very* sick, Jupiter!—why didn't you say so at once? Is he confined to bed?"

"No, dat he aint!—he aint find nowhar—dat's just whar de shoe pinch—my mind is got to be berry hebby bout poor Massa Will."

"Jupiter, I should like to understand what it is you are talking about. You say your master is sick. Hasn't he told you what ails him?"

"Why, massa, taint worf while for to git mad about de matter—Massa Will say noffin at all aint de matter wid him—but den what make him go bout looking dis here way, wid he head down and he soldiers up, and as white as a gose? And den he keep a syphon all de time —"

"Keeps a what, Jupiter?"

"Keeps a syphon wid de figgurs on de slate—de queerest figgurs I ebber did see. Ise gitting to be skeered, I tell you. Hab for to keep mighty tight eye pon him noovers. Todder day he gib me slip fore de sun up and was gone de whole ob de blessed day. I had a big stick ready cut for to giv him d—n good beatin when he did come—but Ise sich a fool dat I hadn't de heart arter all—he look so berry poorly."

"Eh?—what?—ah yes!—upon the whole I think you had better not be too severe with the poor fellow—don't flog him, Jupiter—he can't very well stand it—but can you form no idea of what has occasioned this illness, or rather this change of conduct? Has anything unpleasant happened since I saw you?"

"No, massa, dey aint bin noffin onpleasant *since* den— 'twas *fore* den I'm feared—'twas de berry day you was dare."

"How? what do you mean?"

"Why, massa, I mean de bug—dare now."

"The what?"

"De bug—I'm berry sartain dat Massa Will bin bit somewhere bout de head by dat d—n goole-bug."

"And what cause have you, Jupiter, for such a supposition?"

"Claws enuff, massa, and mouff too. I nebber did see sich a d—n bug—he kick and he bite ebery ting what cum near him. Massa Will cotch him fuss, but had for to let him go gin mighty quick, I tell you—den was de time he must ha got de bite. I didn't like de look ob de bug mouff, myself, no how, so I wouldn't take hold ob him wid my finger, but cotch him wid a piece ob paper dat I found. I rap him up in de paper and stuff piece ob it in he mouff—dat was de way."

"And you think, then, that your master was really bitten by the beetle, and that the bite made him sick?"

"I don't tink noffin bout it—I nose it. What make him dream bout do goole so much, if taint cause he bit by de goole-bug? Ise heerd bout dem goole-bugs fore dis."

"But how do you know he dreams about gold?"

"How I know? why cause he talk about it in he sleep—dat's how I nose."

"Well, Jup, perhaps you are right; but to what fortunate circumstance am I to attribute the honor of a visit from you to-day?"

"What de matter, massa?"

"Did you bring any message from Mr. Legrand?"

"No, massa, I bring dis here pissel;" and here Jupiter handed me an note which ran thus:

My Dear — —

Why have I not seen you for so long a time? I hope you have not been so foolish as to take offence at any little brusquerie *of mine; but no, that is improbable.*

Since I saw you I have had great cause for anxiety. I have something to tell you, yet scarcely know how to tell it, or whether I should tell it at all.

I have not been quite well for some days past, and poor old Jup annoys me, almost beyond endurance, by his well-meant attentions. Would you believe it?—he had prepared a hugh stick, the other day, with which to chastise me for giving him the slip, and spending the day, solus, *among the hills on the main land. I verily believe that my ill looks alone saved me a flogging.*

I have made no addition to my cabinet sense we met.

If you can, in any way, make it convenient, come over with Jupiter. Do come, *I wish to see you to-night, upon business of importance. I assure you that it is of the highest importance.*

Ever yours,

WILLIAM LEGRAND.

There was something in the tone of this note which gave me great uneasiness. Its whole style differed materially from that of Legrand. What could he be dreaming of? What new crotchet possessed his excitable brain? What "business of the highest importance" could *he* possibly have to transact? Jupiter's account of him boded no good. I dreaded lest the continued pressure of misfortune had, at length, fairly unsettled the reason of my friend. Without a moment's hesitation, therefore, I prepared to accompany the negro.

Upon reaching the wharf, I noticed a scythe and three spades, all apparently new, lying in the bottom of the boat in which we were to embark.

"What is the meaning of all this, Jup?" I inquired.

"Him syfe, massa, and spade."

"Very true; but what are they doing here?"

"Him de syfe and de spade which Massa Will sis pon my buying for him in de town, and de debbil's own lot of money I had to gib for em."

"But what, in the name of all that is mysterious, is your 'Massa Will' going to do with scythes and spades?"

"Dat's more dan *I* know, and debbil take me if I don't

blieve 'tis more dan he know, too. But it's all cum ob de bug."

Finding that no satisfaction was to be obtained of Jupiter, whose whole intellect seemed to be absorbed by "de bug," I now stepped into the boat and made sail. With a fair and strong breeze we soon ran into the little cove to the northward of Fort Moultrie, and a walk of some two miles brought us to the hut. It was about three in the afternoon when we arrived. Legrand had been awaiting us in eager expectation. He grasped my hand with a nervous *empressement* which alarmed me and strengthened the suspicions already entertained. His countenance was pale even to ghastliness, and his deep-set eyes glared with unnatural lustre. After some inquiries respecting his health, I asked him, not knowing what better to say, if he had yet obtained the *scarabæus* from Lieutenant G——.

"Oh, yes," he replied, coloring violently, "I got it from him the next morning. Nothing should tempt me to part with that *scarabæus*. Do you know that Jupiter is quite right about it?"

"In what way?" I asked, with a sad foreboding at heart.

"In supposing it to be a bug of *real gold*." He said this with an air of profound seriousness, and I felt inexpressibly shocked.

"This bug is to make my fortune," he continued, with a triumphant smile, "to reinstate me in my family possessions. Is it any wonder, then, that I prize it? Since Fortune has thought fit to bestow it upon me, I have only to use it properly and I shall arrive at the gold of which it is the index. Jupiter, bring me that *scarabæus*!"

"What! de bug, massa? I'd rudder not go fer to trubble dat bug—you mus git him for your own self." Hereupon Legrand arose, with a grave and stately air, and brought me the beetle from a glass case in which it was enclosed. It was a beautiful *scarabæus*, and, at that time, unknown to naturalists—of course a great prize in a scientific point of view. There were two round, black spots near one extremity of the back, and a longer one near the other. The scales were exceedingly hard and glossy, with all the appearance of burnished gold. The weight of the insect was very remarkable, and, taking all things into consideration, I could hardly blame Jupiter for his opinion respecting it; but what to make of Legrand's concordance with that opinion, I could not, for the life of me, tell.

"I sent for you," said he, in a grandiloquent tone, when I had completed my examination of the beetle, "I sent for you, that I might have your counsel and assistance in furthering the views of Fate and of the bug"—

"My dear Legrand," I cried, interrupting him, "you are certainly unwell, and had better use some little precautions. You shall go to bed, and I will remain with you a few days, until you get over this. You are feverish and"—

"Feel my pulse," said he.

I felt it, and, to say the truth, found not the slightest indication of fever.

"But you may be ill and yet have no fever. Allow me this once to prescribe for you. In the first place, go to bed. In the next"—

"You are mistaken," he interposed, "I am as well as I can expect to be under the excitement which I suffer. If you really wish me well, you will relieve this excitement."

"And how is this to be done?"

"Very easily. Jupiter and myself are going upon an expedition into the hills, upon the main land, and, in this expedition, we shall need the aid of some person in whom we can confide. You are the only one we can trust. Whether we succeed or fail, the excitement which you now perceive in me will be equally allayed."

"I am anxious to oblige you in any way," I replied; "but do you mean to say that this infernal beetle has any connection with your expedition into the hills?"

"It has."

"Then, Legrand, I can become a party to no such absurd proceeding."

"I am sorry—very sorry—for we shall have to try it by ourselves."

"Try it by yourselves! The man is surely mad!—but stay!—how long do you propose to be absent?"

"Probably all night. We shall start immediately, and be back, at all events, by sunrise."

"And will you promise me, upon your honor, that when this freak of yours is over, and the bug business (good God!) settled to your satisfaction, you will then return home and follow my advice implicitly, as that of your physician?"

"Yes; I promise; and now let us be off, for we have no time to lose."

With a heavy heart I accompanied my friend. We started about four o'clock—Legrand, Jupiter, the dog, and myself. Jupiter had with him the scythe and spades—the whole of which he insisted upon carrying—more through fear, it seemed to me, of trusting either of the implements within reach of his master, than from any excess of industry or complaisance. His demeanor was dogged in the extreme, and "dat d—n bug" were the sole words which escaped his lips during the journey. For my own part, I had charge of a couple of dark lanterns, while Legrand contented himself with the *scarabæus*, which he carried attached to the end of a bit of whip-cord; twirling it to and fro, with the air of a conjuror, as he went. When I observed this last, plain evidence of my friend's aberration of mind, I could scarcely refrain from tears. I thought it best, however, to humor his fancy, at least for the present, or until I could adopt some more energetic measures with a chance of success. In the mean time I endeavored, but all in vain, to sound him in regard to the object of the expedition. Having succeeded in inducing me to accompany him, he seemed unwilling to hold conversation upon any topic of minor importance, and to all my questions vouchsafed no other reply than "we shall see!"

We crossed the creek at the head of the island by means of a skiff, and, ascending the high grounds on the shore of the main land, proceeded in a northwesternly direction, through a tract of country excessively wild and desolate, where no trace of a human footstep was to be seen. Legrand led the way with decision; pausing only for an instant, here and there, to consult what appeared to be certain landmarks of his own contrivance upon a former occasion.

In this manner we journeyed for about two hours, and the sun was just setting when we entered a region infinitely more dreary than any yet seen. It was a species of table land, near the summit of an almost inaccessible hill, densely wooded from base to pinnacle, and interspersed with huge crags that appeared to lie loosely upon the soil, and in many cases were prevented from precipitating themselves into the valleys below, merely by the support of the trees against which they reclined. Deep ravines, in various directions, gave an air of still sterner solemnity to the scene.

The natural platform to which we had clambered was thickly overgrown with brambles, through which we soon discovered that it would have been impossible to force our way but for the scythe; and Jupiter, by direction of his master, proceeded to clear for us a path to the foot of an enormously tall tulip-tree, which stood, with some eight or ten oaks, upon the level, and far surpassed them all, and all other trees which I had then ever seen, in the beauty of its foliage and form, in the wide spread of its branches, and in the general majesty of its appearance. When we reached this tree, Legrand turned to Jupiter, and asked him if he thought he could climb it. The old man seemed a little staggered by the question, and for some moments made no reply. At length he approached the tree, walked slowly round its huge trunk, and examined it with minute attention. When he had completed his scrutiny, he merely said,

"Yes, massa, Jup climb any tree he ebber see in he life."

"Then up with you as soon as possible, for it will soon be too dark to see what we are about."

"How far mus go up, massa?" inquired Jupiter.

"Get up the main trunk first, and then I will tell you which way to go—and here—stop! take this beetle up with you."

"De bug, Massa Will!—do goole bug!" cried the negro,

drawing back in dismay—"what for mus tote de bug way up de tree?—d—n if I do!"

"If you are afraid, Jup, a great big negro like you, to take hold of a harmless little dead beetle, why you can carry it up by this string—but, if you do not take it up with you in some way, I shall be under the necessity of breaking your head with this shovel."

"What de matter now, massa?" said Jup, evidently shamed into compliance; "always want for to raise fuss wid old nigger. Was only funnin any how. *Me* feered de bug! what I keer for de bug?" Here he took cautiously hold of the extreme end of the string, and, maintaining the insect as far from his person as circumstances would permit, prepared to ascend the tree.

In youth, the tulip-tree, or *Liriodendron tulipiferum*, the most magnificent of American foresters, has a trunk peculiarly smooth, and often rises to a great height without lateral branches; but, in its riper age, the bark becomes gnarled and uneven, while many short limbs make their appearance on the stem. Thus the difficulty of ascension, in the present case, lay more in semblance than in reality. Embracing the huge cylinder, as closely as possible, with his arms and knees, seizing with his hands some projections, and resting his naked toes upon others, Jupiter, after one or two narrow escapes from falling, at length wriggled himself into the first great fork, and seemed to consider the whole business as virtually accomplished. The *risk* of the achievement was, in fact, now over, although the climber was some sixty or seventy feet from the ground.

"Which way mus go now, Massa Will?" he asked.

"Keep up the largest branch—the one on this side," said Legrand. The negro obeyed him promptly, and apparently with but little trouble; ascending higher and higher, until no glimpses of his squat figure could be obtained through the dense foliage which enveloped it. Presently his voice was heard in a sort of halloo.

"How much fudder is got for go?"

"How high up are you?" asked Legrand.

"Ebber so fur," replied the negro; can see de sky fru de top of de tree."

"Never mind the sky, but attend to what I say. Look down the trunk and count the limbs below you on this side. How many limbs have you passed?"

"One, two, three, four, fibe—I done pass fibe big limb, massa, pon dis side."

"Then go one limb higher."

In a few minutes the voice was heard again, announcing that the seventh limb was attained.

"Now, Jup," cried Legrand, evidently much excited, "I want you to work your way out upon that limb as far as you can. If you see anything strange, let me know."

By this time what little doubt I might have entertained of my poor friend's insanity, was put finally at rest. I had no alternative but to conclude him stricken with lunacy, and I became seriously anxious about getting him home. While I was pondering upon what was best to be done, Jupiter's voice was again heard.

"Mos feerd for to ventur pon dis limb berry far—tis dead limb putty much all de way."

"Did you say it was a *dead* limb, Jupiter?" cried Legrand in a quavering voice.

"Yes, massa, him dead as de door-nail—done up for sartain—done departed dis here life."

"What in the name of heaven shall I do?" asked Legrand, seemingly in the greatest distress.

"Do!" said I, glad of an opportunity to interpose a word, "Why come home and go to bed. Do—that's a fine fellow. It's getting late, and besides, you remember your promise."

"Jupiter," cried he, without heeding me in the least, "do you hear me?"

"Yes, Massa Will, hear you ebber so plain."

"Try the wood well, then, with your knife, and see if you think it *very* rotten."

"Him rotten, massa, sure nuff," replied the negro in a few moments, "but not so berry rotten as mought be. Mought ventur out leetle way pon de limb by myself, dat's true."

"By yourself!—what do you mean?"

"Why I mean de bug. 'Tis *berry* hebby bug. Spose I drop him down fuss, and den de limb won't break wid just de weight ob one nigger."

"You infernal scoundrel!" cried Legrand, apparently much relieved, "what do you mean by telling me such nonsense as that? As sure as you drop that beetle I'll break your neck. Look here, Jupiter, do you hear me?"

"Yes, massa, needn't hollo at poor nigger dat style."

"Well! now listen!—if you will venture out on the limb as far as you think safe, and not let go of the beetle, I'll make you a present of a silver dollar as soon as you get down."

"I'm gwine, Massa Will—deed I is," replied the negro very promptly—"mos out to de eend now."

"*Out to the end*!" here fairly screamed Legrand, "do you say you are out to the end of that limb?"

"Soon be to do eend, Massa—o-o-o-o-oh! Lor-gol-a-marcy! what *is* dis here pon de tree?"

"Well!" cried Legrand, highly delighted, "what is it?"

"Why taint noffin but a skull—somebody bin lef him head up de tree, and de crows done gobble every bit ob de meat off."

"A skull, you say!—very well!—how is it fastened to the limb—what holds it on?"

"Sure nuff, massa; mus look. Why dis berry curous sarcumstance, pon my word—dare's a great big nail in de skull, what fastens ob it on to de tree."

"Well now, Jupiter, do exactly as I tell you—do you hear?"

"Yes, massa."

"Pay attention then!—find the left eye of the skull."

"Hum! hoo! dat's good! why dare aint no eye lef at all."

"Curse your stupidity! do you know your right hand from your left?"

"Yes, I nose dat—nose all bout dat—tis my lef hand what I chops de wood wid."

"To be sure! you are left-handed; and your left eye is on

the same side as your left hand. Now, I suppose, you can find the left eye of the skull, or the place where the left eye has been. Have you found it?"

Here was a long pause. At length the negro asked, "Is de lef eye of de skull pon de same side as de lef hand of de skull, too?—cause de skull aint got not a bit ob a hand at all—nebber mind! I got de lef eye now—here de lef eye! What mus do wid it?"

"Let the beetle drop through it, as far as the string will reach—but be careful and not let go your hold of the string."

"All dat done, Massa Will; mighty easy ting for to put de bug fru de hole—look out for him dare below!"

"Very well!—now just keep as you are for a few minutes."

During this colloquy no portion of Jupiter's person could be seen; but the beetle, which he had suffered to descend, was now visible at the end of the string, and glistened, like a globe of burnished gold, in the last rays of the setting sun, some of which still faintly illumined the eminence upon which we stood. The *scarabæus* hung quite clear of any branches, and, if allowed to fall, would have fallen at our feet. Legrand immediately took the scythe, and cleared with it a circular space, three or four yards in diameter, just beneath the insect, and, having accomplished this, ordered Jupiter to let go the string and come down from the tree.

Driving a peg, with great nicety, into the ground, at the precise spot where the beetle lay, my friend now produced from his pocket a tape-measure. Fastening one end of this at that point of the trunk of the tree which was nearest the peg, he unrolled it till it reached the peg, and thence farther unrolled it, in the direction already established by the two points of the tree and the peg, for the distance of fifty feet— Jupiter clearing away the brambles with the scythe. At the spot thus attained a second peg was driven, and about this, as a centre, a rude circle, about four feet in diameter, described. Taking now a spade himself, and giving one to Jupiter and one to me, Legrand begged us to set about digging as quickly as possible.

To speak the truth, I had no especial relish for such amusement at any time, and, at that particular moment, I would most willingly have declined it; for the night was coming on, and I felt much fatigued with the exercise already taken; but I saw no mode of escape, and was fearful of disturbing my poor friend's equanimity by a refusal. Could I have depended, indeed, upon Jupiter's aid, I would have had no hesitation in attempting to get the lunatic home by force; but I was too well assured of the old negro's disposition, to hope that he would assist me, under any circumstances, in a personal contest with his master. I made no doubt that the latter had been infected with some of the innumberable Southern superstitions about money buried, and that his phantasy had received confirmation by the finding of the *scarabæus,* or, perhaps, by Jupiter's obstinacy in maintaining it to be "a bug of real gold." A mind disposed to lunacy would readily be led away by such suggestions—especially if chiming in with favorite preconceived ideas—and then I called to mind the poor fellow's speech about the beetle's being "the index of his fortune." Upon the whole, I was sadly vexed and puzzled, but, at length, I concluded to make a virtue of necessity—to dig with a good will, and thus the sooner to convince him, by ocular demonstration, of the fallacy of the opinions he entertained.

The lanterns having been lit, we all fell to work with a zeal worthy a more rational cause; and, as the glare fell upon our persons and implements, I could not help thinking how picturesque a group we composed, and how strange and suspicious our labors must have appeared to any interloper who, by chance, might have stumbled upon our whereabouts.

We dug very steadily for two hours. Little was said; and our chief embarrassment lay in the yelpings of the dog, who took exceeding interest in our proceedings. He, at length, became so obstreperous that we grew fearful of his giving the alarm to some stragglers in the vicinity;—or, rather, this was the apprehension of Legrand;—for myself, I should have rejoiced at any interruption which might have enabled me to get the wanderer home. The noise was, at length, very effectually silenced by Jupiter, who, getting out of the hole with a dogged air of deliberation, tied the brute's mouth up with one of his suspenders, and then returned, with a grave chuckle, to his task.

When the time mentioned had expired, we had reached a depth of five feet, and yet no signs of any treasure became manifest. A general pause ensued, and I began to hope that the farce was at an end. Legrand, however, although evidently much disconcerted, wiped his brow thoughtfully and recommenced. We had excavated the entire circle of four feet diameter, and now we slightly enlarged the limit, and went to the farther depth of two feet. Still nothing appeared. The gold-seeker, whom I sincerely pitied, at length clambered from the pit, with the bitterest disappointment imprinted upon every feature, and proceeded, slowly and reluctantly, to put on his coat, which he had thrown off at the beginning of his labor. In the mean time I made no remark. Jupiter, at a signal from his master, began to gather up his tools. This done, and the dog having been unmuzzled, we turned in a profound silence towards home.

We had taken, perhaps, a dozen steps in this direction, when, with a loud oath, Legrand strode up to Jupiter, and seized him by the collar. The astonished negro opened his eyes and mouth to the fullest extent, let fall the spades, and fell upon his knees.

"You scoundrel," said Legrand, hissing out the syllables from between his clenched teeth—"you infernal black villain!—speak, I tell you!—answer me this instant, without prevarication!—which—which is your left eye?"

"Oh, my golly, Massa Will! aint dis here my lef eye for sartain?" roared the terrified Jupiter, placing his hand upon his *right* organ of vision, and holding it there with desperate pertinacity, as if in immediate dread of his master's attempt at a gouge.

"I thought so!—I knew it!—hurrah!" vociferated Legrand, letting the negro go, and executing a series of curvets and caracols, much to the astonishment of his valet, who, arising from his knees, looked, mutely, from his master to myself, and then from myself to his master.

"Come! we must go back," said the latter, "the game's not up yet;" and he again led the way to the tulip-tree.

"Jupiter," said he, when we reached its foot, "come here! was the skull nailed to the limb with the face outwards or with the face to the limb?"

"De face was out, massa, so dat de crows could get at de eyes good, widout any trubble."

"Well, then, was it this eye or that through which you dropped the beetle?"—here Legrand touched each of Jupiter's eyes.

"Twas dis eye, massa—de lef eye—jis as you tell me," and here it was his right eye that the negro indicated.

"That will do—we must try it again."

Here my friend, about whose madness I now saw, or fancied that I saw, certain indications of method, removed the peg nearest the tree, to a spot about three inches to the westward of its former position. Taking, now, the tape-measure from the nearest point of the trunk, as before, and continuing the extension in a straight line to the distance of fifty feet, a spot was indicated, removed, by several yards, from the point at which we had been digging.

Around the new position a circle, somewhat larger than in the former instance, was now described, and we again set to work with the spades. I was dreadfully weary, but, scarcely understanding what had occasioned the change in my thoughts, I felt no longer any great aversion from the labor imposed. I had become most unaccountably interested—nay, even excited. Perhaps there was something, amid all the extravagant demeanor of Legrand—some air of forethought, or of deliberation, which impressed me. I dug eagerly, and now and then caught myself actually looking, with something that very much resembled expectation, for the fancied treasure, the vision of which had demented my unfortunate companion. At a period when such vagaries of thought most fully possessed me, and when we had been at work perhaps an hour and a half, we were again interrupted by the violent howlings of the dog. His uneasiness, in the first instance, had been, evidently, but the result of playfulness or caprice, but he now assumed a bitter and serious tone. Upon Jupiter's again attempting to muzzle him, he made furious resistance, and, leaping into the hole, tore up the mould frantically with his claws. In a few seconds he had uncovered a mass of human bones, forming two complete skeletons, and intermingled with several buttons of metal, and what appeared to be the dust of decayed woollen. One or two strokes of a spade upturned the blade of a large Spanish knife, and, as we dug farther, three or four loose pieces of gold and silver coin came to light.

At sight of these the joy of Jupiter could scarcely be restrained, but the countenance of his master wore an air of extreme disappointment. He urged us, however, to continue our exertions, and the words were hardly uttered when I stumbled and fell forward, having caught the toe of my boot in a large ring of iron that lay half buried in the loose earth.

We now worked in good earnest, and never did I pass ten minutes of more intense excitement. During this interval we had fairly unearthed an oblong chest of wood, which, from its perfect preservation and wonderful hardness, had plainly been subjected to some mineralizing process—perhaps that of the Bichloride of Mercury. This box was three feet and a half long, three feet broad, and two and a half feet deep. It was firmly secured by bands of wrought iron, riveted, and forming a kind of open trellis-work over the whole. On each side of the chest, near the top, were three rings of iron—six in all—by means of which a firm hold could be obtained by six persons. Our utmost united endeavors served only to disturb the coffer very slightly in its bed. We at once saw the impossibility of removing so great a weight. Luckily, the sole fastenings of the lid consisted of two sliding bolts. These we drew back—trembling and panting with anxiety. In an instant, a treasure of incalculable value lay gleaming before us. As the rays of the lanterns fell within the pit, there flashed upwards a glow and a glare, from a confused heap of gold and of jewels, that absolutely dazzled our eyes.

I shall not pretend to describe the feelings with which I gazed. Amazement was, of course, predominant. Legrand appeared exhausted with excitement, and spoke very few words. Jupiter's countenance wore, for some minutes, as deadly a pallor as it is possible, in the nature of things, for any negro's visage to assume. He seemed stupified— thunderstricken. Presently he fell upon his knees in the pit, and, burying his naked arms up to the elbows in gold, let them there remain, as if enjoying the luxury of a bath. At length, with a deep sigh, he exclaimed, as if in a soliloquy, "And dis all cum ob de goole-bug! de putty goole-bug! de poor little goole-bug, what I boosed in dat sabage kind ob style! Aint you shamed ob yourself, nigger?—answer me dat!"

It became necessary, at last, that I should arouse both master and valet to the expediency of removing the treasure. It was growing late, and it behooved us to make exertion, that we might get every thing housed before daylight. It was difficult to say what should be done and much time was spent in deliberation—so confused were the ideas of all. We, finally, lightened the box by removing two thirds of its contents, when we were enabled, with some trouble, to raise it from the hole. The articles taken out were deposited among the brambles, and the dog left to guard them, with strict orders from Jupiter neither, upon any pretence, to stir from the spot, nor to open his mouth until our return. We then hurriedly made for home with the chest; reaching the hut in safety, but after excessive toil, at one o'clock in the morning. Worn out as we were, it was not in human nature to do more immediately. We rested until two, and had supper; starting for the hills immediately afterwards, armed with three stout sacks, which, by good luck, were upon the premises. A little before four we arrived at the pit, divided the remainder of the booty, as equally as might be, among us, and leaving the holes unfilled, again set out for the hut, at which, for the second time, we deposited our golden burthens, just as the first faint streaks of the dawn gleamed from over the tree-tops in the East.

We were now thoroughly broken down; but the intense excitement of the time denied us repose. After an unquiet slumber of some three or four hours' duration, we arose, as if by preconcert, to make examination of our treasure.

The chest had been full to the brim, and we spent the whole day, and the greater part of the next night, in a scrutiny of its contents. There had been nothing like order or arrangement. Everything had been heaped in promiscuously. Having assorted all with care, we found ourselves possessed of even vaster wealth than we had at first supposed. In coin there was rather more than four hundred and fifty thousand dollars—estimating the value of the pieces, as accurately as we could, by the tables of the period. There was not a particle of silver. All was gold of antique date and of great variety—French, Spanish, and German money, with a few English guineas, and some counters, of which we had never seen specimens before. There were several very large and heavy coins, so worn that we could make nothing of their inscriptions. There was no American money. The value of the jewels we found more difficulty in estimating. There were diamonds—some of them exceedingly large and fine—a hundred and ten in all, and not one of them small; eighteen rubies of remarkable brilliancy;—three hundred and ten emeralds, all very beautiful; and twenty-one sapphires, with an opal. These stones had all been broken from their settings and thrown loose in the chest. The settings themselves, which we picked out from among the other gold, appeared to have been beaten up with hammers as if to prevent identification. Besides all this, there was a vast quantity of solid gold ornaments;—nearly two hundred massive finger and ear rings;—rich chains—thirty of these, if I remember;—eighty-three very large and heavy crucifixes;—five gold censers of great value;—a prodigious golden punch-bowl, ornamented with richly chased vine-leaves and Bacchanalian figures; with two sword-handles exquisitely embossed, and many other smaller articles which I cannot recollect. The weight of these valuables exceeded three hundred and fifty pounds avoirdupois; and in this estimate I have not included one hundred and ninety-seven superb gold watches; three of the number being worth each five hundred dollars, if one. Many of them were very old, and as time keepers valueless; the works having suffered, more or less, from corrosion— but all were richly jewelled and in cases of great worth. We estimated the entire contents of the chest, that night, at a million and a half of dollars; and, upon the subsequent disposal of the trinkets and jewels (a few being retained for our own use), it was found that we had greatly under-valued the treasure.

When, at length, we had concluded our examination, and the intense excitement of the time had, in some measure, subsided, Legrand, who saw that I was dying with impatience for a solution of this most extraordinary riddle, entered into a full detail of all the circumstances connected with it.

"You remember," said he, "the night when I handed you the rough sketch I had made of the *scarabæus*. You recollect also, that I became quite vexed at you for insisting that my drawing resembled a death's-head. When you first made this assertion I thought you were jesting; but afterwards I called to mind the peculiar spots on the back of the insect, and admitted to myself that your remark had some little foundation in fact. Still, the sneer at my graphic powers irritated me—for I am considered a good artist—and, therefore, when you handed me the scrap of parchment, I was about to crumple it up and throw it angrily in the fire."

"The scrap of paper, you mean," said I.

"No; it had much of the appearance of paper, and at first I supposed it to be such, but when I came to draw upon it, I discovered it, at once, to be a piece of very thin parchment.

It was quite dirty, you remember. Well, as I was in the very act of crumpling it up, my glance fell upon the sketch at which you had been looking, and you may imagine my astonishment when I perceived, in fact, the figure of a death's-head just where, it seemed to me, I had made the drawing of the beetle. For a moment I was too much amazed to think with accuracy. I knew that my design was very different in detail from this—although there was a certain similarity in general outline. Presently I took a candle, and seating myself at the other end of the room, proceeded to scrutinize the parchment more closely. Upon turning it over, I saw my own sketch upon the reverse, just as I had made it. My first idea, now, was mere surprise at the really remarkably similarity of outline—at the singular coincidence involved in the fact, that unknown to me, there should have been a skull upon the other side of the parchment, immediately beneath my figure of the *scarabæus,* and that this skull, not only in outline, but in size, should so closely resemble my drawing. I say the singularity of this coincidence absolutely stupified me for a time. This is the usual effect of such coincidences. The mind struggles to establish a connection—a sequence of cause and effect—and, being unable to do so, suffers a species of temporary paralysis. But, when I recovered from this stupor, there dawned upon me gradually a conviction which startled me even far more than the coincidence. I began distinctly, positively, to remember that there had been *no* drawing upon the parchment when I made my sketch of the *scarabæus.* I became perfectly certain of this; for I recollected turning up first one side and then the other, in search of the cleanest spot. Had the skull been then there, of course I could not have failed to notice it. Here was indeed a mystery which I felt it impossible to explain; but, even at that early moment, there seemed to glimmer, faintly, within the most remote and secret chambers of my intellect, a glow-worm-like conception of that truth which last night's adventure brought to so magnificent a demonstration. I arose at once, dismissing all farther reflection until I should be alone.

"When you had gone, and when Jupiter was fast asleep, I betook myself to a more methodical investigation of the affair. In the first place I considered the manner in which the parchment had come into my possession. The spot where we had discovered the *scarabæus* was on the coast of the main land, about a mile eastward of the island, and but a short distance above high water mark. Upon my seizing it, it gave me a sharp bite, which caused me to let it drop. Jupiter, with his accustomed caution, before seizing the insect, which had flown towards him, looked about him for a leaf, or something of that nature, by which to take hold of it. It was at this moment that his eyes, and mine also, fell upon the scrap of parchment, which I then supposed to be paper. It was lying half buried in the sand, a corner sticking up. Near the spot where we found it, I observed the remnants of the hull of what appeared to have been a ship's long boat. The wreck seemed to have been there for a very great while; for the resemblance to boat timbers could scarcely be traced.

"Well, Jupiter picked up the parchment, wrapped the beetle in it, and gave it to me. Soon afterwards we turned to go home, and on the way met Lieutenant G——. I showed him the insect, and he begged me to let him take it to the fort. Upon my consenting, he thrust it forthwith into his waistcoat pocket, without the parchment in which it had been wrapped, and which I had continued to hold in my hand during his inspection. Perhaps he dreaded my changing my mind, and thought it best to make sure of the prize at once—you know how enthusiastic he is on all subjects connected with Natural History. At the same time, without my being conscious of it, I must have deposited the parchment in my own pocket.

"You remember that when I went to the table, for the purpose of making a sketch of the beetle, I found no paper where it was usually kept. I looked in the drawer, and found none there. I searched my pockets, hoping to find an old letter, when my hand fell upon the parchment. I thus detail the precise mode in which it came into my possession; for the circumstances impressed me with peculiar force.

"No doubt you will think me fanciful—but I had already established a kind of *connection*. I had put together two links of a great chain. There was a boat lying upon a sea-coast, and not far from the boat was a parchment—*not a paper*—with a skull depicted upon it. You will, of course, ask 'where is the connection?' I reply that the skull, or death's-head, is the well-known emblem of the pirate. The flag of the death's-head is hoisted in all engagements.

"I have said that the scrap was parchment, and not paper. Parchment is durable—almost imperishable. Matters of little moment are rarely consigned to parchment; since, for the mere ordinary purposes of drawing or writing, it is not nearly so well adapted as paper. This reflection suggested some meaning—some relevancy—in the death's-head. I did not fail to observe, also, the *form* of the parchment. Although one of its corners had been, by some accident, destroyed, it could be seen that the original form was oblong. It was just such a slip, indeed, as might have been chosen for a memorandum—for a record of something to be long remembered and carefully preserved."

"But," I interposed, "you say that the skull was *not* upon the parchment when you made the drawing of the beetle. How then do you trace any connection between the boat and the skull—since this latter, according to your own admission, must have been designed (God only knows how or by whom) at some period subsequent to your sketching the *scarabæus?*"

"Ah, hereupon turns the whole mystery; although the secret, at this point, I had comparatively little difficulty in solving. My steps were sure, and could afford but a single result. I reasoned, for example, thus: When I drew the *scarabæus,* there was no skull apparent upon the parchment. When I had completed the drawing I gave it to you, and observed you narrowly until you returned it. *You,* therefore, did not design the skull, and no one else was present to do it. Then it was not done by human agency.

And nevertheless it was done.

"At this stage of my reflections I endeavored to remember, and *did* remember, with entire distinctness, every incident which occurred about the period in question. The weather was chilly (oh rare and happy accident!), and a fire was blazing upon the hearth. I was heated with exercise and sat near the table. You, however, had drawn a chair close to the chimney. Just as I placed the parchment in your hand, and as you were in the act of inspecting it, Wolf, the Newfoundland, entered, and leaped upon your shoulders. With your left hand you caressed him and kept him off, while your right, holding the parchment, was permitted to fall listlessly between your knees, and in close proximity to the fire. At one moment I thought the blaze had caught it, and was about to caution you, but, before I could speak, you had withdrawn it, and were engaged in its examination. When I considered all these particulars, I doubted not for a moment that *heat* had been the agent in bringing to light, upon the parchment, the skull which I saw designed upon it. You are well aware that chemical preparations exist, and have existed time out of mind, by means of which it is possible to write upon either paper or vellum, so that the characters shall become visible only when subjected to the action of fire. Zaffre, digested in *aqua regia*, and diluted with four times its weight of water, is sometimes employed; a green tint results. The regulus of cobalt, dissolved in spirit of nitre, gives a red. These colors disappear at longer or shorter intervals after the material written upon cools, but again become apparent upon the reapplication of heat.

"I now scrutinized the death's-head with care. Its outer edges—the edges of the drawing nearest the edge of the vellum—were far more *distinct* than the others. It was clear that the action of the caloric had been imperfect or unequal. I immediately kindled a fire, and subjected every portion of the parchment to a glowing heat. At first, the only effect was the strengthening of the faint lines in the skull; but, upon persevering the experiment, there became visible, at the corner of the slip, diagonally opposite to the spot in which the death's-head was delineated, the figure of what I at first supposed to be a goat. A closer scrutiny, however, satisfied me that it was intended for a kid."

"Ha! ha!" said I, "to be sure I have no right to laugh at you—a million and a half of money is too serious a matter for mirth—but you are not about to establish a third link in your chain—you will not find any especial connection between your pirates and a goat—pirates, you know, have nothing to do with goats; they appertain to the farming interest."

"But I have just said that the figure was *not* that of a goat."

"Well, a kid then—pretty much the same thing."

"Pretty much, but not altogether," said Legrand. "You may have heard of one *Captain* Kidd. I at once looked upon the figure of the animal as a kind of punning or hieroglyphical signature. I say signature; because its position upon the vellum suggested this idea. The death's-head at the corner diagonally opposite, had, in the same manner, the air of a stamp, or seal. But I was sorely put out by the absence of all else—of the body to my imagined instrument—of the text for my context."

"I presume you expected to find a letter between the stamp and the signature."

"Something of that kind. The fact is, I felt irresistibly impressed with a presentiment of some vast good fortune impending. I can scarcely say why. Perhaps, after all, it was rather a desire than an actual belief;—but do you know that Jupiter's silly words, about the bug being of solid gold, had a remarkable effect upon my fancy? And then the series of accidents and coincidences—these were so *very* extraordinary. Do you observe how mere an accident it was that these events should have occurred upon the *sole* day of all the year in which it has been, or may be, sufficiently cool for fire, and that without the fire, or without the intervention of the dog at the precise moment in which he appeared, I should never have become aware of the death's-head, and so never the possessor of the treasure?"

"But proceed—I am all impatience."

"Well; you have heard, of course, the many stories current—the thousand vague rumors afloat about money buried, somewhere upon the Atlantic coast, by Kidd and his associates. These rumors must have had some foundation in fact. And that the rumors have existed so long and so continuous, could have resulted, it appeared to me, only from the circumstance of the buried treasure still *remaining* entombed. Had Kidd concealed his plunder for a time, and afterwards reclaimed it, the rumors would scarcely have reached us in their present unvarying form. You will observe that the stories told are all about money-seekers, not about money-finders. Had the pirate recovered his money, there the affair would have dropped. It seemed to me that some accident—say the loss of a memorandum indicating its locality—had deprived him of the means of recovering it, and that this accident had become known to his followers, who otherwise might never had heard that treasure had been concealed at all, and who, busying themselves in vain, because unguided attempts, to regain it, had given first birth, and then universal currency, to the reports which are now so common. Have you ever heard of any important treasure having been unearthed by the diggers for money along the coast?"

"Never."

"But that Kidd's accumulations were immense, is well known. I took it for granted, therefore, that the earth still held them; and you will scarcely be surprised when I tell you that I felt a hope, nearly amounting to certainty, that the parchment so strangely found, involved a lost record of the place of deposit."

"But how did you proceed?"

"I held the vellum again to the fire, after increasing the heat; but nothing appeared. I now thought it possible that the coating of dirt might have something to do with the failure; so I carefully rinsed the parchment, by pouring warm water over it, and, having done this, I placed it in a tin pan, with the skull downwards, and put the pan upon a furnace of lighted charcoal. In a few minutes, the pan having become thoroughly heated, I removed the slip, and, to my inexpressible joy, found it spotted, in several places, with what appeared to be figures arranged in lines. Again I placed it in the pan, and suffered it to remain another minute. Upon taking it off, the whole was just as you see it now."

Here Legrand submitted the parchment to my inspection. The following characters were rudely traced in a red tint, between the death's-head and the goat:

53‡‡†305))6*;4826)4‡.)4‡);806*;48†8¶60))85;
;]8*;:‡*8†83(88)5*†;46(;88*96*?;8)*‡(;485);5
†2:‡(;4956*2(5*—4)8¶8*;4069285);)6†8)4‡‡
;1(‡9;48081;8:8‡1;48†85;4)485†528806*81(‡9;
48;(88;4(‡?34;48)4‡;161;:188;‡?;

"But," said I, returning him the slip, "I am as much in the dark as ever. Were all the jewels of Golconda awaiting me upon my solution of this enigma, I am quite sure that I should be unable to earn them."

"And yet," said Legrand, "the solution is by no means so difficult as you might be led to imagine from the first hasty inspection of the characters. These characters, as any one might readily guess, form a cipher—that is to say, they convey a meaning; but then, from what is known of Kidd, I could not suppose him capable of constructing any of the more abstruse cryptographs. I made up my mind, at once, that this was of a simple—species-such, however, as would appear, to the crude intellect of the sailor, absolutely insoluble without the key."

"And you really solved it?"

"Readily; I have solved others of an abstruseness ten thousand times greater. Circumstances, and a certain bias of mind, have led me to take interest in such riddles, and it may well be doubted whether human ingenuity can construct an enigma of the kind which human ingenuity may not, by proper application, resolve. In fact, having once established connected and legible characters, I scarcely gave a thought to the mere difficulty of developing their import.

"In the present case—indeed in all cases of secret writing—the first question regards the *language* of the cipher; for the principles of solution, so far, especially, as the more simple ciphers are concerned, depend upon, and are varied by, the genius of the particular idiom. In general, there is no alternative but experiment (directed by probabilities) of every tongue known to him who attempts the solution, until the true one is attained. But, with the cipher now before us, all difficulty was removed by the signature. The pun upon the word 'Kidd' is appreciable in no other language than the English. But for this consideration I should have begun my attempts with the Spanish and French, as the tongues in which a secret of this kind would most naturally have been written by a pirate of the Spanish main. As it was, I assumed the cryptograph to be English.

"You observe there are no divisions between the words. Had there been divisions, the task would have been comparatively easy. In such case I should have commenced with a collation and analysis of the shorter words, and, had a word of a single letter occurred, as is most likely (*a* or *I*, for example,) I should have considered this solution as assured. But, there being no division, my first step was to ascertain the predominant letters, as well as the least frequent. Counting all, I constructed a table, thus:

Of the character 8 there are 33.

;	"	26.
4	"	19
‡)	"	16.
*	"	13.
5	"	12.
6	"	11.
†1	"	8.
0	"	6.
92	"	5.
:3	"	4.

?	"	3.
¶	"	2.
]—.	"	1.

"Now, in English, the letter which most frequently occurs is *e*. Afterwards, the succession runs thus: *a o i d h n r s t u y c f g l m w b k p q x z*. *E* predominates so remarkably that an individual sentence of any length is rarely seen, in which it is not the prevailing character.

"Here, then, we have, in the very beginning, the groundwork for something more than a mere guess. The general use which may be made of the table is obvious—but, in this particular cipher, we shall only very partially require its aid. As our predominant character is 8, we will commence by assuming it as the *e* of the natural alphabet. To verify the supposition, let us observe if the 8 be seen often in couples—for *e* is doubled with great frequency in English—in which words, for example, as 'meet,' 'fleet,' 'speed,' 'seen,' 'been,' 'agree,' &c. In the present instance we see it doubled no less than five times, although the cryptograph is brief.

"Let us assume 8, then, as *e*. Now, of all *words* in the language, 'the' is most usual; let us see, therefore, whether there are not repetitions of any three characters, in the same order of collocation, the last of them being 8. If we discover repetitions of such letters, so arranged, they will most probably represent the word 'the.' Upon inspection we find no less than seven such arrangements, the characters being ;48. We may, therefore, assume that the semicolon represents *t*, 4 represents *h*, and 8 represents *e*—the last being now well confirmed. Thus a great step has been taken.

"But, having established a single word, we are enabled to establish a vastly important point; that is to say, several commencements and terminations of other words. Let us refer, for example, to the last instance but one, in which the combination ;48 occurs—not far from the end of the cipher. We know that the semicolon immediately ensuing is the commencement of a word, and, of the six characters succeeding this 'the,' we are cognizant of no less than five. Let us set these characters down, thus, by the letters we know them to represent, leaving a space for the one unknown—

t eeth.

"Here we are enabled, at once, to discard the '*th*,' as forming no portion of the word commencing with the first *t*; since, by experiment of the entire alphabet for a letter adapted to the vacancy, we perceive that no word can be formed of which this *th* can be a part. We are thus narrowed into

t ee,

and, going through the alphabet, if necessary, as before, we arrive at the word 'tree,' as the sole possible reading. We thus gain another letter, *r*, represented by (, with the words 'the tree' in juxtaposition.

"Looking beyond these words, for a short distance, we again see the combination of ;48, and employ it by way of *termination* to what immediately precedes. We have thus this arrangement:

the tree ;4(‡?34 the,

or, substituting the natural letters, where known, it reads thus:

the tree thr‡?3h the.

"Now, if, in place of the unknown characters, we leave blank spaces, or substitute dots, we read thus:

the tree thr...h the,

when the word '*through*' makes itself evident at once. But this discovery gives us three new letters, *o*, *u* and *g*, represented by ‡? and 3.

"Looking now, narrowly, through the cipher for combinations of known characters, we find, not very far from the beginning, this arrangement,

83(88, or egree,

which, plainly, is the conclusion of the word 'degree,' and gives us another letter, *d*, represented by †.

76

"Four letters beyond the word 'degree,' we perceive the combination ;

46(;88*

"Translating the known characters, and representing the unknown by dots, as before, we read thus:

th.rtee.

an arrangement immediately suggestive of the word 'thirteen,' and again furnishing us with two new characters, *i* and *n*, represented by 6 and *.

"Referring, now, to the beginning of the cryptograph, we find the combination,

53‡‡†.

"Translating, as before, we obtain

.good,

which assures that the first letter is *A*, and that the first two words are 'A good.'

"It is now time that we arrange our key, as far as discovered, in a tabular form to avoid confusion. It will stand thus:

5	represents	a
†	"	d
8	"	e
3	"	g
4	"	h
6	"	i
*	"	n
‡	"	o
(	"	r
;	"	t

"We have, therefore, no less than ten of the most important letters represented, and it will be unnecessary to proceed with the details of the solution. I have said enough to convince you that ciphers of this nature are readily soluble, and give you some insight into the *rationale* of their development. But be assured that the specimen before us appertains to the very simplest species of cryptograph. It now only remains to give you the full translation of the characters upon the parchment, as unriddled. Here is is:

'*A good glass in the bishop's hostel in the devil's seat forty-one degrees and thirteen minutes northeast and by north main branch seventh limb east side shoot from the left eye of the death's-head a bee line from the tree through the shot fifty feet out.*'"

"But," said I, "the enigma seems still in as bad a condition as ever. How is it possible to extort a meaning from all this jargon about 'devil's seats,' 'death's-heads,' and 'bishop's hotels?'"

"I confess," replied Legrand, "that the matter still wears a serious aspect, when regarded with a casual glance. My first endeavor was to divide the sentence into the natural division intended by the cryptographist."

"You mean, to punctuate it?"

"Something of that kind."

"But how was it possible to effect this?"

"I reflected that it has been a *point* with the writer to run his words together without division, so as to increase the difficulty of solution. Now, a not over-acute man, in pursuing such an object, would be nearly certain to overdo the matter. When, in the course of his composition, he arrived at a break in his subject which would naturally require a pause, or a point, he would be exceedingly apt to run his characters, at this place, more than usually close together. If you will observe the MS., in the present instance, you will easily detect five such cases of unusual crowding. Acting upon this hint, I made the division thus:

'*A good glass in the Bishop's hostel in the Devil's seat—forty-one degrees and thirteen minutes—northeast and by north—main branch seventh limb east side—shoot from the left eye of the death's-head—a bee-line from the tree through the shot fifty feet out.*'"

"Even this division," said I, "leaves me still in the dark."

"It left me also in the dark," replied Legrand, "for a few days; during which I made diligent inquiry, in the neighborhood of Sullivan's Island, for any building which went by the name of the 'Bishop's Hotel;' for, of course, I dropped the obsolete word 'hostel.' Gaining no information on the subject, I was on the point of extending my sphere of search, and proceeding in a more systematic manner, when, one morning, it entered into my head, quite suddenly, that this 'Bishop's Hostel' might have reference to an old family, of the name of Bessop, which, time out of mind, had held possession of an ancient manor-house, about four miles to the northward of the island. I accordingly went over to the plantation, and re-instituted my inquiries among the older negroes of the place. At length one of the most aged of the women said that she had heard of such a place as *Bessop's Castle*, and thought that she could guide me to it, but that it was not a castle, nor a tavern, but a high rock.

"I offered to pay her well for her trouble, and, after some demur, she consented to accompany me to the spot. We found it without much difficulty, when, dismissing her, I proceeded to examine the place. The 'castle' consisted of an irregular assemblage of cliffs and rocks—one of the latter being quite remarkable for its height as well as for its insulated and artificial appearance. I clambered to its apex, and then felt much at a loss as to what should be next done.

"While I was busied in reflection, my eyes fell upon a narrow ledge in the eastern face of the rock, perhaps a yard below the summit on which I stood. This ledge projected about eighteen inches, and was not more than a foot wide, while a niche in the cliff just above it, gave it a rude resemblance to one of the hollow-backed chairs used by our ancestors. I made no doubt that here was the 'devil's-seat' alluded to in the MS., and now I seemed to grasp the full secret of the riddle.

"The 'good glass,' I knew, could have reference to nothing but a telescope; for the word 'glass' is rarely employed in any other sense by seamen. Now here, I at once saw, was a telescope to be used, and a definite point of view, *admitting no variation*, from which to use it. Nor did I hesitate to believe that the phrases, 'forty-one degrees and thirteen minutes,' and 'northeast and by north,' were intended directions for the levelling of the glass. Greatly excited by these discoveries, I hurried home, procured a telescope, and returned to the rock.

"I let myself down to the ledge, and found that it was impossible to retain a seat upon it except in one particular position. This fact confirmed my preconceived idea. I proceeded to use the glass. Of course, the 'forty-one degrees and thirteen minutes' could allude to nothing but elevation above the visible horizon, since the horizontal direction was clearly indicated by the words, 'northeast and by north.' This latter direction I at once established by means of a pocket-compass; then, pointing the glass as nearly at an angle of forty-one degrees of elevation as I could do it by guess, I moved it cautiously up or down, until my attention was arrested by a circular rift or opening in the foliage of a large tree that overtopped its fellows in the distance. In the centre of this rift I perceived a white spot, but could not, at first, distinguish what it was. Adjusting the focus of the telescope, I again looked, and now made it out to be a human skull.

"Upon this discovery I was so sanguine as to consider the enigma solved; for the phrase 'main branch, seventh limb, east side,' could refer only to the position of the skull upon the tree, while 'shoot from the left eye of the death's-head' admitted, also, of but one interpretation, in regard to a search for buried treasure. I perceived that the design was to drop a bullet from the left eye of the skull, and that a bee-line, or, in other words, a straight line, drawn from the nearest point of the trunk through 'the shot,' (or the spot where the bullet fell,) and thence extended to a distance of fifty feet, would indicate a definite point—and beneath this point I thought it at least *possible* that a deposit of value lay concealed."

"All this," I said, "is exceedingly clear, and, although ingenious, still simple and explicit. When you left the Bishop's Hotel, what then?"

"Why, having carefully taken the bearings of the tree, I turned homewards. The instant that I left 'the devil's seat,' however, the circular rift vanished; nor could I get a glimpse of it afterwards, turn as I would. What seems to me the chief ingenuity in this whole business, is the fact (for repeated experiment has convinced me that it *is* a fact) that the circular opening in question is visible from no other attainable point of view than that afforded by the narrow ledge upon the face of the rock.

"In this expedition to the 'Bishop's Hotel' I had been attended by Jupiter, who had, no doubt, observed, for some weeks past, the abstraction of my demeanor, and took especial care not to leave me alone. But, on the next day, getting up very early, I contrived to give him the slip, and went into the hills in search of the tree. After much toil I found it. When I came home at night my valet proposed to give me a flogging. With the rest of the adventure I believe you are as well acquainted as myself."

"I suppose," said I, "you missed the spot, in the first attempt at digging, through Jupiter's stupidity in letting the bug fall through the right instead of through the left eye of the skull."

"Precisely. This mistake made a difference of about two inches and a half in the 'shot'—that is to say, in the position of the peg nearest the tree; and had the treasure been *beneath* the 'shot,' the error would have been of little moment; but the 'shot' together with the nearest point of the tree, were merely two points for the establishment of a line of direction; of course the error, however trivial in the beginning, increased as we proceeded with the line, and by the time we had gone fifty feet, threw us quite off the scent. But for my deep-seated impressions that treasure was here somewhere actually buried, we might have had all our labor in vain."

"I presume the fancy of *the skull*—of letting fall a bullet through the skull's eye—was suggested to Kidd by the piratical flag. No doubt he felt a kind of poetical consistency in recovering his money through this ominous insignium."

"Perhaps so; still I cannot help thinking that common-sense had quite as much to do with the matter as poetical consistency. To be visible from the Devil's seat, it was necessary that the object, if small, should be *white;* and there is nothing like your human skull for retaining and even increasing its whiteness under exposure to all vicissitudes of weather."

"But your grandiloquence, and your conduct in swinging the beetle—how excessively odd! I was sure you were mad. And why did you insist upon dropping the bug, instead of a bullet, from the skull?"

"Why, to be frank, I felt somewhat annoyed by your evident suspicions touching my sanity, and so resolved to punish you quietly, in my own way, by a little bit of sober mystification. For this reason I swung the beetle, and for this reason I dropped it from the tree. An observation of yours about its great weight suggested the latter idea."

"Yes, I perceive; and now there is only one point which puzzles me. What are we to make of the skeletons found in the hole?"

"This is a question I am no more able to answer than yourself. There seems, however, only one plausible way of accounting for them—and yet it is dreadful to believe in such atrocity as my suggestion would imply. It is clear that Kidd—if Kidd indeed secreted this treasure, which I doubt not—it is clear that he must have had assistance in the labor. But this labor concluded, he may have thought it expedient to remove all participants in his secret. Perhaps a couple of blows with a mattock were sufficient, while his coadjutors were busy in the pit; perhaps it required a dozen—who shall tell?"

[June 21, 1843]

Early Twentieth Century Influences

Henry James

from *The American Scene*

There was literally no single object that, from morn to
nightfall, it was not more possible to consider with
tenderness, a rich consistency of tenderness, than to
consider without it: *such* was the subtle trick that
Charleston could still play. There echoed for me as I looked
out from the Battery the recent speech of a friend which had
had at the time a depressing weight; the Battery of the long,
curved sea-front, of the waterside public garden furnished
with sad old historic guns, with live-oaks draped in trailing
moss, with palmettos that, as if still mindful of their State
symbolism, seem to try everywhere, though with a
melancholy skeptical droop, to repeat the old escutcheon;
with its large, thrilling view in particular—thrilling to a
Northerner who stands there for the first time. "Filled as I
am, in general, while there," my friend had said, "with the
sadness and sorrow of the South, I never, at Charleston,
look out to the old betrayed Forts without feeling my heart
harden again to steel." One remembered that, on the spot,
and one waited a little—to see what was happening to one's
heart. I found this to take time indeed; everything differed,
somehow, from one's old conceived image—or if I had
anciently grasped the remoteness of Fort Sumter, near the
mouth of the Bay, and of its companion, at the point of the
shore forming the other side of the passage, this lucidity had
so left me, in the course of the years, that the far-away
dimness of the consecrated objects was almost a shock. It
was a blow even to one's faded vision of Charleston
viciously firing on the Flag; the Flag would have been, from
the Battery, such a mere speck in space that the vice of the
act lost somehow, with the distance, to say nothing of the
forty years, a part of its grossness. The smitten face,
however flushed and scarred, was out of sight, though the
intention of smiting and the force of the insult were of
course still the same. This reflection one made, but the old

fancied perspective and proportions were altered; and then the whole picture, at that hour, exhaled an innocence. It was as blank as the face of a child under mention of his naughtiness and his punishment of week before last. The Forts, faintly blue on the twinkling sea, looked like vague marine flowers; innocence, pleasantness ruled the prospect: it was as if the compromised slate, sponged clean of all the wicked words and hung up on the wall for better use, dangled there so vacantly as almost to look foolish. Ah, there again was the word: the air still just tasted of the antique folly; so that in presence of a lesson so sharp and so prolonged, of the general *sterilized* state, of the brightly-lighted, delicate dreariness recording the folly, harshness was conjured away. There was that in the impression which affected me after a little as one of those refinements of irony that wait on deep expiations: one could scarce conceive at this time of day that such a place had ever been dangerously moved. It was the *bled* condition, and mostly the depleted cerebral condition, that was thus attested—as I had recognized it at Richmond; and I asked myself, on the Battery, what more one's sternest justice could have desired. If my heart wasn't to harden to steel, in short, access to it by the right influence had found perhaps too many other forms of sensibility in ambush.

To justify hardness, moreover, one would have had to meet something hard; and if my peregrination, after this, had been a search for such an element, I should have to describe it as made all in vain. Up and down and in and out, with my companion, I strolled from hour to hour; but more and more under the impression of the consistency of softness. One could have expressed the softness in a word, and the picture so offered would be infinitely touching. It was a city of gardens and absolutely of no men—or of so few that, save for the general sweetness, the War might still have been raging and all the manhood at the front. The gardens were matter for the women; though even of the women there were few, and that small company—rare, discreet, flitting figures that brushed the garden walls with noiseless skirts in the little melancholy streets of interspaced, over-tangled abodes—were clad in a rigour of mourning that was like the garb of a conspiracy. The effect was superficially prim, but so far as it savoured of malice prepense, of the Southern, the sentimental *parti-pris*, it was delightful. What was it all most like, the incoherent jumble of suggestions?—the suggestion of a social shrinkage and an economic blight unrepaired, irreparable; the suggestion of by-ways of some odd far East infected with triumphant women's rights, some perspective of builded, plastered lanes over the enclosures of which the flowering almond drops its petals into sharp deep bands of shade or of sun. It is not the muffled ladies who walk about predominantly in the East; but that is a detail. The likeness was perhaps greater to some little old-world quarter of quiet convents where only priests and nuns steal forth—the priests mistakable at a distance, say, for the nuns. It was indeed thoroughly mystifying, the whole picture—since I was to get, in the freshness of that morning, from the very background of the scene, my quite triumphant little impression of the "old South." I remember feeling with intensity at two or three points in particular that I should never get a better one, that even this was precarious—might melt at any moment, by a wrong touch or a false note, in my grasp—and that I must therefore make the most of it. The rest of my time, I may profess, was spent in so doing. I made the most of it in several successive spots: under the south wall of St. Michael's Church, the sweetest corner of Charleston, and of which there is more to say; out in the old Cemetery on the edge of the lagoon, where the distillation of the past was perhaps clearest and the bribe to tenderness most effective; and even not a little on ground thereunto almost adjacent, that of a kindly Country-Club installed in a fine old semi-sinister mansion, and holding an afternoon revel at which I was privileged briefly to assist. The wrong touch and the false note were doubtless just sensible in this last connection, where the question, probed a little, would apparently have been of some new South that has not yet quite found the effective way romantically, or at least insidiously, to appeal. The South that is cultivating country-clubs is a South presumably, in many connections, quite in the right; whereas the one we were invidiously "after" was the one that had been so utterly in the wrong. Even there, none the less, in presence of more than a single marked sign of the rude Northern contagion, I disengaged, socially speaking, a faint residuum which I mention for proof of the intensity of my quest and of my appreciation.

There were two other places, I may add, where one could but work the impression for all it was, in the modern phrase, "worth," and where I had, I may venture to say, the sense of making as much of it as was likely ever to be made again. Meanings without end were to be read, under tuition, into one of these, which was neither more nor less than a slightly shy, yet after all quite serene place of refection, a luncheon-room or tea-house, denominated for quaint reasons an "Exchange"—*the* very Exchange in fact lately commemorated in a penetrating study, already much known to fame, of the little that is left of the local society. My tuition, at the hands of my ingenious comrade, was the very best it was possible to have. Nothing, usually, is more wonderful than the quantity of significant character that, with such an example set, the imagination may recognize in the scantest group of features, objects, persons. I fantastically feasted here, at my luncheon-table, not only, as the genius of the place demanded, on hot chocolate, sandwiches and "Lady Baltimore" cake (this last a most delectable compound), but on the exact *nuance* of oddity, of bravery, of reduced gentility, of irreducible superiority, to which the opening of such an establishment, without derogation, by the proud daughters of war-wasted families, could exquisitely testify. They hovered, the proud impoverished daughters, singly or in couples, behind the counter—a counter, again, delectably charged; they waited, inscrutably, irreproachably, yet with all that peculiarly chaste *bonhomie* of the Southern tone, on the customers' wants, even coming to ascertain these at the little thrifty tables; and if the drama and its adjusted theatre really contained all the elements of history, tragedy, comedy, irony, that a pair of expert romancers, closely associated for the hour, were eager to evoke, the scene would have been, I can only say, supreme of its kind. That desire of the artist to linger where the breath of a "subject," faintly stirring the air, reaches his vigilant sense, would here stay my steps—as this very influence was in fact, to his great good fortune, to stay those of my companion. The charm I speak of, the charm to cherish, however, was most exhaled for me in other conditions—conditions that scarce permit of any direct reference to their full suggestiveness. If I alluded above to the vivid Charleston background, where its "mystification" most scenically persists, the image is all rounded and complete, for memory, in this connection at which—as the case is of an admirably mature and preserved interior—I can only glance as I pass. The puzzlement elsewhere is in the sense that though the elements of earth and air, the colour, the tone, the light, the sweetness in fine, linger on, the "old South" could have had no such unmitigated mildness, could never have seen itself as subject to such strange feminization. The feminization is there just to promote for us some eloquent antithesis; just to make us say that whereas the ancient order was masculine, fierce and moustachioed, the present is at the most a sort of sick lioness who has so visible parted with her teeth and claws that we may patronizingly walk all round her.

This image really gives us the best word for the general effect of Charleston—that of the practically vacant cage which used in the other time to emit sounds, even to those of the portentous shaking of bars, audible as far away as in the listening North. It is the vacancy that is a thing by itself, a thing that makes us endlessly wonder. How, in an at all complex, a "great political," society, can *everything* so have gone?—assuming indeed that, under this ægis, very much ever had come. How can everything so have gone that the only "Southern" book of any distinction published for many a year is *The Souls of Black Folk*, by that most accomplished of members of the negro race, Mr. W. E. B. Du Bois? Had the *only* focus of life then been Slavery?— from the point onward that Slavery had reached a quarter of a century before the War, so that with the extinction of that interest none other of any sort was left. To say "yes" seems the only way to account for the degree of the vacancy, and yet even as I form that word I meet as a reproach the face of the beautiful old house I just mentioned, whose ample spaces had so unmistakably echoed to the higher amenities that one seemed to feel the accumulated traces and tokens gradually come out of their corners like blest objects taken one by one from a reliquary worn with much handling. The note of such haunted chambers as these—haunted structurally, above all, quite as by the ghost of the grant style—was not, certainly a thinness of reverberation; so that I had to take refuge here in the fact that everything appeared thoroughly to *antedate*, to refer itself to the larger, the less vitiated past that had closed a quarter of a century or so before the War, before the fatal time when the South, monomaniacal at the parting of the ways, "elected" for extension and conquest. The admirable old house of the stately hall and staircase, of the charming coved and vaulted drawing-room, of the precious mahogany doors, the tall unsophisticated portraits, the delicate dignity of welcome, owed nothing of its noble identity, nothing at all appreciable, to the monomania. However that might be, moreover, I kept finding the mere melancholy charm reassert itself where it could—the charm, I mean, of the flower-crowned waste that was, by my measure, what the monomania had most prepared itself to bequeathe. In the old Cemetery by the lagoon, to which I have already alluded, this influence distils an irresistible poetry—as one has courage to say even in remembering how disproportionately, almost anywhere on the American scene, the general place of interment is apt to be invited to testify for the presence of charm. The golden afternoon, the low, silvery, seaward horizon, as of wide, sleepy, game-haunted inlets and reed-smothered banks, possible site of some Venice that had never mustered, the luxury, in the mild air, of shrub and plant and blossom that the pale North can but distantly envy; something that I scarce know how to express but as the proud humility of the whole idle, easy loveliness, made even the restless analyst, for the hour, among the pious inscriptions that scarce ever belie the magniloquent clime or the inimitable tradition, feel himself really capable of the highest Carolinian pitch.

Amy Lowell

CHARLESTON. SOUTH CAROLINA

FIFTEEN years is not a long time,
But long enough to build a city over and destroy it.
Long enough to clean a forty-year growth of grass from
between cobblestones,
And run street-car lines straight across the heart of
romance.
Commerce, are you worth this?
I should like to bring a case to trial:
Prosperity versus Beauty,
Cash registers teetering in a balance against the comfort
    of the soul.
Then, to-night, I stood looking through a grilled gate
At an old, dark garden.
Live-oak trees dripped branchfuls of leaves over the
    wall,
Acacias waved dimly beyond the gate, and the smell
    of their blossoms
Puffed intermittently through the wrought-iron
    scroll-work.
Challenge and solution —
O loveliness of old, decaying, haunted things!
Little streets untouched, shamefully paved,
Full of mist and fragrance on this rainy evening.
"You should come at dawn," said my friend,
"And see the orioles, and thrushes, and mockingbirds
In the garden."

"Yes," I said absent-mindedly,
And remarked the sharp touch of ivy upon my hand
    which rested against the wall.
But I thought to myself,
There is no dawn here, only sunset,
And an evening rain scented with flowers.

THE MIDDLETON PLACE

CHARLESTON, S.C.

What would Francis Jammes, lover of dear, dead
    elegancies,
Say to this place?
France, stately, formal, stepping in red-heeled shoes
Along a river shore.
France walking a minuet between live-oaks waving
    ghostly fans of Spanish moss.
La Caroline, indeed, my dear Jammes,
With Monsieur Michaux engaged to teach her
    deportment.
Faint as a whiff of flutes, and hautbois,
The great circle of the approach lies beneath the
    sweeping grasses.
Step lightly down these terraces, they are records of a
dream.
Magnolias, pyrus japonicas, azaleas,
Flaunting their scattered blooms with the same bravura
That lords and ladies used in the prison of the Conciergerie.
You were meant to be so gay, so sophisticated, and
    you are so sad,
Sad as the tomb crouched amid your tangled growth,
Sad as the pale plumes of the Spanish moss
Slowly strangling the live-oak trees.

Sunset wanes along the quiet river.
The afterglow is haunted and nostalgic,
Over the yellow woodland it hangs like the dying
    chord of a funeral chant;
And evenly, satirically, the mosses move to its
    ineffable rhythm,
Like the ostrich fans of palsied dowagers
Telling one another contentedly of the deaths they
    have lived to see.

EPITAPH IN A CHURCH-YARD
IN CHARLESTON, SOUTH CAROLINA

GEORGE AUGUSTUS CLOUGH
A NATIVE OF LIVERPOOL,
DIED SUDDENLY OF "STRANGER'S FEVER"
NOV'R 5TH 1843
AGED 22

He died of "Stranger's Fever" when his youth
   Had scarcely melted into manhood, so
   The chiselled legend runs; a brother's woe
Laid bare for epitaph. The savage ruth
Of a sunny, bright, but alien land, uncouth
   With cruel caressing dealt a mortal blow,
   And by this summer sea where flowers grow
In tropic splendor, witness to the truth
Of ineradicable race he lies.
   The law of duty urged that he should roam,
Should sail from fog and chilly airs to skies
   Clear with deceitful welcome. He had come
With proud resolve, but still his lonely eyes
   Ached with fatigue at never seeing home.

Owen Wister

from *Lady Baltimore*

Thus it was that I came to sojourn in the most appealing, the most lovely, the most wistful town in America; whose visible sadness and distinction seem also to speak audibly, speak in the sound of the quiet waves that ripple round her Southern front, speak in the church-bells on Sunday morning, and breathe not only in the soft salt air, but in the perfume of every gentle, old-fashioned rose that blooms behind the high garden walls of falling mellow-tinted plaster: Kings Port the retrospective, Kings Port the belated, who from her pensive porticoes looks over her two rivers to the marshes and the trees beyond, the live-oaks, veiled in gray moss, brooding with memories! Were she my city, how I should love her!

But though my city she cannot be, the enchanting image of her is mine to keep, to carry with me wheresoever I may go; for who, having seen her, could forget her? Therefore I thank Aunt Carola for this gift, and for what must always go with it in my mind, the quiet and strange romance which I saw happen, and came finally to share in. Why it is that my Aunt no longer wishes to know either the boy or the girl, or even to hear their names mentioned, you shall learn at the end, when I have finished with the wedding; for this happy story of love ends with a wedding, and begins in the Woman's Exchange, which the ladies of Kings Port have established, and (I trust) lucratively conduct, in Royal Street.

Royal Street! There's a relevance in this name, a fitness to my errand; but that is pure accident.

The Woman's Exchange happened to be there, a decorous resort for those who became hungry, as I did, at the hour of noon each day. In my very pleasant boarding-house, where to be sure, there was one dreadful boarder, a tall lady, whom I soon secretly called Juno—but let unpleasant things wait—in the very pleasant house where I boarded (I had left my hotel after one night) our breakfast was at eight, and our dinner not until three: sacred meal hours in Kings Port, as inviolable, I fancy, as the Declaration of Independence, but a gap quite beyond the stretch of my Northern vitals. Therefore, at twelve, it was my habit to leave my Fanning researches for a while, and lunch at the Exchange upon chocolate and sandwiches most delicate in savor. As, one day, I was luxuriously biting one of these, I heard his voice and what he was saying. Both the voice and the interesting order he was giving caused me, at my small table, in the dim back of the room, to stop and watch him where he stood in the light at the counter to the right of the entrance door. Young he was, very young, twenty-two or three at the most, and as he stood, with hat in hand, speaking to the pretty girl behind the counter, his head and side-face were of a romantic and high-strung look. It was a cake that he desired made, a cake for a wedding; and I directly found myself curious to know whose wedding. Even a dull wedding interests me more than other dull events, because it can arouse so much surmise and so much prophecy; but in this wedding I instantly, because of his strange and winning embarrassment, became quite absorbed. How came it he was ordering the cake for it? Blushing like the boy that he was entirely, he spoke in a most engaging voice: "No, not charged; and as you don't know me, I had better pay for it now."

Self-possession in his speech he almost had; but the blood in his cheeks and forehead was beyond his control.

A reply came from behind the counter: "We don't expect payment until delivery."

"But—a—but on that morning I shall be rather particularly engaged." His tones sank almost away on these words.

"We should prefer to wait, then. You will leave your address. In half-pound boxes, I suppose?"

"Boxes? Oh, yes—I hadn't thought—no—just a big, round one. Like this, you know!" His arms embraced a circular space of air. "With plenty of icing."

I do not think that there was any smile on the other side of the counter; there was, at any rate, no hint of one in the voice. "And how many pounds?"

He was again staggered. "Why—a—I never ordered one before. I want plenty—and the very best, the very best. Each person would eat a pound, wouldn't they? Or would two be nearer? I think I had better leave it all to you. About like this, you know." Once more his arms embraced a circular space of air.

Before this I had never heard the young lady behind the counter enter into any conversation with a customer. She would talk at length about all sorts of Kings Port affairs with the older ladies connected with the Exchange, who were frequently to be found there; but with a customer, never. She always took my orders, and my money, and served me, with a silence and a propriety that have become, with ordinary shopkeepers, a lost art. *They* talk to one indeed! But this slim girl was a lady, and consequently did the right thing, marking and keeping a distance between herself and the public. To-day, however, she evidently felt it her official duty to guide the hapless young man amid his errors. He now appeared to be committing a grave one.

"Are you quite sure you want that?" the girl was asking.

"Lady Baltimore? Yes, that is what I want."

"Because," she began to explain, then hesitated, and looked at him. Perhaps it was in his face; perhaps it was that she remembered at this point the serious difference between the price of Lady Baltimore (by my small bill-of-fare I was now made acquainted with its price) and the cost of that rich article which convention has prescribed as the cake for wedding; at any rate, swift, sudden delicacy of feeling prevented her explaining any more to him, for she saw how it was; his means were too humble for the approved kind of wedding cake! She was too young, too unskilled yet in the world's ways, to rise above her embarrassment; and so she stood blushing at him behind the counter, while he stood blushing at her in front of it.

At length he succeeded in speaking. "That's all, I believe.

Good-morning."

At his hastily departing back she, too, murmured: "Good-morning."

Before I knew it I had screamed out loudly from my table: "But he hasn't told you the day he wants it for!"

Before she knew it she had flown to the door—my cry had set her going, as if I had touched a spring—and there he was at the door himself, rushing back. He, too, had remembered. It was almost a collision, and nothing but their good Southern breeding, the way they took it, saved it from being like a rowdy farce.

"I know," he said simply and immediately. "I am sorry to be so careless. It's for the twenty-seventh."

She was writing it down in the order-book. "Very well. That is Wednesday of next week. You have given us more time than we need." She put complete, impersonal business into her tone; and this time he marched off in good order, leaving peace in the Woman's Exchange.

No, not peace; quiet, merely; the girl at the counter now proceeded to grow indignant with me. We were alone together, we two; no young man, or any other business, occupied her or protected me. But if you suppose that she made war, or expressed rage by speaking, that is not it at all. From her counter in front to my table at the back she made her displeasure felt; she was inaudibly crushing; she did not do it even with her eye, she managed it—well, with her neck, somehow, and by the way she made her nose look in profile. Aunt Carola would have embraced her—and I should have liked to do so myself. She could not stand the ideal of my having, after all these days of official reserve that she had placed between us, startled her into that rush to the door, annihilated her dignity at a blow. So did I finish my sandwiches beneath her invisible but eloquent ire. What affair of mine was the cake? And what sort of impertinent, meddlesome person was I, shrieking out my suggestions to people with whom I had no acquaintance? These were the things that her nose and her neck said to me the whole length of the Exchange. I had nothing but my own weakness to thank; it was my interest in weddings that did it, made me forget my decorum, the public place, myself, everything, and plunge in. And I became more and more delighted over it as the girl continued to crush me. My day had been dull, my researches had not brought me a whit nearer royal blood; I looked at my little bill-of-fare, and then I stepped forward to the counter, adventurous, but polite.

"I should like a slice, if you please, of Lady Baltimore," I said with extreme formality.

I thought she was going to burst; but after an interesting second she replied, "Certainly," in her regular Exchange tone; only, I thought it trembled a little.

I returned to the table and she brought me the cake, and I had my first felicitous meeting with Lady Baltimore. Oh, my goodness! Did you ever taste it? It's all soft, and it's in layers, and it has nuts—but I can't write any more about it; my mouth waters too much.

Delighted surprise caused me once more to speak aloud, and with my mouth full. "But, dear me, this is delicious!"

A choking ripple of laughter came from the counter. "It's I who make them," said the girl. "I thank you for the unintentional compliment." Then she walked straight back to my table. "I can't help it," she said, laughing still, and her delightful, insolent nose well up; "how can I behave myself when a man goes on as you do?" A nice white curly dog followed her, and she stroked his ears.

"Your behavior is very agreeable to me," I remarked.

"You'll allow me to say that you're not invited to criticise it. I was decidedly put out with you for making me ridiculous. But you have admired my cake with such enthusiasm that you are forgiven. And—may I hope that you are getting on famously with the battle of Cowpens?"

I stared. "I'm frankly very much astonished that you should know about that!"

"Oh, you're just known all about in Kings Port."

I wish that our miserable alphabet could in some way render the soft Southern accent which she gave to her words. But it cannot. I could easily misspell, if I chose; but how, even then, could I, for instance, make you hear her way of saying "about"? "Aboot" would magnify it; and besides, I decline to make ugly to the eye her quite special English, that was so charming to the ear.

"Kings Port just knows all about you," she repeated with a sweet and mocking laugh.

"Do you mind telling me how?"

She explained at once. "This place is death to all incognitos."

The explanation, however, did not, on the instant, enlighten me. "This? The Woman's Exchange, you mean?"

"Why, to be sure! Have you not heard ladies talking together here?"

I blankly repeated her words. "Ladies talking?"

She nodded.

"Oh!" I cried. "How dull of me! Ladies talking! Of course!"

She continued. "It was therefore widely known that you were consulting our South Carolina archives at the library—and then that notebook you bring marked you out the very first day. Why, two hours after your first lunch we just knew all about you!"

"Dear me!" said I.

"Kings Port is ever ready to discuss strangers," she further explained. "The Exchange has been going on five years, and the resident families have discussed each other so thoroughly here that everything is known; therefore a stranger is a perfect boon." Her gayety for a moment interrupted her, before she continued, always mocking and always sweet: "Kings Port cannot boast intelligence offices for servants; but if you want to know the character and occupation of your friends, come to the Exchange!" How I wish I could give you the raciness, the contagion, of her laughter! Who would have dreamed that behind her primness all this frolic lay in ambush? "Why," she said, "I'm only a plantation girl; it's my first week here, and I know every wicked deed everybody has done since 1812!"

She went back to her counter. It had been very merry; and as I was settling the small debt for my lunch I asked: "Since this is the proper place for information, will you kindly tell me whose wedding that cake is for?"

She was astonished. "You don't know? And I thought you were quite a clever Ya—I beg your pardon—Northerner."

"Please tell me, since I know you're quite a clever Reb—I beg your pardon—Southerner."

"Why, it's his own! Couldn't you see that from his bashfulness?"

"Ordering his own wedding cake?" Amazement held me. But the door opened, one of the elderly ladies entered, the girl behind the counter stiffened to primness in a flash, and I went out into Royal Street as the curly dog's tail wagged his greeting to the newcomer.

THE POETRY SOCIETY OF SOUTH CAROLINA
IN THE 1920S

Hervey Allen

ALCHEMY

Some souls are strangers in this bourne;
  Beauty is born from such men's discontent;
  Earth's grass and stones,
  Her seas, her forests, and her air
Are seas and forests till they mirror on some pool
  Unusually reflecting in an exile's mind,
  Who tarries here protesting and alone;
And then they get strange shapes from memories of
       other stars
  The banished knew, or spheres he dreams will be.
  Thus is the fivefold vision of the earth recast
    By ghostly alchemy.

  But there are favored spots
Where all earth's moods conspire to make a show
    Of things to be transmuted into beauty
    By alchemic minds.
Such is this island beach where Poe once walked,
  And heard the melic throbbing of the sea,
    With muffled sound of harbor bells —
      Bells—he loved bells!
And here are drifting ghosts of city chimes
  Come over water through the evening mist,
Like knells from death-ships off the coasts of spectral
  lands.

  I think some dusk their metal voices
      Yet will call him back
  To walk upon this magic beach again,
While Grief holds carnival upon the harbor bar.
  Heralded by ravens from another air,
  The master will pass, pacing here,
  Wrapped in a cape dark as the unborn moon.
  There will be lightning underneath a star;

And he will speak to me
  Of archipelagoes forgot,
Atolls in sailless seas, where dreams have married
  thought.

John Bennett

THE WANDERING MINSTREL'S SONG

Oh, love is like a summer's day!"
  I heard a minstrel sing,
"But fast its glory fades away
  When cometh evening.
So shall thine heart grow old and gray
  Before the roses fall,
And like the wind along the way
Go crying after yesterday,
As empty as a shadow-play
  Upon a garden wall!"

Across the void and stony waste
  I heard that minstrel sing;
The chill, autumnal afternoon
  Rang with his carolling:
"Oh, love is like a summer day
  In which no shadow fall!"
I heard that wandering minstrel say;
But ere the echo died away
  I heard a cuckoo call!

And there's many folk like sunshine,
  And many folk like wine;
But few folk like the rain's bleak song,
  And fewer still like mine.

DuBose Heyward

DUSK

They tell me she is beautiful, my City,
That she is colorful and quaint, alone
Among the cities. But I, I who have known
Her tenderness, her courage, and her pity,
Have felt her forces mould me, mind and bone,
Life after life, up from her first beginning.
How can I think of her in wood and stone!
To others she has given of her beauty,
Her gardens, and her dim, old, faded ways,
Her laughter, and her happy, drifting hours,
Glad, spendthrift April, squandering her flowers,
The sharp, still wonder of her Autumn days;
Her chimes that shimmer from St. Michael's steeple
Across the deep maturity of June,
Like sunlight slanting over open water
Under a high, blue, listless afternoon.
But when the dusk is deep upon the harbor,
She finds *me* where her rivers meet and speak,
And while the constellations ride the silence
High overhead, her cheek is on *my* cheek.
I know her in the thrill behind the dark
When sleep brims all her silent thoroughfares.
She is the glamor in the quiet park
That kindles simple things like grass and trees.
Wistful and wanton as her sea-born airs,
Bringer of dim, rich, age-old memories.
Out on the gloom-deep water, when the nights
Are choked with fog, and perilous, and blind,
She is the faith that tends the calling lights.
Hers is the stifled voice of harbor bells
Muffled and broken by the mist and wind.
Hers are the eyes through which I look on life
And find it brave and splendid. And the stir
Of hidden music shaping all my songs,
And these my songs, my all, belong to her.

BUZZARD ISLAND

A frieze of naked limbs, gaunt, sinister,
Against the sanguine anguish of the West.
No sound except the steady cluck and purr
Of thirsty streams that tap the sky's bared breast,
And crawl through blind canals until they flood
The barren levels of the empty fields,
The fallen dikes, the rotting trunks, with blood.

Now, as the fading horror swoons to night,
Like cinders scattered from a funeral pyre,
Coursing and veering in the upper light,
With bellies ruddy from the ebbing fire,
The buzzards circle down until their breath
Poisons the stagnant air, until the stark
Awaiting trees blossom and leaf with death.

Beyond these rice-fields and their crawling streams,
Young voices ring; white cities lift and spread.
This is the rookery of still-born dreams;
Here, old faiths gather after they are dead,
Out-lived despairs slant by on evil wing,
And bitter memories that time has starved
Home down the closing dusk for comforting.

Josephine Pinckney

SEA-DRINKING CITIES

Sea-Drinking cities have a moon-struck air;
Houses are topped with look-outs; as a dog
Looks up with dumb eyes asking, dormers stare
As stranger-vessels and swart cunning faces.
They are touched with long sleeping in the sea-born moon;
They have heard fabled sails slatting in the dark,
Clearing with no papers, unwritten in any log,
Light as thin leaves before the rough typhoon;
Keels trace a phospher-mark,
To follow to old ocean-drowned green places.

They never lose longing for the never-known,
These ocean-townships moored and hawsered fast,
They welcome ships, salt-jewelled venturers
That up over the curve of the world are blown
With sun-rise in their sails and gold-topped mast;
And in the evening they let them go again
With a twisted lip of pain,
Into the cavernous fog that folds and stirs;
They have not even a faint tenderness
For their own loveliness.

Their loveliness, as of an old tale told. . .
A harbor-goblet with wide-brimming lip
Where morning tumbles in shaken red and gold,
Trinketed and sun-bedizened they sip;
Their tiny tiles all twinkle, fire-bright;
Their strong black people bargain on the docks
In gaudy clothes that catch the beating light. . .
But all bewitched, old cities sit at gaze
Toward the wharves of Mogador. . .Gibraltar,
Where the shawl-selling Arab piles a blaze
Of fiery birds and flowers on Trade's heaped altar.
Sea-drunken sure are these, —
Towns that doze—dream—and never wake at all,
While the soft supple wind slides through the trees,
And the sun sleeps against the yellow wall.

HAG!

Once when I went to see Victoria
As she sat picking shrimp on the kitchen porch —
"Yuh hear dat hollerin' las' night?" she said,
Nodding, brown-paper capped, above the shrimp
That leapt pink-striped into the yellow bowl.
"Dat was a hag; I heared 'er w'en she jump'
Out'n de winduh en' run 'cross de roof
Scr-r-r-r—vlip!" Her tongue and eye-whites rolled
A sharp description.
                  "Hags is human people,
En' dey kin ketch a ol' black cat en' boil it
En' take a bone en' hol' it in dey mout',
Den dey kin go troo any key-hole livin'.
My Gra'ma seen one w'en she was a chile
In lamp-oil times. De hag gone in de key-hole
En' step out'n 'er skin en' lef' it layin'
Down by de hearth en' gone to ride de people.
W'ite mens is scheemy, dough! Dem people come
En' fin de skin en full it full o' crumbs
En' salt en' pepper en' hide it 'hine de do',
En' time de hag git done en' start to skip
She can't git on de skin, en' den dey ketch'er.
She was a human woman, Gra'ma say,
Only she look red, like, bidout de skin,
Kind o' like flannen. Dey put 'er in de guard-house;
En' when de hangin' come a million people —
Mo' 'n a million people, Gra'ma say,
Gone out to see. De hag ain't crack 'er breath,
But she look rale mad w'en dey stan'er on de gallus;
En' w'en dey start to put 'er in de noose
Suddent she squall out —
                       'Skin! Skin!
                       Slip agin!'
Please Gawd! De skin come sailin' troo de air
En' slip right on 'er—vlip! En' den she *laugh*
To kill, an' ride off on de win' en' gone!
Great Day! You ought'a seen dem people run,
My Gra'ma say. Yes, Ma'am, she *seen* dat hag."

110

Beatrice Witte Ravenel

TIDEWATER

I

COASTS

Were the burned sands of Aeaea —
Circe's—stranger than yours,
Wadmalaw?
Myrtles squat beastlike, each crouching inland,
Sand for a spell on their faces.

Is Samos more white
Than the beaches of Kiawah?
Are the knightly spirits of Rhodes more
    fiercely splendid
Than phantoms of Indian warriors?
Their lances more terrible
Than points of palmetto and yucca
Crossed like a sword-dance
On Edisto?
Their towers more arrogant
Than the belfries of thick white bell-flowers
Carved on the air?

Is Marathon richlier echoed
With voices of youthful heroes
Than the swamps of Santee?
When the bloom runs over the moss
In a lost gray glory of tarnished silver,
    of shadowy pearl,
Riders furrow the night —
Marion, Marion's men,
Pass in a voiceless tumult,
Pass like the smoke from a torch,
With dark, unextinguished eyes.

These are the coasts, the haunted coasts and
    the islands
Of Carolina.

II

HARBOR WATER

All through the night I can hear the sound of dancers,
Soft-padding hoofs, and the lipping of the water,
The water, the water patting juba. . .

> *Juba! Juba!*
> *Juba lef' an' juba right,*
> *Juba dance on a moonshine night —*
> *Juba!*

Knobbly palmetto posts,
Matted trunks of sea-gods,
Hairier than monkeys, rise from the water —
The pulpy, the oily-burnished water.

Soft rocking feet of the dancers sway about them,
Long-swelling ripples with their crisp inhibitions,
Filed golden streaks like the pointed feet of dancers,
Pull of the tide, and the netted flopping motion
Of the water, the music-woven, oily-damasked water,
Water patting juba . .

> *Juba! Juba!*
> *Juba lef' an' juba right,*
> *Juba dance on a moonlight night —*
> *Juba!*

III

DEW

The new morning light is a primitive,
A painter of faintly-filled outlines,
    A singer of folk-songs.

The dew-flattened vines by my window
Are all of one innocent green.
Nothing so young as that green —
An outline cut by a child
    From a soft new blotter.

But when the light grows,
They suck up a pert chiaroscuro,
Gold meretricious knowing high-lights
    Hopelessly clever.

    Their poems
    Dry in the sun.

IV

WHITE AZALEAS IN MAGNOLIA GARDENS

Your images in water! Sea-shell grays
And iridescence; like the endless spawn
Of pale sea-jellies on a moonless night —
A milky way that glamors out of sight —
Something of sea and something of the sky.
Drawn from the earth as blossoming dreams are drawn,
Most strange are you in this, that dreams alight and fly,
But you dream on all your translucent days.

Sweeps of divinest nothingness, abyss
Of beauty, you are the stirred subconscious place
Of flowers, you are the rathe and virgin mood
Of young azaleas.
                    Where heaped branches brood
Like bathers, water-girdled to the hips,
Like Undines, every blossom turns her face
Groping above the water, with her parted, winged,
    insatiable lips,
Each for her soul and its white mysteries.

THE PIRATES

The garden of Garret Vanselvin
Swam in the golden spray of October.
The Mexican rose, like a sun-dial,
In tremulous upstaring blossoms
Told off the day:—
Gemmules, white for the dawn; flushing with desperate

hope in the noon;
And drawn into cowering balls of disastrous red —
Thrown-away red—with the sundown.
Into the wide-set windows
Catspaws of south-flavored wind laughed from the harbor,
Where the town, like a giant child, sat on the knees of the
  islands
and played with a lapful
Of silvery ships.

Did they watch it, day after day —
The pirates —
The doomed gold arcs of their hours slip through the
  sun-dial tree?

In the house-place of Garret Vanselvin —
Charles Town, in the province of South Carolina,
Seventeen-hundred-eighteen —
They were trying the pirates;
Men of Stede Bonnet's, shipmates of Vaughn and of
  Blackbeard;
Noisome things of the sea, vicious with spines, smeared
  with abhorrent blood.
They had scooped them a netful and flung it into a corner.
This vile *frutto di mare.*

The pearly swell and the color of coral and amber drained
  out of them,
Flaccid and lax they lay,
Hardly with wills to answer, only waiting the outcome,
The gasp in this cursed, foreign air,
The last alien strangle. . .

What did they dream of day after day, the trammeled
  sea creatures?
It all must have tasted of dreams.
Dry waves and billows of sound, climbing, discharging
  above them;
Voices of lawyers, sleek, desiccate, deadly.
All of eleven judges.

Chief Justice, black-robed, wigged and appurtenanced,
    just as in England.
Goose-Creek gentry the rest, well-born planters come from
    Barbadoes;
Gentlemen laced and red-coated, men of the crack troop
    of horse
Coloneled by Logan.
A shifting of juries.
And all of them, gentle and simple, cut to the quick of
    their pride and their pockets
When the seemly and gravid rice-ships, matronly moving
    out of the harbor,
Plumped in the arms of fell and insolent sea-thieves
Skulking outside.
Wait!
Chief Justice Nicholas Trott, Judge of the Court of
    Vice-Admiralty,
He it is, speaking.
Will he remember?—

Governor once of Providence in the Bahamas,
Not unreputed as over-friendly to rovers,
Not unrebuked for their fellowship.
For the sake of old days, will he. . .
Wait!

His voice! Those are the melting, significant accents
Than won on their lordships in London, that pull at the
    eyelides
Of lattice-bred women. (Their women live here behind
    windows and iron-tusked walls.
You passed them—the narrow, still streets, ambushed with
    eyes—you two who bore Blackbeard's message,
Laying their high-stomached Province under his
contribution.—
Ay, but that flicked them!)
Hearken!

And first he lifts from your shoulder the cover of common
    humanity.

Men? You are not men. You are *hostes humani generis,*
Enemies of all mankind. Neither faith, nay, nor oath need
    be kept with you.
You were formerly ousted of clergy.
Now the law grants you this comfort; and, with a smooth
    lovingkindness
Equal to that of the law, he trusts you will profit.
But—he may allow you no counsel.

He is telling you further
That the God of the land made the ocean,
(He swivels the Scriptures about like a gun, texts spitting
    for grapeshot);
That he parceled it out and placed it under the thumbs of
    Kings and of lawyers.
(O ye fowls of the air, ye wild winds, ye waterspouts,
Praise ye the Lord!)
And against all these three, God, King and lawyers, have
    you offended.
And the witnesses now.
Will they humor the gentry, tickle their notion of pirates'
    ways,
Got from old chap-books, old songs of the Barbary Coast?
Pshaw! This is tame, this has no tang!
No decks swashing in blood? No one walking the plank?
You, James Killing, mate of the ravished sloop, *Francis,*
Did they not cut you down?—Nay, and their captain, he
    that's escaped, Major Bonnet,
Was civil, uncommon civil.—Cutlasses drawn?—Why,
    yes. . .
To cut down the pineapple-nets over the captain's lockers.
Asked me to join in a health in rum punch to the King —
    over the water;
Asked why I looked so melancholy. Told them I looked
    as well as I could.
Sang two-three glees. . . asked me to join'em a-pirating.
And now they are questioning you.
How came you such monsters, outlaws?
Not by your wills? Forced to that way of life? Why did

116

you join then?
How should one tell this Judge, in his awful and spiteful
   majesty,
His sinister magpie dress, —
"Man—or, my lord—or your honor—had you been left
   on a Maroon shore,
With the sea in front and behind you a present death —
   Indians howling at night,
Or worser than Indians, made out of night, broke loose
   from hell —
Just for the smell of a ship and the job of a shipmate's
   elbow
You'd have turned pirate too!"
God! How mouth it
To his honor, a Lord Chief Justice?

What does it profit to listen
To the long, long, day-long drone,
While the sun spills gold through the Mexican rose-tree?
Better to listen instead
To the winding importunate wind, blowing up from
   palm-tasseled Barbadoes;
Wind that damasks the water, silky wind in the sails
When, like an overripe fruit, rolled in the quickening wash,
The ship is tugging at anchor.
Wind like the hair of girls, so soft, so perfumed and
   resilient,
Tangling the memory now. . .

But here, swelled with importance,
Assistant-Judge Thomas Hepworth, dangerous, droll as
   a pincushion-fish, altercative,
Turns to the jury.
Shall the Carolinas be ruined as one hears that Jamaica
   is ruined?
Are not our rice-ships seized at our very gates?
Is not the incredible true? In our own walled town what
   disturbance, what rioting,
What threatenings to burn it—burn Charles Town—burn

it about our ears!
And all with design
To rescue these pestilent pirates.
Only too well have arts and practice effected
The flight of Stede Bonnet. Certain are favorable toward
    him,
Citing his gentle blood, his fortune, his education—
Enhancements these of his crimes.
An example then, gentlemen all, a substantial and speedy
    example:
The times demand it!

And the trial clicks to the verdict.

No record remains
In the ancient records of Charles Town,
No scribble, no note—
Only the outraged, discretionless speech of his judgeship,
Forwarded straight to London, from his Majesty's Court
    of Vice-Admiralty,
Witnesses yet
To the people's love for the pirates.

They threw doubloons on the counters
Of honest taverns fringing the wharves.
It was Fair-day in Charles Town harbor,
Silks to be bought good cheap, spices and loaves of
    blue-coated sugar,
When the sunburned traffickers landed.
Trinkets they fetched and wines. . .
Ah, but richer and fiercer,
Surely they brought Romance!
(Do you notice that burly man, his scared eyes watching
    the captives
As men watch plague-struck comrades?
Do you mark that girl, twisting, with hunted glances,
Her apron-tail in her teeth?)
They brought in their stained red scarves aromas of
    dangerous rapture
That comfort men who live by the sea and resist its

challenge,—
Romance that lifted the blurred, resentful drab of their
    days
As sunrise opals the sea-mist.

As the shop of a Greek near the wharves
Where the quick white sailors cluster like sea-gulls
Over his tubs of grapes, his ropy netting of melons,
I shall stop, I shall buy a pineapple,
Heavy with tropic flavors.
I shall go to the White Point gardens, as near as may be
To the place where we hanged the pirates—
We Carolinians—
Where the gun from Granville Bastion
Ripped the sky with the sunrise;
And the merciful quicksand took them,—
Twisted, discolored sea-things.

I shall study my pineapple,
Its desperate-clinging points. . .
As a man might cling to life with his finger-nails and his
    toe-nails
When the breath is squeezed in his throat!
As one lays flowers on a grave
I shall toss it over the sea-wall.

Because you laughed when you ravished the *Francis;*
Because you drank to your fallen King—over the water;
But most because they once loved you,
The humble, whose very life is in some sort a piracy,
Marauding the sun and air from the well-found and solid
    citizen;
Because they fought for your lives—
May your quicksand, O pirates,
Be soft as the arms of a girl,
May your sleep be forever
And pleasant with dreams of sea-changes,

Interpreters of the sea!

THE YEMASSEE LANDS

I

In the Yemassee Lands
Peace-belts unwind in the Spring on the banks of Savannah;
Flowers like wampum weave in the grass
Reiterate beads of pink-orange, of clouded white, of
    pale, shimmerless ochre,
Mile after mile.

II

Round the curve of the river,
Meshed by conniving impatient shoots of the gum tree,
Streamers of silver dart, muffled lapping of paddles.
Always, just round the turning, the stealthy canoe
    with its naked upstanding warrior
Comes. . . for the wild-fowl rise in a hurtling of
    startled feathers;
Never comes into sight.

III

In the Yemassee Lands
Cypress roots, at the edge of the swamp, roughly
    fluted, age-wrinkled,
Have budded their rufous knobs like dim and reptilian eyes,
That watch.
Orchids, liquid gold, bend from cylindrical sheaths
Under a phantom moccasined tread.
Gossamer webs, barring the overgrown way through
    the woods,
Shudder but do not break, betraying the passage
Of footsteps gone by.

IV

In the undulant mist of the sunsets of summer

Slim pines stand with scarlet and quivering outlines —
Initiate boys whose whipped young blood leaps up
Now, the first time, to the war-path.
Shadows of red, shadows of bronze and of copper
Disengage from the wood-growth;
Cowering, melting, lost, reappearing,
One after one, the long, lithe, menacing war-line
Loops through the stems.
Light cups the crouching knees,
Splinters on polished shoulders,
Ravels in towering head-plumes.

V

In the Yemassee Lands
When with blowing of wood-smoke and throbbing
    of hidden drums
Indian Summer fashions its spell,
Trembling falls on the air.
Wild things flatten themselves in the jeopardy of the
    shade.
Out of the snarling keen-toothed vines
Berries wink with the cunning obsidian gleam
Of the arrow-head, and deep in the shuddering fern
The rattlesnake coils his pattern of war.
Silence, inimical, lurks in the dark:
Softly on buckskinned soles, halting a step behind,
Something follows and waits. . .
And will not be appeased.

VI

But when Autumn unleashes the winds
And storm treads the lowlands,
Trees, like a panic of horses galloping over the sky-line,
(Charging of chestnut and roan and bay,
Tossing their frantic forelocks)
Flee from the rush
Of invisible hunters.

VII

Stars in the coppery afterglow of the sundown
Hang like strings of teeth on the savage breast of a warrior;
Water-willows trail in the shadowy depths of Savannah,
Draggle like scalps from the war-belt;
And the night-wind sings overhead
Like arrows on deadly sendings,
In the Yemassee Lands.

VIII

Gray through young leaves blows the smoke from the
    ancient fires;
The thud of the young men's dances troubles the earth.
Shadows from ambushed boughs
Reach with a plucking hand for the hair.
The lightning-set pine far away blazes with
    hideous cracklings,
Remembering the long black tresses of captive
    squaws
Tied to the death-pyre.

IX

After two hundred years
Has the forest forgotten?
Always the trees are aware
(Significant, perilous, shaken with whispers of dread
and of welcome)
Of the passage of urgent feet.
Violent shoots strain up to the air and the sunshine
Of cut-over land;
Leaves crowd over the barrows of last year's skeleton
    leaves.
Ever and ever again
The Red Man comes back to his own
In the Yemassee Lands.

"Renaissance" Charleston
and Beyond

John Bennett

MADAME MARGOT

In an age so glorious, rich and fine, and so be-starred with splendor that one almost forgets the bottomless abyss into which it plunged at last, there lived a woman in Charleston of whom a very odd story is told.

Among the fugitives from massacre in San Domingo was a young girl of mixed blood, named Marguerite Lagoux. By her intimates called Rita, by familiar acquaintances, Morgoton, by those who envied her beauty, in disparagement, Margot, she was, after all was done, known merely as Old Mother Go-go.

But, among the golden-skinned San Domingans, loveliest of all, admittedly, was Marguerite Lagoux.

Marguerite was beautiful, as is the case with many of her kind. She was almost white, and the lines of her loveliness were something to look on and to desire.

Men, seeing her for the first time, stopped to look, catching their breaths. There was something about her more than beauty which took men like a spell. Her body was cast in a gloriously perfect mold; she was tall, and full of tiger like grace, the envy of other women. She walked as an empress might, if God gave her grace, with perfect and exquisite motion, effortlessly, not striding, but seeming to glide like a swan on untroubled waters.

Dressed in bright merino, crimson, orange and blue, with a blood-colored silken kerchief bound round her head in Oriental fashion, beads of amber around her neck, and in each ear a hoop of gold, she looked like a great golden tiger lily dusted with *sang-dieu.*

Ducie Poincignon was lovely; so was Rose Lemesurier; but there was only one Margot Lagoux.

She was a milliner and mantuamaker, her shop in King Street, on the western side, beyond Mignot's Garden, a little above the bend. Its location is now altogether uncertain, for all that part of King Street was destroyed by fire.

Her home was a small house in a court long since forgotten, to which led a narrow alley, known as Lilac Lane, from two large *melia azederach* trees, Indian lilacs, which arched its entrance.

Lilac Lane entered the block now bounded by King, Calhoun, St. Philip and George Streets, from George Street, just behind the old Hummel apothecary shop. The apothecary shop also is long since forgotten, and the lane exists no more. All that survives of that inner court and its flowery small cottages is a narrow, pinched and abbreviated exit in St. Philip Street, two doors above Greene.

Her shop was the most popular in Charleston; for of all milliners of her day, Margot was foremost. . . first beyond compare. Her taste was beyond criticism; her instinct for color faultless; her choice of fabrics perfect; her knowledge of women complete; her dexterity infinite.

Her lady patrons were patrician. Those who desired perfect taste and material loveliness combined with exquisite charm found what they sought at Margot Lagoux's. She was employed by the very best people of Charleston; she had no successful competitor; beside her work Eloise Couesnon's was but maladroit.

Lilac Lane was but a narrow entry between two estates, and rambled into that interspace like a brook into a wood, growing narrower as it went, until the high hedges which bordered it met and knit themselves together into what seemed a cul-de-sac, or dead-end passage. The footpath ran on a little yet, until it disappeared in green uncertainty. The unfamiliar traveler, bewildered, here turned back to find a bolder thoroughfare, leaving within that entangled green a little tranquil space withdrawn from curious eyes and from the brawling town, as peaceful as a convent close, a sanctuary from the rude intrusions of a troubling world. Where the strait path vanished into the green Margot's cottage stood snug as the stone in a plum.

It was inevitable that when Margot Lagoux came to the full loveliness of her womanhood she should be pursued by men; and that, sooner or later, and rather soon than late,

126

she should become the indulged mistress of a wealthy man, after the habit of the time, by whom she had a daughter of loveliness even more exquisite than her mother's, and of complexion fairer still, so fair, indeed, that none save those who knew the fact could say whether she were white or black.

As this daughter, whom Margot named Gabrielle, grew from infancy to childhood, from childhood to maidenhood, and approached the perilous age of wakening to the heart's desire, fear laid hold of her mother's heart lest Gabrielle should be what she herself was, and nothing more. Such perfect loveliness asked far more, and bespoke a better fate than that of milliner and mistress, forever doomed from birth until death to be only "a free person of color." Gabrielle, as Margot knew but too well, was possessed of perilous loveliness.

Of Gabrielle's parentage further one can only shrug one's shoulders. . . no one can say more certainly. . . aristocratic beyond a doubt. . . else where had she her radiant, fair beauty, her exquisite, slender body, her arched insteps like a Spanish girl's, and her lovely, aristocratic face? God alone knows.

Margot was lovely; but Gabrielle was lovelier, as brier rose is lovelier than pompadour pink. Gabrielle's was an exquisite ivory loveliness; her ankles were the loveliest things that ever a sandal ribbon bound; she was everywhere known as the loveliest girl in all old St. Finbar's parish. Margot was a pottery figurine molded with marvelous skill; Gabrielle was a statuette of exquisite porcelain. She walked like the wind of April through meadows after rain. Her face with its delicate high cheekbones was like the flowers of Normandy; but her lovely color was Eastern, not Western, Persian, like the roses which bloomed in the forgotten gardens of Istakhr, yesterday's flowers, full of yesterday's loveliness, yesterday's happiness, yesterday's tragedy, sweet with passionate, heart-breaking perfume and the pathos of swift-passing beauty. Her cheeks were the hue of peach flowers at dusk, more delicate than japonica color. God who gave them knew whence came both peach-flower color and dusk. Under her transparent skin a shadowy crimson flowed with the beat of her heart like a twilit tide. . . San Domingo's *sang de crépuscule*. She might have been a sister to Scheherezade.

This loveliness made Margot tremble. It is a perilous privilege for a girl to possess beauty rising above her station in life; there is always a price to be paid for it; sorrow the common fee. There was a thought from which Margot shrank as from a draught of poison: Gabrielle degraded and desolate. Such a heritage of beauty too often proves but a legacy of tragedy and shame.

There was nothing on earth so precious to Margot as her daughter's happiness and security, nothing so important; to Margot even more to be desired than her own eternal peace.

She perceived the ominous shadow which overhung her child from her cradle to her grave. She looked from side to side like a deer hard pressed by the dogs. . . can one escape destiny?

Where were the lovely and the fair she had known in her own youth? The graveyard sand lay cold on their lips; their sweetness and their passion were forgotten long ago. Margot knew that youth and summer nights were made for ecstasy. She knew also that in forgotten graveyards are many unmarked graves of hapless innocence and beauty. Life was stripped of all illusions for Margot Lagoux; the truth stood stark and bare before her in all its unmitigated ugliness. Every look into the future was filled with apprehension. She awoke at night, crying out, "No. . . no. . . no. . . it must not. . . cannot. . . shall not be!"

At adolescence Gabrielle Lagoux was a vision of delight. She was in temperament as ardent as a summer shower, which gives, when it gives, all that it has to give, in a rush of wind and rain. Unspoiled by knowledge, unruined by folly, too innocent still to be perplexed by life's anxieties, her soul mistook Earth for the pathway to Paradise, and nothing as yet had discovered her error. Her light feet stood at the smiling gate of the Primrose Way.

But Margot's days and nights were filled with increasing anxiety, as with increasing doubt she confronted destiny.

The inner door of Margot's cottage gave upon a small paved court, where two old fig trees grew. Here, remote from the curious observation of the world, preserved by cloistral hedges from prying indiscretion, flowed Gabrielle's untroubled existence.

Few ever saw her. Such as saw her by chance through some green interstice, dazzled by her loveliness, spread the tale of a princess in an enchanted wood; but few had ever seen her twice. Margot had kept the court a solitude lest Gabrielle suffer corruption, and maintained around her a very nunnery of care, hovering over her, and kept her as withdrawn from the world as a novice in a convent garth.

But beauty cannot be safely sequestered always anywhere. The less seen, the more thought of. Cloistral existence is all very well for souls of the convent sort; but youth and spring hate convents, and will have life's novitiate or none. There is a crevice in every hedge, no matter how tall or how thick it may be.

Spring came with its universal song; all living creatures voiced the universal theme: the blue dove moaned out his heart's desire; the copper beetle wooed and won his lady in the dust; butterflies and dragonflies glittered in the wind, happy in their airy ecstacy. . . all earth rejoiced in having its heart's desire.

Gabrielle was intoxicated by the unknown passion of her own heart; within her breast a questioning wonder grew.

"Mother," she said wistfully, "what is it fills the world with music day and night? What makes the whole world sing?"

"Happiness," said Margot, "and joy of the spring."

"If it be happiness," rejoined Gabrielle, "why does it make my heart ache?"

Margot, startled, stared, wrung with sudden fear.

"And what is this love of which everyone sings?"

"The source of all human wretchedness," cried Margot.

"But, mother, if love be the source of all wretchedness, why is its song so sweet?"

"Because fools have their folly," said Margot. "Worship God, and leave foolishness to the fool."

"Love. . . foolishness?" said Gabrielle. "You told me that God is love."

"What ails you?" demanded Margot.

"Nothing, mother"; but a flush crept up her cheeks. "How does a woman know that she loves, so that she may say surely, 'This is love'?"

"By the despair that tears her heart in two."

"But, mother," persisted Gabrielle, "they tell me that love is sweet."

"Sweet? As wormwood," said Margot hoarsely. "It is nothing but fever and fret."

"Many I see who have it; but none do I see that fret. I would I might know for myself this pretty play of lovers and beloved!"

"What man has snared your silly heart?" demanded Margot, seeing the shadow near, foreseeing the fate of loveliness, perceiving the lips of indiscretion already at the rim of the cup of danger.

"Why should any man snare my heart?" asked Gabrielle in pitiful wonder. "I have never harmed any man. And, mother, feel my heart! It beats as if it would burst. Am I dying? Must I die? My heart aches so that I would I might die. Was not man made by God? Is not what God made good? You told me that God is love. . . and is not love the world's delight?"

Margot's joy in Gabrielle's beauty was turned to bitterness. "I conjure you, by God's sorrow, close your heart against it."

"How can I close my heart against it when I hear it in my sleep?"

Margot recoiled as she faced the future. There is no woe so sickening as the shuddering, interior sense of impending disaster.

Day after day Gabrielle knelt in her garden and pleaded for her heart's desire. Night after night Margot crouched before her crucifix and prayed in agony that her desire might not be given her. Heaven's auditor mixed those prayers in fatal entanglement; one was answered, and one was not: he alone is responsible.

Sunset lay on Margot's garden. Gabrielle, puzzling upon life's unanswered riddle, stood listening to sounds beyond the hedge. Everywhere was the sound of running feet, and the whisper of wordless laughter mockingly borne on the evening wind. The world was full of the golden vision of light-footed maidens with fluttering garments flying through Lilac Lane pursued by breathless and ardent lovers eagerly following where they fled. The sound of laughter floated along the narrow way, and the little, faint echo of flying feet. It was the time of the year when all young maids are sweet as fresh-gathered flowers, and all men a little mad. Even the earth, drab clod, was astir with the ecstacy of approaching night with its quivering, sentient stars.

As she stood there Gabrielle was suddenly aware of a shadow on the grass. There was a face in the hedge, smiling. . . a lad's face, laughing and debonair. Over his head two butterflies hovered; his yellow hair curled round his face like crisp little golden flames; his eyes were bright and blue as the morning; there was confidence in his bearing, easy lordship and high pride. His eyes, incessantly roving, were audaciously bright as two wild stars.

Gabrielle's eyes were wide opened, round, unwinking, full of suddenly frightened tears. Her lips had fallen slightly apart to free her fluttering breath, she sighed, a little shuddering sigh, and crossed her hands upon her breast.

Her beauty startled him: delicate, frail, almost translucent in the golden sun; she seemed a being not of flesh, blood and gross mortality. . . saint, maid, dryad, nymph, or sprite. . . who could tell which? Silently drinking her loveliness he leaned through the hedge.

Again she sighed softly; stared at his face, and shivered a little. Was it a god or a man in the hedge? Had he sprouted from the boxwood or fallen from the sky? Into the crevice between her lips the sunshine had slipped; her lips were aglow, as if she were breathing ethereal flame.

He drew his breath with an audible sound; and, as he stared, longing seized his boy's heart and wrung it bitterly.

The flame which blazed in his bright eyes put an answering glow in hers. For the first time in her life she was awake to the sense of her own loveliness, wonderful and sweet. A throbbing, delicate fire came fluttering up through her breast. Her eyes met his: in his eyes were delight, surprise and longing. His eyes met hers: and all her doubts went out in wordless joy. . . like a wave which breaks along a beach her heart rushed out to greet him. The world seemed suddenly remote, withdrawn into the depths of incalculable space. There remained but two young love-stunned souls, groping to each other in the garden beneath the magnolia trees.

Night fell, and darkness voyaged the uncharted sky. Overhead the blue dome blazed with innumerable stars and golden planets heaving up heaven's arch; the tremulous green lamps of the fireflies filled the earth with winking constellations around them. But the heavens and the earth were as nothing to them; love was there, and he, and she, and the forgotten starlight. And where youth and love are, life, death, good or ill, the bright stars overhead, or the dark mold below, for better or for worse, are nothing, and wisdom of little worth.

Into the house she came, one little slipper upon its foot, one slipper gone. . . what became of that little lost slipper God only knows. Her stockinged foot was wet with the dew which had dripped from the leaves overhead. Her lips stung; her cheeks were on fire; all her soul was singing. She was so transfigured she seemed a winged creature. Her soft lips moved in inarticulate ecstasy. Hands, feet, neck, face, all told one story. Her eyes were like blazing stars. Margot stared with narrowed eyes.

"Mother, I am happy. . . so happy that I want to live forever!"

Margot searched that radiant face, with a cold hand clutching at her heart.

"I was walking in the garden, mother, and the god of

love was there. He kissed me on my mouth, mother; and, oh, mother, love is sweet!"

Margot's heart stopped. "Are you quite mad?" she asked. Then the truth dawned upon her. "Oh, my God!" she whispered. "I should have known! I should have known! Fool, fool, fool! Mother of Jesus! I should have known!" As if stunned, her head fell down upon her breast.

In the dark and breathless stillness of the night was a stern, strange loveliness; yet now something akin to wordless terror, the terror of a child that dreams, and, waking suddenly in the darkness, cries out in fear of unseen, unknown things.

An ill wind which had blown up since sunset with a far-off, moaning sound, had risen to a melancholy, screaming note. Clouds of soot and ashes blown from the fireplace whirled in drifts around the floor. A bird sped round the house with a shrill, terrified cry; the wind bellowed hoarsely in the chimney; the house shook; over the housestops could be heard the coming of the rain.

Before her crucifix Margot knelt, praying for her daughter as she never had prayed for herself:

"Mother of God, all merciful. . . spare my daughter!" But she heard nothing.

"St. Dominique, lover of souls, preserve my daughter from destruction!" Still she heard nothing.

"Mary, Mother, great in grace, defend and preserve my child! Mother of Sorrows, have mercy upon her!" Still she heard nothing.

"All ye Holy Virgins, intercede for her! Lord of Compassion, hear me! O Thou, Most Pitiful Lord of the Innocent, answer my prayer, and protect my child!"

Again she listened; yet she heard nothing but the whine and whistle of the wind.

"Lord, *Seigneur Dieu*, preserve and spare my daughter! Lord God, answer my prayer!"

But all was still.

It was taking too long for her anguish to reach the foot of God's throne. To her dismayed heart the night was

appallingly still. The confident faithful may wait upon the
leisure of Heaven; but the desperate have no time to wait.
To hearts dismayed there is nothing so appallingly still as
God.

She beat her breast; her garments were disarrayed; her
voice grew shrill; by all vicars, saints and intercessors, by all
intermediaries, she pleaded with God to listen and reply.
There was no answer. "Mary, Mother of Sorrows!" she
gasped. "Does God not understand?"

Her appeal arose piercingly shrill: "*Dieu, Dieu, Eternal
Dieu, écoute mes cris! Hatê-toi de ma secourir! Hâte-toi
d'elle delivrer! O Toi, qui écoutes la prière, air petié de
nous! Ne tarde-pas! Écoute mes cris!*"

She waited; there was no sound; no answer; then her
voice went up like the cry of delirium:

"*O Dieu, très-haut, réveille-toi! Réveille-toi mon Dieu!*"
Then in a tone of amazement and pathos, "Mary, Mother
of Sorrows, do I have to explain to God?"

She paused a moment, while despair rose like a swelling
flood; then through the night went up a bitter cry:
"*Seigneur Dieu! Tout-puissant Dieu! sois attentif à ma
prière. . . Gabrielle, ma fille, mon Dieu!* Forgive in her my
transgressions; pardon in her my sins; deliver her from her
inheritance. . . Oh, my God!. . . let her be white!"

The wind sucked through the chimney with a sound like
awful laughter; but from Heaven there was no answer.

Then she cried out pitifully, the cry which through the
unending ages stands archetype of despair: "*Mon Dieu,
mon Dieu! pourquoi m'as-tu abandonné?*"

She crouched a moment, listening, her head on one side.
There was no reply. She turned her back on her crucifix,
saying bitterly, "I will call upon You no more!"

The candles sank to dull blue sparks. Over her shoulder a
deep voice said, "Then why not try me awhile? I remember
when God forgets."

It was Satan himself, outcast god of the discontented,
who ever waits at the door of opportunity. "Why not try
me awhile?" he said.

"You pray for loving-kindness," he continued sardonically. "If this be loving-kindness, why not try damnation awhile? You have seen all the piety under the sun, that its wages are vanity. God sends you grief. Has he sent you also a cure? or had compassion on you? If this be loving-kindness, why not try damnation instead? It can surely be no worse; and may be vastly better.

"My daughter, you have been cajoled. Come unto me, and I will give you your heart's desire."

"Master. . . Lord," whispered Margot, shivering as with cold, "give me my heart's desire!"

"What is your heart's desire?"

"That my daughter, Gabrielle, shall be white to all eternity. All that I have, all that I am, will I give. . . yea, for this will I give my soul!"

Satan smiled a saturnine smile: "Then lay down your burden at my feet, daughter. You shall have your heart's desire."

Forthwith she bargained with Satan that her daughter, Gabrielle, should be white to all eternity.

And by his eternal damnation Satan swore that she should have her heart's desire. Margot laid down her burden of fear at the feet of the Prince of the Powers of Darkness, and by her rejected hope of salvation swore to abide by their covenant.

She never knelt at a confessional again.

There is a convent school for orphaned girls kept by the nuns in New Orleans. The liveliest girl seen there in years was Gabrielle Lagoux, carried there between two nights, lest young love, like Death, insist. To that school, her origins unknown, went Gabrielle.

Her mother kissed her twice with feverish lips like dry leaves. The coach was at the gate. She said to the coach-boy who guarded her gown from the wheels, "Tell him that I love him." She paused again in the coach door, a dazed look on her face: "Tell him not to forget me. I love him."

She never came back. She never saw her golden lad again. When she entered the coach young love was done for forever. The days became weeks, weeks months, months grew into years. She passed in through the convent's sheltering doors to a world of unfamiliar faces, and forgot.

God made memory cruel, that men might know remorse; but the Devil devised forgetfulness, anodyne of regret. She never returned to the place of her birth, nor saw her mother again.

Reputed heiress to great estates, provided with apparently boundless means, and gifted with rare loveliness, coming of age, Gabrielle was wedded to a substantial planter's son, whose love for her was very great.

She never knew want; her years were filled with happiness and peace; she had a thousand slaves to do her bidding; and bore her husband three children, fair as the morning and with hair like golden fire.

But she never returned to the place of her birth, nor saw her mother again.

The Devil in everything was as good as his promise. But, for favors granted, the Devil takes his pay in his own way.

That is why this story is singular.

Something inscrutable had come over Margot Lagoux.

Her work was oddly altered: it had more air, less ease; more spell, less charm; more force, and less dexterity. Her work retained distinction, but of a queer sort; reserve gave way to novelty; simple beauty was replaced by meretricious charm; her taste, which had been perfect, suffered gradual corruption; her exquisite craft was marked by crudity. She had style, to be sure; but it was style *malade du rouvieux*. Every line of her work was slurred by subtle default; always too much, or too little; never the happy mean. Everything she did was like sweet wine soured, the worse for having been so much better. A queerly degenerated taste marked everything she did. Her custom fell from *vendre cher* to *bon marché*. The air of distinction which had attracted gentility utterly faded away. Calls for her work became infrequent; more infrequent; came no more. One morning the milliner's shop was shut. It never was opened again. Cobwebs hung on the moldy walls; the trade which had known and frequented the place knew it no more.

Wealth was given to Margot Lagoux. Its source it is useless to question. She had money in quantity that made bankers bow. She had women to wait on her, deferential menservants, boys to run at her beck and call, maids to go before her, bond and free. Her cellar was famous for its wines; her dress for its wild extravagance; her riches increased beyond all bounds of reason; she was spoken to with deference, referred to with finesse. She had her carriage, lined with yellow silk; her beauty laughed at sumptuary laws; despite all ordinance she rode the streets like a charioted queen, dressed in *outré*, unstudied colors, wild as Barbary, in amber gown and canary-colored turban fastened with a golden brooch; despite the law, she rode through the community like a lovely malady.

Time but increased the singularity of her beauty. It was gossiped about in the market stalls; it was babbled about in the streets. Her face was like beauty seen in dreams, incredible and untrue; even wise men's souls were disturbed; piety itself was troubled by her golden loveliness; more than one fervent sermon from Solomon's Song was inspired by Margot Lagoux; she was known as the woman with a face like a beautiful blasphemy.

Then a strange, indefinable torpor fell upon her loveliness; though not notably altered, she was greatly changed; her beauty took a dull and leaden look. Her beautiful face had lost something, no one could say just what; had gained something, no one could exactly define. There was a foreignness in her features, and the look of alien things. She looked like a portrait of herself painted in irony.

On the day that her daughter was married in faraway New Orleans, Margot stood before her mirror, motionless, staring at her own reflection. Suddenly she burst into wild, shrill laughter, cheerless, tragic; with body shaking and hands wrung together she turned away with an epithet, reversed the glass, and never looked into a mirror again. Something had passed across her face like a strange, ambiguous stain; a shadow had fallen across her beauty like the dimness beneath a passing cloud.

Margot Lagoux was changing. Sultry beauty such as hers has always an earlier afternoon; but this was more than early afternoon; Margot Lagoux was changing; she was becoming tawny, *bisblanc*, as the Creoles say, as though a somber fountain was playing in her veins.

There were many women at that day on whom fate laid dreadful hands; Louise Briaud, who was blinded by the smallpox; Fanchette Bourie, whom God pitied with death; Hélène Richemont, the leper; Floride Biez, Doucie Baramont, Francesca Villeponteaux, wrecked by disfiguring maladies. God gave them peace! But on none was laid so ruthless, unrelenting, deliberate a hand as fell upon Margot Lagoux. She had changed, like a portrait whose shadows, painted in bitumen, have stuck through and distempered the rest.

The Devil was as good as his promise; but he took his pay in his own way. The old enchantment was gone like a necromancer's spell. Like some strange, nocturnal creature Margot seemed to absorb the gloom. Her glorious eyes grew jaundiced; her rose-brown lips grew dun; the webs which joined her fingers grew yellow as baker's saffron.

Days turned to weeks, weeks to months, months to years. Margot grew swarthy; she put aside beauty like an outworn, bright castoff garment, and grew as grotesque as a teakwood carving.

As her daughter went to white, Margot went to black, by merciless shadowy, gathering degrees. She was paying the price of her daughter's deliverance by her own deterioration. With the passage of the years she grew darker; grew more and more dark; more and more sloven, dingy and daubed, until from the high place of her prosperity, from the riches and luxury in which her patron had installed her while her exotic loveliness was still his pleasure, she sank down, down, down into the slums of the town, as foul, ugly and unclean an old hag as ever haunted the lowest tenement. She became gross, misshapen and debased; of her once-unexampled beauty there was not even the remembrance left.

A young man, with the face of Adonai and hair like curling gold, came once to her door, asking for Marguerite Lagoux. "Is that Marguerite Lagoux?" he asked, shrinking away from the door. . . for her cheeks were blotched and flecked with brown like a decaying peach. "No," he said, "oh, no, no, no! That cannot be Marguerite Lagoux. . . Marguerite Lagoux was lovely. . . and had a beautiful daughter named Gabrielle!" And with that, shuddering, he went away wringing his hands.

She fell apart like an old house with nobody living in it; her sun of glory set. She went down, down, down to oblivion, down to the dusty corner of death. . . and one night died, during a great West Indian storm, in a dirty little hovel, in an unkempt alley, in the middle of a Negro quarter, foul, fallen, filthy, and filled with beggary.

All night long the thunder rolled; the storm was wild beyond comparison. Yet Margot's hovel was ablaze with light. The little taylor who dwelt next door said, "Aha! Old Mother Go-go has company!" But the only person seen to enter her house was a tall man, handsomely attired, but with a face like an unpleasant smell.

The thunder was terrific; the wind blew with a sound like mad, gigantic laughter; the gusts howled through the tailor's house; the wind sucked down the chimney with a sound like awful weeping; the little tailor's soul was filled with a sense of enormous terror.

All night the thunder rolled like the laughter of an angry god. Dislodged by the tremendous concussions, the cockroaches flew out of the walls; and in the morning all the parakeets in that alley were turned as gray as ashes.

The windows and doors of old Mother Go-go's house were standing open wide; it was plain that they had stood open all night, and that the rain had beaten into the house unopposed.

This, however, occasioned but brief surprise. When they peered in at the door the rats were playing about the floor with the scattered beads of a broken rosary.

The priest came early, hurrying in. He did not stay long; and when he came out his face was white as a sheet and his lips pinched and gray as lead. Then those who prepare the dead came.

All over the floor the soot which had fallen from the chimney and been blown around the room was trodden and trampled by great hoofprints, like those of the neighbor's goat.

And Madame Margot? Heh! God had perhaps designed her for tragedy; but here was gross comedy. Margot lay stretched out on the floor, dead, among the ashes and soot, charred like a fallen star, and black as ebony.

The coroner, douce man, found that the woman had died of a visitation of God; but the little tailor said simply, "Has God feet like a goat?"

That was why, everyone was sure, the bishop declined to have masses said for the repose of her soul, and why they would not permit her body to be buried in St. Sebastian's graveyard: her color was too peculiar. Too black to be buried among the white, too white to be buried among the black, too well-to-do to be buried in the Potter's Field, she was secretly buried in her own garden, under the magnolia trees.

And that was the end of Madame Margot.

Yet not even death could purge away the ambiguous spell which surrounded her and her possessions. Every place in which she had dwelt sank into irremediable decay, the swifter where it had seemed to be most permanent and secure. The great house in which she had spent the days of her beauty and power stood a ruin above a decaying court, a wreck of its former pride and splendor. Of Margot's cottage there was no trace, other than a heap of moldering brick, the rafters of a fallen roof, and one bleak, tumbling gable: of Gabrielle's garden nothing whatsoever remained. Even Lilac Lane was gone; there was no lane there any more.

Yet, strangely, about the forgotten lane there hung a something obscure and malign. After a woman had hanged herself at the crook of the lane it was closed to public passage as an abandoned thoroughfare and its entries barred. Yet still for years about the forgotten thoroughfare hung a spell grotesque and anomalous: that every boy who dared to cross the former entry to the lane on his way to school was certain as the sun to shine to be thrashed at school that day, and thrashed most thoroughly.

John Galsworthy

A HEDONIST

What is the highest and final aim of human activity? If the answer is, Feelings of pleasure or happiness, we have hedonism.—PAULSEN.

Rupert K. Vaness remains freshly in my mind because he was so fine and large, and because he summed up in his person and behavior a philosophy which, budding before the war, hibernated during that distressing epoch, and is now again in bloom.

He was a New-Yorker addicted to Italy. One often puzzled over the composition of his blood. From his appearance, it was rich, and his name fortified the conclusion. What the K. stood for, however, I never learned; the three possibilities were equally intriguing. Had he a strain of Highlander with Kenneth or Keith; a drop of German or Scandinavian with Kurt or Knut; a blend of Syrian or Armenian with Khalil of Kassim? The blue in his fine eyes seemed to preclude the last, but there was an encouraging curve in his nostrils and a raven gleam in his auburn hair, which, by the way, was beginning to grizzle and recede when I knew him. The flesh of his face, too, had sometimes a tired and pouchy appearance, and his tall body looked a trifle rebellious within his extremely well-cut clothes; but, after all, he was fifty-five. You felt that Vaness was a philosopher, yet he never bored you with his views, and was content to let you grasp his moving principle gradually through watching what he ate, drank, smoked, wore, and how he encircled himself with the beautiful things and people of this life. One presumed him rich, for one was never aware of money in his presence. Life moved round him with a certain noiseless ease or stood still at a perfect temperature, like the air in a conservatory round a choice blossom which a draft might shrivel.

This image of a flower in relation to Rupert K. Vaness

142

pleases me, because of that little incident in Magnolia Gardens, near Charleston, South Carolina.

Vaness was the sort of man of whom one could never say with safety whether he was revolving round a beautiful young woman or whether the beautiful young woman was revolving round him. His looks, his wealth, his taste, his reputation, invested him with a certain sun-like quality; but his age, the recession of his locks, and the advancement of his waist were beginning to dim his luster, so that whether he was moth or candle was becoming a moot point. It was moot to me, watching him and Miss Sabine Monroy at Charleston throughout the month of March. The casual observer would have said that she was "playing him up," as a young poet of my acquaintance puts it; but I was not casual. For me Vaness had the attraction of a theorem, and I was looking rather deeply into him and Miss Monroy.

That girl had charm. She came, I think, from Baltimore, with a strain in her, they said, of old Southern French blood. Tall and what is known as willowy, with dark chestnut hair, very broad, dark eyebrows, very soft, quick eyes, and a pretty mouth,—when she did not accentuate it with lip-salve,—she had more sheer quiet vitality than any girl I ever saw. It was delightful to watch her dance, ride, play tennis. She laughed with her eyes; she talked with a savoring vivacity. She never seemed tired or bored. She was, in one hackneyed word, attractive. And Vaness, the connoisseur, was quite obviously attracted. Of men who professionally admire beauty one can never tell offhand whether they definitely design to add a pretty woman to their collection, or whether their dalliance is just matter of habit. But he stood and sat about her, he drove and rode, listened to music, and played cards with her; he did all but dance with her, and even at times trembled on the brink of that. And his eyes, those fine, lustrous eyes of his, followed her about.

How she had remained unmarried to the age of twenty-six was a mystery till one reflected that with her power of enjoying life she could not yet have had the time. Her perfect physique was at full stretch for eighteen hours out of the twenty-four every day. Her sleep must have been like that of a baby. One figured her sinking into dreamless rest the moment her head touched the pillow, and never stirring till she sprang up into her bath.

As I say, for me Vaness, or rather his philosophy, *erat demonstrandum.* I was philosophically in some distress just then. The microbe of fatalism, already present in the brains of artists before the war, had been considerably enlarged by that depressing occurrence. Could a civilization basing itself on the production of material advantages do anything but insure the desire for more and more material advantages? Could it promote progress even of a material character except in countries whose resources were still much in excess of their population? The war had seemed to me to show that mankind was too combative an animal ever to recognize that the good of all was the good of one. The coarse-fibered, pugnacious, and self-seeking would, I had become sure, always carry too many guns for the refined and kindly.

The march of science appeared, on the whole, to be carrying us backward. I deeply suspected that there had been ages when the populations of this earth, though less numerous and comfortable, had been proportionately healthier than they were at present. As for religion, I had never had the least faith in Providence rewarding the pitiable by giving them a future life of bliss. The theory seemed to me illogical, for the more pitiable in this life appeared to me the thick-skinned and successful, and these, as we know, in the saying about the camel and the needle's eye, our religion consigns wholesale to hell. Success, power, wealth, those aims of profiteers and premiers, pedagogues and pandemoniacs, of all, in fact, who could not see God in a dewdrop, hear Him in distant goat-bells, and scent Him in a pepper-tree, had always appeared to me akin to dry rot. And yet every day one saw more distinctly that they were the pea in the thimblerig of life, the hub of a universe which, to the approbation of the majority they represented, they were fast making uninhabitable. It did not even seem of any use to help one's neighbors; all efforts at relief just gilded the pill and encouraged our stubbornly contentious leaders to plunge us all into fresh miseries. So I was searching right and left for something to believe in, willing to accept even Rupert K. Vaness and his basking philosophy. But could a man bask his life right out? Could just looking at fine pictures, tasting rare fruits and wines, the mere listening to good music, the scent of azaleas and the best tobacco, above all the society of pretty women, keep salt in my bread, an ideal in my brain? Could they? That's what I wanted to know.

Every one who goes to Charleston in the spring soon or late visits Magnolia Gardens. A painter of flowers and trees, I specialize in gardens, and freely assert that none in the world is so beautiful as this. Even before the magnolias come out, it consigns the Boboli at Florence, the Cinnamon Gardens of Colombo, Concepcion at Malaga, Versailles, Hampton Court, the Generaliffe at Granada, and La Mortola to the category of "also ran." Nothing so free and gracious, so lovely and wistful, nothing so richly colored, yet so ghostlike, exists, planted by the sons of men. It is a kind of paradise which has wandered down, a miraculously enchanted wilderness. Brilliant with azaleas, or magnolias, it centers round a pool of dreamy water, overhung by tall trunks wanly festooned with the gray Florida moss. Beyond anything I have ever seen, it is other-worldly. And I went there day after day, drawn as one is drawn in youth by visions of the Ionian Sea, of the East, or the Pacific isles. I used to sit paralyzed by the absurdity of putting brush to canvas in front of that dream-pool. I wanted to paint of it a picture like that of the fountain, by Hellen, which hangs in the Luxembourg. But I knew I never should.

I was sitting there one sunny afternoon, with my back to a clump of azaleas, watching an old colored gardener—so old that he had started life as an "owned" negro, they said, and certainly still retained the familiar suavity of the old-time darky—I was watching him prune the shrubs when I heard the voice of Rupert K. Vaness say, quite close:

"There's nothing for me but beauty, Miss Monroy."

The two were evidently just behind my azalea clump, perhaps four yards away, yet as invisible as if in China.

"Beauty is a wide, wide word. Define it, Mr. Vaness."

"An ounce of fact is worth a ton of theory: it stands before me."

"Come, now, that's just a get-out. Is beauty of the flesh or of the spirit?"

"What is the spirit, as you call it? I'm a pagan."

"Oh, so am I. But the Greeks were pagans."

"Well, spirit is only the refined side of sensuous appreciations."

"I wonder."

"I have spent my life in finding that out."

"Then the feeling this garden rouses in me is purely sensuous?"

"Of course. If you were standing there blind and deaf, without the powers of scent and touch, where would your feeling be?"

"You are very discouraging, Mr. Vaness."

"No, madam; I face facts. When I was a youngster I had plenty of fluffy aspiration toward I didn't know what; I even used to write poetry."

"Oh, Mr. Vaness, was it good?"

"It was not. I very soon learned that a genuine sensation was worth all the uplift in the world."

"What is going to happen when your senses strike work?"

"I shall sit in the sun and fade out."

"I certainly do like your frankness."

"You think me a cynic, of course; I am nothing so futile, Miss Sabine. A cynic is just a posing ass proud of his attitude. I see nothing to be proud of in my attitude, just as I see nothing to be proud of in the truths of existence."

"Suppose you had been poor?"

"My senses would be lasting better than they are, and when at last they failed, I should die quicker, from want of food and warmth, that's all."

"Have you ever been in love, Mr. Vaness?"

"I am in love now."

"And your love has no element of devotion, no finer side?"

"None. It wants."

"I have never been in love. But, if I were, I think I should want to lose myself rather than to gain the other."

"Would you? Sabine, *I am in love with you.*"

"Oh! Shall we walk on?"

I heard their footsteps, and was alone again, with the old gardener lopping at his shrubs.

But what a perfect declaration of hedonism! How simple and how solid was the Vaness theory of existence! Almost Assyrian, worthy of Louis Quinze.

And just then the old negro came up.

"It's pleasant settin'," he said in his polite and hoarse half-whisper; "dar ain't no flies yet."

"It's perfect, Richard. This is the most beautiful spot in the world."

"Sure," he answered, softly drawling. "In deh war-time de Yanks nearly burn deh house heah—Sherman's Yanks. Sueh dey did; po'ful angry wi' ol' massa dey was, 'cause he hid up deh silver plate afore he went away. My ol' fader was de factotalum den. De Yanks took 'm, suh; dey took 'm, and deh major he tell my fader to show 'm whar deh plate was. My ol' fader he look at 'm an' say: 'Wot yuh take me foh? Yuh take me foh a sneakin' nigger? No, suh, you kin du wot yuh like wid dis chile; he ain't goin' to act no Judas. No, suh!' And deh Yankee major he put 'm up ag'in' dat tall live-oak dar, an' he say: 'Yuh darn ungrateful nigger! I's come all dis way to set yuh free. Now, whar's dat silver plate, or I shoot yuh up, sueh!' 'No, suh,' says my fader; 'shoot away. I's neber goin' t' tell.' So dey begin to shoot, and shot all roun' 'm to skeer 'm up. I was a li'l' boy den, an' I see my ol' fader wid my own eyes, suh, standin' thar's bold's Peter. No, suh, dey didn't neber git no word from him. He loved deh folk heah; sure he did, suh."

The old man smiled, and in that beatific smile I saw not only his perennial pleasure in the well-known story, but the fact that he, too, would have stood there, with the bullets raining round him, sooner than betray the folk he loved.

"Fine story, Richard; but—very silly, obstinate old man, your father, wasn't he?"

He looked at me with a sort of startled anger, which slowly broadened into a grin; then broke into soft, hoarse laughter.

"Oh, yes, suh, sure; berry silly, obstinacious ol' man. Yes, suh, indeed." And he went off cackling to himself.

He had only just gone when I heard footsteps again behind my azalea clump, and Miss Monroy's voice.

"Your philosophy is that of faun and nymph. Can you play the part?"

"Only let me try." Those words had such a fevered ring that in imagination I could see Vaness all flushed, his fine eyes shining, his well-kept hands trembling, his lips a little protruded.

There came a laugh, high, gay, sweet.

"Very well, then; catch me!" I heard a swish of skirts against the shrubs, the sound of flight, an astonished gasp from Vaness, and the heavy *thud, thud* of his feet following on the path through the azalea maze. I hoped fervently that they would not suddenly come running past and see me sitting there. My straining ears caught another laugh far off, a panting sound, a muttered oath, a faraway *"Cooee!"* And then, staggering, winded, pale with heat and vexation, Vaness appeared, caught sight of me, and stood a moment. Sweat was running down his face, his hand was clutching at his side, his stomach heaved—a hunter beaten and undignified. He muttered, turned abruptly on his heel, and left me staring at where his fastidious dandyism and all that it stood for had so abruptly come undone.

I know not how he and Miss Monroy got home to Charleston; not in the same car, I fancy. As for me, I traveled deep in thought, aware of having witnessed something rather tragic, not looking forward to my next encounter with Vaness.

He was not at dinner, but the girl was there, as radiant as ever, and though I was glad she had not been caught, I was almost angry at the signal triumph of her youth. She wore a black dress, with a red flower in her hair, and another at her breast, and had never looked so vital and so pretty. Instead of dallying with my cigar beside cool waters in the lounge of the hotel, I strolled out afterward on the Battery, and sat down beside the statue of a tutelary personage. A lovely evening; from some tree or shrub close by emerged an adorable faint fragrance, and in the white electric light the acacia foliage was patterned out against a thrilling, blue sky. If there were no fireflies abroad, there should have been. A night for hedonists, indeed!

And suddenly, in fancy, there came before me Vaness's well-dressed person, panting, pale, perplexed; and beside him, by a freak of vision, stood the old darky's father, bound to the live-oak, with the bullets whistling past, and his face transfigured. There they stood alongside—the creed of pleasure, which depended for fulfillment on its waist measurement; and the creed of love, devoted unto death!

"Aha!" I thought, "which of the two laughs *last*?"

And just then, I saw Vaness himself beneath a lamp, cigar in mouth, and cape flung back so that its silk lining shone. Pale and heavy, in the cruel white light his face had a bitter look. And I was sorry, very sorry at that moment for Rupert K. Vaness.

DuBose Heyward

from Porgy

"Fish runnin' well outside de bar, dese days," remarked Jake one evening to several of his seagoing companions.

A large, bronze-colored negro paused in his task of rigging a line, and cast an eye to sea through the driveway.

"An' we mens bes' make de mores ob it," he observed. "Dem Septumbuh storm due soon, an' fish ain't likes eas' win' an' muddy watuh."

Jake laughed reassuringly.

"Go 'long wid yuh. Ain't yuh done know we hab one stiff gale las' summer, an' he nebber come two yeah han' runnin'."

His wife came toward him with a baby in her arms, and, giving him the child to hold, took up the mess of fish which he was cleaning in a leisurely fashion.

"Ef yuh ain't mans enough tuh clean fish no fastuh dan dat, yuh bes' min' de baby, an' gib um tuh a 'oman fuh clean!" she said scornfully, as she bore away the pan.

The group laughed at that, Jake's somewhat shamefaced merriment rising above the others. He rocked the contented little negro in his strong arms, and followed the retreating figure of the mother with admiring eyes.

"All right, mens," he said, returning to the matter in hand. "I'm all fuh ridin' luck fer as he will tote me. Turn out at fo' tuhmorruh mornin', and we'll push de 'Seagull' clean tuh de blackfish banks befo' we wets de anchor. I gots er feelin' in my bones dat we goin' be gunnels undeh wid de pure fish when we comes in tuhmorruh night."

The news of Jake's prediction spread through the negro quarter. Other crews got their boats hastily in commission and were ready to join the "Mosquito Fleet" when it put to sea.

On the following morning, when the sun rose out of the Atlantic, the thirty or forty small vessels were mere specks teetering upon the water's rim against the red disc that forged swiftly up beyond them.

Afternoon found the wharf crowded with women and children, who laughed and joked each other as to the respective merits of their men and the luck of the boats in which they went to sea.

Clara, Jake's wife, sought the head of the dock long before sundown, and sat upon the bulkhead with her baby asleep in her lap. Occasionally she would exchange a greeting with an acquaintance; but for the most part she gazed toward the harbor mouth and said no word to any one.

"She always like dat," a neighbor informed a little group. "A conjer 'oman once tell she Jake goin' git drownded; an' she ain't hab no happiness since, 'cept when he feet is hittin' de dirt."

Presently a murmur arose among the watchers. Out at the harbor mouth, against the thin greenish-blue of the horizon, appeared the "Mosquito Fleet." Driven by a steady breeze, the boats swept toward the city with astonishing rapidity.

Warm sunlight flooded out of the west, touched the old city with transient glory, then cascaded over the tossing surface of the bay to paint the taut, cupped sails salmon pink, as the fleet drove forward directly into the eye of the sun.

Almost before the crowd realized it, the boats were jibing and coming about at their feet, each jockeying for a favorable berth.

Under the skillful and daring hand of Jake, the "Seagull" took a chance, missed a stern by a hairbreadth, jibed suddenly with a snap and boom, and ran in, directly under the old rock steps of the wharf.

A cheer went up from the crowd. Never had there been such a catch. The boat seemed floored with silver which rose almost to the thwarts, forcing the crew to sit on gunnels, or aft with the steersman.

Indeed the catch was so heavy that as boat after boat docked, it became evident that the market was glutted, and the fisherman vied with each other in giving away their surplus cargo, so that they would not have to throw it overboard.

By the following morning the weather had become unsettled. The wind was still coming out of the west; but a low, solid wall of cloud had replaced the promising sunset of the evening before, and from time to time the wind would wrench off a section of the black mass, and volley it with great speed across the sky, to accumulate in unstable pyramids against the sunrise.

But the success of the day before had so fired the enthusiasm of the fishermen that they were not easily to be deterred from following their luck, and the first grey premonition of the day found the wharf seething with preparation.

Clara, with the baby in her arms, accompanied Jake to the pier-head. She knew the futility of remonstrance; but her eyes were fearful when the heavy, black clouds swept overhead. Once, when a wave slapped a pile, and threw a handful of spray in her face, she moaned and looked up at the big negro by her side. But Jake was full of the business in hand, and besides, he was growing a little impatient at his wife's incessant plea that he sell his share of the "Seagull" and settle on land. Now he turned from her, and shouted: "All right, mens!"

He bestowed a short, powerful embrace upon his wife, with his eyes looking over her shoulder into the Atlantic's veiled face, turned from her with a quick, nervous movement, and dropped from the wharf into his boat.

Standing in the bow, he moistened his finger in his mouth, and held it up to the wind.

"You mens bes' git all de fish yuh kin tuhday," he admonished. "Win' be in de eas' by tuhmorruh. It gots dat wet tas' ter um now."

One by one the boats shoved off, and lay in the stream while they adjusted their spritsails and rigged their full jibs abeam, like spinnakers, for the free run to sea. The vessels were similar in design, the larger ones attaining a length of thirty-five feet. They were very narrow, and low in the waist, with high, keen bows, and pointed sterns. The hulls were round-bottomed, and had beautiful running lines, the fishermen, who were also the designers and builders, taking great pride in the speed and style of their respective craft. The boats were all open from stem to stern and were equipped with thole-pins for rowing, an expedient to which the men resorted only in dire emergency.

Custom had reduced adventure to commonplace; yet it was inconceivable that men could put out, in the face of unsettled weather, for a point beyond sight of land, and exhibit no uneasiness or fear. Yet bursts of loud, loose laughter, and snatches of song, blew back to the wharf long after the boats were in mid-stream.

The wind continued to come in sudden flaws, and, once the little craft had gotten clear of the wharves, the fleet made swift but erratic progress. There were moments when they would seem to mark time upon the choppy waters of the bay; then suddenly a flaw would bear down on them, whipping the water as it came, and, filling the sails, would fairly lift the slender bows as it drove them forward.

By the time that the leisurely old city was sitting down to its breakfast, the fleet had disappeared into the horizon, and the sun had climbed over the obstructions to flood the harbor with reassuring light.

The mercurial spirits of the negroes rose with the genial warmth. Forebodings were forgotten. Even Clara sang a lighter air as she rocked the baby upon her lap.

But the sun had just lifted over the eastern wall, and the heat of noon was beginning to vibrate in the court, when suddenly the air of security was shattered. From the center of town sounded the deep, ominous clang of a bell.

At its first stroke life in Catfish Row was paralyzed. Women stopped their tasks, and, not realizing what they did, clasped each other's hands' tightly, and stood motionless, with strained, listening faces.

Twenty times the great hammer fell, sending the deep, full notes out across the city that was holding its breath and counting them as they came.

"Twenty!" said Clara, when it had ceased to shake the air.

She ran to the entrance and looked to the north. Almost at the end of vision, between two buildings, could be seen the flagstaff that surmounted the custom-house. It was bare when she looked—just a thin, bare line against the intense blue, but even as she stood there, a flicker of color soared up its length; then fixed and flattened, showing a red square with a black center.

"My Gawd!" she called over her shoulder. "It's de trut'. Dat's de hurricane signal on top de custom-house."

Bess came from her room, and stood close to the terrified woman. "Dat can't be so," she said comfortingly. "Ain't yuh 'member de las' hurricane, how it tek two day tuh blow up. Now de sun out bright, an' de cloud all gone."

But Clara gave no sign of having heard her.

"Come on in!" urged Bess. "Ef yuh don't start tuh git yuh dinner, yuh won't hab nottin' ready fuh de mens w'en day gits in."

After a moment the idea penetrated, and the half-dazed woman turned toward Bess, her eyes pleading.

"You come wid me, an' talk a lot. I ain't likes tuh be all alone now."

"Sho' I will," replied the other comfortingly. "I min' de baby fuh yuh, an' yuh kin be gittin' de dinner."

Clara's face quivered; but she turned from the sight of the far red flag and opened her door for Bess to pass in.

After the two women had remained together for half an hour, Bess left the room for a moment to fetch some sewing. The sun was gone, and the sky presented a smooth, leaden surface. She closed the door quickly so that Clara might not see the abrupt change, and went out of the entrance for a look to sea.

Like the sky, the bay had undergone a complete metamorphosis. The water was black, and strangely lifeless. Thin, intensely white crests rode the low, pointed waves; and between the opposing planes of sky and sea a thin westerly wind roamed about like a trapped thing and whined in a complaining treble key. A singularly clear half-light pervaded the world, and in it she could see the harbor mouth distinctly, as it lay ten miles away between the north and south jetties that stretched on the horizon like arms with the finger-tips nearly touching.

Her eyes sought the narrow opening. Guiltless of the smallest speck, it let upon utter void.

"It'd take 'em t'ree hour tuh mek harbor from de banks wid good win'," said a woman who was also watching. "But dere ain't no powuh in dis breeze, an' it a head one at dat."

"Dey kin row it in dat time," encouraged Bess. "An' de storm ain't hyuh yit."

But the woman hugged her forebodings, and stood there shivering in the close, warm air.

Except for the faint moan of the wind, the town and harbor lay in a silence that was like held breath.

Many negroes came to the wharf, passed out to the pier-head, and sat quietly watching the entrance to the bay.

At one o'clock the tension snapped. As though it had been awaiting St. Christopher's chimes to announce "Zero Hour," the wind swung into the east, and its voice dropped an octave, and changed its quality. Instead of the complaining whine, a grave, sustained note came in from the Atlantic, with an undertone of alarming variations, that sounded oddly out of place as it traversed the inert waters of the bay.

The tide was at the last of the ebb, and racing out of the many rivers and creeks toward the sea. All morning the west wind had driven it smoothly before it. But now, the stiffening eastern gale threw its weight against the water, and the conflict immediately filled the bay with large waves that leapt up to angry points, then dropped back sullenly upon themselves.

"Choppy water," observed a very old negro who squinted through half-closed eyes. "Dem boat nebbuh mek headway in dat sea."

But he was not encouraged to continue by the silent, anxious group.

Slowly the threatening undertone of the wind grew louder. Then, as though a curtain had been lowered across the harbor mouth, everything beyond was blotted by a milky screen.

"Oh, my Jedus!" a voice shrilled. "Here he come, now! Le's we go!"

Many of the watchers broke for the cover of buildings across the street. Some of those whose men were in the fleet crowded into the small wharf-house. Several voices started to pray at once, and were immediately drowned in the rising clamor of the wind.

With the mathematical precision that it had exhibited in starting, the gale now moved its obliterating curtain through the jetties, and thrust it forward in a straight line across the outer bay.

There was something utterly terrifying about the studied manner in which the hurricane proceeded about its business. It clicked off its moves like an automaton. It was Destiny working nakedly for the eyes of men to see. The watchers knew that for at least twenty-four hours it would stay, moving its tides and winds here and there with that invincible precision, crushing the life from those whom its preconceived plan had seemed to mark for death.

With that instant emotional release that is the great solace of the negro, the tightly packed wharf-house burst into a babblement of weeping and prayer.

The curtain advanced to the inner bay and narrowed the world to the city, with its buildings cowering white and fearful, and the remaining semi-circle of the harbor.

And now from the opaque surface of the screen came a persistent roar that was neither of wind or water, but the articulate cry of the storm itself. The curtain shot forward again and became a wall, grey and impenetrable, that sunk its foundations into the tortured sea and bore the leaden sky upon its soaring top.

The noise became deafening. The narrow strip of water that was left before the wharves seemed to shrink away. The buildings huddled closer and waited.

Then it crossed the strip, and smote the city.

From the roofs came the sound as though ton after ton of ore had been dumped from some great eminence. There was a dead weight to the shocks that could not conceivably be delivered by so unsubstantial a substance as air, yet which was the wind itself, lifting abruptly to enormous heights, then hurling its full force downward.

These shocks followed the demoniac plan, occurring at exact intervals, and were succeeded by prying fingers, as fluid as ether, as hard as steel, that felt for cracks in roofs and windows.

One could not long say with certainty, "This which I breathe is air, and this upon which I stand is earth." The storm had possessed itself of the city and made it its own. Tangibles and intangibles alike were whirled in a mad, inextricable nebula.

The waves that moved upon the bay could be dimly discerned for a little distance. They were turgid, yellow, and naked; for the moment they lifted a crest, the wind snatched it and dispersed it, with the rain, into the warm semi-fluid atmosphere with which it delivered its attack upon the panic-stricken city.

Notch by notch the velocity increased. The concussions upon the roofs became louder, and the prying fingers commenced to gain a purchase, worrying small holes into large ones. Here and there the wind would get beneath the tin, roll it up suddenly, whirl it from a building like a sheet of paper, and send it thundering and crashing down a deserted street.

Again it would gain entrance to a room through a broken window, and, exerting its explosive force to the full, would blow all of the other windows outward, and commence work upon the walls from within.

It was impossible to walk upon the street. At the first shock of the storm, the little group of negroes who had sought shelter in the wharf-house fled to the Row. Even then, the force of the attack had been so great that only by bending double and clinging together were they able to resist the onslaughts and traverse the narrow street.

Porgy and Bess sat in their room. The slats had been taken from the bed and nailed across the window, and the mattress, bundled into a corner, had been pre-empted by the goat. Bess sat wrapped in her own thoughts, apparently unmoved by the demoniac din without. Porgy's look was one of wonder, not unmixed with fear, as he peered into the outer world between two of the slats. The goat, blessed with an utter lack of imagination, revelled in the comfort and intimacy of his new environment, expressing his contentment in suffocating waves, after the manner of his kind. A kerosene lamp without a chimney, smoking straight up into the unnatural stillness of the room, cast a faint, yellow light about it, but only accentuated the heavy gloom of the corners.

From where Porgy sat, he could catch glimpses of what lay beyond the window. There would come occasional moments when the floor of the storm would be lifted by a burrowing wind, and he would see the high, naked breakers racing under the sullen pall of spume and rain.

Once he saw a derelict go by. The vessel was a small river sloop, with its rigging blown clean out. A man was clinging to the tiller. One wave, larger than its fellows, submerged the little boat, and when it wallowed to the surface again, the man was gone, and the tiller was kicking wildly.

"Oh, my Jedus, hab a little pity!" the watcher moaned under his breath.

Later, a roof went by.

Porgy heard it coming, even above the sound of the attack upon the Row, and it filled him with awe and dread. He turned and looked at Bess, and was reassured to see that she met his gaze fearlessly. Down the street the roar advanced, growing nearer and louder momentarily. Surely it would be the final instrument of destruction. He held his breath, and waited. Then it thundered past his narrow sphere of vision. Rolled loosely, it loomed to the second story windows, and flapped and tore at the buildings as it swept over the cobbles.

When a voice could be heard again, Porgy turned to his companion.

"You an' me, Bess," he said with conviction. "We *sho'* is a little somet'ing attuh all."

After that, they sat long without exchanging a word. Then Porgy looked out of the window and noticed that the quality of the atmosphere was becoming denser. The spume lifted for a moment, and he could scarcely see the tormented bay.

"I t'ink it mus' be mos' night," he observed. "Dey ain't much light now on de outside ob dis storm."

He looked again before the curtain descended, and what he saw caused his heart to miss a beat.

He knew that the tide should be again at the ebb, for the flood had commenced just after the storm broke. But as he looked, the water, which was already higher than a normal flood, lifted over the far edge of the street, and three tremendous waves broke in rapid succession, sending the deep layers of water across the narrow way to splash against the wall of the building.

This reversal of nature's law struck terror into the dark places of Porgy's soul. He beckoned to Bess, his fascinated eyes upon the advancing waves.

She bent down and peered into the gloom.

"Oh, yes," she remarked in a flat tone. "It been dis way in de las' great storm. De win' hol' de watuh in de jetty mout' so he can't go out. Den he pile up annoder tide on him."

Suddenly an enormous breaker loomed over the backs of its shattered and retreating fellows. The two watchers could not see its crest, for it towered into, and was absorbed by, the low-hanging atmosphere. Yellow, smooth, and with a perpendicular, slightly concave front, it flashed across the street, and smote the solid wall of the Row. They heard it roar like a mill-race through the drive, and flatten, hissing in the court. Then they turned, and saw their own door give slightly to the pressure, and a dark flood spurt beneath it, and debouch upon the floor.

Bess took immediate command of the situation. She

threw an arm about Porgy, and hurried him to the door. She withdrew the bolt, and the flimsy panels shot inward. The court was almost totally dark. One after another now the waves were hurtling through the drive and impounding in the walled square.

The night was full of moving figures, and cries of fear; while, out of the upper dark, the wind struck savagely downward.

With a powerful swing, Bess got Porgy to a stairway that providentially opened near their room, and leaving him to make his way up alone, she rushed back, and was soon at his heels with an armful of belongings.

They sought refuge in what had been the great ball-room of the mansion, a square, high-ceilinged room on the second story, which was occupied by a large and prosperous family. There were many refugees there before them. In the faint light cast by several lanterns, the indestructible beauty of the apartment was evident, while the defacing effects of a century were absorbed in shadow. The noble open fireplace, the tall, slender mantel, with its Grecian frieze and intricate scrollwork, the high panelled walls were all there. And then, huddled in little groups on the floor, or seated against the walls, with eyes wide in the lantern-shine, the black, fear-stricken faces.

Like the ultimate disintegration of a civilization—there it was; and upon it, as though to make quick work of the last, tragic chapter, the scourging wrath of the Gods—white, and black.

The night that settled down upon Catfish Row was one of nameless horror to the inhabitants, most of whom were huddled on the second floor in order to avoid the sea from beneath, and deafening assaults upon the roof above their heads.

With the obliteration of vision, sound assumed an exaggerated significance, and the voice of the gale, which had seemed by day only a great roar, broke up in the dark into its various parts. Human voices seemed to cry in it; and there were moments when it sniffed and moaned at the windows.

Once, during a silence in the room, a whinny was distinctly heard.

"Dat my old horse!" wailed Peter. "He done dead in he stall now, an' dat he woice goin' by. Oh, my Gawd!"

They all wailed out at that; and Porgy, remembering his goat, whimpered and turned his face to the wall.

Then someone started to sing:
"I gots uh home in de rock, don't yuh see?"

With a feeling of infinite relief, Porgy turned to his Jesus. It was not a charm that he sought now for the assuaging of some physical ill, but a benign power, vaster perhaps even than the hurricane. He lifted his rich baritone above the others:

> "Oh, between de eart' an' sky,
> I kin see my Sabior die.
> I gots uh home in de rock,
> Don't yuh see!"

Then they were all in it, heart and soul. Those who had fallen into a fitful sleep, awoke, rubbed their eyes, and sang.

Hour after hour dragged heavily past. Outside, the storm worked its will upon the defenceless city. But in the great ball-room of Catfish Row, forty souls sat wrapped in an invulnerable garment. They swayed and patted, and poured their griefs and fears into a rhythm that never missed a beat, which swept the hours behind it into oblivion, and that finally sang up the faint grey light that penetrated the storm, and told them it was again day.

At about an hour after daybreak the first lull came. Like the other moves of the hurricane, it arrived without warning. One moment the tumult was at its height. The next, there was utter suspension. Abruptly, like an indrawn breath, the wind sucked back upon itself, leaving an aching vacuum in its place. Then from the inundated waterfront arose the sound of the receding flood.

The ebb-tide was again over due, and with the second tide piled upon it, the whole immeasurable weight of the wind was required to maintain its height. Now, with the pressure removed, it turned and raced beneath the low-lying mist toward the sea, carrying its pitiful loot upon its back.

To the huddled figures in the great room of the Row came the welcome sound, as the court emptied itself into the street. The negroes crowded to the windows, and peered between the barricades at the world without.

The water receded with incredible speed. Submerged wreckage lifted above the surface. The street became the bed of a cataract that foamed and boiled on its rush to the sea. Presently the wharf emerged, and at its end even a substantial remnant of the house could be descried. How it had survived that long was one of the inexplicable mysteries of the storm.

Suddenly Peter, who was at one of the windows, gave a cry, and the other negroes crowded about him to peer out.

The sea was still running high, and as a large wave lifted above the level of the others, it thrust into view the hull of a half-submerged boat. Before the watchers could see, the wave dropped its burden into a trough, but the old man showed them where to look, and presently a big roller caught it up, and swung it, bow on, for all to see. There was a flash of scarlet gunnel, and, beneath it, a bright blue bird with open wings.

"De 'Seagull'!" cried a dozen voices together. "My Gawd! dat Jake' boat!"

All night Clara had sat in a corner of the room with the baby in her arms, saying no word to anyone. She was so still that she seemed to be asleep, with her head upon her breast. But once, when Bess had gone and looked into her face, she had seen her eyes, wide and bright with pain.

Now the unfortunate women heard the voices, and sprang to the window just in time to see the craft swoop into a hollow at the head of the pier.

She did not scream out. For a moment she did not even speak. Then she spun around on Bess with the dawn of a wild hope in her dark face.

"Tek care ob dis baby 'til I gits back," she said, as she thrust the child almost savagely into Bess's arms. Then she rushed from the room.

The watchers at the window saw her cross the street, splashing wildly through the knee-deep water. Then she ran the length of the wharf, and disappeared behind the sheltering wall of the house.

It was so sudden, and tired wits move slowly. Several minutes had passed before it occurred to anyone to go with her. Finally Peter turned from the window.

"Dat 'oman ain't ought tuh be out dey by sheself," he said. "Who goin' out dey wid me, now?"

One of the men volunteered, and they started for the door.

A sound like the detonation of a cannon shook the building to its foundations. The gale had returned, smashing straight downward from some incredible height to which it had lifted during the lull. The men turned and looked at one another.

Shock followed shock in rapid succession. Those who stood by the windows felt them give inward, and instinctively threw their weight against the frames. The explosions merged into a steady roar of sound that surpassed anything that had yet occurred. The room became so dark that they could no longer see one another. The barricaded windows were vaguely discernible in bars of muddy grey and black. Deeply rooted walls swung from the blows, and then settled slowly back on the recoil.

A confused sound of praying filled the room. And above it shrilled the terror of the women.

For an appreciable space of time the spasm lasted. Then, slowly, as though by the gradual withdrawing of a lever, the vehemence of the attack abated. The muddy grey bars at the windows became lighter, and some of the more courageous of the negroes peered out.

The wharf could be seen dimly extending under the low floor of spume and mist. The breakers were higher than at any previous time, but instead of smashing in upon the shore, they raced straight up the river and paralleled the city. As each one swung by it went clean over the wharf, obliterating it for the duration of its passage.

Suddenly from the direction of the lower harbor a tremendous mass appeared, showing first only a vast distorted stain against the grey fabric of the mist. Then a gigantic wave took it, and drove it into fuller view.

"Great Gawd A'mighty!" some one whispered. "It's dat big lumbuh schooner bruck loose in de harbor."

The wave hunched its mighty shoulders under the vessel and swung it up—up, for an interminable moment. The soaring bowsprit lifted until it was lost in mist. Tons of water gushed from the steep incline of the deck, and poured over the smooth, black wall of the side, as it reared half out of the sea. Then the wave swept aft, and the bow descended in a swift, deadly plunge.

A crashing of timbers followed that could be heard clearly above the roaring of the storm. The hull had fallen directly across the middle of the wharf. There was one cataclysmic moment when the whole view seemed to disintegrate. The huge timbers of the wharf up-ended, and were washed out like straws. The schooner rolled half over, and her three masts crashed down with their rigging. The shock burst the lashings of the vessel's deck load, and as the hull heeled, an avalanche of heavy timbers took the water. The ruin was utter.

Heavy and obliterating, the mist closed down again.

Bess turned from the window holding the sleeping infant in her arms, raised her eyes and looked full at Porgy.

With an expression of awe in his face, the cripple reached out a timid hand and touched the baby's cheek.

The windows of the great ball-room were open to the sky, and beyond them, a busy breeze was blowing across its washed and polished expanse, gathering cloud-remnants into little heaps, and sweeping them in tumbling haste out over the threshold of the sea.

Most of the refugees had returned to their rooms, where sounds of busy salvaging could be heard. Porgy's voice arose jubilantly announcing that the goat had been discovered, marooned upon the cook-stove; and that Peter's old horse had belied his whinny, and was none the worse for a thorough wetting.

Serena Robbins paused before Bess, who was gathering her things preparatory to leaving the room, placed her hands upon her hips, and looked down upon her.

"Now, wut we all goin' do wid dis po' mudderless chile?" she said, addressing the room at large.

The other occupants of the room gathered behind Serena, but there was something about Bess's look that held them quiet. They stood there waiting and saying nothing.

Slowly Bess straightened up, her face lowered and pressed against that of the sleeping child. Then she raised her eyes and met the gaze of the complacent older women.

What Serena saw there was not so much the old defiance that she had expected, as it was an inflexible determination, and, behind it, a new-born element in the woman that rendered the scarred visage incandescent. She stepped back, and lowered her eyes.

Bess strained the child to her breast with an elemental intensity of possession, and spoke in a low, deep voice that vested her words with sombre meaning.

"Is Clara come back a'ready, since she dead, an' say somet'ing 'bout 'we' tuh yuh 'bout dis chile?"

She put the question to the group, her eyes taking in the circle of faces as she spoke.

There was no response; and at the suggestion of a possible return of the dead, the circle drew together instinctively.

"Berry well den," said Bess solemnly. "Ontell she do, I goin' stan' on she las' libbin' word an' keep dis chile fuh she 'til she do come back."

Serena was hopelessly beaten and she knew it.

"Oh, berry well," she capitulated. "All I been goin' tuh do wuz jus' tuh puhwide um wid er propuh Christian raisin'. But ef she done gib um tuh yuh, dere ain't nuttin' mo' I kin do, I guess."

Ludwig Lewisohn

from *The Case of Mr. Crump*

To Herbert the word home never meant anything else than the house in Calhoun Street into which his parents moved when he was a small boy. Like all the old-fashioned Queenshaven houses it turned its gable end toward the street so that the piazzas, the upstairs and the downstairs, could face the breezes of the south and west. The house stood flush with the street. Behind it, to the very end of the deep yard, stretched a line of tiny, black, two-story cottages inhabited by Negroes. In Herbert's early boyhood Calhoun Street was still paved with half-hewn palmetto logs. Opposite the house on the other side of the street there stood, newly completed except for the steeple which was never built, the large Afro-American Methodist Church. The house next door to the Crumps, which belonged to an Irish family named Delaney, was set far back in a narrow garden, so that from his upper piazza Herbert watched all through his childhood and youth a great clear stretch of the Southern heavens and thus grew up familiar with strong blues and golds, the pomp of sunsets, the grave glitter of crowded constellations.

The visible world intoxicated him from the beginning. More clearly and elementarily the world of sound. He was four years old, as his mother told him later, and had followed his grandfather into the cool, slightly musty church one summer afternoon. He had climbed with the old gentleman into the organ-loft. The sonorous vibrations of sound had made the child tremble and turn pale and the ecstasy had become so insupportable that he had dropped sobbing on the floor and had had to be carried home. Herbert barely remembered this incident. But he remembered clearly, remembered with a quickening of his blood and a tingling of his skin, how music had affected him from his earliest years. At five he himself began to play. He would stop his practice, which seemed an impediment only, to strike chords, simple chords which, by their rich uncomplicated consonance, sufficed to flood him with well-being. Gradually, of course, he became more hardened to the ecstasy of mere sound. But always there recurred moments of its unbelievable poignancy. There were things that for years he could never play through to the end. They broke him. Things by Chopin, such as the "Nocturne in F," quite simple things by Schumann, certain adagios in Beethoven's sonatas. He fled to Handel and Mozart and his father thought that he boy had perhaps inherited his grandfather's sobriety of temper. But Herbert's mother always knew better. For she would sing the *"Möricke Lieder"* of Hugo Wolf and Herbert would sit in a dim corner of the room with tears streaming down his face. *"Lass, O Welt, O lass mich sein. . ."* The boy would grasp his dark, tousled hair; the mother watching him, stopped playing and drew him to her bosom.

There was another world of sound about Herbert, a world to which his father and mother paid little attention. But it thrilled and haunted him and remained forever memorable to him. There were Negroes in the back-yard, as it was called; there was the Negro Church across the street; there were Negroes all around. Herbert would to to Paul Fludd, the butcher, to buy two cents worth of meat for his cat. And the enormous black man would be singing in his vibrant bass voice: "Dee—ee—ee—eep rivah. . ." Hack! The cleaver came down on the meat and the marvelous melody was interrupted. Herbert was too shy to ask Paul to go on and finish his song. So whenever he left the house he would first go a bit eastward toward the Cooper River and listen for the singing of Paul the butcher. But that was not all. He waked up early sometimes in his garret room and would go to the window and see Queenshaven in the dawn like a city carved of mother of pearl under a sky as faintly iridescent as the inner curve of a seashell. He would watch the elderly Negresses coming from the bay. On their red head-kerchiefs they carried large flat wooden platters full of fresh, fainly coral-tinted shrimps to be boiled early and

served with hominy at the white folks' breakfast tables. In
their rich untutored voices the women would cry their
wares: "O you shrimps! O you oysters!" And there was one
old Negro man who sang up and down the scale in a
dreamy, strange sing-song: "Buy fresh buttermilk . . . "
Herbert caught tones and cadences in these Queenshaven
street cries of his childhood that many years later puzzled
the critics in his works.

Sunday was a great day for the boy. He was permitted to
attend church, not in the pew with his mother, but in the
organ-loft watching his father play the handsome new
triple-manual organ and treading the pedals and desperately
but softly keeping the amateur choir in order. These
flirtatious young persons wanted to show off; they wanted
to sing new and attractive music. They thought the
Lutheran Church of their fathers with German song and
sermon a little common anyhow. The frowsy, freckled pale-
eyed popular soprano had once turned languishingly to the
stern choir-master. "Do you know, Professor Crump, what
my friend Agnes Bayer sang for offertory at Grace Church
last Sunday?" Crump's eyes turned severely on the fluffy,
diminutive person. "Well, what?" The girl answered with a
pert gesture of the head: "The Intermezzo from *Cavalleria
Rusticana.*" Herbert always remembered with a profound
pride his father's dry, infinitely decisive: "Good; let her. Not
here!" The soprano was the daughter of a very rich pew-
holder. But Herman Crump was a righteous man. In his
small obscure place in the world he stood firm for the good.
He closed his near-sighted eyes after such an episode, leaned
forward, played a Fugue of Bach and relented with
Beethoven's *"Die Himmel rühmen des Ewigen Ehre . . . "* In
that organ-loft Herbert learned both music and morals.
Memories of those Sunday mornings came to sustain him in
dark and tortured hours of his later years.

Sunday afternoons were drowsy. In the snowless
Queenshaven winters they were usually mild and golden.
After dinner Herbert would climb up to his attic and dream
over a book. Above his dream he listened. In the Afro-

American Church with its stump of a tower across the street the Sunday service was an all-day service and people came and went and chanted and "shouted." And now and again the sisters who had "seen Jesus" were carried into the cottages in the Crump back-yard and were prayed and crooned over. And whatever else was going on in the church, even during the early sermon whenever the preacher's voice fell, the congregation chanted a single chant. Sunday after Sunday the congregation chanted that chant, year in year out. All through Herbert's childhood and boyhood and youth he heard that melancholy chant. And he used often to think, as time went on and on and life turned out so strangely for him, that if he could only go alone to visit Queenshaven and walk from Marion Square eastward to Calhoun Street and stand in front of the old house and hear the Negroes chant that chant again, that then the foul ice which fate had made to congeal in his bosom might melt and a miracle happen within him to placate the seemingly implacable powers.

It was a very simple chant that the Negroes across the street so tirelessly chanted. When Herbert was about fifteen it suddenly occurred to him one Sunday afternoon that the chant must not be lost. He wrote it down, jotted it down quite simply without any bass. And in that first simple version of his boyhood it looked like this:

But he knew at once that the notes held neither the great resignation nor the terribly moving aspiration of simple souls that sounded in the endless, dragging, clinging chant. The C natural at the beginning of the sixth measure—did it not create an interval of infinitude? Did not the souls of the overburdened liberate themselves in it for one moment of eternity? Only to return to earth, to be sure, but with a vision and a hope that sounded full and strong and sonorous—for all its undertone of wailing—in the breadth and large peace of the final measure. Herbert, at all events, believed steadily that this chant, interwoven with all the memories of his earlier years, had an extraordinary musical value. It furnished him with the groundwork of the thematic material of the tone-poem "Renunciation" with its motto from Goethe ("*Entsagen sollst du, sollst entsagen . . .*") the performance of which by the Society of the Friends of Music came too late to do him any good. Curiously enough, he never, during his boyhood spoke to his parents of the absorption of so many of his hours by the magic of the Negro music. He had an obscure feeling that they might not share his taste. And then, as later, he had an unconquerable aversion from the strain and futility of disagreement and debate.

The earliest years of school were like a dream. But it was school that at last created the division between day and dream. It could be dismissed no longer, but threw its jagged shadow into the home. A little conflict arose which was symbolized in Herbert's memory by one brief colloquy between his father and his mother that took place one Friday afternoon when he had brought home a shockingly bad report of his week's work. His father arose in wrath. He could hear his mother's rich contralto speaking voice and her soft Viennese accent: "*Lass mir den Bub in Ruh, Hermann, seine Begabung liegt halt in einer andern Richtung!*" His father turned to his mother, severe and sorrowful: "*Und die Pflicht, Meta, die Pflicht?*" Then he left the room. The mother turned to the boy. "Papa is quite right—as always. You simply must do better, darling." But the boy knew that there was no real conviction behind her words. The North German conception of duty for duty's sake, irrespective of temperament or aim, was foreign to her nature. The boy perceived and, of course, passionately embraced his mother's point of view. The day came when he saw that there was much more than he had imagined to be said for his father's too.

The trouble with school, in actual fact, was not the studies. Herbert could have mastered these. It was the teachers, the atmosphere, the boys. It cannot be said that he was pampered at home. He obeyed his parents without question. He was by nature the reverse of forward. But he was, after all, an only child. There was no friction and no corrective rivalry in the home. When the little daughters of his father's sister, Flora and Annabelle Schott, came to visit, he was very gentle and polite. In fact he liked them, especially Flora, who had a long thick braid of chestnut brown hair and very red lips and liked to play a game with kisses as forfeits. Yet he was always relieved and very tired when the girls went. They were all over the house; they touched things and pulled them out of place in what seemed to him a restless and unreasonable way. It was from his father's side that he must have gotten his innate and almost pedantic love of order. It was a source of quiet amusement to his mother to see Bertie follow the little girls from room to room and with polite unobtrusiveness straighten things out after them.

School was to Herbert a leashed chaos at best, namely in the classroom, an open pandemonium before and between and after classes. The boys' spirit of raising hell for its own sake irritated him obscurely but deeply. He liked some of the teachers and studies no more than they. He would far rather have been at home or playing or walking with Ralph Greene or even with Eddie Bierfischer. But spit-balls and pea-shooters seemed to him, years before he could formulate such feelings in words, stupidly and nastily irrelevant to the situation. Ralph and Eddie more or less

171

shared his attitude. Once in a long while the three boys would simply "play hookey;" they would quietly disappear after the noon recess. But this method wasn't satisfactory either. For the boys, in spite of the quiet bravado with which they didn't quite deceive one another, were all three darkly oppressed by a sense of the consequences of their truancy, especially of the annoyance it might cause their fathers. So they wandered rather forlornly about and ended by planning excuses to be presented at school and at home. Sometimes they envied the "Birdie" Reynolds type who, tall, wiry, sheer muscle and sinew, smote all the other boys hip and thigh surreptitiously in the classroom, openly on the playground and lied to the teachers with an impenetrable impudence on his blue-eyed and angelic countenance. They envied "Birdie;" occasionally they tried to imitate him and always, of course, came to grief. At last one day, in the second year of high school, when Eddie and Herbert were joining in a game of fastening pins, points forward, into your shoes and jabbing the boys in front of you Ralph, the oldest of the three, turned a disgusted face to his friends. "For Christ's sake, quit your foolishness! I want to work!" It was like a liberation to Herbert. He didn't have to pretend any more. He practised for three hours that afternoon and that evening threw his "pony" into the attic closet and found that he could construe his thirty lines of Caesar in just about the same time that it took him to fit the pidgin English of Hinds and Noble's hacks to the Latin on the page before him. School still nauseated him often enough. But the worst was over. By applying his natural methodicalness to his actual circumstances he discovered that he could find time for school, for his music, for his play. He had to sacrifice his great secret occupation—the constant scribbling of music. With a strength of character rare in a boy of thirteen, he deliberately put it off until summer. But vacations were fifteen weeks long and seemed endless in those days.

Sometimes, of course, he broke his resolution. Strange circumstances would arise. Ralph Greene came with a flicker in his eyes that were usually reserved and steady. "Come on, Bert, let's go for a walk." "Where to?" "To Society Street." "Shucks, that isn't much of a walk." Ralph tugged at Herbert's sleeve. There was an urgency and an appeal in his gesture. "Aw, come on!" Suddenly a sense of feverish expectancy communicated itself to Herbet. His throat went hot and dry. "Oh, all right, if you want to." By a common impulse the two boys now hurried along the few blocks down Meeting Street. At the corner of Society Street stood the two Gallagher girls slim, tall for their age, with sweet, identical, oval faces, a few freckles over their tilted noses, large, empty eyes. "How do you do?" they said in a very grown-up way. The boys lifted their caps: "How do you do?" they said in an equally seemly fashion. Ralph paired off with Kate, Herbert with Estelle. A choking silence followed. "Have you ever played circus?" Estelle asked. "No," said Herbert, "but I'd like to if"—a sudden inspiration leaped out of the hot sweetness in his belly— "I'd like to if you're in it!" The girl giggled and looked pleased and let her white sleeve brush Herbert's shoulder.

In the middle of the block they met Hen Hanahan, a boy with a curved mouth that went almost from ear to ear, and a clownlike head, round as an apple. With him was a girl who had fiercely red hair and a slatternly appearance. Estelle turned to Herbert. "Did you ever see the circus? It's in the basement of Hen's house." They were in front of the narrow four-story house. The basement could be entered from the street. Three steps down. It was an ordinary paved cellar strewn with sawdust. The boys and girls went in and sat down on boxes ranged along the wall. The pretence at playing circus was brief and feeble. Hen stood on his head in the middle of the floor. Then he sprang up and slammed and latched the wooden door to the street. Silence and black darkness. Herbert thought that his heart would literally leap into his throat as he felt the head of Estelle on his shoulder and inhaled the fresh odor of the girl's hair. It was she who found his lips and pushed his hands. After that he needed no guidance. There were giggles; there were jokes. All speech was seemly and calculated to fortify the pretence that there was no harm in this game. Nothing fatal and ultimate did in fact happen. But these children of the South had a strong, dumb, ecstatic eroticism—fierce, earnest, almost exalted. The sharp voice of Hen Hanahan came suddenly; "Must be most supper time!" All voices babbled with a cool assumption of naturalness; the door was opened and a calming breeze swept in. The boys and girls wandered out into the dusk and separated casually. Ralph said to Herbert: "Want to come again?" And Herbert answered with the same affected carelessness: "Oh, I guess so." But that night, after the first broken feeling wore off, he covered sheet after sheet of paper with notes and dropped the sheets on the floor. In the early dawn he gathered the sheets and locked them in his little oak desk.

Rafael Sabatini

from *The Carolinian*

Everything concerned with Myrtle's marriage fell out precisely as her ladyship promised and subsequently planned, which was the way of things of which her ladyship had the planning.

To quiet Myrtle's grievous misgivings on the score of her father, her ladyship undertook that after the departure of the bridal couple she would, herself, not merely inform Sir Andrew of what had been done, but compel him to see reason and obtain his pardon for the runagates.

'And never doubt that I shall,' said Lady William [Campbell] with convincing emphasis. 'What men can't alter they soon condone.'

Thus, out of her own splendid confidence, she allayed at last Myrtle's lingering fears and only abiding regrets.

So much accomplished, her ladyship unfolded the further details of her plan for getting the couple safely away. The Brewtons' ball that same Thursday night, being of an almost official character, Lady William's viceregal position demanded that she should go attended by two ladies of honour. From the position of one of these she would depose her Cousin Jane in favour of Myrtle. As a result, Myrtle would be expected to attend her throughout, and to facilitate this, Lady William would arrange with Sir Andrew that Myrtle be allowed to spend the night at the Governor's residence. Thus the bridal couple would be ensured a clear and unhampered start whilst all Charles Town was still entirely unsuspicious. For the rest, the real arrangement was that Harry Latimer should be at hand with a travelling-carriage, and that, as soon as Myrtle could conveniently leave the ball without being missed, she should join him, and they should immediately start for his plantation at Santee Broads, a drive of fifty miles, which would consume the whole of the night. Thence, after resting, they were to push on to a distant estate of Mr. Latimer's in the hills above Salisbury, where for the present they were to abide. There, in the cotton-fields of North Carolina, their honeymoon might peacefully be spent without fear of pursuit from any save Sir Andrew, who would in any case be powerless to untie the knot which the law of England was so securely to tie aboard the *Tamar*.

And so, soon after breakfast on Thursday morning, Myrtle departed from Tradd Street, on the pretext that her ladyship had bidden her come early. There would be a deal to do in preparation for the ball, she casually announced in explanation.

'Not a doubt,' said her father. And when he beheld the dimensions of the clothes-box that was being borne after her, he raised eyes and hands to heaven. 'Lord! The vanity of woman!'

But Myrtle was already down the steps and into her sedan chair, lest he should detect the tears that had suddenly come to fill her eyes at the thought that she was definitely leaving her father's home, and leaving it under cover of a deceit.

It needed all Lady William's stout cheeriness and confidence to dispel the black clouds that were gathering about Myrtle's soul when presently she came into her ladyship's radiant presence. Nor was she given much time for further brooding. Within a half-hour of reaching the Governor's residence, she was taking boat at the Exchange Wharf with her ladyship, a boat manned by four British tars and commanded by a pert boy-officer.

Out in the bay, as they drew near the *Tamar*, with her black-and-white hull, the snowy sails furled along her yards and the gleam of brass from her deck, they were joined by another boat, rowed by blacks in linsey-woolsey jackets, and carrying Harry Latimer and Tom Izard.

In the waist of the warship they found a guard of honour drawn up, whilst Captain Thornborough, the handsome sunburnt officer in command of the sloop, came forward to receive them.

All was ready, as her ladyship had predisposed. But to

satisfy the pretext on which they came, there was first a tour of inspection of the ship. When this was over, the Captain invited the guests to a glass of Madeira in his cabin before leaving. He contrived unostentatiously to include in the invitation the chaplain, who had, somehow, got in the way at the last moment.

In the cabin no time was wasted. No sooner had the steward retired after pouring for them than with naval despatch Captain Thornborough made them come to business. The chaplain was brisk, and confined himself to the essentials of the ceremony. Within a few minutes all was accomplished, and the Captain of the *Tamar* was raising his glass to toast Mrs. Henry Latimer.

'I'd fire a salute in your honour, ma'am, but it would occasion questions we may not be prepared to answer.'

In the vessel's waist, where they had met scarcely an hour ago, husband and wife parted again for the present, and Myrtle and Lady William went down the steps to the waiting cockboat.

Myrtle bore now on her finger the ring that had belonged to Harry's mother, the very ring that once, and not so long ago, she had returned to him. In her heart she bore perhaps the oddest conflict of emotions that has ever been a bride's. There was happiness in the thought that Harry now belonged to her, and that nothing could ever again come between them; there was happiness, too, in the reflection that thus she had conquered Harry's obstinacy and jealous doubts and prevailed upon him to save his life by leaving Charles Town. But there were regrets at the manner of her marriage, and infinitely more poignant regrets at the thought of what her father must suffer in his affection and his pride when he learnt of these hole-and-corner nuptials between herself and a man against whom he bore a prejudice that was amounting almost to hatred.

There were tears blurring her vision as she looked back over the waves on which the sunlight was dancing to that other boat that the foot of the ship's ladder into which her husband and his friend were stepping. And the boy-officer, chatting briskly with Lady William, gave her ladyship no opportunity to offer Myrtle any of the comfort of which she perceived the poor child to stand in need.

They reached at last the Exchange Wharf, and, whilst a sailor held the boat firmly alongside by means of a boathook, the gallant stripling of an officer, standing on the wet slippery steps, handed the ladies ashore, to set them face to face with Captain Mandeville.

Delayed until then by official duties, the Captain was on his way to Fort Johnson to inform Major Sykes that his services that night would no longer be required. He was looking about for a wherry to convey him at the very moment that the cockboat from the *Tamar* containing her ladyship and Myrtle drew alongside the wharf.

Lady William, conscious as she was of being engaged upon a deed of secrecy, paused to stare at him, suspecting an excess of coincidence in his presence. Nor did his air of surprise allay her suspicions, as it should have done, for Captain Mandeville was not the man to show surprise when he actually felt it.

He doffed his black three-cornered hat and bowed.

'I did not know your ladyship addicted to water-jaunts.'

Myrtle, esteeming him, persuaded of his sincere and selfless friendship, and detesting fraud beyond what was absolutely necessary to her safety and Harry's, would there and then have given him the real reason for her journeyings by water, had not her ladyship forestalled her.

'I am not,' she told the equerry. 'But Captain Thornborough offered to show his ship to Myrtle, and the child had never been aboard a man-of-war. But we detain you, Captain,' she added, bethinking her of the second boat that followed, and preferring that he should not stay to meet its occupants.

'No, no,' he answered. 'I am not pressed. I am only going to Fort Johnson. I was looking for a boat. I trust you found the man-of-war all that you expected it, Myrtle?'

'Why, yes,' she said, and lowered her lids under his sharp gaze lest he should perceive the signs of tears about her eyes.

'But we have no enthusiasm,' he faintly rallied her, smiling.

Her ladyship promptly rescued her.

'Come, Myrtle. The man will keep us talking here all day.'

'Nay, a moment of your mercy. This may be my only chance before the ball to-night.'

'Your chance of what?'

'To ensure myself the dance I covet. The first minuet, Myrtle, if you will honour me so far?'

'But, of course, Robert.' And impulsively she held out her hand.

He took it, and, bareheaded as he had remained, bowed low over it. For an instant, as he did so, his eyes dilated; but his bowed head screened this from both the ladies. And then her ladyship whirled Myrtle away without further ceremony.

He stood watching them until they were lost in the bustling crowd about the New Exchange. Then, slowly resuming his hat, a deep line of thought between his fine brows, he turned his attention once more to that other craft which had already caught his eye.

He signalled to a wherry to stand by, but made no move to enter it until the boat he watched was alongside, and out of it sprang Latimer and Tom Izard. They exchanged bows formally, and without words, despite the fact that the equerry was—or had been—on easy terms with her ladyship's brother. Then Captain Mandeville stepped into the boat he had summoned, and sat down in the sternsheets.

'Push off!' he curtly bade the negroes.

The four men bent to their oars, and the boat shot away from the wharf.

'Where does yo' honour want fer to go?' the nearest negro asked him.

Captain Mandeville considered a long moment. Then he stretched out a hand to grasp the tiller.

'To the sloop *Tamar*,' he answered.

When he reached her decks, her captain was below, but he came instantly upon being informed that the Governor's equerry had come aboard.

'Ah, Mandeville! Good-day to you,' he greeted him.

Mandeville gave him a short good-day in return. 'I want a word with you in private, Thornborough.'

The sailor looked at him, mildly surprised by his tone.

'Come aft to my cabin,' he invited, and led the way.

Mandeville sat down upon a locker with his back to the square windows that opened upon the stern gallery. On the table before him he observed a book, a decanter at a low ebb, and six glasses, in two of which a little wine remained. He could account for five of the glasses and assumed the sixth to have been for some other officer of the *Tamar*.

Thornborough, standing straight and tall in his blue uniform with white facings, looked at him questioningly across the table.

'Well?' he asked. 'What brings you?'

'Mr. Harry Latimer has been aboard your ship this morning.'

He had deliberately placed himself so that the light was on Thornborough's face, and his own in shadow. Watching the sailor now, he fancied that his eyes shifted a little to avoid his own. Also there was a perceptible pause before Thornborough answered him.

'That is so. What, then?'

'What do you know of him?'

'I? What should I know? He is a wealthy colonial gentleman. But you should know more about him, yourself.'

'I do. That is why I am questioning you. What was he doing aboard your ship?'

Thornborough stiffened. 'Sink me, Mandeville! What's the reason for this catechism?'

'This fellow Latimer is a rebel, a dangerous spreader of sedition, and a daring spy. That is the reason. That is why I ask you what he came to do aboard your ship.'

Thornborough laughed. 'It had nothing to do with spying. Of that I can assure you. What should he have spied here that could profit him?'

'You are not forgetting that you have Kirkland on board?' Mandeville asked him.

'All Charles Town knows that. What should Mr. Latimer discover by spying on Kirkland?'

'Possibly he came to ascertain whether he is still here. But if you were to tell me on what pretext he did come, I might be able to obtain a glimpse of his real reason.'

It happened, however, that Thornborough's instructions from Lady William were quite explicit; and in nothing that Mandeville had said could he see any reason for departing from them.

'Mandeville, you're hunting a mare's nest. Mr. Latimer came aboard with Lady William Campbell and one or two others so as to view a British man-of-war. To suppose that he could discover here anything of possible advantage to his party or of detriment to ours is ridiculous.'

'You may find that you take too much for granted, Thornborough.' Mandeville spoke mysteriously. As he spoke, he rose, and proceeded to relate to the sailor how Latimer had visited the Governor only yesterday in disguise and pumped him dry on more than one subject. 'If I had not subsequently discovered this, and ascertained the extent of the information he drew from us, I might have remained as unsuspecting as yourself.'

Whilst speaking, he had idly picked up the book from the table, to make the surprising discovery that it was a book of Common-Prayer. A bookmark of embroidered silk hung from its pages, and the book opened naturally in Mandeville's hands at the Marriage Service, which was the place marked. Idly he continued to turn its leaves. He even looked at the name on the fly-leaf, which was 'Robert Flaversham.' It was odd to find such a volume on the Captain's table. He set it down again, and assuming at last that Thornborough really had nothing to tell him beyond the fact which he had desired to ascertain—namely that Latimer actually had been on board the ship in Myrtle's company—he took his leave.

With a final admonition to Thornborough to be careful

of whom he admitted to his sloop, the equerry went down the entrance ladder to his waiting boat, with intent to resume his voyage to the fort. But within a dozen cables' length of the *Tamar*, he abruptly changed his mind.

'Put about,' he ordered, and added curtly: 'Back to Charles Town.'

He was obeyed without question, and the clumsy boat swung round to pull against the tide, which was beginning to ebb.

Ahead of them, drenched in brilliant sunshine, and looking dazzlingly white, the low-lying town appeared to float like another Venice upon the sea, the water-front dominated by the classical pile of the Custom-House with its Ionic pillars and imposing entablature, whilst above the red roofs towered the spires of Saint Philip's and Saint Michael's, the latter so lofty that it served as a landmark for ships far out at sea.

Captain Mandeville, however, beheld nothing but a slender woman's hand, with white tapering fingers protruding from mittens of white silk, and round one of these fingers a circlet of gold, gleaming through the strained silken meshes.

That in some mysterious way Myrtle and Harry had become reconciled was clear from their joint presence aboard the *Tamar*, whilst the discovery of that restored ring betrayed the fact that the reconciliation had gone the extent of renewing their betrothal.

That was reason enough to restrain him from going to Fort Johnson to bid Sykes hold his hand. At all costs, and whatever the consequence with which the Governor might afterwards visit him, Mandeville must allow the plan laid with Sykes to be carried out. He was in a difficult position. But he must deal with one difficulty at a time, and in dealing first with Harry Latimer he dealt with the more imminent danger to himself and all his hopes.

He sat there, elbow on knee and chin in hand, absorbed in thought, piecing together little tenuous scraps of evidence, and plagued to irritation the while by the obstinate association in his mind of the ring he had seen on her finger and the book he had found on Captain Thornborough's table. Those things and that visit of theirs to the sloop that morning forced a dreadful suspicion on his mind, a suspicion too dreadful to be entertained. He rejected it, as wildly fantastic; and yet the thought of the ring and the book persisted until he was landing on the wharf at Charles Town. Finally he shook it off. 'What can it matter, after all?' he asked himself. 'Sykes will make it all of no account to-night. I rid the State of a dangerous enemy and myself of a dangerous rival at one stroke. And I shall be treading a minuet whilst it is done.'

*   *   *

The Executive of the General Assembly, which had by now replaced the old Provincial Congress, was in the hands of a legislative and privy council. John Rutledge had been elected President and invested with all the powers of Governor.

Despite a temperamental antipathy, which he believed mutual, and some lingering remains of that rancour provoked by Rutledge's hard, unsentimental criticisms of his conduct in the Featherstone affair, Harry Latimer could not withhold his admiration of the sagacity, energy, and strength with which the new President went to work to establish and maintain order, to levy troops, and to advance the fortification of the town materially and morally against all emergencies.

In those first days of June there arrived in Charles Town that English soldier of fortune Major-General Charles Lee, sent by Washington to command the troops engaged in the defence of the Southern seaboard. He was a man of great experience and skill, who had spent his life campaigning wherever campaigns were being conducted; and Moultrie tells us that his presence in Charles Town was equivalent to a reinforcement of a thousand men. But his manners, Moultrie adds, were rough and harsh.

The unfinished state in which he found the great fort of palmetto logs seems to have fretted him considerably. His correspondence with Moultrie in these days bears abundant witness to that, and we have a glimpse of the irritation caused him by the calm, unexcited manner in which the stout-hearted Moultrie continued the works as if he still had months in which to complete them. Two things Lee was frenziedly demanding: the completion of the fort, and the building of a bridge to secure the retreat to the mainland of the force on Sullivan's Island.

If Moultrie was leisurely in the matter of the former, he was entirely negligent on the subject of the latter. He had not, he said, come there to retreat, and there was no need to be wasting time, energy, and material in providing the means for it.

Lee's great experience of war had taught him to leave nothing to chance. Moreover, in this instance he was fully persuaded that the fort could not be held—particularly in its unfinished state—against the powerful fleet under Sir Peter Parker standing off the bar. He reckoned without two factors: the calm, cool courage of its defender and the peculiar resisting quality of palmetto wood, experience of which was not included in all his campaignings, extensive and varied though they had been.

Action by the fleet was delayed until the end of June, in order that with it might be combined the operation of a land force under Sir Henry Clinton. This had been put ashore on Long Island with the same object of reducing the fort, which was the key to the harbour. To this end Clinton erected a battery which should cover the transport and fording of troops across the narrow neck of shallow water dividing the two islands. But to defend the passage there was a battery on the east end of Sullivan's Island commanded by Colonel Thomson with a picked body of riflemen.

The defence of Fort Sullivan is one of the great epics of the war, and few of its battles were of more far-reaching effect than this, coming as it did in a time of some uncertainty in the affairs of the Americans.

At half-past ten o'clock on the morning of the 28th of June, Sir Peter Parker on board the flagship *Bristol* gave the signal for action, and the fleet of ten vessels, carrying two hundred and eighty-four guns, advanced to anchor before the fort, confidently to undertake the work of pounding it into dust.

At eleven o'clock that night, nine shattered ships dropped down to Five Fathom Hole, out of range, leaving the tenth—the frigate *Actæon* crippled and aground to westward of the fort, there to be destroyed by fire the next morning.

Throughout the action, Moultrie's supplies of powder had been inadequate. Hence the need, not only for economy of fire, but for greater marksmanship, so that as few shots as possible should be wasted. And whilst the careful, steady fire from the fort battered the ships and made frightful carnage on their decks, the British shot sank more or less harmlessly into the soft, spongy palmetto logs or fell into the large moat in the middle of the fort where the fuses were extinguished before the shells could explode. It is said that of over fifty shot thrown by the *Thunder-Bomb* alone into the fort, not a single one exploded.

But if these did not, there were others that did, and although the casualties of the garrison were surprisingly small, yet throughout that terrible day of overpowering heat the Carolinians in Fort Sullivan may well have deemed themselves in hell. Toiling there, naked to the waist for the most part, under a pall of acrid smoke that hung low and heavy upon them and at times went near to choking them, and amid an incessant roar of guns, with shells bursting overhead, they fought on desperately and indomitably against a force they knew greatly superior to their own. And amongst them, ever where the need was greatest, hobbling hither and thither—for he was sorely harassed by gout at the time—was Moultrie in his blue coat and three-cornered hat, his rugged face calm, smoking his pipe as composedly as if he had been at his own fireside.

Only once did he and his officers, who in this matter emulated their leader, lay aside their pipes; and that was out of respect for General Lee, when in the course of the action he came down to see how things were with them, and to

185

realize for himself that it was possible that with all his great experience of war he had been wrong in his assumption that the place could not be held.

The thing he chiefly dreaded had by then been averted. He had perceived that the fort's alarming weakness lay in the unfinished western side—the side that faced the main. Thence it might easily be enfiladed by any ship that ran past and took up a position in the channel. This vulnerable point had not been overlooked by Sir Peter Parker, and comparatively early in the battle he had ordered forward the *Sphynx*, the *Actæon*, and the *Syren* to attack it. But here Fortune helped the garrison that was so stoutly helping itself. In the haste of their advance the three ships fouled one another's rigging, became entangled, and drifted thus on to the shoal known as the 'Middle Ground.' Before they could clear themselves, the guns of the fort had been concentrated upon them, and poured into them a fire as destructive as it was accurate. The *Sphynx* and the *Syren* eventually got off in a mangled condition, one of them trailing her broken bowsprit. The *Actæon* remained to be destroyed at leisure.

And all this while, Myrtle, in apprehension which was increased to anguish when she remembered the manner of her parting with Harry, lay on the roof of the house on the Bay endeavouring thence by the aid of a telescope to follow the action that was being fought ten miles away, whilst the windows below rattled and the very world seemed to shake with the incessant thunder of the British guns and the slow, deliberate replies from the fort.

Once she saw that the flag—the first American flag displayed in the South; a blue flag with a white crescent in the dexter corner—was gone from the fort. And her dismay in that moment made her realize, as once before she had realized, the true feelings that underlay the crust of vain prejudice upon her soul. There followed a pause of dreadful uncertainty as to whether this meant surrender—the pause during which the heroic Sergeant Jasper leapt down from one of the embrasures in the face of a withering fire to

186

rescue the flag which had been carried away by a chance shot. Attaching it to a sponge staff, he hoisted it once more upon the ramparts, and when she saw it fluttering there again, a faint cheer broke from her trembling lips and was taken up by the negro servants who shared her eyrie and some of her anxiety for the garrison among which was the master they all loved.

There she remained until after darkness had fallen, a darkness still rent and stabbed by the flashes from the guns, and until a terrific thunderstorm broke overhead and the artillery of heaven came to mingle with the artillery of man.

Then at last, unable to follow the combat with her eyes, and already drenched by the downpour which descended almost without warning, she allowed the slaves to lead her down from the roof, and went within to spend a sleepless night of anguish.

In the morning the news of victory filled Charles Town with joy and thanksgiving. It was a victory less complete than it might have been if Moultrie had not been starved of powder. With adequate ammunition, every ship of the British fleet would have been sunk or forced to surrender. But it was complete enough. The battered and defeated vessels were beaten off, and Charles Town was safe for the present.

Whole-heartedly Myrtle shared the general joy and thanksgiving. She knew herself now, she thought, beyond possibility of ever again being mistaken in her feelings. She had been through an experience of anguish, which had sharpened the sight of her soul so that she had come to see her own fault in the discords that had poisoned her married life. It should never, never be so again, she vowed, if only Harry were now safely restored to her. That was the abiding anxiety. Was he safe?

But amid the general rejoicing how could she doubt it? It was known that the casualties and been few in the fort, only some ten killed and twice that number wounded. Surely Heaven would not be so cruel as to include her husband among these.

She went actively about the house during that endless morning, stimulating all into preparations for welcoming Harry home, confident that he would come to her soon in the course of the day.

And come to her he did somewhere about noon, inanimate upon a stretcher borne by two of his men. The click of the garden-gate and the sound of steps on the gravel brought her, swift-footed, eager, to the porch, to swoon there under the shock of what she beheld, believing that it was a dead body those men bore.

When, restored to her senses, she was told that he still lived, though sorely wounded, she would have gone to him at once. But they restrained her—old Julius, Mauma Dido, and Dr. Parker, the latter having flown instantly to Harry's side in response to the news borne him by Hannibal of his master's homecoming.

The doctor, elderly and benevolent, and an old friend of Harry's, very gently broke to her the news that, although her husband's life was not to be despaired of, yet it hung by the most tenuous of threads, and that only the utmost care and vigilance could avoid the severing of this. He had been shot through the body in two places. One of these was a slight wound; but the other was grave, and Dr. Parker had only just extracted the bullet. He was easier now; but it would be better if she did not see him yet.

'But who is to tend and nurse him?' she inquired.

'We must provide for that.'

'Who better than myself?'

'But you have not the strength, my dear,' he demurred. 'The very sight of him wounded has so affected you that . . .'

She interrupted him. 'That shall not happen again,' she promised firmly, and rose commanding her still trembling limbs. Although very white, she was so calm and so resolved, that presently Dr. Parker gave way, and permitted her at once to take up her duties by Harry's side.

He was delirious and fever-tossed, so that there was no danger of any excitement to him from her presence. She received the doctor's instructions attentively, displaying now the calm of an intrepid combatant, preparing for battle. And save for one concession to her emotions, when she knelt by his bedside and offered up a prayer that he might be spared to her, she did not again depart from that stern role.

Down in her heart there was an instinctive knowledge that she, herself, was in part responsible for his condition, even before Moultrie came, as he did later that day, to leave her, by the admissions she drew from him, no doubt upon that score.

It was like the kindly, easy-going soldier to find time amid the many preoccupations of the moment to seek her, all battle-stained as he was, to offer comfort and obtain news of Harry's condition.

'It is precarious,' she answered him. 'But Dr. Parker assures me that he is to be saved by care and vigilance, and these I can provide. Be sure that Harry shall get well again.'

He marvelled at her calm confidence; marvelled, admired, and was reassured. Here was the spirit in which the battle of Fort Sullivan had been won by his gallant lads, the spirit which conquers all material things.

He spoke of the fight of yesterday and of Harry's conduct in it, conduct of a valour amounting to recklessness.

'If I had not known him for a man with every inducement to live, with everything to make life dear for him, I might almost have suspected him of courting death. Twice I had to order him down from the parapet, where he was needlessly exposing himself in his zeal to stimulate the men. And when the flag was carried away a second time by a shot from the *Bristol,* before I could stop him he had done what Jasper did on the first occasion of that happening. He was over the parapet and out on the sand under fire to rescue and bring back our standard. He was standing on the ramparts waving it to the men when he was shot. I caught him in my arms, and, desperately wounded as he was, at the moment I really think my chief emotion was anger with him that he should so recklessly have exposed himself.'

When presently he left her, and she went back to Harry's bedside, where her place had been filled in her absence by Mauma Dido, she took back with her the burning memory of Moultrie's words.

'If I had not known him for a man with every inducement to live, with everything to make life dear for him . . .'

And the truth, she told herself, was that, through her, he was become a man with every inducement to die. Deliberately he had sought death, that he might deliver her from a bond which had been forged by charity instead of love. For this was the lie she had led him to believe; this was the lie which, for a time, she had almost believed herself. Because he imagined that bond grown odious to her—and she had given him all cause so to imagine it—he had sought to snap it, that he might set her free.

How like him was that! How like the high-spirited selfless Harry she had always known! Impetuous and impulsive always, but always upon impulses to serve others. It was the service of others had made him a patriot, where a self-seeker of his wealth and prosperity under the Royal Government would have striven to avoid all change. Whether his political views were right or wrong, noble and altruistic they certainly were. For that she must honour him, and for that, too, since she was his wife, she must make his faith her own.

Never again, if it should please God in His infinite mercy to spare him, would she give him occasion to doubt her, or to suppose that anything but love had brought her, or to suppose that anything but love had brought about that precipitate marriage of theirs. And if he should now be spared, why, then she would spend the wealth that she would inherit to the last penny in forwarding the cause he had espoused.

In such a spirit did she address herself to wrestle with the Angel of Death.

Herbert Ravenel Sass

CAROLINA MARSHES

A sandy point on a lonely beach, with a little river coming down to the sea, is a spot where in March and early April I have spent many mornings watching the spring come up from the summer lands away to the south. You can see her come. She is there before you, white, radiant, graceful—a presence not only felt but, if the right mood is upon you, visible to the eye. She is not the divinity of the ancient Greeks nor the being that poets have imagined: a goddess like a lovely woman but lovelier than any woman of flesh and blood. For me she has no definite shape, yet I can see her; she is very real. She comes riding up from the summer lands on the waving, rhythmic wings of flocks of milk-white herons, flock after flock, drifting slowly along under the bright blue sky, coming nearer and nearer, shining like silver in the sun.

It is a beautiful thing to see on the wild, lonely Carolina beaches—this coming of spring. But seeing it, drinking in its beauty, rejoicing over all that it means, my thoughts fly swiftly from the open beaches and marshes along the edge of the sea to other and very different scenes. Faster than the heron flocks themselves, I am transported in fancy to deep swamps hidden in the woods, to still cypress lagoons, shaded by tall, straight trees and curtained with gray Spanish moss, where presently those heron flocks will come to rest.

For the swamps are their goal, their haven, their true home. They come along the sea's edge, following the beaches northward on their journey from the tropics and the lower South, perhaps guided at night by the everlasting music of the surf; but when they have reached the South Carolina coast, they turn inland (at least, many of them do) away from the ocean and the broad salt marshes, and, flying on and on, over forests and fields and wastes of rushes, they come down at last in the deep heart of the swamp woods and end their journey there.

That is how spring comes to the swamps. The herons bring her—the little flocks of milk-white herons that in March and early April come drifting along above the palm-fringed ocean beaches like fragments of snowy, sun-lit cloud.

With her coming the swamps are transformed. They are beautiful at all seasons. Even in winter, when the cypresses are bare and there is comparatively little visible life, they are not dreary and melancholy, as many suppose. They have a gray, silvery loveliness then that, in certain moods, delights and even exhilarates; it is then that they are most mysterious, that the effect of strangeness, of unreality, as though one had passed from the world of to-day into an earlier and more fantastic epoch, is strongest. But the swamps in winter are asleep. There is a sense of waiting—waiting. At last spring touches them, and gradually, yet swiftly, they awake. It is the soft caress of a white heron's wing that brings the change.

To see the swamps at their best, to enjoy them to the fullest, one must see them in spring after the awakening has taken place. Comparatively few people know them at that season. By that time most of the thousands of visitors who come to the South for the winter are homeward bound again; and the impression that they carry away with them is an impression of gray, dismal wastes of leafless, moss-shrouded trees—silent, colorless, lifeless fastnesses which, seen from the outside, from the window of a train or from an automobile speeding along a highway, appear both melancholy and forbidding.

Go into them and you will find, even in winter, that gray, silvery beauty and that atmosphere of mystery of which I have spoken. But there is little then to indicate what will come later; there is scarcely a hint of the transfiguration which the spring will bring—that strange loveliness of another kind which can hardly be surpassed anywhere on earth.

To reach the heart of the swamp you must paddle, sometimes for miles, in a small flat-bottomed punt along the narrow water-lanes of a flooded forest of cypress or black gum. These water-lanes are inexpressibly beautiful. Sometimes they are straight, so that the eye, wandering down the shadowy vista ahead, looks for a great distance along a dim tunnel through the flooded woods, walled in on each side and above by the smooth trunks and the green feathery foliage of cypresses, curtained and festooned with long, graceful pennons of Spanish moss. Sometimes the water-paths wind in and out like serpents, so that there is always, just in front, the mystery of a curve, a bend in the watery road, beyond which one may see one knows not what.

For a time, perhaps, there will be little visible life. Nor will you see, when you are afloat in the swamp woods, the brightness and prettiness of wild flowers except the pink glow of an occasional swamp rose. There is a grander, more solumn beauty here, yet there is nothing of melancholy in it.

There is bright sunshine and dark shadow. The cypress boughs overhead are a vivid living green; the moss pennons, hanging from the trees and swathing their slim trunks, are gray or silver or pink or lavender, for the sunlight striking on it or through it works miracles with the moss. So, too, the trunks of the cypresses, flaring outward at the base and often hedged about with cypress-knees, are not of one color, monotonous and unchangeable. There also the wonder-working sunlight, pouring down through openings in the green roof overhead or filtering through the tracery of the cypress boughs, changes the brown of the straight, smooth cypress boles into many delicate tints, brilliant or soft, varying endlessly.

Perhaps even more beautiful, the still waters underneath, black on clear-brown like wine, are a mirror in which the world above is not merely reflected but glorified. The darker, richer hues reflected there, especially the many shades of green, often appear deeper and richer, so that the watery floor of the swamp is neither black nor brown (the actual color of the clear water) but becomes a varicolored translucent or transparent glossy surface, as of a dark polished crystal, brighter and clearer where the sunlight falls upon it; and in this vast crystal, luminous with sunshine or dark with deep-green shadow, the blue sky above, the bright green roof of cypress foliage, the exquisite tints of the hanging moss, and the soaring tree-trunks are reproduced in softer tones and yet with an added richness and luster.

The water-lane leads on and on. Sometimes there is only one way amid the crowding tree trunks, one narrow channel barely wide enough for the punt; sometimes the serried ranks of the trees divide and you have choice of several paths; sometimes you come to openings in the flooded forest where there are no trees at all or only a few small cypresses standing by themselves in a little lake walled in at a distance of twenty or perhaps fifty yards by the encircling woods.

These open spaces have a beauty of another kind. A bright-green carpet of duckweed spreads across the water; in shallows along the edges, beds of tall rushes, of dense telanthera and wampee and other aquatic plants flourish in the sun. Where the water is a little deeper, the lily-pads and the much larger circular leaves, often two feet in diameter, of the magnificent yellow lotus, the most gorgeous flower of the swamps, impede the passage of the boat.

All this is the background, the setting. It is, I like to think, the touch of a white heron's wing that wakes the swamps from their winter sleep; and when that awakening has taken place, when spring has fairly come, the herons are among the most abundant and most beautiful of the swamp's inhabitants.

They are of several sizes and species, but the most beautiful of them are the great white egrets—tall, graceful creatures, white as the whitest marble, adorned with long, slender plumes or aigrettes which droop beyond their tails. Deep in the swamp lagoons, the egrets and herons of other kinds build their nests in the cypresses, not singly but in communities sometimes containing hundreds of birds; and in these heron cities, in late April and May, the life of the lagoons is at its crest and the beauty and strangeness of the swamps overwhelm the eye and the mind.

No one can ever forget his first visit to a heron city in one of the Carolina swamps; and the experience is all the more memorable if the city of herons which he visits is situated on one of the larger lagoons so that a considerable journey along the devious water-ways of the swamp is necessary in order to reach the place.

He passes then through scenes of indescribable beauty before attaining his goal: down shadowy, moss-tapestried water-lanes so mysteriously lovely that they are like secret byways through some Kingdom of Dreams: along broader, sun-dappled channels through the flooded woods where the magic of the sunlight in the trees, in the trailing veils of moss, and in the clear, placid water works miracles of color; across sun-bathed openings, golden and mellow, lying like secret enchanted lakes embosomed in the woods.

Against this background he sees, as he journeys on, the abundant life of the swamp: a flash of white, slowly waving wings far ahead along a narrow water-path as an egret takes flight at his approach; the glowing orange-gold of tiny prothonotary warblers flitting here and there in the feathery green of the cypresses; wood ducks rising from the water with their high, thin notes of protest and alarm; long-necked, long-tailed anhingas or water-turkeys, strangest and most fantastic of all the swamp birds, sailing high overhead like airplanes against the blue; perhaps a flock of great wood ibises, soaring at an even greater height, their long necks and legs outstretched, their wide, white, black-edged wings rigid and motionless.

The swamp lagoons teem with life. Often it is brilliant, vivid, flashing, aglow with the rich colors of the tropics from which many of the swamp birds come. Sometimes it is fantastic, grotesque, prehistoric in its strangeness.

In all the swamp waters alligators are at home; in some of the larger lagoons and in many of the creeks and rivers they abound and attain a great size, twelve feet or more in length, though these monsters are uncommon. On a trip to a heron city in one of the larger lagoons not long ago, we counted thirty alligators, none of them, however, more than eight feet long from nose to tail-tip. Terrapins of various sizes sit in rows on the half-submerged logs and dive overboard as the punt draws near. Now and again, though rarely (for, contrary to popular belief, snakes are not numerous in the cypress lagoons), a water snake, sunning himself on some log or in the lower branches of a willow or buttonwood bush, slithers downward into the depths.

The snakes are seldom seen and are most of them harmless; afloat on the lagoons there is practically no danger from them at all. The alligators, even the grim and powerful leviathans of their race, learned long ago to keep out of man's way. The life of the swamp waters, grotesque but only rarely sinister, is comparatively inconspicuous; it is the abundant life of the air that gives the lagoons their most compelling charm. The herons are the most characteristic and perhaps the most spectacular of the birds of the lagoons; and when at last the voyager along the water-paths of the flooded woods reaches the heron city for which he has been bound, he finds himself in the midst of a bewildering panorama of life such as, in all likelihood, he has never dreamed of or imagined.

The cypresses are crowded with nests, ten or fifteen perhaps in a single tree. On the nests, in the branches, in the air, herons in scores or perhaps in hundreds—herons of various sizes and hues, dark-blue or parti-colored or glittering spotless white—stand or sail in a maze of interweaving circles amid an astonishing swelling clamor of innumerable voices.

Little blue herons are there, airy, graceful Louisiana herons, burly, deep-voiced black-crowned night herons, fantastic anhingas, perhaps great blue herons also and wood ibises, the largest of the swamp birds; and, most wonderful of all, stately, immaculate great egrets, white as snow, trailing their long nuptial plumes behind them as they fly, sweep back and forth overhead or stand like tall, slender statuettes of shining marble in the green cypress tops.

Sometimes one species predominates, sometimes another. The most fascinating of the heron cities are those in which the great egrets are most numerous, for there the trees are sometimes white with the splendid snowy birds, while the void above is bright with their shining, buoyant bodies, as they sail, like white stately ships of the air, above the feathery tree tops or swing slowly 'round and 'round under the blue sky on their radiant, slowly waving wings.

It is, above all else, the life of the swamps that gives them their enchantment; and since this life is most abundant on the swamp lagoons, they are always to my mind the most interesting parts of these fastnesses. The lagoons are of various kinds. Most of them are small; some are natural ponds or lakes, while others—and these include many of the loveliest— are old backwaters or "reserves" of the rice-planting days when lower South Carolina was a region of great plantations where the finest rice in the world was grown.

These were, in the beginning, artificial or semi-artificial bodies of water. A low bank thrown across a swamp would flood a large area behind it; and periodically the water from this submerged area or "reserve" would be drawn off to flood the rice fields below. The rice-planting days are over, but the old reserves remain; and in most cases nature has hidden effectively all signs of man's handiwork around them, so that they are as wild now and as beautiful as the natural ponds or lagoons.

The lagoons vary endlessly in appearance and in character. In fact, no two of them are alike; but two main types may be distinguished—those that are wooded, grown up with cypress or tupelo or black gum (or with all of these) so that the effect is that of a flooded forest, a forest whose floor is water instead of earth; and, second, those that are open—that is to say, devoid of trees, though large parts of the surface are generally covered with water growths and with floating islands sometimes solid enough to support willows and low bushes.

The former are, I think, the more beautiful; but the open lagoons have their distinctive charm also. Their bird-life is of a different kind. There, for instance, in reeds and rushes and wampee beds and amid rafts of lily pads and other aquatic plants, you will find least bitterns, king rails, and gorgeous purple gallinules, birds rarely or never seen in the wooded swamps; and in summer, when the yellow lotus is in bloom, the open lagoons and the old rice fields themselves are often scenes of unimaginable beauty.

The lotus is not found everywhere but only in certain spots. It comes and it goes mysteriously, taking possession of a lagoon or an abandoned rice field, then disappearing perhaps for years. In places only a few plants are to be seen, or, again, an acre of water may be covered with them. Occasionally these wild lotus gardens cover areas many acres in extent; and the spectacle then, in early morning or late afternoon, with white herons standing amid the great golden flowers and perhaps a pair of purple gallinules walking lightly about over the hugh circular lotus leaves, is one that will never be forgotten.

The swamps are friendly, not inimical. You will not, if you will observe a few simple rules, be eaten alive by mosquitoes, poisoned by deadly snakes, or infected with prostrating fevers. You must, in the warm season, get out of the swamp before nightfall; you must, in walking through thick places, be careful where you put your foot. Once afloat on the lagoons you are safe; there is no more likelihood that a venomous moccasin will drop from an overhanging bough into your lap than there is that one of the big alligators of the lagoons will take it into his head to climb into your boat. Nor are the swamp lagoons intolerably hot, as is commonly believed. In the dry portions of the swamps the summer heat is intense, and on the open lagoons at midday it may become actually unbearable. But on the wooded lagoons, shielded from the rays of the sun by a high canopy of boughs, the voyager, even on a sultry summer day, will suffer little or no discomfort.

And always the swamps are beautiful. There are places in the swamps of the South Carolina low country which are the most beautiful places that I have ever seen. Perhaps that is because I have lived close to them and know them more familiarly than I know the mountains or the hills; but others, seeing them for the first time in their spring loveliness, drifting along their shadowy water paths under the moss-hung cypresses, watching the living beings of many shapes and hues that make their homes in those columned solitudes, come quickly under the spell of their enchantment.

I have not begun to describe them here. I cannot put into words their loveliness as I see it, still less their mystery and their strange fascination; but in the exquisite pictures of Alice R. Huger Smith, all her life a lover of the Carolina swamps, knowing them better than any other artist who has ever tried to paint them, not only the physical beauty which the eye sees but also the very spirit of the swamps is expressed. These lovely canvases tell the story of the swamps far better than the pen can portray them.

CONTEMPORARY POETRY

James Dickey

THE SALT MARSH

Once you have let the first blade
Spring back behind you
To the way it has always been,
You no longer know where you are.
All you can see are the tall
Stalks of sawgrass, now sawing,
But each of them holding its tip
Exactly at the level where your hair

Begins to grow from your forehead.
Wherever you come to is
The same as before,
With the same blades of oversized grass,
And wherever you stop, the one
Blade just in front of you leans,
That one only, and touches you
At the place where your hair begins

To grow; at that predestined touch
Your spine tingles crystally, like salt,
And the image of a crane occurs,
Each flap of its wings creating
Its feathers anew, this time whiter,
As the sun destroys all points
Of the compass, refusing to move
From its chosen noon.

Where is the place you have come from
With your buried steps full of new roots?
You cannot leap up to look out,
Yet you do not sink,
But seem to grow, and the sound,
The oldest of sounds, is your breath
Sighing like acres.
If you stand as you are for long,

Green panic may finally give
Way to another sensation,
For when the embodying wind
Rises, the grasses begin to weave
A little, then all together,
Not bending enough for you
To see your way clear of the swaying,
But moving just the same,

And nothing prevents your bending
With them, helping their wave
Upon wave upon wave upon wave
By not opposing,
By willing your supple inclusion
Among fields without promise of harvest,
In their marvelous, spiritual walking
Everywhere, anywhere.

SLAVE QUARTERS

In the great place the great house is gone from   in the sun
Room, near the kitchen of air   I look across at low walls
Of slave quarters, and feel my imagining loins

Rise with the madness of Owners
To take off the Master's white clothes
And slide all the way into moonlight
Two hundred years old with this moon.
Let me go,

Ablaze with my old me-
scent, in moonlight made by the mind
From the dusk sun, in the yard where my dogs would smell
For once what I totally am,
Flaming up in their brains as the Master
They but dimly had sensed through my clothes:
Let me stand as though moving

204

At midnight, now at the instant of sundown
When the wind turns

From sea wind to land, and the marsh grass
Hovers, changing direction:
                                        there was this house
That fell before I got out. I can pull
It over me where I stand, up from the earth,
Back out of the shells
Of the sea:
                  become with the change of this air
A coastal islander, proud of his grounds,
His dogs, his spinet
From Savannah, his pale daughters,
His war with the sawgrass, pushed back into
The sea it crawled from. Nearer dark, unseen,
I can begin to dance
Inside my gabardine suit
As though I had left my silk nightshirt

In the hall of mahogany, and crept
To slave quarters to live out
The secret legend of Owners. Ah, stand up,
Blond loins, another
Love is possible! My thin wife would be sleeping
Or would not mention my absence:

                                        the moonlight

On these rocks can be picked like cotton
By a crazed Owner dancing-mad
With the secret repossession of his body

Phosphorescent and mindless, shedding
Blond-headed shadow on the sand,
Hounds pressing in their sleep
Around him, smelling his footblood
On the strange ground that lies between skins

With the roof blowing off slave quarters
To let the moon in burning
The years away
In just that corner where crabgrass proves it lives
Outside of time.
Who seeks the other color of his body,
His loins giving off a frail light
On the dark lively shipwreck of grass   sees
Water live where
The half-moon touches,
The moon made whole in one wave
Very far from the silent piano   the copy of Walter Scott
Closed on its thin-papered battles
Where his daughter practiced, decorum preventing the one
Bead of sweat in all that lace   collected at her throat
From breaking and humanly running
Over Mozart's unmortal keys —

                     I come past
A sand crab pacing sideways   his eyes out
On stalks   the bug-eyed vision of fiddler
Crabs sneaking a light on the run
From the split moon   holding in it a white man stepping
Down the road of clamshells and cotton   his eyes out
On stems   the tops of the sugar
Cane soaring   the sawgrass walking:

                     I come past
The stale pools left
Over from high tide   where the crab in the night sand
Is basting himself with his claws   moving ripples outward
Feasting on brightness
                and above
A gull also crabs slowly,
Tacks, jibes   then turning the corner
Of wind, receives himself like a brother
As he glides down upon his reflection:

My body has a color not yet freed:
In that ruined house let me throw

Obsessive gentility off;
Let Africa rise upon me like a man
Whose instincts are delivered from their chains
Where they lay close-packed and wide-eyed
In muslin sheets
As though in the miserly holding
Of too many breaths by one ship.   Now

Worked in silver   their work lies all
Around me   the fields dissolving
Into the sea   and   not on a horse
I stoop to the soil   working
Gathering   moving to the rhythm of a music
That has crossed the ocean in chains

In the grass the great singing void of slave

Labor about me   the moonlight bringing
Sweat out of my back as though the sun
Changed skins upon me   some other
Man moving near me on horseback   whom I look in the eyes
Once a day:
                    there in that corner

Her bed turned to grass. Unsheltered by these walls
The outside fields form slowly
Anew, in a kind of barrelling blowing,
Bend in all the right places   as faintly Michael rows
The boat ashore   his spiritual lungs
Entirely filling the sail.   How take on the guilt

Of slavers?   How shudder like one who made
Money from buying a people
To work as ghosts
In this blowing solitude?
I only stand here upon shells   dressed poorly
For nakedness   poorly
For the dark wrecked hovel of rebirth

Picking my way in thought
To the black room
Where starlight blows off the roof
And the great beasts that came in the minds
Of the first slaves, stand at the door, asking
For death, asking to be
Forgotten: the sadness of elephants
The visionary pain in the heads
Of incredibly poisonous snakes
Lion   wildebeest   giraffe   all purchased also
When one wished only
Labor
          those beasts becoming
For the white man the animals of Eden
Emblems of sexual treasure   all beasts attending
Me now   my dreamed dogs snarling at the shades
Of eland and cheetah
On the dispossessed ground where I dance
In my clothes beyond movement:
In nine months she would lie
With a knife between her teeth to cut the pain
Of bearing
A child who belongs in no world   my hair in that boy
Turned black   my skin
Darkened by half   his, lightened
By that half exactly   the beasts of Africa reduced
To cave shadows flickering on his brow
As I think of him: a child would rise from that place
With half my skin. He could for an instant
Of every day   when the wind turns   look
Me in the eyes. What do you feel when passing

Your blood beyond death
To another in secret: into
Another who takes your features   and adds
A misplaced Africa to them,
Changing them forever
As they must live?   What happens

To you, when such a one bears
You after your death into rings
Of battling light   a heavyweight champion
Through the swirling glass of four doors,
In epauletted coats   into places
Where you learn to wait
On tables   into sitting in all-night cages
Of parking lots   into raising
A sun-sided hammer in a gang
Of men on a tar road working
Until the crickets give up?
What happens when the sun goes down

And the white man's loins still stir
In a house of air   still draw him toward
Slave quarters? When Michael's voice is heard
Bending the sail like grass,
The real moon begins to come
Apart on the water
And two hundred years are turned back
On with the headlights of a car?

When you learn that there is no hatred
Like love in the eyes
Of a wholly owned face?   When you think of what
It would be like   what it has been
What it is to look once a day
Into an only
Son's brown, waiting, wholly possessed
Amazing eyes, and not
Acknowledge, but own?

August Kleinzahler

LONGITUDE LANE

The oleander on Longitude Lane
flares among the langours and fevers of June
below the south-facing piazzas
the sea breezes find
or don't quite find
along the corridors of ivy-colored brick
Carolina *gray* brick and wrought iron
that wind away inland from the Battery

History just sits out there, a kind of weather
in the harbor and beyond
on the plantations and through the low country
with its bogs and herons
its skirmishes never forgotten

And the manners in town so antique, so elegant
an underwater Kabuki in summer dresses
The old families and Huguenot names

The long siege and storied cannonades

Turkey buzzards over the market
water rats under the pantry

The precious settee and the wild, wild daughters

Nick Lindsay

PILOT BOAT

Does my work have a face?
Suppose I meet it in some public place,
Outside the church, in the store, does it have hands
To make things with, or paws? What about its walk?
Does it search avidly for some trace
Of me, whimper and dig like an abandoned dog
With yellow teeth? Beaten away from new tin garbage cans.
(O my work's an enemy's gift, an axe wound chopped wide,
Then sewed up by a blind drunk using phone calls
For all his needle stitches, and missed tides.)

There is a pilot boat out in the yard
Humped with her keel upward toward the sky.
Thirty years ago a neighbor dumped her there,
"Patch her, plank her, put new butt blocks, caulk. . ."
Neither he nor I have bothered to pay for her,
Or haul her away. She's still here, a grey hulk
Once stormworthy as a stone. Her strong-framed lines
Flow with the live oaks, palmettos, lofty pines,
Lines ancient, powerful, and most ordinary.
Along her crumbling gunwales wild grapes root,
  down-grasp,
Bind her to earth as they climb up to offer
Like a girl her breast their new chaste-wanton blossoms
To the high wild-cherry winds of February.

I may then know my work; this is its sign:
It's an abandoned boat with rotten garboards
Beneath a blossoming tree.
It's hallowed by the signs of humanness:
Signature, wholeness, rootedness, binding.
This rootedness, I set out upon it
As upon the open sea.

POEM

Dry November, dry
Leaves' russet rustle, we
Came there, she and I in the secret
Woods, scarce a path, marked by our feet, ours
Alone in the way they like to walk, then by small
Animals, rabbits, coons, wildcats, who liked the way we
    found. Here slaves
Had their village, "We willage," as they
Called it. Here, brambles, by the creek, the street
Ran back to the well, hid now, lost in high thicket
Oak, pine. She stepped over fallen trunks, ducked
Through vines, ran ahead, flew, dis-
Appeared, bright knees' wink, blue denim a swirl escaping
Me, laughed at clumsiness she so easily
Easily outran. A wren, her wings thrust with carolling
Courage, owns
All wildness, makes her high
Home there. Sandalled
Feet, a pause on the rubble.
From below leaf mold, vines, roots, oyster shells break
Through, mark a house door, tumbled rock here a chimney.
Sandalled feet, an instant, spring
Aside, astride, startled, intent, stopped in
Flight. I win our game, seize a slim waist between my
    elbows, lock
Hands beneath her ribs, but?

    "There," she points.
A copperhead who had been taking his last
Lazy look at the woods before winter's
Sleep stones and the earth surround: stepped on in her run
Has drawn into himself, coiled among the rocks, includes
Feet in his peevish acceptance, our grandfather, includes the
    green
Glinting creek, us on hands and knees taking in his smell,
    leafmold
Smell.

The sky for us sometimes, the high warm
Branches, sugarshell branches, or sometimes the sparse dry
Of grass. The grey salt marsh, the swift
Guzzle of tide beyond, the clapping oysters. Applaud. A stormy
Tumble. Our grandfather's disgruntled benediction follows us
Home. A benediction then, each new
Serpent-crescent moon, each full moon. The tenth one brings

Excitement. Not the nurse-and-doctor-emergency in the temple
Of the fear of death and debt, no. But this: under the tenth full moon
Midnight before the break of day, among the bed
Time books, sheets, the pillowcases of go to work
Times without number,
A fuzzy head, a nose, shoulders doing push ups against
His mother's newly-emptied womb,
A son, a brother.

Wendy Salinger

SEASMOKE

On an island near this island
Poe blew on his fingertips,
red and stinging from the salt wind.
Was it the floaters
brooding in his eyes
or these white fibers
carded from the foam?
Forms steam
off the wet sand.
Tufts of spilt lining flock the air.
He saw the last palmettos lift
their gray trunks above the mist.
One by one their bristling
heads get taken
as if by Turner's brushwork.
Each thing wears its shroud.
Out where nothing is, a dog
barks at some discovery.

A man kneeling
nears me as I walk.
He crouches in the chemical smell of oysters
over his machine propped on the jetty.
The wooden posts, rotted almost black
and scrofulous with barnacles, suck the dregs
of brown tide like a drain
and wet his boot.
The hands that fit the motorcycle chain
are pale
with wedges of darkness under the nails.
The black jacket straining in the smoke
pulls up to bare his back
swirled with hair.
Orange wings are blazoned on the helmet
laid carefully beside him.
Gulls and turnstones skirt him

pecking for midges.
Their cries rust on the air.
I glide past him like the clouds of spume
that walk the beach.
Then I am once again turbaned in mist.
Then once again his dark machine materializes;
his blazing forehead, the red light in his wake.

He too is trying to get more lost.
His noise sputters before me
and goes out.
He thinks he can drop me off
in his cloud trail.
He thinks what disappears doesn't exist —
like a child craving the life of a hero or orphan —
he drives his deed into the cottonmouthed air.
He tightens his knees on the sweating,
metal flanks.
He thinks I can't follow him
into the cataract,
I can't hear
his feathery chest
or see the bird pulse move
up and down his rough throat.
He thinks he can be sifted
into nothing.
He is so restless
with the dream of rest.
He leaves me to the wind,
he leaves me blind.
Only this ectoplasm
is clear to the eye,
though I know the ocean
by its white noise.
Dim to everything
I meant
to walk
into the shadow of my own heart.

CHARLESTON, SOUTH CAROLINA, 7 P.M.

Vapors of musk and oyster rise,
a fine perspiring from the streets.
Blue bends toward purple:
a voice growing husky.
Things seek their silhouettes.
Green gathers darkness into the palm trees,
and the houses seem to rush out.
How whitely the stucco flowers and the pillar
that wavers as if seen through water.
So it is with consequences, the sun's aftertaste,
its resonances pool out in clapboard and stone.
Light hesitates between the streetlamp and the sky,
and distance is palpable as it is between those
who turn to each other with eyes downcast.

We lean from our bones but we don't leave,
we hang about, we hover at the edges,
we live in our mouths, heaviness on our tongues.
The tongue could do all the work tonight
of sight and sound and most surely of thought.
We hover at surfaces like moths
at our white linen, our moon silks,
at our own flesh. Surely under the fresh
ironing our genitals are cool and strange.
Surely they are fronds and gardenia flowers.

A weedy draft of ocean floods our lungs.
I know this now. How the past waits
coiled in an odor,
wet for the drinker of a limpid sound,
to be unbottled, to assail the blood.
I know the past exists.
And I could enter anywhere and find you, arranged
in the mime, for example, of just such an evening,
when lifting the cigarette through its steam
your arm inscribes forever that arc in space.
I know the rich molecules collect.

But who can court a balcony that commands
the bay to shine from its dark height?
My music's wrong, I'm not my own
bent low in the folds of a polished gown,
bowing to a man whose forehead shames the moon,
whose wrists flash steel.
A moisture films his formal lip
and sticks the shirt to the moving chest
and lifts the light on the beaded glass.
Is it possible that other histories covet us?

A stray dance can find our forms,
an incomplete gesture usurp our arms.
We shudder against the humid seizures
that wrestle us out of modern motion,
curve us, bow us,
wheel our waists through the watery air
where the ocean lives in its altered state
of brine and oyster musk, and smoke
from the factories braids with the swerve
of the black kids on their bicycles
who criss-cross the northend traffic.

CONTEMPORARY PROSE

Pat Conroy

from *The Prince of Tides*

My wound is geography. It is also my anchorage, my port of call.

I grew up slowly beside the tides and marshes of Colleton; my arms were tawny and strong from working long days on the shrimp boat in the blazing South Carolina heat. Because I was a Wingo, I worked as soon as I could walk; I could pick a blue crab clean when I was five. I had killed my first deer by the age of seven, and at nine was regularly putting meat on my family's table. I was born and raised on a Carolina sea island and I carried the sunshine of the low-country, inked in dark gold, on my back and shoulders. As a boy I was happy above the channels, navigating a small boat between the sandbars with their quiet nation of oysters exposed on the brown flats at the low watermark. I knew every shrimper by name, and they knew me and sounded their horns when they passed me fishing in the river.

*   *   *

My family lived in splendid isolation on Melrose Island in a small white house my grandfather had helped build. The house faced the inland waterway, and the town of Colleton could be seen down the river, its white mansions set like chess pieces above the marsh. Melrose Island was a lozenge-shaped piece of land of twelve hundred acres surrounded on four sides by salt rivers and creeks. The island country where I grew up was a fertile, semitropical archipelago that gradually softened up the ocean for the grand surprise of the continent that followed. Melrose was only one of sixty sea islands in Colleton County. At the eastern edge of the county lay six barrier islands shaped by their daily encounters with the Atlantic. The other sea islands, like Melrose, enscarved by vast expanses of marshland, were the green sanctuaries where brown and white shrimp came to spawn in their given seasons. When they came, my father and other men like him were waiting in their fine and lovely boats.

*   *   *

To describe our growing up in the lowcountry of South Carolina, I would have to take you to the marsh on a spring day, flush the great blue heron from its silent occupation, scatter marsh hens as we sink to our knees in mud, open you an oyster with a pocketknife and feed it to you from the shell and say, "There. That taste. That's the taste of my childhood." I would say, "Breathe deeply," and you would breathe and remember that smell for the rest of your life, the bold, fecund aroma of the tidal marsh, exquisite and sensual, the smell of the South in heat, a smell like new milk, semen, and spilled wine, all perfumed with seawater. My soul grazes like a lamb on the beauty of indrawn tides.

I am a patriot of a singular geography on the planet; I speak of my country religiously; I am proud of its landscape. I walk through the traffic of cities cautiously, always nimble and on the alert, because my heart belongs in the marshlands. The boy in me still carries the memories of those days when I lifted crab pots out of the Colleton River before dawn, when I was shaped by life on the river, part child, part sacristan of tides.

*   *   *

I was ten when I first saw the white porpoise known as Carolina Snow following our shrimp boat as we returned to the dock after a day dragging the beaches along Spaulding Point. It was the only white porpoise ever sighted along the Atlantic seaboard in the memories of the shrimping brotherhood, and some said the only white porpoise ever to inhabit the earth. Throughout Colleton County, with its endless miles of salt rivers and tidal creeks, the sighting of the Snow was always cause for wonder. She was never seen with other porpoises, and some shrimpers, like my father, surmised that porpoises, like humans, were not kind to their freaks and that the Snow was sentenced by her remarkable whiteness to wander the green waters of Colleton, exiled and solitary. That first day, she followed us almost all the way to the bridge before she turned back toward the sea. Snow lent to the county a sense of specialness, and all who saw her remembered the first moment for the rest of their lives. It was like being touched by a recognition that the sea would never forfeit its power to create and astonish.

Through the years, the Snow had become a symbol of luck in the town. Colleton would prosper and flourish as long as the Snow honored these waters with her visitations. There were times when she disappeared for long periods and then suddenly would return to the waters of the Carolina sea islands. Even the paper noticed her comings and goings. Her entrance to the main channel and her slow, sensual passage through the town would bring the entire citizenry to the river's banks. Commerce would cease and collectively the people of the town would stop what they were doing to acknowledge her return. She visited the main river rarely, and because of its rarity, her appearance was a precious town-stopping thing. She approached us always as a symbol, monarch, and gift; she approached us always alone, banished, and the people on the shore, calling her by name, shouting out in greeting, acknowledging her divine white passage, formed the only family she would ever know.

Grandpa started the motor and headed the small boat out toward the channel. The Snow rose out of the river ahead of us, her back lilying in the dimming light.

"She's going our way," Grandpa said, steering the boat toward her. "Now if that ain't proof of a living God then nothing is. You'd think he'd be satisfied with just a plain porpoise. That's as beautiful as any creature on earth. But no, he's still up there dreaming up things even more beautiful to please man's eye."

"I've never seen her this close," Savannah said. "She's pure white, like a tablecloth."

But it was not a pure white we were seeing when she surfaced twenty yards from us. Faint ores of colors shimmered across her back as she cut through the water, a brief silvering of her fins, evanescent color that could not be sustained. You knew she could never be the same color twice.

We watched her as she circled the boat, saw her beneath

us, and she flowed like milk through water. Rising, she hung suspended, concolorous with peaches and high-risen moons, then down as milk again.

These are the quicksilver moments of my childhood I cannot recapture entirely. Irresistible and emblematic, I can recall them only in fragments and shivers of the heart. There is a river, the town, my grandfather steering a boat through the channel, my sister fixed in that suspended rapture she would later translate into her strongest poems, the metallic perfume of harvested oysters, the belling voices of children on the shore. . . When the white porpoise comes there is all this and transfiguration too. In dreams, the porpoise remains in memory's waters, a pale divinity who nourishes the fire and deepest cold of all the black waters of my history. There were many things wrong with my childhood but the river was not one of them, nor can the inestimable riches it imparted be traded or sold.

As we passed under the bridge I looked back and saw the shadows of people who had gathered to watch the Snow's passage. Their heads appeared in clusters above the bridge's cement railing, at intervals, like the beads of a damaged rosary. I heard the voice of a small girl begging the Snow to return beneath the bridge. Men and women began assembling on the floating docks, which bobbed in the moving tide; they were all pointing toward the last spot the porpoise had surfaced.

When the white porpoise came, it was for my grandfather like seeing the white smile of God coming up at him from below.

"Thank you, God," my grandfather said behind us in one of those unrehearsed prayers that burst naturally from him when he was deeply moved by the external world. "Thank you so much for this."

I turned. My sister turned. And that good man smiled at us.

Later, long after my grandfather was dead, I would regret that I could never be the kind of man that he was. Though I adored him as a child and found myself attracted to the safe protectorate of his soft, uncritical maleness, I never wholly appreciated him. I did not know how to cherish sanctity; I had no way of honoring, of giving small voice to the praise of such natural innocence, such generous simplicity. Now I know that a part of me would like to have traveled the world as he traveled it, a jester of burning faith, a fool and a forest prince brimming with the love of God. I would like to have walked his southern world, thanking God for oysters and porpoises, praising God for birdsong and sheet lightning, and seeing God reflected in pools of creekwater and the eyes of stray cats. I would like to have talked to yard dogs and tanagers as if they were my friends and fellow travelers along the sun-tortured highways, intoxicated with a love of God, swollen with charity like a rainbow, in the thoughtless mingling of its hues, connecting two distant fields in its glorious arc. I would like to have seen the world with eyes incapable of anything but wonder, and with a tongue fluent only in praise.

*   *   *

It was almost summer when the strangers arrived by boat in Colleton and began their long, inexorable pursuit of the white porpoise. My mother was baking bread and the suffusion of that exquisite fragrance of the loaves and roses turned our house into a vial of the most harmonious seasonal incense. She took the bread fresh from the oven, then slathered it with butter and honey. We took it steaming in our hands down to the dock to eat, the buttery honey running through our fingers. We attracted the ornery attention of every yellow jacket in our yard, and it took nerve to let them walk on our hands, gorging themselves on the drippings from our bread. They turned our hands into gardens and orchards and hives. My mother brought the lid of a mayonnaise jar full of sugar water down to the dock to appease the yellow jackets and let us eat in peace.

We had almost finished the bread when we saw the boat, *The Amberjack*, bearing Florida registry, move through the channels of the Colleton River. No gulls followed the boat, so we were certain it was not a fishing vessel. It lacked the clean, luxurious lines of a yacht, yet there was a visible crew of six men whose sun-stained burnt-amber color announced them as veteran mariners. We would learn the same day that it was the first boat ever to enter South Carolina waters whose function was to keep fish alive.

The crew of *The Amberjack* were not secretive about their mission and their business in these waters was known all over Colleton late that afternoon. Captain Otto Blair told a reporter from the *Gazette* that the Miami Seaquarium had received a letter from a Colleton citizen, who wished to remain anonymous, that an albino porpoise frequented the waters around Colleton. Captain Blair and his crew planned to capture the porpoise, then transport it back to Miami, where it would be both a tourist attraction and a subject for scientific inquiry. The crew of *The Amberjack* had come to Colleton in the interest of science, as marine biologists, inspired by a report that the rarest creature in the seven seas was a daily sight to the people of the lowcountry.

They may have known all there was to know about porpoises and their habits, but they had badly misjudged the character of the people they would find in the lower part of South Carolina. The citizens of Colleton were about to give them lessons free of charge. A collective shiver of rage passed invisibly through Colleton; the town was watchful and alarmed. The plot to steal Carolina Snow was an aberrant, unspeakable act to us. By accident, they had brought the rare savor of solidarity to our shores. They would feel the full weight of our dissent.

To them the white porpoise was a curiosity of science; to us she was the disclosure of the unutterable beauty and generosity of God among us, the proof of magic, and the ecstasy of art.

The white porpoise was something worthy to fight for.

The Amberjack, mimicking the habits of the shrimpers, moved out early the next morning, but it did not sight the porpoise that day and it set no nets. The men returned to the shrimp dock grim-lipped and eager for rumors about recent sightings of the Snow. They were met with silence.

After the third day, Luke and I met their boat and listened to the crew talk about the long fruitless days on the river, trying to sight the white porpoise. Already, they were feeling the eloquent heft of the town's censure and they seemed eager to talk to Luke and me, to extract any information about the porpoise they could from us.

Captain Blair brought Luke and me on board *The Amberjack* and showed us the holding tank on the main deck where specimens were kept alive until they could reach the aquariums in Miami. He showed us the half mile of nets that they would use to encircle the porpoise. A man's hand could pass easily through the meshing of their nets. The captain was a cordial middle-aged man and the sun had burned deep lines in his face, like tread marks. In a soft, barely discernible voice he told us how they trained a porpoise to eat dead fish after a capture. A porpoise would fast for two weeks or more before it would deign to feed on prey it would ignore in the wild. The greatest danger in the capture of a porpoise was that the animal would become entangled in the nets and drown. Hunting dolphins required a swift and skilled crew to ensure that drowning did not occur. He then showed us the foam rubber mattresses they laid the porpoises on once they got them on board.

"Why don't you just throw them in the pool, Captain?" I asked.

"We do usually, but sometimes we've got sharks in the pool and sometimes a porpoise will hurt himself thrashing around in a pool that small. Often it's better to just lie 'em down on these mattresses and keep splashing 'em with seawater so their skin won't dry out. We move 'em from side to side to keep their circulation right and that's about all there is to it."

"How long can they live out of the water?" Luke asked.

"I don't rightly know, son," the captain answered. "The longest I ever kept one out of the water was five days, but he made it back to Miami just fine. They're hardy creatures. When's the last time you boys spotted Moby in these waters?"

"Moby?" Luke said. "Her name is Snow. Carolina Snow."

"That's what they've named her down at Miami, boys. Moby Porpoise. Some guy in the publicity department came up with that one."

"That's the dumbest name I've ever heard," Luke said.

"It'll bring the tourists running, son," Captain Blair answered.

"Speaking of tourists, a whole boatful spotted the Snow yesterday morning in Charleston Harbor as they were heading out for Fort Sumter," said Luke.

"Are you sure, son?" the captain asked, and one of the crewmen leapt to his feet to hear the rest of the conversation.

"I didn't see it," Luke said, "but I heard it on the radio."

The Amberjack left for Charleston Harbor the next day, cruising the Ashley and the Cooper rivers looking for signs of the white porpoise. For three days they searched the waters around Wappoo Creek and the Elliott Cut before they realized that my brother Luke was a liar. They had also taught my brother how to keep a porpoise alive if the need ever arose.

The call to arms between *The Amberjack* crew and the town did not begin in earnest until the evening in June when the crew tried to capture the white porpoise in full view of the town. They had sighted the Snow in Colleton Sound, in water much too deep to set their nets for a successful capture. All day, they had followed the porpoise, remaining a discreet distance behind her, stalking her with infinite patience until she began moving into the shallower rivers and creeks.

Just as the crew tracked the porpoise, the shrimpers of the town kept issuing reports on the position of *The Amberjack* on their short-wave radios. Whenever the boat changed course, the eyes of the shrimp fleet noted and remarked upon the shift of position, and the airwaves filled up with the voice of shrimpers passing messages from boat to boat, from boat to town. The shrimpers' wives, monitoring their own radios, then got on the telephone to spread the news. *The Amberjack* could not move through county waters without its exact bearings being reported to a regiment of secret listeners.

"*Amberjack* turning into Yemassee Creek," we heard one day through the static of the radio my mother kept above the kitchen sink. "Don't look like they found any Snow today."

"Miami Beach just left Yemassee Creek and appears to be settin' to poke around the Harper Dogleg up by Goat Island."

The town carefully listened to these frequent intelligence reports of the shrimpers. For a week the white porpoise did not appear, and when she did it was one of the shrimpers who alerted the town.

"This is Captain Willard Plunkett and Miami Beach has got the Snow in sight. They are pursuing her up the Colleton River and the crew is preparing the nets on deck. It looks like Snow is heading for a visit to town."

Word passed through the town in the old quicksilvering of rumor, and the prefigured power of that rumor lured the whole town to the river's edge. People kept their eyes on the river and talked quietly. The sheriff pulled into the parking lot behind the bank and monitored the shrimpers' reports. The eyes of the town were fixed on the bend in the Colleton River where *The Amberjack* would make its appearance. That bend was a mile from the point where the river joined three of its sister rivers and bloomed into a sound.

For twenty minutes we waited for *The Amberjack* to make the turn, and when it did a collective groan rose up in the throats of us all. The boat was riding high above the marsh on an incoming tide. One of the crewmen stood on the foredeck with a pair of binoculars trained on the water in front of the boat. He stood perfectly still, rapt and statuesque, his complete immersion a testament to the passion he brought to his task.

Luke, Savannah, and I watched from the bridge, along with several hundred of our neighbors who had gathered to witness the moment of capture of the town's living symbol of good luck. The town was only curious until we saw Carolina Snow make her own luxurious appearance as she rounded the last curve of the river and began her silken, fabulous promenade through the town. She silvered as the sunlight caught her pale fin buttering through the crest of a small wave. In her movement through town she achieved a fragile sublimity, so unaware was she of her vulnerability. Burnished by perfect light, she dazzled us again with her complete and ambient beauty. Her dorsal fin broke the surface again like a white chevron a hundred yards nearer the bridge, and to our surprise, the town cheered spontaneously and the apotheosis of the white porpoise was fully achieved. The ensign of Colleton's wrath unfurled in the secret winds and our status as passive observers changed imperceptibly as a battle cry, unknown to any of us, formed on our lips. All the mottoes and passwords of engagement appeared like fiery graffiti on the armorial bearings of the town's unconscious. The porpoise disappeared again, then rose up, arcing toward the applause that greeted her sounding. She was mysterious and lunar. Her color was a delicate alchemy of lily and mother-of-pearl. The porpoise passed argentine beneath the sun-struck waters. Then we looked up and saw *The Amberjack* gaining ground on the Snow and the crew getting the nets into a small boat they were going to lower into the water.

The town needed a warrior and I was surprised to find him standing beside me.

Traffic jammed the bridge as drivers simply parked their cars and went to the bridge's railing to watch the capture of the porpoise. A truck loaded down with tomatoes from one of Reese Newbury's farms was stuck on the bridge and the driver was leaning on his horn in vain, trying to get the other drivers back into their cars.

I heard Luke whisper to himself, "No. It just ain't right," and he left my side and mounted the back of the truck and began to toss crates of tomatoes down among the crowd. I thought Luke had gone crazy, but suddenly I understood, and Savannah and I bashed a crate of tomatoes open and began to pass them along the railing. The driver got out and screamed for Luke to stop, but Luke ignored him and continued passing the wooden crates down to the outstretched arms of his friends and neighbors. The driver's voice grew more and more frantic as people began taking tire tools from their trunks and splitting the crates wide open. The sheriff's car moved out of the parking lot and headed out toward the Charleston highway on the opposite side of town.

When *The Amberjack* neared the bridge, two hundred tomatoes hit the deck in a green fusillade that put the man with the binoculars to his knees. The tomatoes were hard and green and one of the other crewmen working on the nets was holding his nose near the aft of the boat, blood leaking through his fingers. The second salvo of tomatoes followed soon afterward and the crew scrambled, dazed and insensible, toward the safety of the hold and cabin. A tire tool cracked against a lifeboat and the crowd roared its approval. Boxes of tomatoes were passed down the line, the driver still screaming and not a single soul listening to his pleadings.

The Amberjack disappeared beneath the bridge and two hundred people crossed to the other side in a delirious, headlong rush. When the boat reappeared we showered it with tomatoes again, like archers on high ground pouring arrows on an ill-deployed infantry. Savannah was throwing hard and with accuracy, finding her own good rhythm, her own style. She was screaming with pure pleasure. Luke threw a whole crate of tomatoes and it smashed on the rear deck, sending ruined tomatoes skittering like marbles toward the battened-down hold.

The Amberjack pulled out of range of all but the strongest arms when the porpoise, in a thoughtless gesture of self-preservation, reversed her course and turned back toward the town, passing the boat trailing her on its starboard side. She returned to our applause and our advocacy. We watched her move beneath the waters below the bridge, grizzling the bright waves like some abstract dream of ivory. When the boat made its long, hesitant turn in the river, even more crates of tomatoes were passed through the mob. By this time, even the truck driver had surrendered to whatever mass hysteria had possessed the rest of us and he stood with his arm cocked, holding a tomato, anticipating with the rest of us *The Amberjack's* imminent return. The boat started back for the bridge, then turned abruptly away from us and moved north on the Colleton River as Carolina Snow, the only white porpoise on our planet, moved back toward the Atlantic.

The next day the town council passed a resolution enfranchising Carolina Snow as a citizen of Colleton County and making it a felony for anyone to remove her from county waters. At the same time, the South Carolina state legislature passed a similar law rendering it a felony for anyone to remove genus *Phocaena* or genus *Tursiops* from the waters of Colleton County. In less than twenty-four hours, Colleton County became the only place in the world where it was a crime to capture a porpoise.

Captain Blair went straight to the sheriff's office when he reached the shrimp dock that night and demanded that Sheriff Lucas arrest everyone who had thrown a tomato at *The Amberjack*. Unfortunately, Captain Blair could not provide the sheriff with a single name of even one of the miscreants, and the sheriff, after making several phone calls, could produce four witnesses who would swear in a court of law that no one had been on the bridge when *The Amberjack* passed beneath it.

"Then how did I get a hundred pounds of tomatoes on the deck of my boat?" the captain had asked.

And in a laconic reply that was well received in each Colleton household, the sheriff had answered, "It's tomato season, Captain. Those damn things will grow anywhere."

But the men from Miami quickly recovered their will and developed a new plan for the capture of the porpoise. They kept out of sight of the town and did not enter the main channel of the Colleton River again. They began to haunt the outer territorial limits of the county, waiting for that perfect moment when the Snow would wander out of county waters and beyond the protection of those newly contracted laws. But *The Amberjack* was shadowed by boats from the South Carolina Game and Fish Commission and by a small flotilla of recreational boats commanded by the women and children of the town. Whenever *The Amberjack* picked up the trail of the porpoise, the small crafts would maneuver themselves between the porpoise and the pursuing vessel and slow their motors. *The Amberjack* would try to weave between the boats, but these women and children of Colleton had handled small boats all their lives. They would interfere with the Florida boat's progress until the white porpoise slipped away in the enfolding tides of Colleton Sound.

Each day Luke, Savannah, and I would take our boat and ride up the inland waterway to join the flotilla of resistance. Luke would move the boat in front of *The Amberjack's* bow, ignoring the warning horn, and slow the Whaler by imperceptible degrees. No matter how skillfully Captain Blair maneuvered his boat, he could not pass Luke. Savannah and I had our fishing gear rigged and we trolled for Spanish mackerel as Luke navigated between *The Amberjack* and the white porpoise. Often, the crew would come out to the bow of the ship to threaten and taunt us.

"Hey, kids, get out of our goddamn way before we get pissed off," one crewman yelled.

"Just fishing, mister," Luke would shoot back.

"What're you fishing for?" The man sneered in exasperation.

"We hear there's a white porpoise in these waters," said Luke slowing the motor with a delicate movement of his wrist.

"Is that right, smartass? Well, you're not doing such a good job catching it."

"We're doing as good as you are, mister," Luke answered pleasantly.

"If this were Florida, we'd run right over you."

"It ain't Florida, mister. Or haven't you noticed?" Luke said.

"Hicks," the man screamed.

Luke pulled back the throttle and we slowed almost to a crawl. We could hear the big engines of *The Amberjack* throttling down behind us as the bow of the boat loomed over us.

"He called us hicks," Luke said.

"Me, a hick?" Savannah said.

"That hurts my feelings," I said.

Up ahead, the white porpoise turned into Langford Creek, the alabaster shine in her fin disappearing behind a green flange of marsh. There were three boats waiting at the mouth of the creek ready to intercept *The Amberjack* if it managed to get past Luke.

After thirty days of delay and obstruction, *The Amberjack* left the southern boundaries of Colleton waters and returned to its home base of Miami without the white porpoise. Captain Blair gave a final embittered interview to the *Gazette,* listing the many obstacles the citizens of Colleton had erected to disrupt the mission of *The Amberjack.* Such deterrence, he said, could not be allowed to frustrate the integrity of scientific investigation. But on their last day, he and his crew had taken sniper fire from Freeman's Island and he, as captain, had made the irrevocable decision to discontinue the hunt. The shrimp fleet observed *The Amberjack* as it passed the last barrier islands, maneuvered through the breakers, then turned south, angling toward the open seas.

But *The Amberjack* did not go to Miami. It traveled south for forty miles, then turned into the mouth of the Savannah River, putting in to the shrimp dock at Thunderbolt. There it remained for a week to resupply and to let the passions in Colleton County cool, still monitoring the short-wave radio, following the travels of the white porpoise by listening to the Colleton shrimpers give accurate reports of her soundings. After a week *The Amberjack* left the harbor in Savannah in the middle of the night and turned north out beyond the three-mile limit. They cruised confidently out of sight of the shore-bound shrimp trawlers. They were waiting for one signal to come over the radio.

They had been offshore for three days when they heard the words they had been waiting for.

"There's a submerged log I just netted in Zajac Creek, shrimpers. You boys be careful if you're over this way. Out."

"There's no shrimp in Zajac Creek anyhow, Captain," a voice of another shrimp boat captain answered. "You a long way from home, ain't you, Captain Henry? Out."

"I'll catch the shrimp wherever I can find them, Captain. Out," my father answered, watching the Carolina Snow moving a school of fish toward a sandbar.

Zajac Creek was not in Colleton County and *The Amberjack* turned west and came at full throttle toward the creek, the crew preparing the nets as the shoreline of South Carolina filled the eyes of Captain Blair for the last time. A shrimper from Charleston witnessed the capture of the white porpoise at 1130 hours that morning, saw Carolina Snow panic and charge the encircling nets, saw when she entangled herself, and admired the swiftness and skill of the crew as they got their ropes around her, held her head above the water to keep her from drowning, and maneuvered her into one of the motorboats.

By the time the word reached Colleton, *The Amberjack* was well outside the three-mile limit again, set on a southerly course that would take them into Miami in fifty-eight hours. The bells of the church were rung in protest, an articulation of our impotence and fury. It was as if the river had been deconsecrated, purged of all the entitlements of magic.

"Submerged log" was the code phrase my father had worked out with Captain Blair and the crew of *The Amberjack*. He had agreed to fish the boundary waters at the edge of the county until he sighted the white porpoise moving into the territorial waters of Gibbes County to the north. My father was the anonymous Colletonian who had written the Miami Seaquarium informing them of the presence of an albino porpoise in our county. Two weeks after the abduction of Snow and a week after her picture appeared in the *Colleton Gazette* being lowered into her aquarium tank in her new Miami home, my father received a letter of gratitude from Captain Blair and a check for a thousand dollars as a reward for his assistance.

"I'm ashamed of what you did, Henry," my mother said, barely able to control her temper as my father waved the check in front of us.

"I earned a thousand big ones, Lila, and it was the easiest money I ever made in my life. I wish every porpoise I passed was an albino so I could spend all my time eating chocolate and buying banks."

"If anybody in this town had any guts, they'd go to Miami and set that animal free. You'd better not let anyone in town hear that you're responsible, Henry. Folks are still steaming mad about that porpoise."

"How could you sell our porpoise, Daddy?" Savannah asked.

"Look, sweetie, that porpoise is gonna be in fat city, chowing down on gourmet mackerel and jumping through hoops to make kids happy. Snow doesn't have to worry about a shark the rest of her life. She's retired in Miami. You got to look at it in a positive light."

"I think you've committed a sin that not even God can forgive, Daddy," Luke said darkly.

"You do?" My father answered. "Hey, I never saw 'Property of Colleton' tattooed on her back. I just wrote the Seaquarium that Colleton had a natural phenomenon that could lure in the crowds and they rewarded me for being on my toes."

"They couldn't have found him if you hadn't radioed every time you spotted him in the river," I said.

"I was their liaison officer in the area Look, it's not that great a shrimping season. This thousand bucks is going to put food on the table and clothes on your back. This could pay for a whole year of college for one of you kids."

"I wouldn't eat a bit of food you bought with that money," Luke said. "And I wouldn't wear a pair of Jockey shorts you bought with it either."

"I've been watching the Snow for more than five years now," my mother said. "You once punished Tom for killing a bald eagle, Henry. There's a lot more eagles in the world than white porpoises."

"I didn't kill the porpoise, Lila. I delivered it to a safe harbor where it will be free of all fear. I look upon myself as the hero of this affair."

"You sold Snow into captivity," my mother said.

"They're going to make her a circus porpoise," Savannah added.

"You betrayed yourself and your sources," Luke said. "If it was a businessman, I could understand. Some low-life creepy Jaycee with shiny hair. But a shrimper, Dad. A shrimper selling Snow for money."

"I sell shrimp for money, Luke," my father shouted.

"Not the same," Luke said. "You don't sell what you can't replace."

"I saw twenty porpoises in the river today."

"And I promise you, Daddy, not one of them was white. None of them was special," Luke said.

"Our family is the reason they captured the Snow," said Savannah. "It's like being the daughter of Judas Iscariot, only I bet I'd have liked Judas a lot better."

"You shouldn't have done what you did, Henry," my mother said. "It'll bring bad luck."

"I couldn't have had any worse luck than I've had," my father answered. "Anyway, it's done. There's nothing anyone can do about it now."

"I can do something about it," said Luke.

Three weeks later, in the languorous starry dark, when my parents were asleep and we could hear the soft chaos of my father's snoring, Luke whispered a plan to us. It should not have surprised us, but years later, Savannah and I would talk and wonder about the exact hour when our older brother turned from a passionate, idealistic boy into a man of action. Both of us were terrified and exhilarated by the boldness of his proposal, but neither of us wanted any part of it. But Luke continued to urge us quietly until we found ourselves imprisoned by the magnetic originality of his gentle eloquence. His decision was already made and he spent half the night enlisting us as recruits in his first real dance on the wild side. Ever since the night we watched him facing the tiger alone in the barn, we had known Luke was brave, but now we were faced with the probability that Luke was also reckless.

Three mornings later, after Luke had made exhaustive preparations, we were on Highway 17, thundering south, with Luke stepping hard on the accelerator, and the radio turned up high. Ray Charles was singing "Hit the Road, Jack" and we were singing it along with him. We were drinking beer iced down in a cooler and had the radio tuned to the Big Ape in Jacksonville as we shot across the Eugene Talmadge Memorial Bridge in Savannah. We slowed up at the toll gate and Luke handed the old man who was doling out tickets a dollar for a round tripper.

"You gonna do a little shopping in Savannah, kids?" the old man asked.

"No, sir," Luke replied, "we're on our way to Florida to steal us a porpoise."

Shelby Foote

from *The Civil War: A Narrative*

Pierre Gustave Toutant Beauregard was as flamboyant by nature as by name, and over the course of the past two years this quality, coupled all too often with a readiness to lay down the sword and take up the pen in defense of his reputation with the public, had got him into considerable trouble with his superiors, who sometimes found it difficult to abide his Creole touchiness off the field of battle for the sake of his undoubted abilities on it. Called "Old Bory" by his men, though he was not yet forty-five, the Hero of Sumter had twice been relieved of important commands, first in the East, where he had routed McDowell's invasion attempt at Manassas, then in the West, where he had saved his badly outnumbered army by giving Halleck the slip at Corinth, and now he was back on the scene of his first glory in Charleston harbor. Here, as elsewhere, he saw his position as the hub of the wheel of war. Defying Union sea power, Mobile on the Gulf and Wilmington, Savannah, and Charleston on the Atlantic remained in Confederate hands, and of these four it was clear at least to Beauregard that the one the Federals coveted most was the last, variously referred to in their journals as "the hotbed of treachery," "the cradle of secession," and "the nursery of disunion." Industrious as always, the general was determined that this proud South Carolina city should not suffer the fate of his native New Orleans, no matter what force the Yankees brought against it. Conducting frequent tours of inspection and keeping up as usual a voluminous correspondence—a steady stream of requisitions for more guns and men, more warships and munitions, nearly all of which were returned to him regretfully unfilled—he only relaxed from his duties when he slept, and even then he kept a pencil and a note pad under his pillow, ready to jot down any notion that came to him in the night. "Carolinians and Georgians!" he exhorted by proclamation. "The hour is at hand to prove your devotion to your country's cause. Let all able-bodied men, from the seaboard to the mountains, rush to arms. Be not exacting in the choice of weapons; pikes and scythes will do for exterminating your enemies, spades and shovels for protecting your friends. To arms, fellow citizens! Come share with us our dangers, our brilliant success, or our glorious death."

Two approaches to Charleston were available to the Federals. They could make an amphibious landing on one of the islands or up one of the inlets to the south, then swing northeastward up the mainland to move upon the city from the rear; or they could enter through the harbor itself, braving the massed batteries for the sake of a quick decision, however bloody. Twice already they had tried the former method, but both times—first at Secessionville, three months before Beauregard's return from the West in mid-September, and again at Pocotaligo, one month after he reassumed command—they had been stopped and flung back on their naval support before they could gather momentum. This time he thought it probable that they would attempt the front-door approach, using their new flotilla of vaunted ironclads to spearhead the attack. If so, they were going to find they had taken on a good deal more than they expected; for the harbor defenses had been greatly improved during the nearly two years that had elapsed since the war first opened here. Fort Moultrie, Castle Pinckney, and Fort Sumter, respectively on Sullivan's Island, off the mouth of the Cooper River, and opposite the entrance to the bay, had not only been strengthened, each in its own right, but now they were supported by other fortifications constructed at intervals along the beaches and connected by a continuous line of signal stations, making it possible for a central headquarters, itself transferrable, to direct and consolidate their fire. First Beauregard, then Pemberton, and now Beauregard again—both accomplished engineers and artillerists, advised moreover by staffs of specialists as expert as themselves—had applied all their skill and knowledge to make the place as nearly impregnable as military science and Confederate resources would allow. A total of seventy-seven guns of various calibers now frowned from their various embrasures, in addition to which the harbor channels were thickly sown with torpedoes and other obstructions, such as floating webs of hemp designed to entangle rudders and snarl propellers. Not content with this, the sad-eyed little Creole had not hesitated to dip into his limited supply of powder in order to improve the marksmanship of his cannoneers with frequent target practice. Like his idol Napolean he believed in a lucky star, but he was leaving as little as possible to chance; for which reason he had set marker buoys at known ranges in the bay, with the corresponding elevations chalked on the breeches of the guns. As a last-ditch measure of desperation, to be employed if all else failed, he encouraged the organization of a unit known as the Tigers, made up of volunteers whose assignment was to hurl explosives down the smokestacks of such enemy ships as managed to break through the ring of fire and approach the fortress walls of the city docks. The ironclads might indeed be invincible; some said so, some said not; but one thing was fairly certain. The argument was likely to be settled on the day their owners tested them in Charleston harbor.

This was not to say that Beauregard had abandoned all notion of assuming the offensive, however limited his means. He had at his disposal two homemade rams, the *Palmetto State* and the *Chicora,* built with funds supplied by the South Carolina legislature and the Ladies' Gunboat Fair. The former mounted an 80-pounder rifle aft and an 8-inch shell gun on each broadside, while the latter had two 9-inch smoothbores and four rifled 32-pounders. Both were balky and slow, with cranky, inadequate engines and armor improvised from boiler plate and railroad iron, but as January drew to a close the general was determined to put them to the test by challenging the blockade squadron off the Charleston bar. Orders were handed Flag Officer Duncan Ingraham on the 30th, instructing him to make the attempt at dawn of the following day. Beauregard meanwhile had in mind a more limited offensive of his own, to be launched against the 9-gun screw steamer *Isaac Smith*, which had been coming up the Stono River almost nightly to shell the Confederate camps on James and John's islands. That night he lay in wait for her with batteries of field artillery, allowed her to pass unchallenged, then took her under fire as she came back down. The opening volley tore off her stack, stopped her engines, riddled her lifeboats, and killed eight of her crew. Her captain quickly surrendered himself and his ship and the 94 survivors, including 17 wounded. Repaired and rechristened, the *Smith* became the *Stono* and served under that name as part of Charleston's miniature defense squadron, the rest of which was already on its way across the bay, under cover of darkness, in accordance with Ingraham's orders to try his hand at lifting the Union blockade.

Palmetto State and *Chicora*, followed by three steam tenders brought along to tow them back into the harbor in case their engines failed, were over the bar and among the wooden-walled blockaders by first light. Mounting a total of one hundred guns, the Federal squadron included the 1200-ton sloop-of-war *Housatonic,* two gunboats, and seven converted merchantmen. A lookout aboard one of these last, the 9-gun steamer *Mercedita,* was the first to spot the misty outline of an approaching vessel. "She has black smoke!" he shouted. "Watch, man the guns! Spring the rattle! Call all hands to quarters!" This brought the captain out on deck, clad only in a pea jacket. When he too spotted the stranger, nearer now, he cupped his hands about his mouth and called out: "Steamer, ahoy! You will be into us! What steamer is that?" It was the *Palmetto State*, but for a time she did not deign to answer. Then: "Halloo!" her skipper finally replied, and with that the ram put her snout into the quarter of the *Mercedita* and fired her guns. Flames went up from the crippled steamer. "Surrender," the rebel captain yelled up, "or I'll sink you!" The only answer was a cloud of oily smoke shot through with steam. "Do you surrender?" he repeated. This brought the reply, "I can make no resistance; my boiler is destroyed!" "Then do you surrender?" "Yes!" So the *Palmetto State* backed off, withdrawing her snout, and turned to go to the help of the *Chicora,* which meanwhile had been serving the 10-gun sidewheel steamer *Keystone State* in much the same fashion. Riddled and aflame, the Federal hauled down her flag to signify surrender, then ran it up again and limped out to sea as the two rams moved off in the opposite direction. At the far end of the line, the *Housatonic* and the gunboats held their station, thinking the racket had been provoked by a blockade runner venturing out. By full daylight the two improvised ironclads were back in Charleston harbor, their crews accepting the cheers of a crowd collected on the docks.

Beauregard was elated by the double coup. Quick to claim that the blockade had been lifted, at least for a time, he took the French and Spanish consuls out to witness the truth of his words that "the outer harbor remained in the full possession of the two Confederate rams. Not a Federal sail was visible, even with spyglasses." Next day the blockaders were back again, presumably too vigilant now to permit him to risk another such attempt, but he did not admit that this detracted in the slightest from the brilliance of the exploit. He bided his time, still improving his defenses for the all-out attack which he believed was about to be launched. "Already six monitors. . . are in the waters of my department, concentrating about Port Royal, and transports with troops are still arriving from the North," he reported in mid-March. "I believe the drama will not much longer be delayed; the curtain will soon rise." Three more weeks went past before his prediction was fulfilled. Then on Monday, April 6, the day after Easter—it was also the first anniversary of Shiloh and within a week of the second anniversary of the opening of the war in this same harbor— not six but nine brand-new Union ironclads, some single- and some doubled-turreted, crossed the Charleston bar and dropped anchor in the channel, bringing their great 15-inch guns to bear on the forts and batteries Beauregard had

would "go to the roof on a hot summer day, talk to half a dozen degenerates, descend to the basement, drink tepid water full of iron rust, climb to the roof again, and repeat the process at intervals until she was fagged out, then go to bed with everything shut tight." Individual reactions to this monotony, which was scarcely relieved by an unbroken diet of moldy beans, stale biscuits, and sour pork, varied from fisticuffs and insubordination to homosexuality and desertion. Officers fraternized ashore with Negro women, a practice frowned on by the Navy, and mess crews specialized in the manufacture of outlaw whiskey distilled from almost any substance that would ferment in the southern heat—as in fact nearly everything would, including men. Rheumatism and scurvy kept the doctors busy, along with breakbone fever, hemorrhoids, and damage done by knuckles. These they could deal with, after their fashion, but there was no medicine for the ills of the spirit, brought on the strain of monotony, poor food, and unhealthy living conditions, which produced much longer casualty lists than did rebel shells or torpedoes. "Give me a discharge, and let me go home," a distraught but articulate coal heaver begged his skipper after months of duty outside Charleston. "I am a poor weak, miserable, nervous, half crazy boy. . . . Everything jars upon my delicate nerves."

Inside the harbor, Beauregard was about as deep in the doldrums as were the blue-clad sailors beyond the bar. Disappointed that he had not been ordered west to resume command of the army Bragg had inherited from him, privately he was telling friends that his usefulness in the war had ended, and he predicted defeat for the Confederacy no later than spring or summer. He gave as the cause for both of these disasters "the persistent inability and obstinacy of our rulers." Primarily he meant Davis, of whom he said: "The curse of God must have been on our people when we chose him out of so many noble sons of the South, who would have carried us safely through this Revolution."

In addition to the frustration proceeding from his belief that presidential animosity, as evidenced by slights and

snubs, had cost him the western command he so much
wanted, the Creole's gloom was also due to the apparent
failure of a new weapon he had predicted would
accomplish, unassisted, the lifting of the Union blockade by
the simple process of sinking the blockaders. There had
arrived by rail from Mobile in mid-August, disassembled
and loaded on two flatcars, a cigar-shaped metal vessel
about thirty feet in length and less than four feet wide and
five feet deep. Put back together and launched in Charleston
harbor, she resembled the little *David*-class torpedo boats
whose low silhouette made them hard for enemy lookouts
to detect. Actually, though, she had been designed to carry
this advantage a considerable step further, in that she was
intended to travel under as well as on the water, and thus
present no silhouette at all. She was, in short, the world's
first submarine. Christened the *H. L. Hunley* for one of her
builders, who had come from Alabama with her to instruct
the Carolinians in her use, she was propeller-driven but had
no engine, deriving her power from her eight-man crew,
posted at cranks along her drive shaft, which they turned on
orders from her coxswain-captain. Water was let into
ballast tanks to lower her until she was nearly awash; then
her two hatches were bolted tight from inside, and as she
moved forward the skipper took her down by depressing a
pair of horizontal fins, which were also used to level and
raise her while in motion. To bring her all the way up, force
pumps ejected the water from her tanks, decreasing her
specific gravity; or in emergencies her iron keel could be
jettisoned in sections by disengaging the bolts that held it
on, thus causing her to bob corklike to the surface. A glass
port in the forward hatch enabled the steersman to see
where he was going while submerged, and interior light was
supplied by candles, which also served to warn of the
danger of asphyxiation by guttering when the oxygen ran
low. Practice dives in Mobile Bay had demonstrated that the
Hunley could stay down about two hours before coming up
for air, and she had proved her effectiveness as an offensive
weapon by torpedoing and sinking two flatboats there. Her

method of attack was quite as novel as her design. Towing at the end of a 200-foot line a copper cylinder packed with ninety pounds of powder and equipped with a percussion fuze, she would dive as she approached her target, pass completely under it, then elevate a bit and drag the towline across the keel of the enemy ship until the torpedo made contact and exploded, well astern of the submarine, whose crew would be cranking hard for a getaway, still underwater, and a return to port for a new torpedo to use on the next victim. Beauregard looked the strange craft over, had her workings explained to him by Hunley, and predicted an end to the Yankee blockade as soon as her newly volunteered crew learned to handle her well enough to launch their one-boat offensive against the U.S. Navy.

Such high hopes were often modified by sudden disappointments, and the *Hunley* was no exception to the general application of the rule. Certain drawbacks were soon as evident here as they had been at Mobile earlier: one being that she was a good deal easier to take down than she was to bring back up, particularly if something went wrong with her machinery, and something often did. She was, in fact—as might have been expected from her combination of primitive means and delicate functions—accident-prone. On August 29, two weeks after her arrival, she was moored to a steamer tied to the Fort Johnson dock, resting her "engine" between dives, when the steamer unexpectedly got underway and pulled her over on her side. Water poured in through the open hatches, front and rear, and she went down so fast that only her skipper and two nimble seamen managed to get out before she hit the bottom. This was a practical demonstration that none of the methods providing for her return to the surface by her own devices would work unless she retained enough air to lift the weight of her iron hull; a started seam or a puncture, inflicted by chance or by enemy action while she was submerged, would mean her end, or at any rate the end of the submariners locked inside her. If this had not been clear before, it certainly was now. Still, there was no difficulty in finding more volunteers to man her, and Hunley himself, as soon as she had been raised and cleared of muck and corpses, petitioned Beauregard to let him take command. He did so on September 22 and began at once a period of intensive training to familiarize his new crew with her quirks. This lasted just over three weeks. On October 15, after making a series of practice dives in the harbor, she "left the wharf at 9.25 A.M. and disappeared at 9.35. As soon as she sank," the official post-mortem continued, "air bubbles were seen to rise to the surface of the water, and from this fact it is supposed the hole at the top of the boat by which the men entered was not properly closed." That was the end of Hunley and all aboard, apparently because someone had been careless. It was also thought to be the end of the vessel that bore his name, for she was nine fathoms down. A diver found her a few days later, however, and she was hauled back up again. Beauregard was on hand when her hatch lids were removed. "The spectacle was indescribably ghastly," he later reported with a shudder of remembrance. "The unfortunate men were contorted into all sorts of horrible attitudes, some clutching candles. . . others lying in the bottom tightly grappled together, and the blackened faces of all presented the expression of their despair and agony."

Despite this evidence of the grisly consequences, a third crew promptly volunteered for service under George E. Dixon, an army lieutenant who transferred from an Alabama regiment to the *Hunley* and was also a native of Mobile. Trial runs were renewed in early November, but the method of attack was not the same. Horrified by what he had seen when the unlucky boat was raised the second time, Beauregard had ordered that she was never again to function underwater, and she was equipped accordingly with a spar torpedo like the one her rival *David* had used against the *Ironsides*, ten days before she herself went into her last intentional dive. A surface vessel now like all the rest, except that she was still propelled by muscle power, she continued for the next three months to operate out of her base on Sullivan's Island, sometimes by day, sometimes by night. But conditions were never right for an attack; tide and winds conspired against her, and at times the under-powered craft was in danger of being swept out to sea because of the exhaustion of the men along her crankshaft. Finally though, in the early dusk of February 17, with a near-full moon to steer her by, a low-lying fog to screen her, and a strong-running ebb tide to increase her normal four-knot speed, Dixon maneuvered the *Hunley* out of the harbor and set a course for the Federal fleet, which lay at anchor in the wintry darkness, seven miles away.

At 8.45 the acting master of the 1200-ton screw sloop *Housatonic*—more than two hundred feet in length and mounting a total of nine guns, including an 11-inch rifle—saw what he thought at first was a "plank moving [towards us] in the water" about a hundred yards away. By the time he knew better and ordered "the chain slipped, engine backed, and all hands called to quarters" in an attempt to take evasive action and bring his guns to bear, it was too late; "The torpedo struck forward of the mizzen mast, on the starboard side, in line with the magazine." Still trembling from the shock, the big warship heeled to port and went down stern first. Five of her crew were killed or drowned, but fortunately for the others the water was shallow enough for them to save themselves by climbing the rigging, from which they were plucked by rescuers before the stricken vessel went to pieces.

There were no Confederate witnesses, for there were no Confederate survivors; the *Hunley* had made her first and last attack and had gone down with her victim, either because her hull had been cracked by the force of the explosion, only twenty feet away, or else because she was drawn into the vortex of the sinking *Housatonic*. In any case, searchers found what was left of the sloop and the submarine years later, lying side by side on the sandy bottom, just beyond the bar.

William Price Fox

COLEY MOKE

In order to get back to Coley Moke's place outside Monck's Corner, South Carolina, you have to run down a Peevy or a Taylor or another Moke and make him take you back. Charley, Jim and I got us a Taylor and went back one day.

There were too many dogs in the yard to count but there were four runty gray pigs who'd been talked into believing they were hounds. When we petted the dogs we had to scratch the pigs. It was hot and the dogs were panting so Coley led us into his front room. There was a bed and a wood stove in the room and nothing else. No tables, no chairs, no lights; it was the only room in the house.

"Make yourself to home."

And then, "You bring any funny books?"

Charley pulled a roll out of his back pocket. Coley thumbed through them and said, "Fine."

He emptied a Mason jar of corn whisky into a water bucket, placed a tin dipper in the bucket and set it down on the floor.

Three of the older dogs got up on the bed with Coley. One of the little razorbacks tried to make it but couldn't.

We sat down against the wall near the bucket and when we started drinking, Coley started talking.

"See this dog here. . . his name's Brownie."

He was a long thin brown dog; his eyes were closed.

"Well, when I tell him the law is coming he picks up that steel bucket and runs out into the swamp, and I mean he doesn't come back until I call him. Couple of the others would do that for me but they got so they were spilling too much.

"Brownie here knows I got me only one small still going now and he don't waste a drop. One old timer—Trig—he's gone now—would take it out there by the creek. He was a mess. He'd drink a while and then swim a while and then sleep until he was sober and then start in all over again. . . ."

251

Charley nudged Jim and Jim nudged me. We drank some more.

Coley laughed and rasseled the head of the red bone hound on his left. "This here's Bob, and they don't come any smarter than him. One day he convinced these Federal men he would lead them back to the house. And they followed him. He led them poor bastards between the quicksand and the 'gators and showed them every cottonmouth moccasin in the swamp. He got them so scared they were just begging him to lead them back on the road—any road. They promised him steaks and that they'd never raid me again. Well, sir, Bob kept them going until it was dark and after he walked them over a couple long 'gators that looked like logs he finally put them up on the road. It was the right road but it was about twelve miles from their car. Old Bob sure had himself some fun that night. He told Brownie here all about it and Brownie told me."

Charley took a big drink; Jim and I took a big drink. There was more. About how Spot and Whip would team up on a moccasin or a rattlesnake and while one faked the snake out of his coil the other would grab him by the tail and pop his head off like a buggy whip.

Jim said, "Man, that is some dog to do that."

Coley began to drink a little more and when he started talking about his wife his voice changed. "Yeah, I suspect I miss that old gal. Wonder what she looks like now. She was something, all right. Up at dawn, cook a first-class meal and then go out and outplow any man and mule in the county and every Sunday, rain or shine we had white linen on the table and apple pie. . . ain't nothing I like better than apple pie.

"Sometimes we didn't speak for a week. It was nice then, real nice. As long as I kept quiet and minded the still and my dogs everything was fine. But we started talking and then the first thing you know we were arguing and then she began to throw the dogs up in my face. Let's see. . . it was right in the middle of the Compression. Right here in this room. She had to go and try and turn me against my dogs. . . . Well, the Compression hit us bad—real bad. I had no money, no copper for the still, and no way of getting any up. I was doing a lot of fishing and hunting then. . . . Yeah, right here. . . oh, it was different then. There were four cane chairs and a dresser and a mirror from Sears Roebuck against that wall, and there was a couple insurance calendars from the Metropolitan Life Insurance Company hanging over there."

He took a big drink. The light was fading but we could still see his face. A bull alligator deep in the swamp rumbled once and decided it was too early.

"Yeah, I was lying here with old Sport. He was Brownie here's father. He was young then and high-spirited and, you know, sensitive. When Emma Louise got up from her chair and came over he must have seen it in her face. They never had gotten along. He crawled off the bed and went outside. If I live to be two hundred, I'll never forget those words. . . .

"She said, 'Coley Moke, you are the sorriest man on God's green earth. Here it is almost winter, we got no money, we got no food, and you just lay there and stare up at that leaky roof. And what's more, you've gone out and taken our last hog and traded it for another dog.'"

Coley smiled and leaned forward. Then his face set mean and hard. "'Emma, Emma Louise.' I said, 'if I told you once I told you a hundred times. . . . But since you seem to not hear I'm going to tell you one more time. I traded that hog and I got me a dog for the plain and simple reason that I can't go running no fox with no hog.'

"Come one men, drink her up. When that's gone there's more where it came from. And if we get too drunk to walk we can send my old buddy Brownie here."

He rasseled the dog's head. "How about it, boy, what d'you say?"

We drank until it was time to eat. Coley lighted a fire in the wood stove and warmed up some red-horse bread. He served it on folded newspapers and with the little light from the stove we sat back down where we had been sitting and ate.

Later he chased the two pigs outside and we heard their hooves clopping down the porch and on the steps. The pigs slept under the house with the dogs. Colcy said they generally got to bed a littler earlier than the dogs.

An owl sounded, a bull alligator answered, and the moon glided out of the tall cypress trees in the swamp and the room began to streak with silver light. We slept. . . .

It was raining in the morning and all the dogs and hogs were in the living room. Spot, Trig and Buckles were on the bed with Coley. The two hogs were under the unlit stove and the rest of the dogs were against the wall. Charley, Jim and I were sitting on the floor.

Coley was talking. "Bob's father—that was Earl Brown— he's been dead a long time now. Let's see, next month it'll be eleven years. It doesn't seem like it was that long ago. Eleven years, man, but don't it drive by?"

Charley took a drink and handed me the dipper. I took one and gave it to Jim.

"Buried him out on that hill knuckle in front. He always liked it up there. Some mornings I'd wake up and look out and there he'd be sitting up there just as pretty as you please. All the other dogs would still be sleeping. But not Earl Brown, he was always the first one up.

"He wasn't like the others. Now I ain't saying the others weren't smart, but it was a different kind of smartness. You know how it is with hounds. They'll do anything you tell them. But there's a lot of them that just don't have any initiative. Now that's right where Earl Brown was different. Earl Brown was always trying to better himself, trying to improve himself, you might say.

"I could tell it when he was a pup. The other dogs would fall all over one another getting at the food and when they'd get to it they'd bolt it down like they hadn't eaten in a month. But not Earl Brown, no sir. He'd wait and let them take their places at the trough. Then he'd walk over, slow-like, and commence eating. He wouldn't rush. He even chewed his food longer."

Coley got down off the bed and took a drink. He studied the bottom of the empty dipper.

"Yeah, they don't make any finer dog than Earl Brown."

He put the dipper in the bucket of whisky on the floor

and sat back down on the bed.

"That dog was a loner, too. The others would all sleep in the wood box. Sometimes there'd be as many as seventeen all flopped in there on top of one another. But not Earl Brown. From the day that scutter was weaned he slept by himself outside the box.

"I guess I miss Earl Brown as much or more than any of them. He was a marvelous dog, all right. Marvelous, that's what he was.

"I told you how he'd sit up on the hill early in the mornings. Well, he wasn't out there lapping the dew off the grass for nothing. He was working on something.

"Boys, I want you to know what that dog was working on. I wouldn't tell this to just anyone else. They'd say that fool Coley Moke has gone slap out of his mind, living out there with all them dogs.

"First of all I wouldn't have known a thing if it hadn't been for the chickens. But they started a lot of noise during the night. I thought a weasel or a snake was getting at them so I started watching from the window. It wasn't no weasel and it wasn't no snake. It was two foxes. Big red ones, long as dogs, and five times smarter. But those foxes didn't go inside the coop. They just stood there. They must have been there five minutes and then I thought I saw another fox. I looked again and you know who it was?

"It was Earl Brown. Well sir, those two red foxes and Earl Brown stood outside that chicken coop for ten minutes. My other dogs were all inside the house and they were going crazy. The poor hens were clucking and screeching for help. I didn't know what to do. Finally I heard Earl Brown growl and then the next thing you know the three of them ran off into the woods.

"I kind of figured Earl Brown was setting those foxes up for me to shoot, so I decided to wait until he gave me some kind of sign. Well, next night it happened again. Same time, right around three o'clock they came out of the woods. Well, they had their little meeting right outside the coop and then they ran off again.

"Of course, during all this I had to make sure Earl Brown got out at night and my other dogs stayed in. That took some doing. The others all knew that Earl Brown was getting special treatment and they got mad as hell. And they smelled those foxes on him and they wouldn't have a thing to do with him.

"But Earl Brown didn't care what they thought about him. He even liked it better that way. But he got to looking peaked and red-eyed. Like he wasn't getting any sleep. I put a couple extra eggs in his rations. That boy was on a rough schedule. He'd go to sleep around ten with the others but he'd be up at two and off with his friends.

"Things began looking bad. My dogs were giving me a fit to be let out at night. I wasn't getting any sleep. And those hens. Lord, those poor hens were going right out of their minds. They got so nervous they were laying eggs at midnight. The rooster worried so he began losing weight and limping. He got so he wouldn't even crow. They were one sad-looking sight in the mornings. Wouldn't eat, couldn't sleep. I mean it got so bad them hens were stumbling around and bumping into one another.

"I decided to give Earl Brown two more nights and then end it. I was determined to shoot those damn foxes and get my chickens back on some decent schedule.

"And that was the very night it happened. . . .

"Earl Brown stepped aside and let one of those foxes go into the coop. Those poor chickens were so scared and tired. I guess they were relieved when that fox walked in and picked one out. He took a Rhode Island Red. That hen didn't even squawk. Just hung there in his mouth and across that red fox's back like she was glad it was all over. Those chickens slept the rest of the night. It was the first good night's sleep they'd had in three weeks."

Coley stopped. "You boys ain't drinking."

Charley said, "I just this minute put the dipper down."

Coley drank again and hunched himself back up between the dogs. "Well, I figured that was the end for Earl Brown. I saw where he had thrown in with the foxes and I knew it would be best if I shot him and foxes. I had it worked out in my mind that those three were going to take a chicken a night until I was stripped clean. So I loaded up my four-ten over and under and got the four-cell flashlight ready and waited. I was praying Earl Brown wouldn't run off that night. But two o'clock came and he sneaked out and lit out through the woods. . . . You know what happened?"

"What?"

"They never showed up."

"Never?"

"Never. . . but still every night Earl Brown would leave the house at two. About a week later, I followed that dog out through the woods. I was downwind and I stood behind a big sweet gum and watched them.

"They were out in this little field and the moon was good and I could see everything. They were playing some kind of game out there in that moonlight. The foxes would run and Earl Brown would chase them in little circles. Then the foxes would chase him back and forth. And then it all ended and Earl Brown started back through the woods home.

"Mind you, I said 'started back.' Because the minute that rascal figured those foxes figured he was going home, he doubled back. I tell you that was one funny sight. Here I'm behind one tree and Earl Brown is behind another tree and we're both watching those foxes.

"They were running around in circles and making little barking sounds like they were laughing. I tell you, I don't know when I've been so fascinated. I shore wish I had had me a camera about then.

"All of a sudden it hits me what was going on. Old Earl Brown was picking up the foxes' secret about running. That rascal had paid them foxes to show him something. He'd paid them with that Rhode Island Red and now he was checking on the foxes to make sure he'd got his money's worth. Well, by God, I thought I knew something about hounds and foxes but I was shore learning something that night standing out behind that sweet gum tree. And Earl Brown not twenty yards away tipping his head around his tree. . . man, that was one funny night.

"Well, that running secret ain't easy and Earl Brown had to go back several nights. And every night he went, I went. It took him, all told, about three weeks but I'll be dogged if he didn't finally get it."

Coley got off the bed and squatted down by us. He took another drink and we followed. He spoke lower now.

"I don't want them dogs hearing the rest of this. They'll get out and try it out and wind up breaking their necks. It's too tricky. As smart as Earl Brown was he had a hard time learning it. He took a few pretty bad falls himself before he got it."

Coley stopped and let the bait trail. . . .

Charley rose to it. "Learned what, Coley?"

Coley spoke even lower than before. "How to run like a fox, that's what. Oh, that was one fine dog. He set his mind to it and he learned it. He was marvelous."

Charley was getting jumpy. "What did he learn, Coley? What did he learn?"

"Don't rush me, boy. You don't know much about foxes, do you, boy?"

"I guess not."

"Well you know a fox can outrun any living dog if he feels like it, don't you?"

"Yes."

"Usually they don't feel like it. They're too smart to just do straight running. Most of the time they work in pairs and they get the dogs so confused they don't know what's going on. They'll be running one way and then all of a sudden the other fox will pop up from another direction. Hell, they have signals. Sometimes they'll run the dogs through briar patches, skunk cabbage, anything, and lots of times round and round in the same circles. A good fox will give a pack of dogs a fit. Lot of times a fox will hide and when the dog pack comes by he'll jump in and run along with them. He'll be barking and carrying on and having himself a marvelous time and the dogs won't know a thing.

"Oh, them red foxes are smart. And a good running fox

on a straightaway, I mean, no cover, no nothing, can burn a dog down to the ground. He can run that hound right into the ground and he'll be as fresh as when he started. He won't even be breathing hard. You think back. You ever seen a tired fox? No. They don't get tired. And it's all because they got this secret way of running."

Coley was whispering. He really didn't want the dogs to hear. "It's like this. When a fox runs he only uses three legs. Next time you see one running, you watch. You gotta look close, those reds are smart devils. They keep it secret and they only do it when they're off by themselves or when they get in trouble. Kind of emergency you might say."

Charley said, "Whoa now. What do you mean three legs?"

"They rotate, that's what they do. They rotate. They run on three and keep rotating. That way they always got one resting. That's why they give the impression that they're limping all the time and got that little hop in their run."

"Coley," Charley said, "I just can't believe that one."

Coley jumped up and walked across the room twice. He raised his hand. "The Lord will snatch out my tongue and strike me dead right here and now if that ain't the God's truth."

It continued raining. . . and the Lord didn't make a move. . . .

MONCK'S CORNER

What I remembered most about Monck's Corner, South Carolina, is leaving it. . . .

Two were in the middle of the road, three were lying alongside the fence by the tobacco field, and Fred Peevy and Dean Brown were sitting down in the drain ditch eating sardines and Zu-Zus and drinking corn out of a half-gallon Mason jar.

Floyd Lovett stopped the car: "They get mad if you don't drink with them."

Dean handed Floyd the jar and he drank. He tried to speak but couldn't. He tried to cough but couldn't. He gasped, wiped his eyes, then closed them, wiped his mouth, shook his head and finally gasped, "Jesus, what is it?"

Dean handed the jar from Floyd to me "No name, ain't got no name."

Floyd said, "It ain't rub, is it?"

Dean said, "Man, you know I'd never give you any rub."

I took a drink and waited. It didn't taste as bad as it smelled, but I could feel the headaches moving down my arms and legs and inching around to the small of my back.

Dean was saying, "Dollar and a half a half gallon and we get a dime deposit back for the jar."

Floyd said, "Dollar and a half. . . let me see it again."

He closed his eyes and drank. He smiled and said, "Yes sir, it appears I've been too hasty. That stuff's got a nice taste. Unique, that's what it is."

So we sat down there in that drain ditch and drank and spat and lied and ate Zu-Zus until it was dark. A breeze came up around seven, and later someone said: "Al's Place. . . ."

Bass fiddle, Hawaiian guitar, long-necked banjo, all-night square and round dancing. Mill workers, spinners, weavers, sweepers, wipers. Print dresses, straw hats, steel-heeled brogans. Room-shaking breakdowns, stomps, swamp shouts. No neckties, no socks, white or red Roy Rogers' scarves with cows' skulls or pairs of dice as slipknots. Thirty-five cents corkage. Room vibration keeps the bead bubbling on the 120-proof whisky standing in marked jars along the wall. Tall fellow on bass takes drink out of Mason jar. Needs both hands to hold jar steady. Uses back of hand for chaser.

We begin to dance. . . four hands across, promenade, all join hands, follow the leader. Intermission.

Catfish stew served in tin pie plates. Hot-peppery. Chase stew with cold beer, chase beer with 120-proof and back to stew.

Dean says stuff is as hot as a weasel's ass in a pepper

patch.

Sounds of fight outside.

Owner locks doors so no one can get out. No windows, can't see, don't care.

Music whangs up again. Return to dancing. . . new caller. . . tall thin ugly man, lips like two dimes pressed together, loud, nasal. Banjo solo. . . same chords only louder, flatter, madder, worse. . . more stew, more 120-proof, more dancing. . . hot, cold flashes. . . .

Palpitations. Lean against wall, can't understand it. It might pass. . . it might not. Head seems to be clamped in some gigantic squeezing machine.

Dean comes over, slaps me on the back. "Tell the truth, now, when you had so much fun?"

I can't think. It wouldn't have mattered because I couldn't speak. Dragged out onto floor. . . promenade. . . become bird in the cage.

Sneak out back door, pass table where catfish were cleaned, hold onto tree, to stomach, to head, try to vomit smoothly. . . pine needles, oak leaves, cool breezes. Lie down carefully and stare up through small trees at the autumn moon and swear I'll call Greyhound and see how much it costs to go north.

Harlan Greene

from *Why We Never Danced The Charleston*

I was born in Savannah but spent most of my life in Charleston. Still this city never really accepted me. I was too nouveau, to outré for it; was born too far away to be taken seriously. I wish, though, that before I started on this journey, someone had told me that only Charlestonians themselves ever really arrive here. I would have gone back to Savannah, or done things differently. I see now that I was but a trespasser all along. I strayed down these streets in just the way I strayed into this story. But there is no one else who can tell it—or, at least, tell it correctly; and that is troublesome. I remember some things as clearly as my own name; others are fuzzy. So please bear with me. It is hard for an old man to begin at the beginning; to do that, I suppose I'll have to go back to Ned Grimke.

For I met Ned first. I met him years before I met Hirsch and long before any of us would ever turn up at the Battery. And even then, even that early, it was never *Ned;* it was always *Ned Grimke.* My family and I spoke and thought of him that way, as if he were too frail to stand alone, as if he had no character or personality not granted him by his family. He always did seem overwhelmed by them and shadowed by their past; but that was not very remarkable: many of my friends in Charleston and even Savannah were, to a degree. History haunted us all, especially those of us born in a sleepy old southern town that had Fort Sumter for a legacy. It rose up from the harbor to stain the sky. We could see it from our school windows, red in the morning. We were used to it, the symbol of the city, its epitome. We'd stare at it in awe and reverence while we said our morning prayers, as if the ruin was Zion, as if Sumter was the Olympus hovering over us. For God, we did not doubt, did dwell in Charleston; or the Lord of the lost cause did anyway. Savannah, we were taught, was not quite so bright a star in the constellation of southern cities. Charleston was the brightest, and many of the boys I went to school with there bore holy names—names that had gathered a romantic sound to them and had garnered the prestige and patina of history—names like Laurens and Middleton and Pinckney. It was not so for Ned. There was a shame of sorts attached back then to being a Grimke, a shame that was traced to two sisters of that name, who in the early nineteenth century had believed that women were equal to men; even more telling than that, they had acknowledged a gentleman's—their father's—indiscretion, and had accepted their half-black half-brother whole-heartedly. There was something not so wonderful in being a Grimke after that; and for their ideas, for their heresies, the sisters had been forced north from the city.

Whoever you are who finds these notes, I wonder if you will believe me if I tell you that their stigma remained all those years later, and that the stain of their name was still there when I was growing up. Something peculiar and unclean seemed to lurk even in its pronouncing; I think I can remember, even as a child, how strange it sounded—as if it were a word from another language. I remember a chill running down my spine as my mother checked my nails and behind my ears and turned me over to my Dah to take me to meet Ned Grimke.

"What's that?" I remember asking my mother.

"He is a boy, just like you," she said. "Take him, Dah."

"I don't want to go," I cried. I was scared by one of those irrational fears in which childhood specializes.

"You must," my mother said; she kneeled beside me to pat my hair. "And you must be kind to him and make him feel welcome while he is here."

My Dah pressed my fingers together. Tightly. When she did that I knew there was no chance. I looked at my mother and waved as if going to Europe. She waved back. My Dah took me down the street to meet Ned Grimke.

That was the beginning. It was the same year that Miss Wragg first came here. I don't even recall if I liked Ned Grimke at first: if we became friends, it was out of

necessity, for it seemed that summer that we were the only
two boys in the whole city.

Like every summer, heat had laid its siege and people
refugeed as they had after Sumter; they went to Flat Rock,
and to the mountains of North Carolina, as my family and I
did usually. But the summer Ned and I first met, my
grandmother lay ill and we could not leave. We were left in
Charleston in the heat, and Grandmama lay gasping for
breath, like a mullet out of water in a shuttered upstairs
room. I tiptoed up to her doorway to listen to her inhales
and her gasps as if they were the pronouncements of some
deity. Dah would shoo me away if she saw me playing with
my puppets in the doorway. I had several. The gendarme
my grandmother had given me was the angel of death.

"He's coming for her," I told Dah.

"Boy," she warned, "don't even think those things."

She was scared of puppets and glass-eyed doll babies.

Often the doctor would appear. In a gloom that gripped
the house as tensely as hands held in prayer, my parents
spoke to him in whispers and interpreted every tiny change:
was it a sign that the end was near, or did it signal a rally?
They could not tell top from bottom in their weariness and
so they felt cross and guilty in the heat. Lost in the shuffle
of emotions, I slipped through people's fingers. Dah, my
black nurse (and that was their generic name, Dah being an
African word for mother, and one that best summed up
their tragedy—that of those black women doomed to raise
white babies), took me out for walks once in a while; but
she spent most of her time with my sickly brother, Hal, who
had been born in April. So I was free to wander the city.

I found Charleston a ghost town that summer—the
houses hollow and the streets empty; the Charlestonians
who could just went to cooler places before air-
conditioning. The fact that we were left in town and were
from Savannah was not lost on the other families. Grass
grew up in the streets, and every afternoon the streetcar
came by, depositing my father for his dinner, which we ate
at three: cold potato salad, cutlets and shrimp, tomato

sandwiches, okra or green beans. While we ate, the shutters of the nearby houses rattled like dice in the breeze and petals of overblown roses fell in green gardens abandoned to the ravages of creepers and ivy. The talk was sparse, mostly of my grandmother—what she had eaten that morning—and of the stranger's fever that had appeared here and there in the black sections of town. Passing a shack on the way home, my father said he had heard a scream and a black woman's malarial delirium. "New York," she had cried, "New York City." Later, nearly every afternoon, purple storm clouds came up from the sea and it rained and thunder boomed in the deserted streets; the old roof tiles were washed in a rainbow, a pigeonlike sheen. On Sunday, we could hear St. Michael's chimes throughout the whole city.

Time was a tunnel that summer, like the one I entered under the cool trees of Broad Street, to be passed through listlessly until September would bring its storms and October would arrive, leading people back to the city. It was halfway or so through that tunnel of summer (I think the hurricane lilies were out and wisteria was blooming again) when my mother came looking for me one morning; she examined me with a look of pride and inevitability. She sighed and suggested with a false brightness in her voice— as if she were suggesting something to which she had been forced to concur—that I go off and visit Ned Grimke.

There was no use resisting; Dah was the disciplinarian in our home and made me do everything my parents said; so we went, Dah and I, passing slowly down the streets, she matching her rhythm to mine. Going through the throbbing heat, we passed the hucksters calling out their wares, singing out for she-crab or "weggutubles" or shrimp; on a corner the ground-nut mauma dipped into a sweet grass basket and gave me a taste of her goods for free; and I thanked her.

"Thank *you*, white gentleman," she said.

They all tipped their hats out of respect for Dah—no mean feat, for some carried their wares on their heads.

Though Standard Oil moved my father and us back and forth between Charleston and Savannah, the Charlestonians, all in all, considered us almost quality; Dah was attached to us and so she held the same ranking.

Finally we drew up in front of a dark green door, so dark it was almost black, and stopped. I lost my nerve. Both of us were scared, I think; both of us had heard tales of what went on behind these walls, but neither of us had ever entered the Confederate Home before that morning. It loomed up above us on Chalmers Street.

It seemed huge that day, the building, as it always did; and eternal; and gray, reaching up to eclipse the sky. Rust-stained and rain-streaked, the earthquake-bolted facade seemed clasped in some iron-clad bitterness; the three-storied back (the front is on Broad Street) rose like a medieval fortress, so abruptly, that I had never known until we summoned up our courage and entered that the building was arranged around an open courtyard, in the middle of which grew a huge and balanced cedar tree. Once we opened the door to the passageway, we could see the tree waving in front of us, green and dazzling, so that it seemed like sunlit water at the end of the dark walkway.

When we reached it, we looked up with eyes blinking; there were porches atop porches surrounding the courtyard; and on them, we could see, watering flowers in tin cans, or sitting in green wicker rocking chairs, or just pausing to look out over the railings, countless old ladies, looking like aged Juliets on their balconies.

"Do, Jedus," Dah moaned.

I said nothing.

They made sounds like bees humming. If they waited up there for their beaux, they waited in vain; for only death would ever come calling. I think they must have realized this, for all the ladies wore black, and it was that fact that frightened me most. To me, they looked like those ominous nuns I had seen circling in front of St. Mary's; my friend Dwin had told me that all nuns carried guns under their black habits, guns that had been issued to them by the Pope for each newborn Catholic baby.

I was scared of them and tried to call to my Dah but my mouth was dry; she stood rooted and all the ladies ignored us. We were mesmerized by them, so that we were surprised when Ned Grimke suddenly appeared.

We had heard him, without knowing that the sound heralded his coming—a funny scraping noise against wood, as if someone were coming downstairs dragging something metal, like a scythe, behind him. He was coming down one of the many ramshackle staircases that seemed to have been added as an afterthought to the building.

Because of the angle of the sun, he was half in and half out of the shadows; like a magician's saw, white light sliced him diagonally. He stood there on the bottom step, holding on to the newel post.

His head was in the sunlight; he was so blond it was almost blinding; and his pale skin was nearly the color of an albino. His eyes were the same blanched blue of the burnt-out sky that hot July morning. He seemed to gleam in the light, all thin elbows and knees. But he had a look my grandmother would have called "lively." We looked him up and down as if he were some vision; and I held onto Dah's hand. His shoes were peculiar: one was normal, while the other's sole was thicker by an inch or two; both were black and shiny.

Ned Grimke looked us over, too, surprise widening his eyes; he hung back, reaching for the banister, and tilted his head to one side, studying us.

Dah pried her fingers free from my moist hand and gently pushed me forward.

"Manners," she whispered.

"Hello," I responded, like her pet monkey.

Ned Grimke held tighter to the post and backed away.

With another prod from Dah, I held out my hand to shake, telling Ned my name and how my mother had sent us. He became solemn; he chewed his lip, clasped his own hand behind his back, and stared at mine, outstretched, as if it were something peculiar, a fish, I was offering.

He worked his jaw; his eyes drew light. He seemed to listen; then he reached out his hand and we shook; he bent from the waist in an old-fashioned bow, all the while saying not a thing.

"Cat got your tongue?" Dah asked.

He smiled, hung his head a little, and shyly shook it. His silence gave him a serious air. He blushed.

And no one moved or said a thing; we were suspended there in the wilting silence, oppressive as the temperature. It came from all around, in waves, like heat; all you could hear were insects shrilling. Some folks said they were so loud that year they drove two colored people crazy.

"Where are your people, boy?" Dah asked gently.

Ned just turned his head to one side and whispered something to no one we could see; then he paused again and seemed to be listening. We were impressed by that—as if it was a sign of wisdom or maturity; he was unlike anyone I had met before and had roused my curiosity if not my sympathy. We knew (only because my mother had told us) that Ned was an orphan—or half a one: his mother was dead and his father had moved away after Ned's birth to Walhalla, South Carolina. I had never met an orphan before that I could remember and wondered if that thick shoe had anything to do with it—a mark of it, a badge maybe.

"Where are your aunts?" Dah asked.

Ned spoke to his shoulder; his eyes turned down, and Dah warned, "Boy, doan you make fun o' me. Where they be?"

We knew he was here visiting his father's two aunts, who lived in the Confederate Home. Those gaunt gray women, Azalea and Eola, though they did not like children, nevertheless insisted that Ned spend as much time as possible with them in his native city. This was not a wish— the thin old women did not give into whims—it was an abstract idea, inbred, against which there was no struggling. For, to them, Walhalla might just as well have been Africa. Azalea and Eola and all their family believed that true civilization existed only in Charleston and the low country, that thin strip of alluvial soil about forty miles in from the sea: plantation country—encompassing a few other populated areas—Richmond, Savannah, and by the grace of geography alone, New Orleans. Civilization existed only where it smelled of salt and seaweed; an almost underwater world in which moss dripped down from the trees; a damp and moist atmosphere that mildewed and moldered everything, one that had molded all of us—the Grimke sisters and all the other old ladies, Ned, my Dah, and me.

We stood there at the foot of the stairway, frozen in a tableau like wax figurines.

"Whooh!" Dah waved a handkerchief under her arm; she was sweating profusely. "I declare," she shook her head and muttered, "you too strange, boy," She looked along the walls of the porch—a chafed pink. There was no one around on the ground floor to appeal to; there were only the ladies on the porches hovering above us and we did not want to ask them anything. They were above us, like insects or chimney swifts swirling across the sky in the evening. There were steps leading up there, but they were useless. We knew the ladies were removed from us by more than mere height; they seemed as evanescent as light, as unearthly. They had been transported up there by their dreams; bereft, they were the wives, daughters, granddaughters, and great-nieces of those men who had fought for the Confederacy. Flesh may have withered; tints had changed from pink to lavender; but the unvanquished ideas of a vanished world still reigned here.

All of us children in Charleston knew of others, maiden aunts and spinster cousins, who had pressed their blossoms, shut them up and lovingly consigned them to where we found them on rainy days (in Bibles or albums), but they—the ladies of the Confederate Home—still clung to them like bridal bouquets, eternal Miss Havershams. They were vestal virgins.

They were not women, they were ideas; each obsessed with an individual past, each a small taper burning in memory:

"I am Richard Henry Duprée, cut down at First Manassas."

"I am my great-uncle Huger."

"I am chivalry."

We suspected them of taking such vows, and accused them of rituals and bizarre ceremonies. My Dah and I knew we had set foot on foreign soil when we entered; and we got no help at all from Ned Grimke. He hung there between the shadow and the light. "What do you think?" he asked himself out loud. "No! I won't!" he answered himself defiantly.

Dah was by now getting nervous—looking about for whom Ned was talking to. She was always on the lookout for plat eye, ghosts and zombies; I saw her touch the match she kept in her hair, knowing the sulfur would keep haints at bay. Ned spoke more to himself, and then with a lurching and not ungraceful movement, he came off the bottom step towards us.

Before we could do anything there was a movement on the stairs and Ned's own Dah appeared; she must have come down with him from the upcountry. She stood behind him and put her hands on his shoulders protectively. She was tall and thin, statuesque, part Indian perhaps; with her scarlet turban on her head she moved with great dignity. Then she mopped her hands on her white apron and, although she and my Dah had never met before, after dropping each other a curtsy, they immediately started speaking to each other in Gullah, their stark and grotesque patois.

She gave Ned a look that between those two, and those two alone, held a meaning. Each nodded slightly. The two black women moved off, speaking together.

Now Ned stood right in front of me. "Hello," he said.

"Who were you talking to?" I asked.

"A friend."

"Who? I didn't see anyone."

"He's tiny."

"Can I see him?"

He nodded.

I stood still, fascinated, as Ned pinched the air above his shoulders as if he were lifting something off that he then put in his other palm, offering it open and flat to me.

"It's Jervey."

He came over and lifted his palm to right in front of my eyes. "I don't see a thing."

"He's invisible." Ned then cocked his ears and listened. "Jervey says he's pleased to meet you."

"Oh." I was taken aback. "Can I hold him?"

Ned looked at his palm and then up at my eyes. He hesitated. "Okay."

I opened my hand next to his, our two index fingers touching in a bridge. "Here he comes," Ned said. "Hold still."

I waited with baited breath. I could feel him. I said, "It tickles like a cricket!"

"He's dancing in your hand. But be careful," Ned worried; he dragged his foot and hovered nearby.

I was not about to admit that I didn't see anything. Jervey, in Ned's behalf, seemd to be some sort of half man, half sprite, with wings.

"Where did he come from?" I asked.

"I found him."

"Where?"

"Over there." He pointed to a patch of deeper green under the cedar tree. "He may have belonged to one of the ladies."

"Why don't you ask?"

"Because then I'd have to give him back." He looked up at them. Ned was thoughtful about that for a while and said, "Jervey's tired."

"How do you know?"

"He told me."

"I didn't hear anything."

Ned snatched him quickly from my hand and put him in the hollow under his arm. "He likes it under there. He's sleeping."

271

"I'm gonna see if I can find me one." I ran over to the patch of clover and Ned followed me. With his hands, he lowered himself to the ground.

"What's wrong with your foot?" I asked. "Why's your shoe so big?"

Ned did not answer. He had turned to Jervey again, having wakened him up and transferred him to his ear. "You can't make me," he said.

I was poring through the clover and Dah called, "You git outta there, boy! Ain't I tell you not to play wit dem stink bugs?"

"I'm not, Dah."

But having issued her warning she paid no attention to me. She and Ned's Dah were already thick as thieves.

All I found in the clover that morning was a dried-out cocoon—some shell an insect had left behind after molting; it was Jervey's, Ned told me; his carriage. "Give it to me," he demanded.

I did. "Why does he need a carriage when he has wings?"

"It's a secret," Ned said.

*   *   *

We were in Hibernian Hall, that white Ionian temple at the foot of Chalmers Street, at some ball, maybe even our grandest of the season, the St. Cecilia; or it might have been a debutante party. I can't remember that; but I can remember that it was a splendid evening. And what with all the candles on the walls and the old gas-light fixtures above us and some of the old gowns, you could almost believe it was the nineteenth century. My father's business contacts, I suppose, had gotten us in here. The Charlestonians did not like that in the least, and they blamed us for their poverty that made this a necessity. The musicians played only waltzes and reels and quadrilles, no modern themes; it was a ritual. The dancers could have been their own ancestors; times mixed; young men danced with old ladies. With the great oaken doors of the hall rolled shut, they could feel that there was nothing else transpiring in all the world. All that mattered was here. A young and foolish boy from

Savannah could pretend that he belonged as well. And then, in a flash, in the whirr of the moment, it was all changed, shattered, like a champagne glass, with a sound that was shrill and disconcerting.

I had been standing along the wall watching the believers dance, trying not to be seen by anyone, when one of the managers silently whisked by. That usually meant some newspaperman was trying to break in to take photographs—a taboo thing by the by-laws of the Society— or some dowager had fainted, or a poor debutante had been caught smoking. That night, it was none of those things. The manager had not been quick enough to stop a couple from committing the unpardonable sin that has ever since been called "fast dancing."

Back then it was shocking. People nearly screamed as suddenly, without warning, as if having fits, Lucas Simons and Suzanne Pinckney broke into the Charleston, the dance that had been spawned on our street corners by colored children and would soon be mimicked across the country. As soon as Lucas and Suzanne began there arose a cry; other couples ran from the floor, holding their hands over their eyes, as if they were afraid they would be blinded by gazing at such deviltry. Lucas just smiled with his hands going wild on his knees and Suzanne reached for the heavens like a Jesus-crazed black lady. You almost expected to hear the screech of whistles or to see the police; but like reporters, they were not allowed in here. The believers had their won watchdogs of society. Men in evening dress quickly pushed past us and ushered the culprits off the dance floor; no one swooned, though many had seemed capable of it; there was a lot of fan snapping and tut-tutting among the old ladies. They issued dark prophecies and there were at least two fates sealed that evening—Suzanne and Lucas were expelled for their heresy, two positions in the elect became open in the St. Cecilia Society.

In the confusion of their dancing and being led away (I watched them as they walked out, heads up and wrists together, unrepentant and proud, as if being led to the guillotine), Lila Lesesne lowered the bodice of her gown and smiled at me. But I had had my fill of debutantes that night; and I was not going to volunteer for any extra duty if my name was not already on a dance card and no dowager sailed up to claim me for a visiting niece. I pretended not to see her. So Lila, undaunted, set her green eyes on Ned, and licked her teeth. He had been following me. I saw him blush bright red and immediately turn his eyes downward. He backed against the wall and tried to disappear. He was slightly taller than me, but still so bleached out, white as a skeleton, so skinny. He seemed out of place here; as if he had just dropped to earth and was not used to this atmosphere. Lila came his way; he gulped and blushed and chewed his lip. He looked to me to save him but I looked away. And that made me wonder if he were not like me. I started to blush too and suddenly was hot; I looked around to see if anyone noticed. As Lila spoke to Ned I slipped away to the punch bowl, and returned armed with two glasses. Ned looked up hopefully, but they weren't for him; people would think I was retrieving for some young lady, so I could wander about freely.

I walked around pretending I was looking for my girl; everyone I passed was whispering about Lucas and Suzanne. Would they leave town? Would they get married? The musicians started up a waltz; and after that, as if regrouping after a battle, people assembled for a Virginia reel. So they had survived; Charlestonians celebrated their own hardihood; it took more than one assault to destroy society. Lila Lesesne came my way with her arm linked through Winfield Huger's, and as they passed, I bowed and presented them with my two cups of punch. Winfield saluted, but Lila ignored me. I stood in the middle of the floor.

In a second, my friends came up; Hilary and Dwin came out of a corner looking like Jack Sprat and his wife, or Laurel and Hardy, Dwin thin and dried up, Hilary pink and pudgy with blond hair. They were always together.

"Where's Swinton?" I asked.

He was our best and we always gravitated to him; and was older than us by a few years; we felt somehow grander in his company. He was slim and dark; there was already some gray in his black hair and he had a refined face, a "French face," we said in Charleston, and an elegant body. We saw him across the room and he motioned us to silence.

The colored waiters in their white jackets were still whispering and flashing their white teeth as Swinton moved behind them and surreptitiously lifted a bottle of champagne from an ice bucket. He wiped it with a napkin and winked. He quickly put it under his coat, became solemn, and crossed the ballroom. In a flash I saw Ned marooned along the wall looking at us longingly with his blanched blue eyes. I looked away.

In the vestibule, I found my father helping my mother into her coat and I told them not to wait up. My mother blew me a kiss; we boys went out into the freezing night; and St. Michael's rang as we ran toward it, hooraying in victory as Swinton lifted the bottle. He held it up in tribute to the white church that loomed up at us like a wedding cake, tasteful and chaste under excesses of decorative white filigree. We went reeling and hallooing under the portico to Swinton's parents' house on Tradd Street. It *must* have been the St. Cecilia ball, for lights were on all over the city.

Josephine Humphreys

from *Rich In Love*

In old cities there are always statues. Charleston had John C. Calhoun, Henry Timrod (Poet of the Confederacy), and a toga-clad woman who was meant to be Confederate Motherhood, sending her naked son into battle with the Yankees.

But my favorite was Osceola, the Seminole chief. Down the road from our house was Fort Moultrie, where his statue rose from the top of a hill, looking seaward. I imagined his view, over the brick fort and the housetops of red and silver, the dark cumulus trees, to the slice of white dunes, blue water, Fort Sumter, and finally in the distance a black, jagged, double line of rocks, jetties that held the channel for incoming ships. From his perch he watched for whatever would be coming over the horizon—freighters, shrimpboats, seabirds, the sun and moon.

Bees lived in him. They appeared to get in through a hole in his neck, which made me wonder if he was hollow. And if hollow, was he filled with honey? He never flinched, in that wild swarm. I had grown up under his watch, and he had come to be a landmark and something of a hero to me, my idea of what a man should be. A warrior, secretly filled with sweetness.

In life Osceola had been betrayed in Florida, captured under a flag of truce, and sent here as a prisoner, where he died under what I considered suspicious circumstances. Caught a cold and died, they said. Well—perhaps. But in the fort was a portrait that the government was careful to get painted of him just weeks before he caught the fatal cold. He knew something was afoot, you can tell from the portrait. The eyes have the gentle serenity of a man who sees fools and traitors all around him. When he died, the attending physician sawed off his head and took it home to Savannah, where he pickled it and hung it on his son's bedpost whenever the child misbehaved. I swear this is true.

The headless body was buried at the fort. A ten-foot cypress representation of the head in profile can now be seen marking the entrance to Osceola Pointe, a bankrupt development on the bypass.

You won't find the whole Osceola story in the history books, of course. I discovered these facts in the South Carolina Room at the library, where I worked on Friday afternoons. The room was kept locked—they said, to keep out winos and children. But I made some discoveries in that room, and I think I know the real reason they locked it. There was a lot of history in there that they didn't want to let out.

*   *   *

The Episcopalians had a picnic area next to the fragrance garden. Nobody ever picnicked there except me and Wayne. We had found it one afternoon and started taking our lunch there, since seniors were allowed to leave the school during the lunch period. The tables were "redwood," i.e., not redwood, with benches attached. They had sunk into the dirt and were beginning to rot at the feet. Every time we went, more wood had gone soft and disintegrated, so that the tables had sunk just a little bit lower. A line of electric lights was strung overhead from a pine to a palmetto, and there was a sort of oyster-roast pit built of brick by somebody who had never laid bricks before.

When I got there, Wayne was asleep on top of a picnic table.

I stood over him and looked down. His shirt was on the bench; he must have taken it off to get some sun, and then fallen asleep. His chest was white and narrow; his nipples were the same color as his lips. I thought he looked sick. His jeans stood away from his hips, showing the elastic of his shorts below his belly button. He wasn't getting the right foods. I had seen Mrs. Frobiness last week at the Piggly Wiggly, her cart loaded with Brie and kohlrabi and artichokes and smoked salmon. No wonder he had moved out.

I looked away. It was dangerous for me to start worrying

about Wayne. I knew how it would go: I'd worry about his well-being, and then I'd think how I could go about straightening his life out for him, the same way I thought about Evelyn. But I had too many people within my own family, whose lives I was trying to straighten out. I couldn't afford to take on outsiders. And if he was such a great crisis counselor, he ought to be able to take care of himself.

I sat on the bench. The churchyard ran to the water's edge, a straight shore where the Army Corps of Engineers had channelized a yacht highway from Miami to New York, the Intracoastal Waterway. No doubt it had once served some military purpose, but the main traffic now was the parade of sparkling white, overpowered, heavily antennaed boats. When they passed, waves cut into the mudbank and undermined it; chunks of slick blue-black mud and marsh grass plopped into the water and bobbed away. Later, when the tide dropped to show a thin sandy beach, pieces of Indian pottery were left high and dry. I had a box full of the gray pocked clay shards, most of them barely big enough to show the curve of the original pot. I loved a number of things in this place. The wide sky above me, tables sinking into the earth, the string of lights, millionaires' boats, relics of ancient men.

A skinny arm snaked around my neck and held me in its crook.

"Don't move, lady. One little snap of my arm, and your head's off. I know karate. Or something like that, the one where one little snap of my arm can take your head off."

I nipped him with my front teeth.

"Hey!" he said. "Damn, teeth marks!" He sat up and examined his forearm.

I opened my hamburger. It was fixed the way I like it, with lettuce and mustard only. I ate it in silence.

He reached for his shirt and took a pack of cigarettes from the pocket. "You were looking at my chest," he said, tapping out a Winston.

"I was not."

"I saw you. I wasn't really asleep. You came over and

stood behind my right shoulder and you looked at me." He took a deep breath to make his chest expand, but he still had a frail look. Then he put his shirt on and lit a cigarette, and raised a finger. "Don't tell me not to smoke," he said. He took a drag. "'Just quit.' I hear it every day. 'Why don't you just quit drinking,' they say to the old wino. 'Why don't you just quit screwing her,' the wife cries to the husband. Why don't people *just quit* these things? I'm glad you asked. I will now explain the Law of Increasing Reality. The older you get, the clearer you see. The clearer you see, the more you need to forget what you saw. So people smoke, drink, stuff things up their noses, eat, and screw. We *need* some of these pleasures. And the clock is ticking, Lucille. You need—"

"I need nothing."

He changed the subject. "Are you aware," he said, "of the various attempts I have made to get in touch with you? I left messages with that man in your house, not knowing who he was—"

"He is my new brother-in-law."

"I heard you say that, but I didn't know it then, did I? The last time I called I accused him of not delivering the messages. Yesterday I came over and beat on the door. I had the feeling you were right there behind it, listening to me slam that little lion's head up and down a hundred times. So I looked through the security peephole. You can see through those things, if there's good light. I saw you."

"You didn't. You can't see through that hole."

"Yes, you can, I swear to God. Try it. There was light behind you. You stood there looking at the door. Admit it! You had on something yellow."

"Okay. Yes. I didn't feel good. I didn't want to get into this with you."

Across the water was the burnt bridge that used to go to Charleston, its black piers now sticking up out of the waterway at angles. Cormorants sat on the stumps, spreading their wings.

"Look at me," he said. "I want to make sure you're

listening, not tuning out like you usually do. I still feel the same way about you as I said before. However, simultaneously, you aggravate the shit out of me. You don't really know what love is. I don't think you have it in you. Your idea of love is a total error, three hundred and sixty degrees off."

"You mean a hundred and eighty," I said. I made a circle with my thumb and finger.

He dropped his cigarette on the ground. It lit some dry grass. The thatch puffed up and sent out a small smoke cloud, but the flame went out. We stared at the blackened bare patch left on the ground.

"I'm not the girl for you," I said.

"Yes, you are."

On the mud flat near the old bridge a Vietnamese family twenty strong was pulling a seine through chest-high water. The men dragged the end poles, and the floats swept out in a wide arc behind; on shore the women set green garbage cans in the mud to receive the catch. To my right curved the Mount Pleasant shoreline, coming into view again across a cove: verandahed houses, live oaks, boathouses, and rickety docks. And way in the distance the harbor, the city under the high bridges. In this light the city skyline was cream-colored again, the sky and water that hazy blue-pink.

"Look at that view," I said.

Wayne knew I was serious. He knew that a really good view had the power to draw me into it, so I seemed to float out along its curls and colors and receding planes. The world, I thought, was losing not only ozone and panthers but also views. Even this one was endangered: a condo complex, built in a Middle Eastern style, rose from a spit of marshland beyond the old bridge. I blocked it out by letting a lock of hair fall over it.

I have seen paintings that devote a whole canvas to vista, i.e., the long view outward from the viewer. Past trees, cascades, and mountains it goes, and humanity, if shown at all, is nothing but a blip of a canoe in the middle ground. Speaking from experience, I know of the human need for vista. Without it, I am in danger of losing myself behind my own eyes. Then, I *need* the Intracoastal Waterway shooting straight for Miami, high tide rising in the spartina, myrtle hummocks brown in the lavender haze. A person has to now and then break out of the head and heart, places that cannot, over any length of time, support life.

I went into a reverie. The Vietnamese picked up the flopping fish. A cormorant tried to tuck its wings back into position, and to my amazement, in spite of its precarious position on the burnt piling and the prodigious amount of wing to be folded, succeeded.

Wayne said, "I feel trapped by the oncoming day. It's going to get me." He gazed with me, as if we were an audience watching some show.

"Quit working so hard," I said. "You can't keep this up. They aren't even paying you."

"As my father is fond of pointing out. But listen who's talking responsibility. The girl who screwed up her exams. I noticed you weren't at the grand ceremony, but I didn't know why till this week."

"I did not screw up. I absented myself. Anyway, who told you about that?"

"Rhody."

"But how did Rhody know?"

"Rhody knows everything. I think she's weirding out. She got laid off from Palmetto Dunes, and you know what she's been doing?"

"Working at Fishbone's."

"I mean in the daytime. Dressing in disguise and going into the city."

"What?"

"She says she's doing research for a book. 'Observing.' She has it all planned out in her head, and she's observing for details."

"She told you this?"

"She called me about Evelyn, and I set her up for an evaluation. We got into a conversation."

"What's wrong with Evelyn?"

He looked at me with his exasperated look. Sometimes I pressed him to tell me the stories his clients called in with. My interest was purely for narrative entertainment, but he said everything he heard at the Center was confidential, and he would not reveal more than the bare bones of a tale. "There's nothing wrong with Evelyn," he said, "besides normal strangeness. She's better off than most of what I get. Jesus, am I sick of troubled youth. They call in with their sullen, dead voices and they think they are the center of the universe. They think if they let all their blood out into the shower stall, that's going to solve their problems. They won't listen to me when I tell them the real solutions. I have *got* solutions, too. I have a list. It's that easy! They can name any problem, and I've got the answer that will turn their life around, guaranteed. Abuse, drugs, acne, parents, money, sex, I don't care what, it can be cured. They won't *listen.*"

"Sex can be cured?"

"You're a laugh riot, Lucille."

"Some of those people listen to you, I know they do."

"Some."

I knew for a fact that Wayne was responsible for getting Paula Govery off cocaine, and that he had talked several people out of doing themselves in. One afternoon I had barged into the phone room at the Center to find him hunched over the desk with the receiver hidden under his head and arms. He was cradling it, talking steady and low. He heard me come in, look up, and pointed toward the door, meaning *get out*. But I was curious. I sat down and listened. I wanted to hear what he said, how he went about convincing somebody that life was worth living. He glared hard at me, then gave up and pretended I wasn't there.

"Listen, Philip," he said. He rested his forehead in one hand. I noticed that the morning paper was spread out flat on the desk under his elbows. "I got another one. 'Alfa Romeo, 1979 Limited Edition Sprint Veloce Millemiglia. Black coupe, sunroof, AC, special alloy wheels, wood steering wheel. 2000cc. electronic fuel injected 4cyl. This car is a rare beauty and a great performer. Needs some minor cosmetic work. Must sell at $4500.' *Give me a break*. 'Minor cosmetic work.' We know what that means, right? I think I saw this car getting towed on 17 South, garbaged. I wouldn't touch it. Now, here you go. '1984 300 ZX Turbo, Black, loaded, digital, t-top, low miles. Ex. condition, paid $20,000, sell $14,000. 883-3722, ask for Rick, nights and Sundays.' What do you think? I mean if it's really excellent condition. You think fourteen would be too much for a car like that?"

I frowned at Wayne and said out loud, "What are you doing?" I had assumed this was a Hot Line call, but he was getting advice on buying a car.

He mouthed "Shut up" to me, then went back to talking. "I don't know, Philip. Frankly, for me fourteen thousand dollars is too damn much money to put into an automobile. Maybe I ought to get a bike. Didn't you say you had one?. . . Is that right? Shit, everything in the paper is Japanese. Honda, Honda, Honda, Yamaha, Suzuki. One Harley, a '73 XLCH, but it's twenty-four hundred bucks. So you would recommend the British over both Japanese and American? Right. Well, I know this isn't what you called me about, but, ah, I'd really like to see that Triumph. What are the chances you might want to unload it?. . . Sure. Bring it by this afternoon. You have an appointment with Dr. Furman, don't you? Great, Phil."

When he hung up, he was white-faced. He looked at me. "Guy had his dad's twelve gauge and a coat-hanger."

"And you tried to *buy his motorcycle?*"

"Get them interested in the affairs of the world," he said. "Whatever it may be, cars, food, making a buck. I find the newspaper helpful. Sometimes I read them the travel section, or what's doing in the malls. Merchandise for sale, that sort of thing. Puppies free to good home, that's the most effective."

My acquaintance with Wayne Frobiness had taught me that genius is not always measurable on the SAT. He hadn't scored so well on that; but here he was a brilliant strategist in the battle for human happiness. I thought his type of intelligence was more useful than the ability to figure the average speed of a locomotive or pick out a word that means the same or nearly the same as another word. Those pieces of measurable intelligence are so minuscule; a person could have them and still not understand the world. Wayne had a large intelligence, wide enough to take in the whole hodge-podge of trouble and joy in modern society. The Crisis Center had trained him to man the Hot Line: let the client know you're listening attentively, give supportive responses, facilitate the client's expression of the problem. But Wayne went beyond the guidelines, inventing his own techniques. He broke a lot of the rules—gave advice, told his own troubles, discussed religion and politics, showed disapproval. And then he'd do something like read the newspaper out loud. One time he sang a song over the phone, the one that says, "I can see clearly now the rain is gone." People called in to say they were considering a Valium overdose and Wayne would arrange to meet them at Cinema East to see a Molly Ringwald movie.

I was proud to know him. But I was not the girl for him. He needed somebody high-spirited, a lively, perky girl. I asked him, as we sat on the picnic table together, if he had been seeing Laura Migo.

"Christ," he said.

"Does that mean yes or no?"

"Okay, yes. On your instructions I took Laura Migo to a movie."

"How did it go?"

"It went great. The nerdy guy got the girl, after she realized he was the one she liked all along rather than the jock she'd been trying to —"

"I mean you and Laura. After the movie. Did you and she get along?"

"Sure."

"Well?"

"This is unhealthy. This conversation. But I'll tell you. Laura wanted to go to her daddy's boathouse after the movie. We went there. Laura wanted to get in the Whaler and take off certain items of her clothing —"

"She didn't."

"She did," he said gloomily.

"Took them off?"

"No, wanted to. The whole situation was too much for me. I thanked her politely, I said she was fantastic, I mean, just so *great* and I felt like the luckiest fellow in the world, but, um, no thanks. Listen, Lucille, I'm not interested in Laura Migo. I want you."

I said, "We tried it and it didn't work."

"It would have gotten better," he said, "You would have grown to like it."

"I don't think so. Please, let's not think about it any more."

"See, I *liked* it, that's the problem. I can't not think about it. I'm thinking about it all the time. I'm thinking about it at the moment," he said.

He looked at me. I smiled.

"You're too young," he said. "You're too young for me, that's what it is. I ought to let you go for four, five years and then come back for you. You're smart as a whip, I looked up your I.Q. But you just aren't grown up yet."

"You looked up my I.Q.?"

"I had to go through some stuff at Wando for Dr. Furman, and the folders were all right there. I didn't look *closely;* I didn't look at your subscores or anything."

"What was it?" I said.

"That's confidential."

"Tell me."

"I'll tell you if you'll go out with me."

"No."

He unwrapped his Whopper and ate it cold.

"I'm the same age as you," I said, "more or less."

"Less."

He shaded his eyes with a hand and looked to where the Vietnamese had drawn their long net out of the water and were culling their catch. They threw away the creek debris—plastic beer harnesses, Styrofoam cups, Baggies, picnic forks—whatever the yachtsmen had tossed overboard yesterday. They kept everything remotely edible: stingrays, mullet, crabs, the thin one-foot sharks called dogfish. Water was rising over the mudflats, a gray that glared to white under the high sun. Because the flats were wide, you could see the water rise, spreading over the green mud, seeping into the courses it had cut on the last run out. Two egrets were forced to move to higher ground. Behind the Vietnamese, up on the bridge, shrimpers readied their drop nets for the moment when the water would cover the mud underneath them, bringing in the little fat creek shrimp.

"And the solution to your problems is easy, too," Wayne said. "You're happy as long as you can see at least three hundred yards. That's when you're at your best. I think you're afraid something is going to sneak up on you."

"Maybe so."

"I have a favor to ask of you."

"Please. I don't want to keep going over this, I—"

"No, it's something else. I want you to go to the Yacht Club with me for lunch."

"We already ate." I didn't even mention the cheese and Snickers and cake I had downed earlier.

"The purpose of the lunch is not to eat. It's to have a little talk with my father."

"Well, I can't just show up. He's not expecting *me*; he wants you."

"Yeah, but I can't do it by myself."

"Hogwash," I said.

"If you're there, I'll behave. If you're not there, I can't take responsibility for what might happen, and it's the Yacht Club and all. One can't overturn one's table and throw soup in there. I need you to keep me in line."

"But I'm not dressed up. Neither are you. You can't go like that."

"We have time for you to change, and I've got a clean shirt and tie in the car. I'm not kidding," he said. "I need for you to go."

"All right."

My house was empty.

I put on one of Rae's dresses; she couldn't get into any of them nowadays. It had a lace collar and a brooch at the neck. I also put on a pair of her black flat shoes, because I owned only sandals and Nikes. When I got back out to the car, Wayne was wearing a yellow dress shirt and a clip-on bow tie.

"He won't like the tie," I said. "Let me get you one of Pop's."

"This is my lucky tie. It lives in the glove compartment and comes out when I need some luck. It works."

"He'll think you're wearing it on purpose."

"I am."

We drove across the bridge and into the city, down to the Carolina Yacht Club. In the parking lot Wayne pulled right up to the steps and parked next to two Jaguars with cellular phones. "They're married," he said, standing between the cars and laying each hand on a Jaguar fender. "Guy practices with my father. He drives the car a year, then gives it to his wife. His is always a year newer than hers."

Dr. Frobiness was waiting in the lounge. He was puzzled to see me, and only vaguely remembered meeting me before, but it did not seem to bother him that I had come along. We went through the buffet line in the dining room. I helped myself to crab casserole, fried flounder, shrimp pie, rice, civvy beans and yellow squash. Wayne stared at my plate. His own contained a slice of watermelon, which he had sawed off the centerpiece, a watermelon cut in the shape of a basket and filled with fruitballs.

I shrugged. I couldn't help loading up, the food was so pretty, and my stomach was hurting. There was the long table and its thick dusky rose cloth, warm lights bathing the dishes in gold. I was adding a crab cleverly deviled in its own shell, when I saw that behind the buffet table was an eight-foot aquarium in which large gray bulldog-faced fish swam slowly from one end to another and around to the start again. I could not tell how it was that they achieved forward motion; they seemed never to flutter their tails or twist their thick bodies, but steadily drifted forward, making the circuit of the tank.

Ordinarily I loved the Yacht Club. From its porch you could see across the harbor to Mt. Pleasant, the very reverse of the view I had seen that morning. You could sit in the dark, cool dining room and eat old-fashioned food and look out into the dazzling sun where young Townsends and Pringles in sailing attire skippered their Sunfish back and forth, barely missing the dock. People eating there were always quiet and well-behaved. There was a high turnover in waiters, but often one of them was a Wando High black guy who would bring me double portions of charlotte russe. But today I didn't feel right in there. The aquarium was a new addition. It is hard to eat seafood while seafood swims in a tank before your eyes, especially when it swims glumly, the corners of its mouth downturned.

Dr. Frobiness started right in on Wayne once we were seated and had been served our iced tea. Wayne was ready to bolt. He had never liked the Yacht Club. I watched him squirm. Everything his father said or did annoyed him, down to the way Dr. Frobiness pronounced words and blinked his eyes. You know a relationship has deteriorated past the point of salvage when one person detests another's gestures.

"I understand your interest in the downtrodden," Dr. Frobiness said. "I like to think that as a young man I was drawn to medicine for similar humanitarian reasons. But look at yourself son. *Look* at yourself. What's happening to you? Don't allow yourself to be pulled into their world. That's the danger. You've got to stay within your own world and help from there, not leap in with these people." He blotted his lips with the dusky rose napkin. Wayne's eyes were glued to the napkin: up to the mouth, blot, blot, down to the lap. Wayne coughed.

"Now, I have a proposal to make." Dr. Frobiness paused for Wayne to respond, but Wayne was staring at something in the vicinity of his father's hand. "What I propose is this," his father said. "You take the remainder of the summer and do with it what you will. Continue at the Center if you like.

Then in September you enroll at the College of Charleston. I know it's not Sewanee, but at this point I'll settle for any four-year accredited institution. I'll pick up the tab for tuition and rent. You get some sort of job, a *paying* job, to cover food and transportation. I'll expect you to maintain a decent average, but nothing spectacular. Just stay in, that's all I hope for. I've lowered my sights considerably." He smiled at me. "What do you think, Lucille? A new bachelor apartment? Maybe you can help me get this young man on the right track."

"What is that on your finger?" Wayne said.

Dr. Frobiness looked at his hand. "It's a ring," he said.

Wayne was aghast. "What for?"

"Why, for nothing. A ring to wear."

"That's a diamond in it."

"Just a small one. It was a good investment. It's called a Man's Diamond. It was advertised in *The New Yorker*. A little less than two carats, but high quality. But, ah, look, son, if you don't mind, don't mention this to your mother. It might upset her."

"Dad, she said you were in debt because of setting up the new office and all the expenses of trying to build up the practice."

"I am, I am. She's absolutely correct. My God, the cost of secretarial equipment alone was over fifteen thousand, and I want you to guess how much I have to pay for liability insurance. Guess."

"I couldn't begin to."

"No, just take a wild guess. What do you think I have to cough up?"

"I don't know." Wayne was stubborn. I knew he wouldn't guess.

"Take a guess, son," Dr. Frobiness insisted.

"A million dollars," I said.

"Heh, no, little lady, not quite that much. No, I'm ponying up *twenty-one thousand* dollars a year for insurance." He pronounced the first syllable of "thousand" with a wide open mouth, and made his eyes big.

"Holy smoke," I said, to be polite. In truth, I thought that was a pretty good bargain. Suppose he botched a liposuction or misaligned an implant? If I were the insurance company, I would not have insured Dr. Frobiness for any amount.

He went on to say that some fathers, himself and Ronald Reagan included, had a lot at stake in the careers of their sons. It wasn't as if the sons of such fathers were free agents. "My heart aches for the President," he said.

"Excuse me," I said. I wanted seconds before they wheeled the roast beef away. It was already three o'clock, and the steamboat round was carved down like a saddle. The waiter in charge of slicing meat was standing over by the aquarium with two other waiters. I waited politely by the meat, plate in hand, but they were engaged in an argument, and a partially melted seahorse made of ice stood between me and them. They didn't notice me. One said, "Maître d' said, get that mother *out.*" Another said, "Get him out how?" "I don't know, but get him out." "Shit, man, I ain't reaching my hand in there. It's crabs in there." "He ain't dead yet anyhow." "Sure he is." "Naw, he ain't. His gills is opening and closing, that's his breathing." "Any fish that is upside down is dead in my book." "Said get him out fast before a member sees him." "Get him out, James." "Go for it, James." "All *right, James."*

From behind the ice sculpture I watched as James took the roast beef fork and speared the ailing bulldog-fish. It was an expert move—not a splash, not a sound. The fish was spirited into the kitchen. James returned to the roast beef table where he carved me a slice of well-done gray beef. I thought I recognized him from school, maybe the basketball team; but I couldn't be sure, he was dressed in a waiter's black pants and coat, and he didn't let on that he saw anything recognizable in me. He only looked at the meat and sawed; he used a regular fork to hold it down, I was glad to see.

When I got back to my seat, I looked at my roast beef and realized I could not eat it. I put my napkin casually across the plate. Probably there was not a good filter system in the tank, not enough oxygen. The fish got sluggish, going round; lost whatever dim sort of consciousness fish possess; and bellied up.

"Wayne," I started to say, but he was gazing at his father, who was writing his club number on the check.

"We are all going to have to tighten our belts, Dr. Frobiness said. "For the time being. I can manage the college tuition and an apartment for you, but that's about it. Your mother's going to have to find an apartment as well and some kind of job. Has she discussed this with you?"

Wayne said nothing.

Dr. Frobiness said, "I spoke with a radiologist whose wife runs a dress shop. She has several gals helping her out part-time, and she needs somebody else in the afternoons."

"Lucille," Wayne said sharply to me. "Do you feel sick?"

"Mmmm."

"Lucille throws up at the drop of a hat," Wayne said.

Dr. Frobiness looked alarmed. He glanced around at the few remaining diners.

"Now?" Wayne said. I nodded. "Excuse us, Dad. We'll talk later." He ushered me out the door and onto the porch, down the steps and into the Ram Charger.

"Fantastic," Wayne said. "What a girl."

"I need air."

"Me, too. Me, too. God*damn*. I'm sorry you had to witness that."

"I need to get some fresh air or I'm going to be sick."

"Sick? I thought you were faking. I thought you were doing it to get me out of there."

"No. The fish in the aquarium made me dizzy."

"You look awful. Your skin is clammy. Here, let's get out and walk down on the dock." He ran around to my side, opened the door, and gave me a hand down. My knees wobbled.

"I never thought your father was the type for a diamond ring," I said.

"He's converting to tangibles. Hidable tangibles. Come the day of reckoning, he turns over his financial records for a settlement, and there won't be as much on paper as she thought."

"I see."

A red Sunfish hit a green Sunfish, and the young sailors hollered blame at each other. They appeared to be no older than nine or ten. Rich people are careless with their children, I observed. A chill ran down my spine to think of letting a child go alone into the harbor on a small plank with a tiny sail. There were tankers and freighters out there. But the children seemed perfectly at ease, even when they wrecked or capsized, and they would be back at it again tomorrow.

"Lucille, give me another chance." He spoke without looking at me. He leaned on the railing and watched the children. "I'm desperate," he said.

Well, that broke me because I knew it was the truth. His bow tie was too small for his neck and had lost its grip on one side. His pain was bright, shining in his eyes and skin and shoulders. I made a mistake that girls commonly make. Out of a sense of honor (he was a good boy who deserved something from a good girl) I said yes. It was the generous and friendly thing to do, but it was a mistake. We agreed to meet the next night on the dock in front of my house. He looked happy.

Nick Lindsay

from *An Oral History of Edisto Island:*

SAM GADSDEN TELLS THE STORY

I was born in 1882. One of my earliest memories is the earthquake of 1886. I was four years old when it came through and tore up Charleston and that whole section all around there.

It didn't shake down any houses on Edisto though. It just damaged some of the big ones a little. It came in the evening of the twentieth day of August and the people had all been out picking cotton all day. My father and my two brothers came home and it was *hot*. After a while my mother came home; she had been over there at Mr. Towney Mikell's plantation, California, picking his cotton. She got supper for us all and after we were done eating, she opened both of the doors of the house—it was a small house—and she put down quilts on the floor. We lay down there to try to get a nap and oh, it was *hot!*

Directly there came a rumbling, RRRRRRRRRR! People jumped out of their houses and started to holler, "Merceeee! Judgemennnnnnt!" And they started to run back and forth to one another's houses.

I did it too. I was four years old; I went to the door and looked out; I enjoyed that kind of doings. The earth was going this way, that way, twisty, twisty, like something was underneath. Water was springing up out of the earth all about. I liked that kind of weather.

The thing went on, it didn't stop, so the people ran up and started a meeting at the meeting house, and they all went crazy with whooping and hollering. That earth didn't settle down at all for two days. People would just get to work in the fields when the ground would start to twist and hump and they would run inside again. They were about to run off, but they didn't know where to run to.

I didn't have much sense. I didn't know and understand what I was looking at, so I took it for a rare pleasure.

The next insurrection we had here in this country was the storm of '93. I was a boy nearly twelve years old then. It was on a Sunday and the day was foggy. There was fog everywhere. I was hanging around the house while my father was getting ready to go to church. Allen AME Church it was, that same church on the corner where we go now.

My father gave my older brother the task to keep the crows out of the cornfield. They had been shucking and eating the corn as fast as they could go. I wasn't needed, so my father sent me to the next neighbor's; he had a boy my same age I went to school with. I went there and my parents went to church. A fog and a stillness were on the whole creation.

The neighbors boy said, "Let's go over to Mikells'," that was a couple of miles west. And the trees were so *still!* We played there a while then we went to play with my cousin two miles east of us. Then they each went about their business and I was alone there at my cousin's house. Then the fog began to get heavier and heavier, and it began to fog-rain. I was in the house looking out when it started to windstorm, Ohhhh! Oooooooooooooh! Oooooooooooooh! And it started to rain steadily.

There I was, all by myself. I looked out and I thought how I was far away from home and nobody knew where I was because nobody had sent me there. I jumped out of that house and ran flat out across the hill in the place they call Scott's. I got to the pond that is in the middle of that hill and all the pine trees that were around that pond were bending down to the ground. Their heads would touch ground, then they would jump back, touch down, jump back.

I was bound for the woods now. When I got to the woods, all the trees in the woods had their heads low, down to the ground. But the wind was behind me. I got through that place, I *fled* through that place. I wanted out. When I got out on the other side, the storm was there, the full storm, wind after wind. I went on until I got to the house of Old Man Peter Wright. He said, "Boy, you go on home."

But I said, "Let me stay here," so he opened the door and let me come in to the house. They were standing or sitting about the parlor, but I wouldn't go in there. I stayed on the stairs they had there going upstairs, sat right there on the one step.

I sat down and watched and the storm was *real* then. I looked down, and there those steps I was sitting on were starting to come apart one from the other. When I saw that, I leaped out of that house into the storm. The wind was behind me and drove me home so quick I didn't even know when I went right past it. I had to cut back, and that one thing was like to have cost me all.

The old man had a corn house on the far side of the yard and the house was on the near side. I got into that corn house and I looked out and that was a *rain!* I looked across to see the house but the rain was so thick I couldn't see across the yard. I looked back down, and in that short time that I was looking across the yard, the water had risen waist deep around me. Water had come on that last flow of wind. I made ready to strike out for the house. A flow of wind came, then went on by, and the storm ceased for one roll. I leaped out there, and the water was already almost up to my neck, salt water. I got to the house how ever I could, crawled up against it, "Knock, knock, knock."

My old man opened the door, "Where you come from?" and he shut it again as quick as he could, but the water was running through. I couldn't see anything; I was almost drowned. I went into the back of the house and pulled off my wet clothes, but then I couldn't get anybody to give me any room on the stairs. They were all on there. I went on up anyhow, climbed up on the underneath side of the stairs, like you climb the back side of a ladder when it's up against the house, hanging upside down like a squirrel. The back of the stairs wasn't closed in with boards. I got up to the top and lay right across the step there and fell fast asleep. I was out and done!

When I woke up next morning and looked out, everything was under water. The storm had abated. All the chickens and turkeys were drowned, all the goods—drowned, dead things everywhere. I thought I must be dreaming, I rubbed my eyes to try and wake up and I looked out again.

Across the face of the island—the Great Atlantic Ocean! Water was across the whole creation. You couldn't see anything but ocean all about, then two miles over there, Mr. Mikell's place still standing, one or two smaller houses, but most of them were down under the water. The tide from the northeast met the tide from the southwest and the whole place was covered.

That water started to run off then. That was a sight to see too. I thought I would die of astonishment. I never saw water run away so fast. The whole place turned into a swift-running river of tide water. You couldn't see anything but a brook here and a river there, a creek here and a run yonder. I dug out the oars to go with the boat and find out what water was.

Late that day the news came out, "Do you know, all the people on Joe Island drowned?" Joe Island, that's the northeast end of Edisto, the place they call Swallow's Bluff now. "They are all drowned, every soul. All the houses are gone."

Peter Wright, his boy, his wife, and James Wright and his daughter—all drowned. A lot of people lived there, and the whole island was drowned off, every soul. In the years before the storm we used to go and pick oysters in the creek beside that settlement of people, and all were drowned. When the news reached us, I had to assimilate that.

Many people on Little Edisto were drowned, and all of them on Whooping Island. Many communities were completely wiped out. It was the worst disaster that ever came to Edisto Island.

The storm of '93 was the hardest time I ever experienced and it brought on the hardest times that anybody ever saw on this island. It didn't really start till sundown and the main body of it came after dark. It washed right in, came up into the houses and then the houses broke up. Many children were drowned. If it had come in the daytime, the people could have saved themselves better, but it came in the night. No one could see, they got up and ran out of the house as it began to break up, and ran out to their deaths. Many swam off and drowned just like the cattle. And almost all the cattle were drowned, the cows, the hogs, the goats.

It was a very hard time for the year after the storm. More people died after the storm than died in it. There was nothing to eat, the whole island stank with dead cattle. We had no time to bury them. The Government sent some relief here: Missy Barton who was giving people some clothes and a few groceries. You could get maybe a peck of yellow corn meal every week, and two pounds of bacon, but it wasn't enough to stem the hardship. The storm came in August and all the crops for that year were wiped out and the land was too salty and wasn't fit to plant the next spring, 1894. I don't see how the people that had no wages to help them out managed to live through that year.

The next two years sickness broke out and killed almost all the old people. They were already starved, so they got sick easily. I had that sickness then too, and like to have gone. When God is ready for you, you go. He send me back. They called that sickness 'malarial grippe.' It was something like influenza.

Almost all the able bodied men went away from here to try to get wages anywhere they could. Many men took work digging phosphate rock for fertilizer in the rock mine at Red Top. They called that the Cherokee Mine. They worked there to make a few pennies to help them beat the hard times for that one year.

After the storm passed, and then the pestilence passed, we started in on some good times. Everybody that had come through made sure that they would make themselves a crop to live on. They had corn, peas, rice, hogs and fowls and tater plenty. They all started up again, they went into good times that year and have never fallen back into anything like the misery of 1893, 1894, 1895.

After 1895, we were suddenly back on our own with that long cotton again, and pretty easy money. We were getting forty, fifty cents and sometimes as much as a dollar a pound. Since each man was raising all his own food, all the money he got from that cotton was clear and free, maybe one or two hundred dollars. Not only that, there was nothing out here he could spend money on. Each man had more money than he could spend; he was living like a prince. The people bought horses and buggies and they must have taken a million rides. Some unusual men actually did save some money and buy land with it. The majority didn't save any.

Egrets were in season then too, and you could get a lot of them before they passed the law against hunting them. A man could make a couple of hundred dollars a year on egret feathers; it was easy to catch them and it didn't take any investment.

The churches played a large part in the way the people knit themselves together and recovered from the storm. That is always the way it has been on this island: there is a group of people who guide the church and the church organizes the rest. There was no one man who stood up and said, "I am the boss. I want this, and I want that." A man like that would get killed. The people on this island work through the church.

That storm came at about the wind-up of Reconstruction times. The official Reconstruction was over when Wade Hampton came in a governor in 1877, but the time trickled on around here a little longer. First came the War, in 1861; then in 1865, in April, peace was declared. That peace time lasted until Reconstruction set in about 1867.

When the war came, the masters all left their plantations, but their colored people stayed on. Some of them stayed home all during that while. They were farming, "We are a free nigger, yes sir, we are free." Boy, they thought they owned that man's place.

Then Peace was declared and the masters came back. They had to be simple residents then. They were very poor and didn't have anything to eat. All their money had gone to run that war and if there was any left, Jefferson Davis had it somewhere. None of the masters had any. And then, oh! but those were hard times! For the white people especially. When they got home they found the house full of "all the niggers," as they called them. It was like a house filled with children, from their point of view.

In some places out around North Charleston there were some fights when the masters came back and tried to enter the house. The colored people wouldn't accept them. Things like that didn't happen on Edisto Island. Around here they thought a lot of their masters.

For those "children" welcomed the hungry master and took him in and fed him from their own gardens, and worked for him and helped him do his chores. They thought a lot of their master. When Maussa come home, everything is going to be all right now.

Some of the masters weren't able to come back; they were killed in the war or had some other trouble. The people on those plantations grieved, for if the master is there and any person wants for any thing, he can tell Maussa and Maussa will help him to it. They are glad to work for Master, feed Master and be his servant and care for him in every way.

Commerce was cut off and there was nothing but what you could make with only your two hands. They used kindling wood to light with. That was still the way in my time. When I came along there was no gas, no electricity, but it was the kindling time. You want a light in your house? You go out into the woods and cut fat lightered pine, called lightwood because you light up the house with it. You split that up, put it in a bundle and have it there to light with. You make a flambeau with lightwood, carry that around the house, out in the yard. That was the dark age. After that, the times grew and grew until there came the time of a little tin lamp. That came in Reconstruction times, at the end of Reconstruction. A little tin lamp with a cup and a spout and it had a wick in there. It was a little brass light. You could read pretty fair with it. It had no chimney, but it didn't smoke. The flame went straight up like a candle. The people in the big, ornamental houses used candles. The poor people were blessed to get a little lamp.

And at the time when the masters just came back, they all lived that way. It wasn't a bad way; they didn't suffer. All the people who were smart enough to make their own food ate well and they all made enough to feed the others that weren't—that's the masters and the ex-slaves that didn't have the gumption to care for themselves. All ate well. They carried the others along until times changed and Reconstruction set in.

Everything changed then, because they started getting money. Commerce started to flow through the island as it had before the war but with the difference that now the commerce and politics included the colored people. It is when they say the good times started. Everything flowed freely and they started to make money off of that long cotton. During slavery times they didn't allow any slave to plant cotton for himself, just vegetables. Some of the good masters would buy the garden truck from their slaves, though more often than not he would just take it. The good masters would allow the slaves to come up to the market at the head of Store Creek and they could sell it. There was a market there for the slaves to sell their pumpkins, potatoes, peas and so on. Some of them made pretty good money even during slavery times. But they must always go back and work that cotton crop for Master, and work Master's corn, and peas for Master's cow. And no slave must plant cotton.

But Reconstruction began and they could make money off that long cotton for themselves. When they started in on the money crops again, the master didn't know anything about how to plant nor how to plow cotton, for he never did any work for himself, but his slaves did it all. Now they were free and they were planting that cotton to their own account instead of his. Master must wait for them to show him how to do it, or he must hire them to do it. In that one way the people held the upper hand in commerce for a brief time.

I was born right in that time, 1882. When Reconstruction first began, we got a dollar a pound for our long cotton and the white people made up to as much as two dollars. By 1890 we were down to forty, fifty, maybe some years seventy five cents. We could have been making a dollar a pound right through that whole time except the buyers and management cut us down to that. During those days short cotton was twelve and fourteen cents a pound. There wasn't anyone around here who fooled with short cotton very much. Short cotton, that is cotton with a short fiber length, is the crop they raise up country and all about the United States. You couldn't raise long cotton anywhere except in these islands along the coast. Can't raise it anywhere now since the boll weevil came.

In the time of masters it was all right so long as the Black people had a really white master. Some of the masters would starve their people and wouldn't give them anything. I'm not talking about them. In slavery times, as long as they had a good master, the Black people didn't worry about anything in their life—how to do and how to get what they needed, what to hold on to or how to hold on. They didn't care so long as the master had it. "If Master has it, it is as good as though I had it for myself." He would say, "Maussa got him? Go for me." That is the way it started back in the slavery days. Some people picked it up and that's the way they do even to this day. This was the days of masters.

But after the war, and then after Peace was declared, then after Reconstruction set in, the Black people didn't have any master, good *or* bad. That meant they had to come together and work things out in some way so they could get along. The difficulty seemed to be within the white people. They didn't like to see the Black people be free. They set up rules and arrangements to keep the power and regard in their own hands.

"You want this, and you want that? Then go to Mister So and So. You work for him and he'll give you this and he'll give you that." They were against your staying free. It was not easy for them. It is as though you had raised some cattle and then the cattle all ran away and were gone. But then they didn't even stay gone, but came back and hung around the place you thought was *your* place and you couldn't control them any more. It's easy to see how you're going to feel. That's the way the white people felt who came back after the war and found the colored people living here all about the place, running free.

At first the white and Black worked together, but then commerce started to spread and all the usual, human feelings left from among them. The white people began to begrudge these niggers their running around and doing just as they chose. That's all there is to segregation, that caused the whole thing. The white people couldn't master these niggers any more so they took up the task of intimidating them. The best of the masters would have liked to keep the old slavery idea alive, "Maussa got him? Go for you." Hang on to the master, believe in the master, just like God Almighty. If he's got it, it will come to you. If he hasn't got it, you don't need to worry.

Just as it was in slavery times, in the Reconstruction times, some of the masters were bad, they would starve you and wouldn't give you anything. They turned that saying around to read, "If you want anything, Master has to get most of it first and then give you a little bit. He gets the meat, leave you the bone; he gets two dollars for his cotton, gives you forty cents. Don't worry or cause a fuss."

I completed my education—the fifth grade at the school that stands now across from Grant's store. That was the top grade for us here in those years. I worked a little around the island, then about 1898 I left and went to follow construction work over on the mainland. I was in my teens and early twenties. We built all in the swamps in Georgia and Florida. I did all kinds of construction work. If I came to a place and liked it and could make a few dollars, I would stay. If I didn't like it, if it was a wild place, I wouldn't stay. I would go back to town and by the next

Sunday I would be back home again. Sometimes the contractor would take us forty miles down a little railroad track, deep into those swamps and out of the way places. When the train stopped, I would look out, and if I didn't see a church anywhere, I might not even get off the train. Or if I did get off and couldn't find a church anywhere around there, I would not stay long.

It's not just because of the way I was raised that I did this, although that had a lot to do with it. Yes, immediately when I would see a church, I would feel myself at home. But if there was none there, I knew I was off my beat. I would leave that place as soon as possible because that was a dangerous place.

It was dangerous because of the kind of people who lived there. They were the murderers, gamblers, pickpockets, men who just got out of the penitentiary, and everything low that wrecks people. They had come in there and they hung around just in order to get money and to hide from the law. There might be money there, and there might not be any, but money was their reason for being there. That was a money jungle where all those rogues and thieves hung out. Money was their only reason for going anywhere or doing anything. They are dangerous people.

But if a church comes into a place like that, those people aren't going to stay long. If they stayed, they would have to confess and turn away from their reckless way of living. So they get out as soon as a church comes in.

I quit that work in 1906. I had worked my way down to Fort Lauderdale, Florida and one day I accidentally met some cousins of mine who were working on the railroad down there. They said, "You ain't heard the news?"

"No what news?"

"The Marion gone down and drowned half the people of Edisto."

That sounded pretty bad. The Marion was a boat that used to carry passengers from Charleston to Beaufort and make stops at all the islands along the way. I went back to my room that night and wrote home to my mother to find out about what my cousins had told me. She wrote me a long letter and she could tell me a whole lot since she knew the people who drowned. I came home right after that and I have been here ever since. The sinking of the steam boat Marion just before I came home helps me keep track of that date. They built that boat back, gave her a new name, name her the Islander.

I have been working only for myself from that time onwards. Sometimes I have made it pretty well and sometimes it's been pretty bad, but I have always made enough to stay off of public work; I have worked only for myself from that time onwards.

I have been a poor rich man. I have done as I chose and worked as I felt like it. Some days it would rain and I couldn't work. I was sorry I couldn't work, but not too sorry. I rested a little and then went back at it again.

I could make a little money. Some years I came out very well. I remember in 1915 I made seven bales of cotton, and that same year I bought up eighteen bales of cotton from these other farmers around here. I held them up a little while and then when I went on through with it and marketed those twenty five bales, I had three thousand dollars, spot cash. I was dealing there for a while in that long staple cotton. I made a nice pile of money just from buying and selling when my hand never touched the crop. I went to the factors who handled that cotton, when to them one at a time—first to Mr. Ravenel, and he gave me a pile of money, then to Mr. Boyle, and he gave me a pile of money, then to Mr. Whaley and Rivers, and he gave me a pile of money. I couldn't take all the cotton to one place, I had to divide it out among those brokers, for if any one of them thought I was bringing in that big a load of cotton, he would cut me down. They had an allotment there for any colored farmer and if you brought in any more than that allotment, thcy would play a bad trick on you. They wouldn't sell your cotton, but put it back in the warehouse until it got old and rotten. We found out about that trick and the safe politics they were playing. When I divided the crop out that way, each one thought I had just an ordinary, little crop and he paid me for it. He didn't pay me but half of what he paid a white farmer, or even less, but still it was a lot better than no pay at all.

I was dealing in that cotton, and I could make enough garden crops to feed us here and I could always make a little money on vegetables. There was never any need for me to go to work for some other man for wages.

I planted long staple cotton until the boll weevil came along that wiped that all out after 1918. After that I tried to make some good crops of short staple cotton, but I never did understand how to manage that correctly. By the time I did understand, the state law came out and gave every man an allotment and it was so small it didn't pay to fool with it. That short cotton sold so cheap there wasn't much money in it for the small farmer at any time.

I raised Irish potatoes and beans, these two crops. I never did plant anything else. Some years those two crops kept me going along fine and I made good money off of them. Some years there wasn't anything to them except the work—no money at all.

During the last twenty years a radical change has come through the whole world. In these days a common man can do his work and get two dollars, three dollars an hour. Some common men get five! A skilled man who can lay concrete block and brick can get six and seven dollars an hour! Who ever dreamed that could happen?

I can lay block and brick and I can do the carpentry work, but in my time there was no wage at all, because there was no work. There was no job to be found, no matter how you would come at it, not here on this island. The country wasn't developed and nothing was going on.

This island is getting into the main stream of things now. It's a necessary thing: get in the stream. Don't just lay there up in the grass, or the tide will leave you out on the marsh. You must kick and kick until you can get in the stream. That's the way the world runs.

In the eighties, if you were lucky enough to get any job, it wouldn't pay you as much as five cents an hour. That is the top price for a skilled man. Some places you would get fifty cents for a ten hour day. Most places you wouldn't get but forty cents for a twelve hour day. You worked from six in the morning till six at night just to make a little bread to eat. Those were very long hours, and no progress at all. That's because the only thing that was going on here was farming, one-crop farming, raising that long staple cotton. There was no job open here except farm labor.

After I came home in 1906 I never did any hourly wage work for anyone else, but I did do some work for Mr. Townsend Mikell at his plantation California in return for the use of some of his land. The rent he charged on his land was one work day a week during growing season for each three acres of land you used. You must give him Mondays from May to July, that's planting time to lay-by time, and then August through November, that's picking time. In July they left that crop alone a month, they laid it by until August, when they started in to pick it. You helped to plant, hoe and pick his crop for that one day each week, and he let you use three acres of his land for the year.

He gave you three tasks of land to be your day's work. Monday was the day. It was a mean Monday too. The way they measured a task of land was with a big wooden compass that stood higher than a man, and they would walk that compass across the field twenty one times, twenty one diameters of that compass was one task. Three tasks of land, either to plant it or to hoe it, that is a very heavy day's work. You would work that three tasks every week from May until the fourth of July. Then they lay by until the last of July. When the time came to pick, they gave you fifty pounds of cotton as your day's work, but you see, you came in better during that part of the year, because they would give you a little money too. They gave you fifteen dollars a month in cash when you gave that one day a week and picked your fifty pounds each week from August until November. Later on they raised it to eighteen dollars a month, but when I started it was fifteen.

I would give Mr. Mikell one day a week, then the rest of the week I could work my own crop which I had planted on his three acres of land and on my own.

On his land, which was good land, I would make better than a bale of that long staple cotton to the acre and I could sell my cotton, even when they low-priced me the way they did, and get three hundred dollars for each bale. When the white farmers brought their cotton to market, they got eighty cents to a dollar a pound, but the cotton brokers had their arrangement made and they wouldn't give a colored farmer but forty or fifty cents a pound in those years. My return on that three acres was three hundred dollars for the season.

Mr. Mikell's three tasks, that averaged an acre of land that he had me tend for him until it was time to pick, then to go ahead and pick it. And then I would get fifteen dollars for that. But I saw that if I had tended an acre of land for myself, I would have made three hundred dollars. It was plain to me that I had better try to make some of that cotton for myself, even though I had to sell it low.

It looks as though I could have been able to get the same price on the market for the same product, but that cotton was an organized game, and if you weren't in that organization, you couldn't get the price the organization got. It is just the same with truck crops today. You can plant four or five acres and make a good crop of fine vegetables, but if you are not in the marketing organization, it's a good chance you can't even sell yours, and you absolutely are not going to get the market price. The buyer will take your crop and hold it and hold it, but the crop can't wait, not fresh vegetables. So he will give you whatever price he wants. He can completely take advantage of you. Some people say there could be a co-op. Is there a co-op? They hide all those co-ops. They are just for the big farmer. There is no co-op for the poor people. The poor people who want to plant those things, they go ahead and plant them, but they have to take them to market on their own.

We raise a lot of tomatoes here and there is a cannery for

tomatoes over on Yonges Island. That canning factory buys on a reduction. They come in after the crop has been shipped and take all the ripe tomatoes you were going to throw away. They bring in their crew and pick those tomatoes, throw them in the truck and take them to the canning factory. At the end of the crop, when the whole field ripens at once, they come and take all. But they don't pay you more than twenty five cents a bushel and they tell you, "That's a *good* price for them."

They might be right, because if it weren't for them, the farmer would have to plow them under, cover them over, because he can't afford to hire anyone to pick them and grade them and box them. The box costs as much as the canning factory is giving him.

The factory claims it is a big price they are giving him, because they say he has already made a lot of money on the tomatoes he has graded and shipped. He has already got plenty of money out of the crop, he ought to *give* the waste stuff to the factory, so they say.

It is better than plowing them under. Some years when the market price is low, even though the people in the cities are hungry, the farmer can't afford to pick any of his crop at all. The dollar rules, not common sense. There will be good tomatoes, the best you could ever see, and the farmer has to plow it all under. It is all a money gambling time that leaves the poor man in the cities hungry and the small farmer poor.

Things are plentiful out on a farm. I was down in Florida back before 1906. They raise grapefruit and oranges and all kinds of fruit along the east coast there. If you would go to any city there, say Miami, and you wanted a banana, you had to pay ten cents for it. But if you would go to where they were grading them, they would let you eat as much as you wanted. They had a pail of them there. A man would bring in a whole truck load and after he had graded out the best, the ones he could take out to the city and sell at twenty five cents a bunch, he would let you have as much as you wanted. He would just give it to you.

It was the same with oranges. If you went in to the field where they were grading them, you could back a cart right up in there and load it up for nothing. They were glad for you to haul them away by the cart load. Those were the cull oranges, the ones they couldn't sell. But in some of the towns right around there you had to pay five cents and ten cents apiece. I have see that myself.

Right here on this island, with the cabbage, if you go to the store for cabbage it will cost you ten cents a pound, but if you go out in the field the farmer will say, "You want some? Oh yeah. Take some and be welcome. We got plenty here."

Things are plentiful on a farm, but the farmers are all kicking about the price they have to pay for labor. The Government has set the wage up to a dollar sixty five, and as high as two dollars some times. No. A farm cannot pay that kind of wage for the labor and compete on the market. He must compete on his price, but if he sells at the price the marketing organizations give him, unless he is very large, he can't afford to pay the wages the Government says he must.

They have thrown the little man out. It's only the big man who can make it, since he sells enough. He plants a big farm, and has a thousand acres of tomatoes. He has his crews pick those tomatoes as soon as they get ripe enough. He picks about three or four thousand lugs of tomatoes that first picking. A lug, that's one of those wooden boxes they use to bring the tomatoes in from the field. For that first picking he will get from five to nine dollars a lug. Some places he will get ten dollars a lug. Now he has made back every dime he spent on that crop. The next time he picks, he picks twice as much, and he gets three dollars a lug. And it's just like shoveling up money with a shovel. He is a big farmer; he has enough tomatoes to cover the market, and at that price too.

The price for the first picking is the highest, the second is lower, and after a while the price falls to a dollar and a half a lug. That's about the time the poor *little* farmer is just getting his crop to market. Poor scoundrel, he bucks himself off a dollar and a half, or a dollar a lug and that doesn't pay him to fool with. But it's all he's got.

The poor farmer doesn't have any thousand acres to work with, no, all he has is a little bit of a place and all he can do with his crop is to carry it in town to the co-op and they will give him whatever they want. No poor man can farm now. You just as well take your little money and dig a hole and bury it as to put it in a farm, because you will never get anything at all, not on any little farm.

The big farmer will be the first on the market every time, because he has money behind him. He can buy fertilizer and he can force his crop to get it to market early, and he has all his bulldozers and tractors to make the land ready so he can plant earlier too. There is no doubt about it, he is going to get that first crop out way ahead of you. And there he goes, that first crop has paid all his expenses; then he gets in there while the price is falling and he racks the second picking in there and puts that money in his pocket; then he gets the third drag—he don't *want* no more.

The whole business is gambling, right now just like it was all along. The gamblers get all the money and the working man is poor. All money business is gambling. The only sure thing is from God Almighty. Any thing that has to depend on man is gambling. If you are a plain working man and your boss pays you a good wage, you can depend on it that he is making ten times as much as you. He gets the wholesale business and you, the man who does the labor, you get only the retail part and the whole thing gone to the devil for you unless you can get into that organization, the money gang. If you can once get on the inside of that money gang, you will get rich quick.

There is no maybe about it, if you get into that association, you will be able to get all the money you want. You will get enough to fulfill your contract and leave you a good stake of clear profit. If you handle your business carefully, you'll have twenty thousand dollars after the first few deals like that: ten thousand to put in the bank and ten to go back into the business.

A working man who just works and saves can never get any stake to start him in business. He will have to get inside that money gang or else he will just be working for a piece of bread and a roof. That will be the limit of what he will ever get.

For a rich man it comes out as nicely as it did with the bossman in slavery days. They thought these Africans could stand more rough living in new construction work than any white people could, so they treated them roughly. They bought them and raised their children and had them trained to clear land and work in the fields. The thing went on so nicely until the bossman, he didn't have to work at all, neither he nor any of his family. He went around wearing his white collar and his necktie and riding his horses and all, just like a Prince of Wales, and put all the rough work off onto the Black people.

Rich people. They! They don't do nothing. They just go from place to place, enjoy the scenery, enjoy the good things they have here or they own there. What, work for their food? Who, them? they have people to do that; they themselves don't do nothing. They just go around inside their houses in this city or visit that country place they own, or the other plantation.

That Doctor Greenway who bought Sea Cloud plantation and the Townsend Place, Bleak Hall, he has places in Connecticut, and a rubber farm in South America too. His son wouldn't even stay here. He came through here once on an airplane and landed on the beach, then he went away again and we will see him no more. He comes and goes between his farm in South America and his place in Connecticut. They have too much money. They don't know what to do with it. But they themselves don't do nothing; their money does all the work. The Greenways are all millionaires.

Doctor Greenway came in here during the depression, around 1930, and bought up those places. He built his house on the Townsend place, Bleak Hall, after he tore down the old plantation house. The Townsends were dead broke and he bought the place pretty cheap. It was the Townsend daughter who ruled the Townsends then. They could have kept the place, paid taxes and all, but they didn't want any fuss with their daughter, so they let the assessor come out and go over the place and they mortgaged it for thirty thousand dollars. During the depression they couldn't find that kind of money, so they let the place go and Doctor Greenway got it.

It was all sold except one piece right next to the sea which still belongs to young John Townsend. He's a doctor in Charleston.

I remember his old granddaddy used to sail in a sailboat all up and down there where we would fish. The colored people used to fish plenty back then, but we didn't use boats for that. Each person had his own catch. He would use a cast net back in the creek. And there is an inlet over there where old Mr. Townsend used to be sailing called Jeremy Inlet, and another one further down called Frampton Inlet. In those inlets you could catch fish by the load at certain times. And if you went out on the beach there you could fish for sea bass in the ocean.

For sea bass you use a long line, swing it round your head two or three times, then let go, and it will sail out way beyond the breakers and you can catch those bass out there. Maybe two or three in a day—that's a cart load. Big old bass! Red channel bass maybe five feet long.

I have caught him many times out there on Edingsville Beach. By now that's about the only place left where you can catch him, because a bass is a scary fish and the people have scared him away from the beaches further down. You can't catch him where the real estate people have developed the place, you must come further down this way where the people aren't mixing up the water.

I'll catch me one about three feet long, fry that fish up, peel him, put him in a cool place and you have a month of fish there. After I get one meal off him on the table with rice or grits or something like that, I don't want him on the table any more, but every time I come in I get a piece and eat it dry, just so. Get a little bread maybe. Presently I will eat that whole fish. That's the way I like to eat fish.

from *An Oral History of Edisto Island:*

THE LIFE AND TIMES OF BUBBERSON BROWN

Care for your own, that's the best thing to learn or know. Care for you own people. I stay with mine—Daddy, Granddaddy, Grandmother and all—until I bury them. I walk with them, I plant and plow for them, gather the crop. When Daddy ain't home, my mother work right with Granddaddy. Granddaddy, he crazy about them daughter. He plant six task of cotton for each of them, plant tater and all. And he cultivate it too. He care for us.

You must care for you own. My wife tell them children we need wood here, tell them cut wood. And then they ain't done nothing but slip off! My own grandchildren! You better believe I tell them a good warning. "I work for you, I care for you myself all these years. When you see me come to the place where I can't do it no more and your grandmother tells you, ain't nothing to do but go and do it." I tell them so. That's the best thing they could learn and know.

*　　　*　　　*

When you live in the country, you can help yourself. I raise hogs, raise poultry of all kinds. I have a big hog here, and one up yonder, she is in pig right now. She'll have pigs here in the next two or three weeks. I fish sometimes, but not this month. By next month the bass will bite. In August and September you can always catch a good fish. But in July, this time of year, you go out there, and set down two or three hours and come back with two or three little fish. Why do that when I could go and catch eight or nine quarts of shrimp and put them up? I went out and got three quarts of shrimp this morning. I work around here all the time, go in the creek, come out with some fish or oysters. I take on little jobs here or there, yarn a net or nail up some screens or jack up a sill of a house. I keep on doing something all the time, make myself useful. If I sit down long, it gets painful.

This is better, home here. Me and my wife been together all these years now, sixty years. Long water run out me eye how thankful the Lord been to me! I sleep so good here, the world turn over. Like I sleep in that dark rain way back yonder, I was a boy. Such a terrible thunder shower. Middle of the afternoon, it was a Friday. Dark, dark, dark. That same time lightning strike a woman, Old Man Lestin daughter, over the other side of the creek. I come in the house, my grandmother house. Lay down, gone to sleep. Done night time for me. Later on, I wake up, sunshine, bird sing. I get up. I gone out, start my Saturday work. "How come? Sun in west? World been turn upside down while I been asleep?" But they show me: sun in the west cause it still Friday. I done the same today. Sleep so good, wake up at two o'clock this afternoon, I figure I done sleep around the clock, couldn't make it out no way, got to call my wife in here, "Hey, old woman! Come here, get me some sense into my head!" She must tell me what day it is. Sleep so good the world turn upside down.

And now I have been living here for the last lifetime, a three and three quarter, a four score of years, a quite a while. I ain't been up to New York from Edisto now for over two straight years. That's all.

Walker Percy

from *The Last Gentleman*

They didn't, the engineer and Jamie, quite cut loose after all, or detour through Norfolk (did Rita mean he should take Jamie to a whorehouse?) or feel any beloveds' warm mouths on theirs. But they had a good time and went their own way for a day or two at a time, wandering down the old Tidewater, sleeping in the piney woods or along the salt marshes and rendezvousing with the Cadillac in places like Wilmington and Charleston.

The camper was everything he had hoped for and more. Mornings on the road, the two young men sat together in the cab; afternoons the engineer usually drove alone. Well as he looked, Jamie tired easily and took to the bunk in the loft over the cab and either read or napped or watched the road unwind. They stopped early in the evening and went fishing or set up the telescope on a lonesome savanna and focused on the faraway hummocks where jewel-like warblers swarmed about the misty oaks.

Nights were best. Then as the thick singing darkness settled about the little caboose which shed its cheerful square of light on the dark soil of old Carolina, they might debark and, with the pleasantest sense of stepping down from the zone of the possible to the zone of the realized, stroll to a service station or fishing camp or grocery store, where they'd have a beer or fill the tank with spring water or lay in eggs and country butter and grits and slab bacon; then back to the camper, which they'd show off to the storekeeper, he ruminating a minute and: all I got to say is, don't walk off and leave the keys in it—and so on in the complex Southern tactic of assaying a sort of running start, a joke before the joke, ten assumptions shared and a common stance of rhetoric and a whole shared set of special ironies and opposites. He was home. Even though he was hundreds of miles from home and had never been here and it was not even the same here—it was older and more decorous, more tended to and a dream with the past—he was home.

A *déjà vu*: so this is where it all started and which is not quite like home, what with this spooky stage-set moss and Glynn marshes but which is familiar nevertheless. It was familiar and droll and somehow small and curious like an old house revisited. How odd that it should have persisted so all this time and in one's absence!

At night they read. Jamie read books of great abstractness, such as *The Theory of Sets*, whatever a set was. The engineer, on the other hand, read books of great particularity, such as English detective stories, especially the sort which, answering a need of the Anglo-Saxon soul, depict the hero as perfectly disguised or perfectly hidden, holed up maybe in the woods of Somerset, actually hiding for days at a time in a burrow of ingenious construction from which he could notice things, observe the farmhouse below. Englishmen like to see without being seen. They are by nature eavesdroppers. The engineer could understand this.

He unlimbered the telescope and watched a fifty-foot Chris-Craft beat up the windy Intercoastal. A man sat in the stern reading the *Wall Street Journal*. "Dow Jones, 894—" read the engineer. What about cotton futures, he wondered.

He called Jamie over. "Look how he pops his jaw and crosses his legs with the crease of his britches pulled out of the way."

"Yes," said Jamie, registering and savoring what the engineer registered and savored. *Yes, you and I know something the man in the Chris-Craft will never know.* "What are we going to do when we get home?"

He looked at Jamie. The youth sat at the picnic table where the telescope was mounted, stroking his acne lightly with his fingernails. His whorled police-dog eye did not quite look at the engineer but darted close in a gentle nystagmus of recognitions, now focusing upon a mote in the morning air just beside the other's head, now turning inward to test what he saw and heard against his own private register. This was the game they played: the sentient tutor knowing quite well how to strike the dread unsounded chords of adolescence, the youth registering, his mouth parted slightly, fingernails brushing backward across his face. *Yes, and that was the wonder of it, that what was private and unspeakable before is speakable now because you speak it.* The difference between me and him, thought the engineer and noticed for the first time a slight translucence at the youth's temple, is this: like me he lives in the sphere of the possible, all antenna, ear cocked and lips parted. But I am conscious of it, know what is up, and he is not and does not. He is pure aching primary awareness and does not even know that he doesn't know it. Now and then he, the engineer, caught flashes of Kitty in the youth, but she had a woman's knack of cutting loose from the ache, putting it out to graze. She knew how to moon away the time; she could doze.

"Why don't we go to college?" he said at last.

"It's forty miles away," said Jamie, almost looking at him.

"We can go where we please, can't we? I mean, do you want to live at home?"

"No, but —"

Ah, it's Sutter he has in mind, thought the engineer. Sutter's at home.

"We could commute," said the engineer.

"Then you'll go?"

"Sure. We'll get up early in the morning."

"What will you take?"

"I need some mathematics. What about you?"

"Yes, me too," nodded the youth, eyes focused happily on the bright mote of agreement in the air between them.

It suited them to lie abed, in the Trav-L-Aire yet also in old Carolina, listening to baseball in Cleveland and reading about set theory and an Englishman holed up in Somerset. Could a certain someone be watching the same Carolina moon?

Or they joined the Vaughts, as they did in Charlestown,

where they visited the gardens even though there was nothing in bloom but crape myrtle and day lilies. Evil-tempered mockingbirds sat watching them, atop tremendous oily camellias. Sprinklers whirled away in the sunlight, leaving drops sparkling in the hairy leaves of the azaleas. The water smelled bitter in the hot sun. The women liked to stand and talk and look at houses. They were built for standing, pelvises canted, and they more or less leaning on themselves. When the men stood still for thirty minutes, the blood ran to their feet. The sun made the engineer sick. He kept close to the women, closed his eyes, and took comfort in the lady smell of hot fragrant cotton. A few years from now and we'll be dead, he thought, looking at tan frail Jamie and nutty old Mr. Vaught, and they, the women, will be back here looking at "places."

It was like home here, but different too. At home we have J. C. Penney's and old ugly houses and vacant lots and new ugly houses. Here were pretty, wooden things, old and all painted white, a thick-skinned decourous white, thick as ship's paint, and presided over by the women. The women had a serious custodial air. They new the place was theirs. The men were not serious. They all but wore costumes. They plied their trades, butcher, baker, lawyer, in period playhouses out in the yard.

Evenings the Vaughts sat around the green chloriniferous pools of the California motels, Rita and Kitty swimming and minding their bodies, Mr. Vaught getting up often to monkey with his Cadillac (he had installed a top-oiler and claimed he got the same mileage as a Chevrolet), Mrs. Vaught always dressed to the nines and rocking vigorously in the springy pool chair and bathing her face with little paper pads soaked in cologne. When she was lucky, she found some lady from Moline who shared her views of fluoridation.

Kitty avoided him. He sought her out, but she damped him down. She must think badly of him, he decided, and quick as he was to see as others saw, was willing to believe she was right. Was it simply that she took the easy way: she was with Rita and not with him and that was that? At any rate, if she didn't love him, he discovered he loved her less.

When they met by chance in motel passageways they angled their shoulders and sidled past like strangers. At Folly Beach they collided at the ice dispenser. He stood aside and said nothing. But when she filled her pitcher, she propped it on the rim of her pelvis and waited for him, a somewhat abstracted Rachel at the well.

"It's a lovely night," she said, stooping to see the full moon through the cloister of the Quality Court.

"Yes," he said politely. He didn't feel much like waiting upon her. But he said, "Would you like to take a walk?"

"Oh yes."

They put their pitchers in the chest and walked on the beach. The moonlight curled along the wavelets. She put her hand in his and squeezed it. He squeezed back. They sat against a log. She took her hand away and began sifting sand; it was cool and dry and left not a grain on the skin.

He sat with his hands on his knees and the warm breeze flying up his pants leg and thought of nothing.

"What's the matter, Bill?" Kitty leaned toward him and searched his face.

"Nothing. I feel good."

Kitty shifted closer. The sand under her sheared against itself and made a musical sound. "Are you mad at me?"

"No."

"You act mad."

"I'm not."

"Why are you different then?"

"Different from what?"

"From a certain nut who kissed a very surprised girl in the automat."

"Hmm."

"Well?"

"I'm different because you are different," said the engineer, who always told the exact truth.

"*Me!* How?"

"I had looked forward to being with you on this trip. But

it seems you prefer Rita's company. I had wanted to be with you during the ordinary times of the day, for example after breakfast in the morning. I did not have any sisters," he added thoughtfully. "So I never knew a girl in the morning. But instead we have become like strangers. Worse, we avoid each other."

"Yes," she said gravely, conscious, he could not help but notice, of saying it so: gravely. "Don't you know why?" she said at last.

"No."

She sifted the cool discrete sand into her palm, where it made a perfect pyramid, shedding itself. "You say you never had sisters. Well, I never had a date, boyfriends—except a few boys in my ballet class who had foreheads this low. Rita and I got used to living quietly."

"And now?"

"I guess I'm clinging to the nest like a big old cuckoo. Isn't that awful?"

He shrugged.

"What do you want me to do?" she asked him.

"What do I want you to do?"

"Tell me."

"How do you feel?"

"How do *you* feel? Do you still love me?"

"Yes."

"Do you? Oh, I love you too."

Why did this not sound right, here on Folly Beach in old Carolina in the moonlight?

One thing I'm sure of, thought he as he held her charms in his arms: I shall court her henceforth in the old style. I shall press her hand. No more grubby epithelial embraces in dogbane thickets, followed by accusing phone calls. Never again! Not until we are in our honeymoon cottage in a cottage small by a waterfall.

But when he kissed her and there she was again looking at him from both sides at once, he had the first inkling of what might be wrong. She was too dutiful and athletic. She worked her mouth against his (is this right, she as good as asked).

"Wonderful," she breathed, lying back. "A perfect setting."

Why is it not wonderful, he wondered, and when he leaned over again and embraced her in the sand, he knowing without calculating the exact angle at which he might lie over against her—about twenty degrees past the vertical—she miscalculated, misread him and moved slightly, yet unmistakably to get plainly and simply under him, then feeling the surprise in him stopped almost before she began. It was like correcting a misstep in dancing.

"What is it?" she whispered presently.

"Nothing," he said, kissing her tenderly and cursing himself. His heart sank. Was is not that she was right and that he made to much of it? What it was, though, was that this was the last thing he expected. It was part of his expectations of the life which lay before him that girls would be girls just as camellias were camellias. If he loved a girl and walked with her on Folly Beach by moonlight, kissed her sweet lips and held her charms in his arms, it should follow that he would be simply he and she she, she as complete as a camellia with her corolla of reticences and allurements. But she, Kitty, was no such thing. She didn't know any better than he. Love, she, like him, was obliged to see as a naked garden of stamens and pistils. But what threw him off worst was that, sentient as always, he found himself catching onto how it was with her: he saw that she was out to be a proper girl and taking every care to do the right wrong thing. There were even echoes of a third person: what, you worry about the boys as good a figure as you have, etc. So he was the boy and she was doing her best to do what a girl does. He sighed.

"What?" she asked again.

"Nothing," he said, kissing her eyes, which were, at any rate, like stars.

He sighed again. Very well, I'll be both for you, boyfriend and girlfriend, lover and father. If it is possible.

They stirred in the musical sand. "We'd better go back," said the gentlemanly engineer and kissed her somewhat lewdly so she wouldn't feel she had failed. It seemed to be his duty now to protect her non-virtue as best he could. After all, he mused, as he reckoned girls must have mused in other ages, if worst comes to worst and all else fails I can let her under me—I shan't begrudge her the sacrifice. What ailed her, him, them, he wondered. Holding her hand as they returned to the Quality Court, he flexed his wrist so that he could count his pulse against her bone.

Mainly their trouble—or good fortune, as the case might be—was that they were still out of phase, their fervors alternating and jostling each other like bad dancers. For now, back at the cooler and she then going ahead of him with her pitcher on the rim of her pelvis, desire like a mighty wind caught him from behind and nearly blew him down. He almost fainted with old motel lewd-longing. "Wait," he whispered—oh, the piercing sorrow of it, this the mortal illness of youth like death to old age. "Wait." He felt his way along the blotting-paper wall like a blind man. She took his outstretched hand.

"What is it, dearest?"

"Let's go in here," he said, opening the door to a closet which housed a giant pulsing Fedders.

"What for" she asked. Her eyes were silvery and turned in.

"Let us go in the service room." For it is here and not by moonlight—he sighed. Her willingness and nurse-tenderness were already setting him at naught again.

"There you are," said Rita, opening the door opposite. "Where in the world was the ice machine?"

And off he went, bereft, careening down the abstract, decent, lewd Quality corridor.

Padgett Powell

from *Edisto*

Then we went to town one last time, for no reason other than the good old days, which you could taste suddenly getting closer to their end and sweeter, like the last pieces of candy. We got up early on a Saturday I was not scheduled for a custody junket. Taurus had his car idling by the shack, mumbling little piffs of hot smoke into the cool cloud of fog which held everything still like a sharecropper photograph. We closed the green shutters on the sea window and one of them fell off, about breaking my foot. I said before they were sorry shutters anyway, which he got from Charleston, and they were sorry even though no dime-store stuff. Each weighed about a hundred pounds, which is why the one fell and why they never departed this world in the hurricanes which probably took a house or two out from under them. That's why Taurus could come to find them out of service yet still for sale, shutters stouter than planters' summer homes and stronger than a cotton economy. When that one fell in the sand, old and spent as it had to be, with scaling paint so thick it could cut your fingers like can lids, it looked like the top of a treasure chest to me. It was green and crooked, with sand already drifting into the louvers.

"Theenie's going to pitch a fit about cutting her wall open," I said.

"We'll put it back later."

"It won't matter," I said. "When she gets back and sees that hole, she'll put a mattress in it until we get a professional carpenter with tar paper and tin tabs and real lumber to shore it back up *right.*"

"Hmmp," he said, just like Theenie. He was a cool jake to the end. We took off.

We had breakfast at an old hotel on the Citadel Square in Charleston. John Calhoun's out there in bronze about forty feet tall, and it seems he's doing something about the Confederacy by standing up there so very proudly, but I don't know what, because I don't know what he did, if he was a decent Reb or a bad one or anything. Looking out the cool dewy windows of the hotel, feeling the cold glass, I could still see that sad shutter in the sand.

We order these country-gentleman breakfasts, and this other waitress than ours comes to the table. She just comes up very close to it, even presses it with her front, and just kind of turns her lips or bites the inside corner of her mouth, tucking her lips to one side.

"Hey," she says to Taurus, but then she looks quickly at me, too. It's a funny way to show them, but I get the idea this girl has manners.

Taurus stands up and takes her hand and bows to kiss it, and she snatches it away with a laugh and sort of slow-motion socks him in the arm. Then she wiggles around like a tail wagging a dog. Her uniform rear had some jelly on it, which she might have already had or got wiggling, I don't know, but it was funny the way she moved sideways to him but watched him straight with large eyes. In fact, they were the largest eyes I had ever seen that weren't in a calf, and very blue or gray. I think I had a romantic stirring.

"Are we all set?" Taurus asked.

"I don't know," she said.

He doesn't say anything. She fiddles with the table a bit. "She's never been on a date, T."

Who? T.? I was figuring a bunch of things at the time, like the eminent sensation I had that this female third party had a lot to do with me, so I missed for a time the significance of "T." That's what she called him for short, I guessed, and it became my only clue to his real name, because that's all she called him and I never asked. But could he really *have* been named Taurus?

"Well," he says. "Simons here is just starting out himself."

"Oh, good." Then she adds, "That's romantic," almost so quiet you can't hear her.

"You get off at eleven? We'll be down there on the green."

We got those country-gentleman breakfasts with pork

chops that had about an ounce of paprika and pepper on them, very tasty, and cut them up in white-sided chunks and pushed the rich broken egg yolks around, making the meat yellow. I was all of a sudden hungry as hell.

"What's happening?"

"We're going sailing," he told me. "With a boatful of willing gentlewomen from the low country."

"Holy God."

"Holy God is right."

Suddenly great old patinaed John Calhoun and the green shutters all vanished before what I was sure was the dawning of the real, present South, a new land full not of ghosts but of willing gentlewomen.

It didn't turn out so marvelous. It's like water-skiing, which is no fun until you know what you're doing. Same with kissing, etc. We picked up this girl from a house on the Battery. She was cute all right, a regular button of a girl. She jumped down the steps in blue tennis shorts and a white cotton shirt with a tiny monogram, her hair pulled back, making her face shinier than it might have been without the tension, which was, I suspected, plenty shiny. She had on blue Keds that looked tight too and little pom-pom socks. She jumped in the car. For some reason, before I could look at her face all I saw was those cinched-up shoes, brand-new and looking as firm as shoe forms or hooves. I wondered if I was going to be a blockhead.

The trouble was, Taurus's girl was shabby where mine was shiny, loose where mine was tight, and I had already taken a heavy fall for her because of those jaw-breaker eyes. And she was developed out. Now, I didn't hold that against mine, because my burning worm was nothing to call the bureau of standards and measures about either, but the whole effect of this big-eyed, wobbling, nervous girl with giant bazongas had got to me, and what I wanted was a little one just like her. What I had looked like something at a recital.

"Oh, wait!" she cried, clapping her hand to her mouth. "Hi" to me. "I forgot" to them. She dropped a pink orthodontic retainer from the roof of her mouth and was out of the car and up the steps and back, smiling, in one motion. "All set."

She and I got through names and grades before we reached the water. We were about even on names—she was a double Jenkins and I had my one-"m" Simons, plus the Manigault—but on schools she had the edge, being at Mrs. Oldfield's famous institution for landed white girls, while I was in Bluffton Elementary with the people. I was going to display some Great Books stuntwork if she pressed about my not going to Cooper Boyd Academy. But she didn't. She was nervous and smiling so hard about nothing at all that every time I looked at her, it sort of hurt my face. I hoped a little weather and salt on the boat would knock the shine off and we could be regular. Her name was Londie. Short for Altalondine Jenkins Jenkins.

At the yacht club we met a gigantic fat dude who was breathing with difficulty. He outfitted us with his boat, an air of a favor he owed Taurus about the proceedings. He made sure to impress Taurus with how irregular lending his boat was without *his* going. And then Taurus's girl came out of the yacht club changed into a purple swimsuit with plenty of everything very obvious and she a little self-conscious, which made her smile and do that dog-wobble ever so slightly. On the front of the suit was a brilliant whale dancing on its fluke and spouting white spume, the figure made of inlays of nylon stitched together in colors resembling a parrot. The fat guy stopped talking when he saw her.

I watched him while Taurus rigged the boat. He had been blubbering about tightening this and battening that and rules of the road, but now he was mostly pointing and grunting, half at Taurus and half at his girl. His wheezing picked up.

He stepped over to Taurus and said, "My health."

Taurus looked up.

"I'm worried about my health."

"What about it?" Taurus said.

He sucked in a big load of wind and said, "It's *deteriorating.*"

Taurus was holding a broken halyard and standing in three inches of stinking bilge water in the open ribs of the cockpit.

"What *isn't?*" he said.

"Good point! Very good point! Ah, sir!" shouted the wheezer. He laughed and then charged Taurus's girl, virtually shouting, "Young lady! There's a *whale* on your stomach!"

She bit her mouth sideways, stretched her suit outward a bit, and looked down at the colorful whale.

"Are you a"—he almost choked—"a *swimmer?*" With reverence in that word.

She looked at him and then at herself again, up and down, her legs, the whale, the bosom she could hardly see over. Now I was excited too, but the big guy was, I swear, fixing to collapse drooling, and she was getting red in the face. He was about two inches from her and standing like Santa Claus, rocked back on his heels with an enormous gut stuck out, which he rubbed absently with tiny hands, and he looked at her through eyes squinted shut with fat, seething, when Taurus said to her, "In the boat." And to me, "Cast off." She did, I did, Londie jumped in as light and precise as a fawn, and we motored out of the club.

That was about the biggest adventure of the day. It got a little rough, but nobody puked. We kept out stomachs full with cold Coca-Cola and nice big chunks of ice. Coke can taste very good in salty conditions, I've noticed.

We went to Fig Island, which is one island too small for the Arabs to bother to take. It was nice. We played in the water. Londie and I worked on our kissing nerve by trying to swim at each other underwater and embrace and then kiss, but each time one or both of us burst out laughing in embarrassment before we got our lips situated, big blasts of bubbles obliterating the target and the moment, and we'd have to surface for air and laugh and laugh more to conceal how scared we were to actually do it. And then I saw something that really took the wind out of my sails.

There was Taurus and his girl about a hundred yards away in chest-deep water, and she had her arms at full length draped on his shoulders, and maybe it was a trick of light and water or something but I swear I saw large pale surfaces between them and I thought it was her tits floating. It destroyed our game, made it so silly. I don't even know if it was her tits, if boobs even float like that, if it wasn't a fish belly. But the idea was enough. Me and old A'londine was way down in the minors, so I suggested we walk the island.

It had a shell ring. That's a ring of oystershells piled about head-high in a circle about fifty yards across. Indians made them, they say for ceremonies and whatnot, and of course even live sacrifices get bandied about, but my information is that they don't really know. The rock hounds and anthropods come out and remove chunks of the rings like bites out of a doughnut, but I don't think they ever find anything but oystershells. The digs are all old-looking. My guess is it's where the Indians had their oyster roasts, and a fine way to use the shells too, because it cuts out the wind for 360 degrees.

Anyway, we thought about the ghosts of Indians and rumrunners and all those old things that took place on a coast, and we didn't really square off the kissing like we wanted to. Just became regular jake friends while Taurus, etc. I felt little.

But at least he went to bat for me, and if I whiffed, it wasn't his fault, maybe not my fault, certainly not button-nosed Altalondine Jenkins's fault, and most certainly not that big wobbly blessing's fault, for if ever there was a walking incitement to riot she was it. Call her my first love, fine with me.

I think that was his plan, really, to show me not cutie-cakes by what you can find if you look for genteel Diane Parkers—big, wonderful, warm girls who are just a hint upset about things. A smudge of abandon. Maybe that's my motto. Me and old Mike can team up. He can worry about being an ignoramus and I can worry about round, wonderful girls with their edges ruined by life's little disasters, who remain solid and tough in their drive to feel good—to themselves and to you—and offer a vision of snug harbor.

Louis D. Rubin, Jr.

FINISTERRE

> Although more and more people are coming to refer to
> boats with the neuter pronoun "it," the traditional "she" remains
> fully correct in speaking or writing about any size of vessel
> —Chapman, *Piloting, Seamanship*
> *and Small Boat Handling*

The city of Charleston, South Carolina, is bounded on three sides by rivers and the harbor. In such a place, with ships and tugboats and small craft always moving about, I was very much aware of the water and wanted to go out on it. But except on very rare occasions when my uncle would take me sailing, I never got the opportunity. No one else that I knew owned a boat of any kind. My father was not an outdoorsman and was utterly uninterested in boats or in fishing. For me to have proposed that we acquire a rowboat would have been as far-fetched as to have suggested the purchase of an airplane or a railroad locomotive. Moreover, I had been declared by my mother to be ineligible for going out on boats except under the most reliable of adult supervision such as my uncle's, because of my failure to learn how to swim.

When we had lived downtown on Rutledge Avenue I was only a few blocks from the Ashley River, and it was a walk of ten blocks down Tradd Street to Adger's Wharf and the Cooper River waterfront, but I seldom thought to go there. Not until we moved far up to the northwest end of town did I begin to get interested in the waterfront.

I was fourteen years old that fall, and on Saturday mornings after the movies I would set off down King Street for the waterfront, pausing to examine the postage stamps, Confederate army buttons, insignias, and belt buckles, and the swords and pistols on display in the window of Bruchner's Antique Store. In the center of the window was a framed picture that fascinated me. It was an old engraving depicting the body of Stonewall Jackson lying in state at the Confederate capitol rotunda in Richmond. Standing behind the coffin were Robert E. Lee, Jefferson Davis, J. E. B. Stuart, and other Confederate heroes, all looking very gloomy. Sometimes I wondered whether any of the various antique pistols and sabers displayed in the window had belonged to soldiers killed in the war, and might actually have been taken from the hands of dead men.

After looking at the window display I would walk on to Broad Street and then eastward toward the Cooper River. Usually I would stop in at the law office where my Aunt Ellen was employed as a secretary, spend a little while there, and then proceed across East Bay Street and along Exchange to the shore. The *Cherokee,* one of the coastal passenger ships of the Clyde-Mallory line, would usually be tied up alongside the pier just upstream, in full sight.

Compared to the Transatlantic liners that put in at ports such as New York and Boston, I knew, the *Cherokee* was no doubt a very small ship, but she seemed enormous to me. Her great black hull took up the entire length of the pier from close to the short all the way to the end, where her stern protruded out into the ship channel, while her cabins and superstructure, painted white and gold, towered above the two-story warehouse on the dock. The *Cherokee* arrived early in the morning, lay alongside the dock while her passengers were off touring the city, and departed in mid-afternoon. While in port the ship was festooned with pennants and flags, and appeared altogether glamorous.

I would remain there for a while to watch, then I would walk southward along the shore. Just downstream, next to a marine railway, there were the remains of several old wooden boats partly buried in the mud and marsh grass, with the weathered ribs and timbers protruding up like arms and legs. At high tide the harbor water would wash about the old hulks, but when the tide was out they were imbedded in the mud, with fiddler crabs scurrying about the surface of the black, viscous tidal flat. There was a salty fragrance in the air that seemed to be part of the scene. No doubt the old craft had been towed there years ago and left to disintegrate gradually in the heat and moisture of the marsh. Once my Aunt Ellen walked down to the waterfront with me, and referred to the place as a "ship's graveyard."

I would pause there briefly, then proceed along the shoreline to Adger's Wharf. It was actually two wharves, and was home port for a variety of shrimp boats and small working craft, several of which were in freight service between Charleston and the various sea islands up and down the coast. There was a packing house, situated on the land side of the north pier, with a tin-covered roof beneath which black women worked at sorting and packing shrimp brought in from off the various boats. Meanwhile the crews of the shrimp boats were working aboard their craft, hosing down the decks and the hold, repairing nets and adjusting lines. The shrimp boats were of all shapes and sizes. Some were painted in bright blues, reds, and greens; others were unpainted and drab. But all held their attractions for me, for they were seagoing boats, and went out beyond the jetties at the harbor mouth and into the ocean.

By far the most interesting craft berthed at Adger's Wharf, however, were the tugboats of the White Stack Tugboat Company, which occupied the far end of the south pier. There were three of them, the *Cecilia*, the *Robert H. Lockwood*, and the *James P. Congdon*. They were painted brick red, with glossy black hulls and white trimming, and their smokestacks were white with black rings.

They were kept in prime condition, and when not at work somewhere about the harbor lay waiting alongside the pier, their boilers always kept fired, with wisps of smoke trailing from their stacks. It was always my hope to see one of them departing or returning, for it was a formidable sight to view the sturdy craft in action, their powerful propellers churning the harbor water at the stern into foamy little hills, as they maneuvered confidently alongside the dock, while crewmen waited to tend the lines. They were owned by the Lockwood brothers, the eldest of whom, Captain Tunker Lockwood, was mayor *pro tem* of the City of

Charleston and had lived next to us on Rutledge Avenue. My father had told me once that the two Lockwood boys, Henry and Edward, would one day succeed to command of the tugboats, and I always viewed them with awe and envy. They were several years older than I, and hardly knew me, but I watched them from afar, as among the more fortunate of the earth.

Berthed at Adger's Wharf along with the shrimp boats, cargo launches, pilot boats, and the White Stack towboats were a few small open boats with make-and-break gasoline engines and several rowboats. They were used for fishing or for work about the waterfront, and sometimes while I was watching, the owner of one of them might show up, climb down to where his boat was moored alongside the dock, and after a time cast loose the lines and proceed out into the harbor. I was deeply envious, for I could envision myself as someday being able to actually to own a boat of that size, and the idea of heading out into the harbor in a boat of my own, rowing along the waterfront past the Clyde Line docks and up toward the Cooper River Bridge, or else downstream past the Carolina Yacht Club and along the sea wall of the High Battery, was marvelous to contemplate. Even better, if more remote, was the hope of possessing one of the larger craft with gasoline engines. With such a boat I could go out to the center of the harbor, explore the wooded shoreline along the southern rim of the harbor up to Fort Johnson and beyond, or even head upstream on the Ashley River, rounding the point of the Battery and up along the Boulevard past the lighthouse station at the head of Tradd Street, to where the river widened and the Intracoastal Waterway entered it at Wappoo Creek across the river.

But if that was beyond any hope of fulfillment for years to come, at least I might someday own a rowboat and keep it at Adger's Wharf. Not anytime soon, to be sure—for even if it were somehow possible for me to buy a rowboat, the fact that I could not swim would be an insurmountable barrier to any such hope, since my mother made it quite clear that until or unless I learned how to swim, I could go out in no boat not supervised by an adult.

Logically I knew that the first step in persuading my parents to acquire a rowboat, or in abetting me in getting one, would be to learn how to swim. But that I had proved unable to do. The summer before when we still lived downtown, I had tried. I had been sent to the YMCA to take swimming lessons, but had failed miserably. I could not force myself to let go of the railing around the pool or to keep my head under water. I was not afraid of the water as such; when not in it I would vow to do what I was supposed to do. But once I felt myself unsupported, I lost all control over my actions, and came raging back to the surface and to the side of the pool, where I hung on for dear life, oblivious to encouragement or expostulation by the instructor. My will power was simply not strong enough to overcome my fear. Where the other boys in the swimming class were soon splashing across the pool and learning to dive deep and come up, breathing hard and blinking water from their eyes, yards distant from where they had gone under, I remained clinging to the side.

"See how easy it is?" the instructor, a pleasant voiced man named Mr. Fudge, would say to me. "There's nothing to be afraid of." But I could not do it.

When my parents realized that I was not learning how to swim, they were exasperated. My mother telephoned the swimming instructor, to my considerable embarrassment, to discuss my failure. "He says you won't try," she reported. "The others have all been swimming for a week now, but you won't let go of the railing." I was informed in no uncertain terms that I was to obey the instructor.

After the next lesson, during which I kept unhappily to the side of the pool, unable to force myself to push loose from the side with my feet and dive under the water, the instructor told me to remain when the others had gone. He got down into the water himself, and took hold of my body by the waist. "Now just let yourself go," he said. "Don't worry, I've got hold of you." Feeling his hands supporting me I did as he asked, and tried to move my arms and kick out with my feet, while he held me up and walked across the pool with me.

"This time I'm going to let go and let you swim," Mr. Fudge said. "I'll have my arms right under you to hold you up if you begin to sink. Now just have confidence in yourself, and you can do it." But when he let go and I felt myself unsupported in the water, I thrust my legs down, groping for the bottom of the pool with my feet, and when I could not touch it I lost all control of myself, grabbed hold of the instructor's arms, pulled myself partly out of the water, and clung to his shoulders and chest, panting and half-sobbing in embarrassment and anger at myself.

After a few minutes, Mr. Fudge climbed out of the pool and told me to do the same. "I can't teach you to swim if you won't try to relax and let go," he said. My lips were tight and my teeth chattering, as if the water were frigid. I felt humiliated and exhausted.

When I returned home I knew he had telephoned my mother to report my failure, for, while my mother said nothing about it, her silence was so studiedly casual that I knew she was very disappointed at my cowardice. At dinnertime my father also made no reference to it, and only told me that there was a new *S. S. Glencairn* story, which he knew I liked, in that week's number of *Collier's*. That evening my mother said that it would not be necessary for me to return to the YMCA swimming classes any more. Though ashamed at my failure, I felt relieved.

So now, a summer afterward, I remained a nonswimmer, and could not hope to own a rowboat. In June school ended, and there was no longer anything to prevent me from sometimes riding my bicycle downtown to the waterfront and spending all morning there, returning only in time for two o'clock dinner. I would take along a pair of inexpensive binoculars that my father had bought for me to observe the occasional ships that moved up the Ashley River past our house. I would ride all the way to the High Battery at the very tip of the city. From there I could see all the way across to where the low form of Fort Sumter lay near the harbor entrance, so that most of the activity in the lower harbor was visible to me. When a ship came into view, she was first a smudge of smoke and a dot of superstructure far out beyond Sumter.

With the binoculars I could observe her all the way in until she disappeared behind Sumter, and afterwards reemerged, much larger in visible size, along the Fort Moultrie side of the fort.

The next minutes were crucial. For if she were a ship from a foreign port she would anchor out in the Roadstead for customs inspection and come no closer that morning, while if she were bound up the Cooper River she would move along the Rebellion Reach channel on the far side of the harbor, pass out of sight beyond Castle Pinckney, which was on an island in the harbor, and at no time come closer than three or four miles from where I stood. But if when the ship rounded Sumter and moved toward the inner harbor she neither anchored nor swung northward, then I knew that I would soon be able to observe her from close by, for the destination would be either the downtown waterfront or else up the Ashley River, and in either event she would pass within less than a half-mile of the High Battery. What I most hoped was that the ship was headed for the Cooper River waterfront, for then she would move right across my line of vision, in front of me, no more than a few hundred yards away, and I should not only be able to observe her every detail but also get a long look at the White Stack tugboat that had gone out to meet her and guide her in.

The tug designated to receive the ship would make its rendezvous with the visitor well out in the harbor. The ship would have stopped her engines to await her escort. There would be a ceremonial (as I thought) exchange of whistled salutes, the tug's high-pitched whistle signal answered by the deep-voiced note of the ship. I would watch through the binoculars to try to catch sight of the passing of the towline from tug to ship, but it was too far out to see. Eventually, however, the tug would take up its position in front and the procession would head for port, the tug in the lead, followed by the much larger ship. As they neared the point at which the Cooper River waterfront channel veered from the Ashley River channel there would be more whistle signals, and then first the tug and then the ship would make the turn, and come slowly, massively toward the waterfront. Past where I stood watching they would steam, the sturdy red tugboat in the lead, the hugh freighter or tanker following obediently behind, still under her own power but linked to the tug by the manila towline that was to be used in the docking operation. The White Stack tugboats never looked more capable and confident than at such times. As they churned their way past the Battery they seemed to be aware of their own importance as worthy stewards of the port, and without ostentation but in entire self-possession and pride they would lead the visitor to the wharf and the waiting slip.

Meanwhile a second White Stack tugboat would by then have cast off its lines from its berth at Adger's Wharf and be waiting off at the far side of the channel, ready to follow along upstream and assist in the docking. As the first tug and its tow moved by, it would take up its station abeam and proceed upstream too, and I would watch until finally the ship and her escorts passed out of view, and only the tall masts of the ship were now visible above the low roofs of the warehouses along the shore.

What I would have liked to be able to do was to own a small boat, so that I could row upstream to where the freighter was being docked, take up a position safely out of the way, and observe the entire operation. As it was, I could only look enviously at the occasional small craft that did come moving along the waterfront. If, as sometimes happened, the occupants of such craft were not adults but boys seemingly only a little older than myself, then my envy was almost beyond bounds. To have to stand there on the Battery, looking out at the harbor, while some fortunate boy was out on the water in a boat, rowing along in splendor past me, perhaps even glancing up, as I imagined, in momentary pity for such as myself, but for the most part too satisfyingly engaged in rowing his boat to have time for mere landlubbers—it was a mournful business.

Our new house was located far up at the northeast end of the city, on a bluff that overlooked the Ashley River. We moved there in the spring of 1935, after my father had recovered from a severe illness and had spent a number of months in the hospital. Twice during those months he had been expected to die. He was much better now, however, and part of the reason for building the new house was that he would be able to plant flowers and shrubs and work in the yard. There were only two other houses within a mile of us, one of them owned by Mr. Herbert Simons, my father's closest friend and Saturday night poker-playing companion, who was in the real estate business and had bought and renovated an old plantation house, Versailles, and was now preparing to develop the surrounding area. Our house was situated across from an avenue of hugh water oaks on Mr. Simons' grounds, and beyond the oaks and Mr. Simons' house the land sloped abruptly down some thirty feet or more to the edge of the salt marsh, which was spread out along the shore in either direction as far as the eye could see.

From the edge of the marsh to the river itself was a distance of a quarter-mile or so. A creek led from the river through the marsh to a small dock behind Mr. Simons' house, though doubtless it had been many years since a boat had been moored there. On summer mornings sometimes my mother and I would go crabbing off the dock, tying hunks of old meat to strings, with weights attached, dropping them into the creek, then waiting for blue crabs to come in with the tide, take hold of the meat, and allow themselves to be netted. Though the creek was narrow, there was a steady procession of crabs, and in a morning's crabbing we could fill half a washtub with them.

Sometimes while we sat there crabbing a freighter might come up the river, bound for the fertilizer docks a mile upstream, preceded by a White Stack tugboat. The river channel led so close to the edge of the marshland that from where we watched the freighter seemed to be floating upon a sea of reed grass as she moved by. Much later the tugboat would come heading back, having completed its task of docking the freighter, en route downstream to the harbor.

At low tide there was only a trickle of water in the creek. Occasionally I would sit down on the dock then and watch the fiddler crabs sunning themselves on the banks of black mud. There were also oyster shells on the sides, and little pools of inky rainbow-hued oil formed by the marsh gases. Sometimes I could hear birds and small animals, swamp rats probably, stirring about off in the marsh grass. There was a continual popping and cracking sound on hot days, caused I supposed by the heat of the sun on the decaying surfaces of the mud and grass.

When the tide was very high, not only the creek but much of the marshland between the shore and the river's edge was also covered by water. It did not take very long for me to come up with the idea that, even if my inability to swim meant that I could not hope to go out on the river in a boat, I might possibly be able to persuade my parents to let me paddle a boat about the marshland at high tide, since there could be little danger involved in going on water that was only a couple of feet deep in most places.

If, that is, I had a rowboat. But where was I to get a rowboat? One of my parents' friends was a woodworking contractor, and I asked him what it would cost to have a small rowboat built. "Oh, about fifteen dollars," he said. Since my weekly allowance was fifty cents, the prospect of my saving enough to buy a boat seemed somewhat remote. If I could bring myself to set aside a dime a week, which was unlikely, it would take three years before I had enough to afford the boat.

In late June my cousin Charles, from Atlanta, came to visit us for two weeks, and one day we went to the waterfront. Since he had no bicycle we rode down on the trolley car. A freighter was coming in along the south channel when we arrived at the Battery, and after we watched her swing by us, preceded by the escorting tug, my cousin was eager to follow them up the waterfront and see the docking take place. I explained to him that the slip where the freighter would be docking was entirely hidden from view from the shore, but he insisted upon seeing for himself, so we headed up Concord Street, which fronted the docks, in pursuit of the ship and tug. It turned out that they were bound for the Bull Line wharf, beyond Market Street, which was not only completely screened from view by several large corrugated tin warehouses but surrounded by a high wire fence as well.

We tried to walk out past the Bull Line dock to find a place from which to observe the operation. There was a swampy field, partly under water, beyond the extremity of the fence, and we picked our way through it, past the ruins of an old brick building. When we reached the edge of the marsh, however, the downstream view was blocked off by the farthest warehouse, which protruded some distance out into the ship channel.

As we were making our way back to solid ground, I noticed, piled near the brick ruins, what appeared to be some boxes. I went over to examine, jumping from one spot of dry ground to another across the boggy ground, with my cousin following. Lying there in the marsh, exposed to the rain and the tidal water, was a mass of deteriorated cartons, filled with papers. Most were waterlogged and soggy, but when I pulled away some of the papers on the exterior of one carton we found beneath them, in quite satisfactory shape, great quantities of postcards, letters, and envelopes. They were all handwritten, were addressed to a firm called F. W. Wagener Company, and consisted of orders and correspondence.

It was the postage stamps that interested me. For the papers were all dated in the 1802 and 1890s, and on the envelopes were stamps that for the most part I had never seen before, older than any in my own stamp collection.

"I bet some of these are worth money," my cousin said.

"I bet they are, too."

And suddenly the thought came to me that I might be able to sell the stamps for enough money to buy a rowboat.

For the next several hours my cousin and I combed through some of the boxes of old correspondence. It was a hot, moist day, and the water lying about us in the marsh and covering some of the cartons of papers had a powerful, cloying odor of decaying sweetness. Beetles and other insects infested the material, but we worked away excitedly. A majority of the stamps, to be sure, were identical two-cent red George Washingtons, but there were numerous other kinds as well. We assembled stacks of postcards and envelopes, with all manner of stamps on them, until finally we had as many as we could possibly carry, even though we stuffed them inside our shirts until we bulged out on all sides.

By now it was early afternoon, and we set out across the field, bound for King Street and Bruchner's Antique Store, which bought and sold stamps. As we walked we speculated on the worth of our find. If each envelope was worth a dime and each postcard a nickel, my cousin declared, we ought to receive at least twenty dollars apiece in payment for them. More than enough to buy a rowboat? "Now don't tell where we found them," my cousin whispered as we opened the door of the store.

Into Bruchner's we walked, down a long aisle between showcases of silverware and old coins, past a glass-front case with a complete Confederate uniform including polished black boots, gauntlets, sash, military belt, grey coat, and trousers with gold buttons, gold epaulets, and wide-brimmed hat, displayed on a mannequin of some sort that looked almost like a ghost. At a desk at the rear of the dark, cavernous showroom the proprietor, an angular, bony-faced man, sat working at some papers. The desk was illuminated by a single gooseneck lamp, which cast a yellow glow on the papers. At first, the man seemed not to notice us in the gloom, but after a moment he looked up.

"We want to know if you want to buy some stamps," I told him.

"Let's see them."

My cousin and I began extracting stamps and postcards from inside our shirts. It took us several minutes to assemble them all. While we were doing so the man did not so much as reach out to examine a single one of the envelopes and cards, but only waited for us to be done. When finally we had placed them all on the counter in a heap, he began to leaf through our cache, while we waited tensely.

"They aren't worth anything," he said after a minute.

The gloom of the dark store now matched my hopes.

"They're all very common," he added.

We stood there, waiting.

The man turned over a few more envelopes. "You go through them," he said after a minute, "and pick out two of each kind for yourself, and I'll take the rest of them off your hands for a dollar."

I looked at my cousin, who looked back at me. My cousin shrugged.

"Okay," I said.

It was some time before we had sorted through all the envelopes and cards and put aside two each of each kind. The man did not seem particularly interested. He went back to what he had been working on, while we sorted stamps. I had not realized just how many envelopes and cards we had collected. Though most were duplicates, and these would be what the man was taking off our hands, there remained a considerable variety in the pile that we were to keep for ourselves.

When we were done the man handed me a paper sack. "Put all those in there," he said, gesturing with his bony hand toward the discards. We complied, and placed the sack full of stamps on the desk.

Then the man reached out for the stack of two each that we were to keep, and took them from me. "Now I'll take these," he said, "and you can keep those in the sack."

He opened the drawer of the desk, extracted a dollar bill, and handed it to me.

It was not until my cousin and I were outside the store

and walking up King Street that we could begin to think about what had happened.

"Why did you let him get away with that?" my cousin asked.

"I don't know," I said. And I didn't. I had been so ill at ease that when he had reached out for and taken the stack of envelopes and cards from me I had been unable to do anything except relinquish them. There was something about his thin, bony hand, with its yellow fingers, that had frozen me into inaction.

"You shouldn't have given them to him. You should have said No," my cousin declared.

"Why didn't you, then?" I retorted. "They were just as much yours as mine." We had both been afraid of the man.

By the time we boarded the Rutledge Avenue trolley car and were headed uptown, most of the fifty cents apiece that we had been paid for the stamps had been spent. We still had the sack of discards, but the best ones were gone. I sought to rationalize my failure by reminding myself that even if the stamps had been marketable for enough money to buy a rowboat, it was unlikely that my parents would have permitted me to have one, anyway.

My cousin, after thinking the matter over, decided that while the man had clearly tricked us, it was unlikely that any of the stamps or postcards were really rare, because in that case the man would have wanted all of them, and not just two of each variety. They might have been worth, say, five or six dollars in all, he said, instead of the single dollar we had been paid. His idea was that since Bruchner's was the only stamp dealer in Charleston, what we would do would be to go back down to the waterfront tomorrow, assemble another cache of stamps, and he would take them along when he went home to Atlanta that weekend, and see whether a stamp dealer there would buy them.

We reckoned, however, without my parents, or more particularly, my mother. For when we related what had happened, my mother was not at all impressed by the possible value of the stamps. Instead she was quite angry at the notion of our foraging about in the marsh for old papers. We might have fallen and cut ourselves on broken glass, or contracted Lord knows what manner of disease, she declared, or been bitten by snakes or rats, or otherwise place our lives in peril. Under no circumstances were we to return for more stamps the next day, nor was I ever again to go poking about in trash or junk or anything of the sort, as if I were no more than some poor white trash myself, on pain of being forbidden absolutely ever to go down to the waterfront again.

She had a good mind, she said, to deduct the dollar from the next several installments of my allowance, and return it to Mr. Bruchner. But the last was an idle threat, as even I recognized, for my mother was no admirer of the sharp practices of shopkeepers. So I made no reply and let the storm blow over, which it did, but only after she ordered us to go into the bathroom at once and run a hot bath, and wash away every trace of the stamps and postcards from our bodies. I sent my cousin in to run the bath, while I went down to the basement where we had left the sackful of discards and hid it in the woodpile. In a few days' time, I knew, I could safely take the stamps up to my room, for she would have ceased to worry about the matter.

My cousin left for home that weekend, and though several times in subsequent weeks I disobeyed instructions, went back to the cache of papers in the marsh on the waterfront, and collected additional varieties of stamps and postcards, I made no further attempt to sell them. Without in any way intimating to my father that I had acquired more envelopes and postcards, I asked him about the F. W. Wagener Company, to which all the envelopes had been addressed. He said that F. W. Wagener had been a very wealthy and prominent wholesale grocery dealer in Charleston at one time, when he was a boy. His own father, my grandfather, had done business with Wagener while operating a grocery store in Florence, South Carolina. I had never known my grandfather, for he had died many years before I was born, when my father was about my present age. Afterwards I looked through the letters and postcards that I had found in the marsh, to see whether any of them might have been from my grandfather, but did not find any.

That September there was a hurricane, which though it did not strike Charleston itself came ashore near enough along the coast to cause extremely high tides and heavy rains. When several weeks afterward I went back to collect more stamps I found that the marsh where they had been located had been thoroughly flooded, and where the boxes of papers had once been were now only standing water and mud.

Any further thoughts about acquiring a rowboat remained only very general and passive during the autumn and winter months that followed. From time to time I went down to the waterfront and observed the goings-on in the harbor, but it was not until the late spring that I began again to meditate ways of getting a boat. My Uncle Edward, my father's brother, who was city editor of the afternoon newspaper and owned a sailboat, invited me to go sailing with him one Sunday in late April. His plan was to sail his boat up the Ashley River from where he kept it, at the foot of Beaufain Street downtown, all the way to where we lived, and to come ashore by way of the creek through the quarter-mile of tidal marsh, and tie up at the dock behind Mr. Simons' house. By leaving in mid-morning he would arrive when the tide was scheduled to be close to high, have Sunday dinner with us, and return downstream on the outgoing tide. "Now be careful and don't jump around in the boat," my mother told me as my father prepared to drive me downtown to join my uncle. "You know you can't swim."

It was a trip of several hours upstream, though the distance by water was only some three miles, for though the incoming tide was with us we had to do considerable tacking and reaching to make progress against the northwest wind. It was past one o'clock when we reached the mouth of the creek. The tide was very high—a spring tide, my uncle called it—so that the water covered all but the tips of the marsh grass alongside the creek. With the centerboard halfway up we were able to sail right along the winding creek with almost no rowing or poling. I found it tremendously exciting to sail up to the dock, where my parents and Mr. and Mrs. Simons stood waiting, and step over the side of the wooden sailboat onto the dock.

Walking up the slope of the bluff toward our house, on dry land once again, I felt most important, and after dinner when we went back down to the dock and my uncle and I prepared to leave on the return journey, I imagined that my Uncle Edward and I were two veteran mariners about to set off from Adger's Wharf for the high seas. The tide had ebbed sufficiently to make it necessary to raise the centerboard all the way to get out of the marsh creek and into the river, and since the wind was against us my uncle had to row, but once we gained the open river we had wind and current with us, and we sailed rapidly down the Ashley, the mainsail swung wide to take the wind, and with no tacking necessary at all.

"I wish I had a boat," I told my parents at supper that evening.

"We haven't any use for one," my mother said.

"I'd like to use it in the marsh."

"You're too young for a boat," my mother replied, "and you can't swim. You might fall overboard and you'd drown."

"Not in the marsh," I said. "I wouldn't go out in the river. I just want to row around in the marsh."

"Well, we don't have a boat and we're not going to get one," my mother declared.

That night, as I lay in bed thinking back on the day's excitement, I told myself that while I was no closer to being able to afford to buy a boat than before, my remark about wanting to row around in the marsh had not been vetoed as such. My mother had said only that they were not going to buy a boat. My argument about not being in danger of drowning so long as I stayed in the marsh had not been refuted. If my mother thought differently about it, she had not said so. Silence, I had read somewhere, gives consent.

Though I could foresee no likelihood of acquiring a boat, I knew that if ever I were somehow to manage to get one, it would be through my father, not my mother, that I should proceed so as to gain consent. He had said nothing during the suppertime discussion. There was no chance whatever that he could ever be coaxed into buying a boat, or even into helping me to buy one, but if a boat were in some undreamed-of way to materialize, I felt, he at any rate would not use the grounds of my inability to swim to forbid my using it. So that was something, anyway.

For several days following the end of school, there was a very high spring tide, with the water converting the salt marsh into what seemed almost a lake, and with only the tips of the reed grass along the edge of the shore and the channel visible. The tide rose so high that it even covered the wooden planks of the dock behind Mr. Simons' house. John Carmody, a friend up from Versailles Street, and I went down to the water's edge to investigate, then decided to climb out on a huge water oak on the shoreline, to a point at which we were suspended in the air some twenty feet up, and well over the edge of the marsh. If I fell, I knew, I would get myself thoroughly ducked, so I clung carefully to the tree.

From our perch we watched the marsh and the river, and I told of how I hoped someday to acquire a rowboat and to go out in the marsh.

"Why don't we build one?" John Carmody asked.

The thought had never occurred to me. It seemed an obvious solution. Within minutes we were scrambling down the tree and headed for my house. We went up to my room, I got out pencil and paper, and we began designing a boat. That night, as soon as it was sufficiently dark, we took a wagon and went up Pendleton Street to the site of a house under construction, and selected an assortment of boards from the scrap lumber pile. From a keg that had been conveniently left open on the uncompleted second floor of the house we collected several pounds of nails. We were careful to take only boards of which a portion had been sawed away, so that we could assure ourselves that we were only using scrap lumber, even though some of the scraps were ten feet or more in length. As for the nails, no such rationale was needed. Once a nail keg had been opened and left exposed it was fair game. My father observed us as we carted our material back into the yard and set up operations under the side porch, but he made no objection, for on more than on occasion he had paid nighttime visits to the scrap lumber pile himself.

Since we would be using the boat in the marsh, we decided it was not necessary to give it a pointed bow. Instead we planned a bateau, with blunt ends and uniform width. It was to be some eight feet long and three feet wide, with sides made of two eight-inch-wide planks, giving us ample freeboard. The bow and stern did not come straight down all the way but were tucked in on an angle about halfway down, to give the boat somewhat greater mobility in the water than a mere box would have.

The next day we built the sides, then the ends, and were preparing to add the planking by nightfall. While we were at work my father came by several times to observe. I knew that he recognized exactly what was being undertaken, even though he made no comment on it, contenting himself by reminding us to be sure to put the tools away when done and to pick up all the scraps of boards lying about and put them in the kindling wood box. If my mother was aware of the project she said nothing about it, and I was careful to avoid making any reference to the boat myself, for if I brought the matter out into the open she would feel obliged, if only for the sake of consistency, to object, and my father would then be equally obliged to support her objections.

The next morning we cut the planks, nailed them into place, then turned the boat right side up and nailed planks across the top at each end and in the middle for seats. In lieu of oars, we built paddles, nailing flat pieces of board to both ends of two-by-twos so that they would be double bladed. Our boat was now ready for launching. While we were loading it on to the wagon, my father came by again. "If you're going to paddle around in that," he said, "you'd better take a can along to bail it out."

"Yes, sir," I agreed, "we sure better," and I hurried off happily to find a coffee can, for now I had formal acknowledgment of and consent for the boat.

We rolled the boat out of the yard, across Mr. Simons' grounds through the oak grove, and down the bluff to the wharf. I tied a length of manila rope to a bolt I had placed at one end, and then we eased the boat out onto the dock, slid it over the end, and into the creek. It rode high, and rocked a little as the current pushed against it.

"It floats good!" John said.

"Let's get in," I proposed. "You hold the rope and I'll climb in, then you can get in."

"How about the paddles?"

"That's right." We had forgotten to load them into the boat. John retrieved them from where we had left them on the shore, and we dropped them into the boat. "Okay, I'll get in the stern," I said, "and you get in the middle."

"How do we know which end's the stern?"

"It doesn't matter. I'll sit in the back, and you sit in the middle facing the same way, and the end we're facing will have to be the bow."

"All right."

I climbed into the boat, scrambled back to the far end, and sat down. John followed, took his seat amidships, and we took up the paddles and prepared to move out.

"It leaks!" John said.

The water was jetting in through the seams in little fountains.

"Give me the coffee can," I said. "I'll bail and you paddle."

I began scooping water out, while John used his paddle to turn the boat around. We moved off down the creek, with John paddling while I bailed away.

"This is great!" John said.

I looked back at the dock. It was twenty-five feet away. "You bail while I paddle," I proposed. I handed him the can and began paddling. The boat moved slugglishly through the water, but it made steady progress.

Though the water kept coming in steadily through the seams, we found that it was not necessary to keep bailing at all times. We could paddle for a while, until the water rose a couple of inches into the bottom, and then one of us could bail while the other paddled. We proceeded along the creek for some distance, until we came into an opening in the wall of marsh grass along the creek and could move out into the wider area of flooded marsh. We paddled through it until I could see our house, back through the oak trees. My parents were standing on the front porch, watching. I waved to them. My father waved back.

"Boy, isn't this fine?" John asked.

I agreed. "We're going to have to do something about these leaks, though." The water kept coming in.

"Let's take it back to the dock," John said.

We paddled back through the marsh and along the creek to the dock, with considerable bailing of water en route. We climbed out, tied the rope to the dock, and stood there for a while, watching our boat swaying in the current. There were several inches of water in it, but now that we were no longer in it, it seemed not to be taking any more water. Meanwhile, there it was, a genuine boat, crude to be sure and given much too much to leaking, perhaps more of a long wooden box than a boat and resembling a crude coffin, but I had gone out into the marsh aboard it, and hereafter could do so whenever I wanted.

We discussed ways whereby our boat might be kept from leaking. My idea was that we might cover the entire bottom with a sheet of tarpaper, but John was dubious. The water would only seep in between the tarpaper and the planks and come in through the seams just as before, he said. We considered getting some lath boards and nailing them over the seams, but decided that the uneven bottom would make it more difficult to paddle the boat, and would also only solve the problem partially, for water would still get in around the lath boards. It was suppertime, so we decided to think upon the problem overnight.

Now that my parents had seen us paddling out in the marsh in the boat, it could be mentioned openly, and at supper I described its performance in glowing terms.

"Did your boat leak much?" my father asked.

I told of our troubles along that line. "You need to caulk the seams," my father said.

"We don't have any cork."

"Not cork, caulk—c-a-u-l-k. It's like string."

"Does it cost much?"

"I doubt it. You have to wedge it into the seams."

My mother was not especially pleased with developments. "You'd better be careful," she repeated several times. "If you fell in you couldn't swim."

I assured her that there was no danger of my falling in, and that even if I did I would be safe enough in the marsh, because I could always stand up in the reed grass.

"You might cut yourself on oyster shells or old pieces of glass," she said. "You don't know what's out there in that mud."

I thought it best to argue no more. She had accepted the fact of my going out in the boat. That was what mattered.

It turned out that when the tide came in the next afternoon and we were able to go out in the boat again, the leaking had diminished considerably. Water still came in, to be sure, but at nothing like the rate of the previous day, so that it was necessary to bail out the boat only every quarter-hour or so. We decided that the wood must have swelled in the water overnight. We also discovered that the boat leaked even less when only one of us was in it.

After a few days my friend John Carmody's interest in paddling around in the marsh creeks subsided, but mine did not. Almost every day, when the tide permitted, I would go out for a trip. I explored up and down the marsh, along all the little creeks leading off the main creek, sometimes venturing along channels so narrow that I could not paddle but had to pole along by pushing from the stern. There were neap tide days when the tide rose much less than at other times and when, standing in the boat, I could scarcely see over the top of the reed grass and went traveling down creeks that seemed like high-walled tunnels through the marsh. At such times, if there was no wind, the marsh was very hot and sticky, with the reed grass screening off any slight breeze. Sometimes, as I threaded my way through the maze of narrow channels, there would be a sudden splash and a flurry of wings up ahead, as a heron or a marsh hen, alarmed at my unexpected appearance, would take to the air and go speeding off across the marsh grass. Sometimes, too, I would come upon hordes of little white insects which swarmed hotly around me, and I would have to pole frantically to get the boat out of range.

The days I liked best were those when there were very high tides, for then I did not have to confine my explorations to the creeks, but could paddle across the expanses of submerged marsh in whichever direction I wished. Though the reed grass just beneath the surface slowed the boat somewhat, at such times there was almost nowhere in the marshland that I could not go, and at times I ventured near the edge of the river itself. But it was a while before I dared to take my boat all the way along the creek to where it emptied into the river. For one thing, it was a long way to paddle—for though the river's edge was only a quarter-mile from the shore, the creek was winding and contained a series of bends and curves. Several times I reached the place at which the creek executed its last turn before opening directly upon the river some seventy-five feet away, but I always stopped there. I was afraid that if I moved any closer, my boat might somehow get caught in the river current and be carried out into the channel. So I held up just beyond the final turn, not venturing to take my boat into the delta-shaped creek mouth even though the water seemed calm enough, and looked at the river flowing past.

Finally, late one afternoon, I resolved that I was going to go all the way to the river itself. I was under strict orders from my parents to remain in the marsh, to be sure, but the mouth of the creek was hidden from view from our front porch by the Simons' house and the oak trees. I paddled along the creek, rounded the final bend, and moved forward, paddling vigorously with the perceptibly stronger current that pushed against the blunt stern of the boat, until I was actually within the delta-like creek mouth itself, and could look over the reed grass about the sides and see the edge of the river upstream and down. For an instant I held there, the channel flowing by in front of me, the low shoreline of the farther side of the river clearly visible across the water, until the current propelled the boat sideways toward the marsh grass. I let it drift into the edge of the grass. The tide was going out. I could feel the river current moving across the creeks and pushing against the boat, which rocked in the flow. I could see the long curving edge of the marsh downstream, and the Seaboard railroad trestle more than a mile distant. Upstream I had a clear view of the fertilizer docks, and could see a freighter tied up alongside one wharf.

It was exciting, but I also felt very uneasy, and after a minute I pushed away from the marsh. Once I did I yielded to panic and began desperately paddling the boat back into the creek, and did not stop until I was safely back at the bend of the creek. There I let the boat swing around and then guided it into the marsh grass, and watched the river from a distance. I breathed easy again. I had taken my boat to the very edge of the river, but had then lost my nerve. And it was silly, I realized, for I had had no trouble paddling the boat back up the creek.

That night, after I had gone to bed, I thought of how exciting it had been to be there at the river's edge, holding my boat in place at the creek mouth, with the current pushing vigorously against the side of the boat, and with the entire panorama of the Ashley River open before me, upstream and downstream. If only I could make myself bold enough to paddle out beyond the marsh, I could swing around the point of reed grass that marked the entrance, and move down the edge. I could take my boat up and down the side of the river, and provided I stayed close to the marsh there could be no danger, for the current had not really been too strong. My panic had been needless. There was nothing to be afraid of; the boat handled well. It was not like the swimming lessons, for I was in a boat, and knew how to handle the boat. Yet I had been afraid, and I had lost control of myself. I had wanted to go out in a boat, and now I had the boat, and I had failed.

It seemed to me—however much I recoiled at the thought—that I *must* take the boat out into the river the next day, no matter what. I was not sure why it was necessary. After all, there would be other days, and besides, the boat had not been built to be taken out into the river. If that had been the intention we would have tried to build it with a pointed bow to handle the current better. But now that I had the boat, I knew that I had to do it. To think about what I was going to do made me tremble. My mother, if she knew what I planned, would forbid it emphatically. If she caught sight of me out there, it would be the end to my boating in the marsh or anywhere else, for she would order me never to go out in the boat again.

I told myself that in any event I could not do it tomorrow, because the tide would be high too late in the day. I felt relieved. But then I thought that I could go early in the morning, when the tide would also be high. So that excuse was invalid.

I tried to think about something else, but my thoughts kept returning to the boat. It occurred to me that now that I had won the right to have a boat in the marsh, I might be able to get a full-fledged boat, one with a pointed bow and a curved design, that would be much better for going on the river. True, I had no money, but I could take my entire stamp collection, which I had been assembling for years and which was worth at least twenty dollars by book value in the Scott catalog, and sell it to Mr. Bruchner. He could not possibly offer me less than that. But I found the idea of going back into Bruchner's Antique Store and dealing with the man disturbing. Besides, my mother would not let me sell the stamps that way.

I was a long time going to sleep, and when I did, I had a dream in which I was being taken by my nurse to play in Hampton Park. I recognized it at once, because when I was a small child I had been taken there every afternoon to play. When we got to the park there was another nurse seated on a bench, and she too was overseeing the play of a child, whom I recognized at once as a girl named Janet Dennis, who was in my seventh grade class at school. Janet suggested that we play hide-and-go-seek, and she went off to hide, while I kept my hands over my eyes and counted up to a hundred. But I had secretly peeked through my fingers, and I knew she had gone down the path to a large stand of bamboo canebrake about seventy-five feet away, so when I was done counting, I ran straight to the canebrake. There was a path in the canebrake, and I hurried along it. The bamboo was so thick that it was almost like nighttime, and several times I had to pass through swarms of insects, while off in the underbrush I could hear animals scurrying about.

I groped my way along until I found her, deep inside the thick canebrake. "This is my hideaway," she told me. She reached down and turned on a single gooseneck electric lamp which was there, and in the darkness it illuminated a white and gold colored box which was lying on the ground under a rosebush. Printed on the box were the words SALT WATER DIVINITY FUDGE, MANUFACTURED BY THE F. W. WAGENER COMPANY. "Do your parents let you eat candy?" Janet Dennis asked. I nodded. She opened the box, but instead of fudge candy inside there were some Confederate army buckles and insignia.

I could hear the nurses calling us, and wanted to leave, but Janet refused. "I'm going to stay here and not go back to my nurse," she insisted, laughing. At that point I saw a length of manila rope lying on the ground, so I picked it up, made a lariat, and dropped the noose over her shoulders. She laughed again, and I began towing her back along the path. She resisted, but not too vigorously, and I had the feeling that she really wanted to come back to the nurses, whom I could hear calling, but her pride dictated that she struggle. After much tugging we were near the edge of the canebrake, but we had taken a different path and a dense thicket blocked our escape. Though it was dark in the canebrake I could see that beyond, outside, it was broad daylight, and I saw a man who was busily pruning an arbor or cherokee roses. It was my uncle, and I wondered why he was there. Meanwhile I kept trying to pull Janet Dennis through the thicket, and she continued to resist. "Watch out!" she said, laughing, "you'll fall on those thorns and cut yourself!" I laughed, and then as I gave another tug on the rope I lost my footing suddenly and fell in the thicket, and the momentum tumbled Janet toward me. "Watch out! Watch out!" she cried. And at that instant I woke up. The dream seemed very real, and it took me a minute or so to realize fully that I was lying in my bed, and it had been only a dream.

The next morning I went right out to my boat after breakfast. The tide, though ebbing, was still quite high. I set out down the creek, rounded the last bend, and paddled straight for the mouth. The current was with me; I went swinging out past the fringes of marsh grass into the river itself.

At once the current swung my boat about, and took it in tow. The bow turned downstream. I tried to steer the boat toward the edge of the marsh. The current took me along, but finally I managed to get the bow up into the marsh grass, grabbed hold of a fistful of reeds to hold the boat in position while the stern swung downstream, and with the paddle I was able to nose it further into the marsh so that the current would not dislodge it. For the moment I was safe.

I sat there, breathing hard. The river was flowing powerfully by, no more than a few feet from where I clung to the marsh. It was, I thought helplessly, a bright clear day, in no way ominous or threatening in itself, and yet here I was. The current was much stronger than I had guessed. If I let the boat get caught in it I might well be swept out to sea, or—worse still—be taken into the rougher water of the lower river, and the boat might capsize. And I had no life preserver.

To get back into the protection of the creek, I had two possible courses of action. One would be to pull the boat all the way through the marsh grass, and get to the creek from the side. But that seemed impossible, for except along the very edge of the marsh up by the creek mouth the reed grass was much too tall and dense.

The other choice was to go back out into the river. What I would have to do, I realized, was to let loose of the marsh grass along the side, push off with the paddle so that the stern of the boat would swing parallel with the current, and the bow point upstream, and then work along the edge, against the current, until I could shove the bow up into the thin grass just at the edge of the creek mouth, from where I could push the boat over into the creek mouth itself.

The thing to do was to remain calm and not to panic. If I failed to make sufficient headway against the current, I thought, I could always slip back into the marsh again, and I would be no worse off. So long as I kept my head and did not let the boat swing broadside to the current, where it would be carried rapidly offshore, I would be safe. The very worst that could happen would be that I should have to stay there alongside the marsh all day until the tide rose that evening.

I wanted to delay, but I knew that the longer I did, the stronger the tide would be running and the more difficult it would be to paddle the boat against it.

Trembling, I let go the reed grass and pushed the paddle against the bank. The boat slid back into the current, was taken by it, began to swing about. I dug the paddle into the water, pulling furiously. The boat straightened out, drifted back a few yards but remained parallel to the marsh, then began moving ahead. I could feel the current throbbing as it pushed against the blunt bow. Slowly, with much effort, I was able to work the boat ahead along the marshside. I paddled steadily, forcing myself to take my time and make each thrust count.

Then after several minutes I realized that I was now in somewhat slacker water, screened from the full force of the river current by the protruding marsh grass at the creek entrance. I paddled ahead, made more progress, nosed the bow into the reed grass, paddled in as far as I could go, then, before the current could shove the boat back, jumped up into the bow and dug the paddle into the mud, pushed, until the boat was up into the fringe of the marsh, balanced there, and then, as I stepped to the stern and pushed again with the paddle, it eased over the point and into the mouth of the creek. Now the current turned it broadside, but it was all right, for the marsh was there to hold it. I pushed against the marsh, paddled, and the boat moved up into the creek. I kept paddling all the way until I had reached the bend of the creek, seventy-five feet distant. There I moved the boat up into the marsh, where it held, secure.

I sat in the boat, panting for breath, exhausted. My arms were shaking from the exertion they had made. My face felt as if it were on fire.

After a few minutes I realized that there were four inches or more of water in the bottom of the boat. I had been too caught up in my efforts to think to bail it. I picked up the coffee can and began dipping water from the boat.

Yet the boat had performed well enough. I had simply not realized how powerful the river current could be. When I ventured out into the river again I must be careful to do so while the tide was right. The thing to do was not to work against the current but to go with it. If I wanted to go upstream I could go at slack tide, or while the tide was still coming in, not when it was ebbing. If I wanted to go downstream I could keep to the side of the marsh and nose in to rest when I grew tired, and when I got ready to return I would need only to swing the boat about and go back with the tide, using my paddle to steer.

While I was waiting there, preparatory to returning up

the creek to the dock, I heard a ship's whistle off toward town. I stood up in the boat and looked over the marsh grass. A half-mile or so downstream, a freighter was coming up the channel, preceded by a tugboat, bound for the fertilizer docks upstream. They would soon be passing right beyond the mouth of the creek.

I knew there would be wake, so I pushed my boat out of the marsh and paddled across the creek to where there would be a belt of reed grass between me and the creek mouth. I pushed up into the grass to wait, next to an old waterlogged tree trunk, or perhaps a piling—it was so decayed that I could not tell for sure—what was lying in the marsh, studded with barnacles and oyster shells.

Toward me they came, the tugboat first, then behind it, the towline slack in the water but ready, linking them, the freighter, many times the size of the tugboat, moving slowly and under control. They passed no more than several hundred feet off the creek mouth. The tugboat was the *Robert H. Lockwood*. I could see the crew of the tugboat, and even the captain in the wheelhouse. I waved my hand, and one of the crew on the deck saw me and waved back. Then the freighter eased by, stately and high-sided, with crewmen standing along the railings watching over the sides. I saw the cargo booms, the wheelhouse, the lifeboats attached to the davits, the air ports, the companionway ladders, the portholes, the deck machinery. At the stern a French tricolor was flying. Beneath the raised stern the blades of a propeller thumped slowly, half out of the water. I read the name and the home port on the stern as the freighter moved upstream: *FINISTERRE:* BORDEAUX.

The wake came surging toward the shoreline, and as it broke along the marsh there was a low, churning sound of water, rolling steadily upstream. Into the delta of the creek mouth the hills of water flooded, to beat against the marsh bank and be contained by the reed grass. Even through the expanse of marsh separating me from the open water I could feel the surge. My little boat rocked as it lifted above the water and dropped back. It bumped against the tree trunk, which momentarily was almost covered by the flowing water. Then it was calm again in the marsh.

The creek was well down as I paddled up to the dock behind Mr. Simons' house. I had simply arrived at the water's edge too late, when the tide was already moving out. In a couple of days' time the tide would be high late enough in the morning so that I could get out in my boat while it was still coming in, I thought. Then there would be no trouble. I would go upstream with the tide a little while, and paddle back to the creek when the current slacked off.

I tied my boat up to the dock and walked on back up the bluff and across the oak grove toward our house. As I entered the gate my father was working in the garden.

"Where've you been for so long?" he asked.

"Just paddling around in the marsh," I said.

EPILOGUE

Andy Warhol

LOVE (PRIME)

A: Should we walk? It's really beautiful out.
B: No.
A: Okay.

Taxi was from Charleston, South Carolina—a confused, beautiful debutante who'd split with her family and come to New York. She had a poignantly vacant, vulnerable quality that made her a reflection of everybody's private fantasies. Taxi could be anything you wanted her to be—a little girl, a woman, intelligent, dumb, rich, poor—anything. She was a wonderful, beautiful blank. The mystique to end all mystiques.

She was also a compulsive liar; she just couldn't tell the truth about anything. And what an actress. She could really turn on the tears. She could somehow always make you believe her—that's how she got what she wanted.

Taxi invented the mini-skirt. She was trying to prove to her family back in Charleston that she could live on nothing, so she would go to the Lower East Side and buy the cheapest clothes, which happen to be little girls' skirts, and her waist was so tiny she could get away with it. Fifty cents a skirt. She was the first person to wear ballet tights as a complete outfit, with big earrings to dress it up. She was an innovator—out of necessity as well as fun—and the big fashion magazines picked up on her look right away. She was pretty incredible.

We were introduced by a mutual friend who had just made a fortune promoting a new concept in kitchen appliances on television quiz shows. After one look at Taxi I could see that she had more problems than anybody I'd ever met. So beautiful but so sick. I was really intrigued.

She was living off the end of her money. She still had a nice Sutton Place apartment, and now and then she would talk a rich friend into giving her a wad. As I said, she could turn on the tears and get anything she wanted.

In the beginning I had no idea how many drugs Taxi took, but as we saw more and more of each other it began to dawn on me how much of a problem she had.

Next in importance for her, after taking the drugs, was having the drugs. Hoarding them. She would hop in a limousine and make a run to Philly crying the whole way that she had no amphetamines. And somehow she would always get them because there was just something about Taxi. Then she would add it to the pound she had stashed away at the bottom of her footlocker.

One of her rich sponsor-friends even tried to set her up in the fashion business, designing her own line of clothes. He'd bought a loft on 29th Street outright from a schlock designer who had just bought a condominium in Florida and wanted to leave the city fast. The sponsor-friend took over the operation of the whole loft with the seven seamstresses still at their machines and brought Taxi in to start designing. The mechanics of the business were all set up, all she had to do was come up with designs that were basically no more than copies of the outfits that she styled for herself.

She wound up giving "pokes" to the seamstresses and playing with the bottles of beads and buttons and trimmings that the previous manager had left lining the wall. The business, needless to say, didn't prosper. Taxi would spend most of the day at lunch uptown at Reuben's ordering their Celebrity Sandwiches—the Anna Maria Alberghetti, the Arthur Godfrey, the Morton Downey were her favorites—and she would keep running into the ladies room and sticking her finger down her throat and throwing each one up. She was obsessed with not getting fat. She'd eat and eat on a spree and then throw up and throw up, and then take four downers and pop off for four days at a time. Meanwhile her "friends" would come in to "rearrange" her pocketbook while she was sleeping. When she'd wake up four days later she'd deny that she'd been asleep.

At first I thought that Taxi only hoarded drugs. I knew that hoarding is a kind of selfishness, but I thought it was only with the drugs that she was that way. I'd see her beg people for enough for a poke and then go and file it in the bottom of her footlocker in its own little envelope with a date on it. But I finally realized that Taxi was selfish about absolutely everything.

One day when she was still in the designing business a friend and I went to visit her. There were scraps and scraps of velvets and satins all over the floor and my friend asked if she could have a piece just large enough to make a cover for a dictionary she owned. There were thousands of scraps all over the floor, practically covering our feet, but Taxi looked at her and said, "The best time is in the morning. Just come by in the morning and look through the pails out front and you'll probably find something."

Another time we were riding in a cab and she was crying that she didn't have any money, that she was poor, and she opened her pocketbook for a Kleenex and I happened to catch site of one of those clear plastic change purses all stuffed with green. I didn't bother to say anything. What was the point? But the next day I asked her, "What happened to that clear plastic change purse you had yesterday that was stuffed with money?" She said, "It was stolen last night at a discothèque." She couldn't tell the truth about anything.

Taxi hoarded brassieres. She kept around fifty brassieres—in graduated shades of beige, through pale pink and deep rose to coral and white—in her trunk. They all had the price tags on them. She would never remove a price tag, not even from the clothes she wore. One day the same friend that asked her for the scrap of material was short on cash and Taxi owed her money. So she decided to take a brassiere that still had the Bendel's tags on it back to the store and get a refund. When Taxi wasn't looking she stuffed it into her bag and went uptown. She went to the lingerie department and explained that she was returning the bra for a friend—it was obvious that this girl was far from an A-cup. The sales lady disappeared for ten minutes and then came back holding the bra and some kind of log book and said, "Madame. This bra was purchased in 1956." Taxi was a hoarder.

Taxi had an incredible amount of makeup in her bag and in her footlocker: fifty pairs of lashes arranged according to size, fifty mascara wands, twenty mascara cakes, every shade of Revlon shadow ever made—iridescent and regular, matte and shiny—twenty Max Factor blush-ons. . . She'd spend hours with her makeup bags Scotch-taping little labels on everything, dusting and shining the bottles and compacts. Everything had to look perfect.

But she didn't care about anything below the neck.

She would never take a bath.

I would say, "Taxi. Take a bath." I'd run the water and she would go into the bathroom with her bag and stay in there for an hour. I'd yell, "Are you in the tub?" "Yes, I'm in the tub." Splash splash. But then I'd hear her tip-toeing around the bathroom and I'd peek through the keyhole and she'd be standing in front of the mirror, putting on more makeup over what was already caked on her face. She would never put water on her face—only those degreasers, those little tissue-thin papers you press on that remove the oils without ruining the makeup. She used those.

A few minutes later I'd peek through the keyhole again and she'd be recopying her address book—or somebody else's address book, it didn't matter—or else she'd be sitting with a yellow legal pad making the list of all the men she'd ever been to bed with dividing them into three categories—"Slept," "Fucked," and "Cuddled." If she made a mistake on the last line and it looked messy, she'd tear it off and start all over. After an hour, she'd come out of the bathroom and I'd say gratuitously, "You didn't take a bath." "Yes. Yes I did."

I slept in the same bed with Taxi once. Someone was after her and she didn't want to sleep with him, so she crawled into bed in the next room with me. She fell asleep and I just couldn't stop looking at her, because I was so fascinated-but-horrified. Her hands kept crawling, they couldn't sleep, they couldn't stay still. She scratched herself constantly, digging her nails in and leaving marks. In three hours she woke up and said immediately that she hadn't been asleep.

Taxi drifted away from us after she started seeing a singer-musician who can only be described as The Definitive Pop Star—possibly of all time—who was then fast gaining recognition on both sides of the Atlantic as the thinking man's Elvis Presley. I missed having her around, but I told myself that it was probably a good thing that he was taking care of her now, because maybe he knew how to do it better than we had.

Taxi died a few years ago in Hawaii where an important industrialist had taken her for a "rest." I hadn't seen her for years.

SELECTED BIBLIOGRAPHY

Allen, Hervey, and DuBose Heyward. *Carolina Chansons: Legends of the Low Country.* New York: The Macmillan Company, 1924.

Allen, Hervey. *Anthony Adverse.* New York: Holt, Rinehart and Winston, 1933.

Allen, Hervey. *Israfel.* New York: Holt, Rinehart and Winston, 1934.

Alpert, Hollis. *The Life and Times of Porgy and Bess: The Story of an American Classic.* New York: Alfred A. Knopf, 1990.

Bartram, William. *The Travels of William Bartram: Naturalist's Edition.* Edited by Francis Harper. New Haven: Yale University Press, 1958.

Bennett, John. *Doctor to the Dead: Grotesque Legends and Folk Tales of Old Charleston.* New York and Toronto: Rinehart and Company, 1943.

Bennett, John. *Madame Margot: A Legend of Old Charleston.* Columbia: University of South Carolina Press, 1951.

Bennett, John. *Master Skylark,* New York: The Century Company, 1922.

Bennett, John. *The Treasure of Peyre Gaillard,* New York: The Century Company, 1906.

Bresee, Clyde. *How Grand a Flame: A Chronicle of a Plantation Family, 1815-1947.* Chapel Hill: Algonquin Books, 1992.

Bresee, Clyde. *Sea Island Yankee.* Chapel Hill: Algonquin Books, 1986.

Chestnut, Mary Boykin. *Mary Chestnut's Civil War.* Edited by C. Vann Woodward. New Haven and London: Yale University Press, 1981.

Chyet, Stanley F. "Ludwig Lewisohn in Charleston." *American Jewish Historical Quarterly 54 (1965):* 296-322.

Conroy, Pat. *The Great Santini.* New York: Houghton Mifflin, 1976.

Conroy, Pat. *The Lords of Discipline,* New York: Houghton Mifflin Company, 1980.

Conroy, Pat. *The Prince of Tides.* New York: Houghton Mifflin Company, 1986.

Conroy, Pat. *The Water is Wide.* New York: Houghton Mifflin Company, 1972.

Davis, R. B., C.H. Holman, and L.D. Rubin, Jr., eds. *Southern Writing 1585-1920.* New York: The Odyssey Press, 1970.

Dickey, James. *Poems: 1957-1967.* Middletown, Conn.: Wesleyan University Press, 1968.

Durant, Mary B., and Michael Harwood. *On the Road with John James Audubon.* New York: Dodd, Mead & Company, Inc., 1980.

Elliott, William. *Carolina Sports by Land and Water; Including Incidents of Devil-Fishing, Wild-cat, Deer and Bear Hunting, etc.* New York: Darby and Jackson, 1859.

Foote, Shelby. *The Civil War: A Narrative.* New York: Vintage Books, 1986.

Fox, William Price. *Southern Fried Plus Six*. Orangeburg, S.C.: Sandlapper Publishing, 1968.

Fraser, Walter J., Jr. *Charleston! Charleston! The History of a Southern City*. Columbia: University of South Carolina Press, 1987.

Galsworthy, John. "A Hedonist." *The Century Magazine* 102, no. 3 (1921): 321-325.

Greene, Harlan. *Charleston: City of Memory*. Photography by N. Jane Iseley. Greensboro, N.C.: Legacy Publications, 1987.

Greene, Harlan. *What the Dead Remember*. New York: Dutton/Signet, 1991.

Greene, Harlan. *Why We Never Danced the Charleston*, New York: Viking Penguin, Inc., 1985.

Griswold, Francis. *A Sea Island Lady*. New York: William Morrow & Co., Inc., 1938.

Guilds, John Caldwell. *Simms: A Literary Life*. Fayetteville: University of Arkansas Press, 1992.

Harris, Alex, ed. *A World Unsuspected: Portraits of Southern Childhood*. Chapel Hill and London: University of North Carolina Press, 1987.

Hayne, Paul Hamilton. *Poems of Paul Hamilton Hayne*. Boston: D. Lothrop and Company, 1882.

Heyward, DuBose. *Mamba's Daughters: A Novel of Charleston*. New York: The Literary Guild, 1929.

Heyward, DuBose. *Peter Ashley*. New York: Farrar and Rinehardt, 1932.

Heyward, DuBose. *Porgy: A Novel*. Charleston: The Tradd Street Press, 1985.

Heyward, DuBose and Dorothy Heyward. *Porgy: A Play in Four Acts*. Garden City, N.Y.: Doubleday, Page and Company, 1927.

Hoffman, Daniel. *Poe, Poe, Poe, Poe, Poe, Poe, Poe*. Garden City, N.Y.: Doubleday and Company, 1972.

Humphreys, Josephine. *Dreams of Sleep*. New York: The Viking Press, 1984.

Humphreys, Josephine. *The Fireman's Fair*. New York: The Viking Press, 1991.

Humphreys, Josephine. *Rich in Love*. New York: The Viking Press, 1987.

James, Henry. *The American Scene*. Introduction and Notes by Leon Edel. Bloomington and London: Indiana University Press, 1968.

Kimball, Robert, and Alfred Simm. *The Gershwins*. New York: Atheneum Publishers, 1973.

King, Susan Pettigru. *Gerald Gray's Wife* and *Lily: A Novel*. Introduction by Jane H. and William H. Pease, Durham and London: Duke University Press, 1993.

Lewisohn, Ludwig. *The Case of Mr. Crump*. New York: Farrar, Straus and Company, 1947.

Lewisohn, Ludwig. *Up Stream: An American Chronicle*. New York: Modern Library, 1926.

Lindsay, Nick, transcriber. *An Oral History of Edisto Island: The Life and Times of Bubberson Brown*. Goshen, Ind.: Pinchpenny Press, 1977.

Lindsay, Nick, transcriber. *An Oral History of Edisto Island: Sam Gadsden Tells the Story*. Goshen, Ind.: Pinchpenny Press, 1975.

Lowell, Amy. *A Dome of Many-Colored Glass*. New York: The Macmillan Company, 1916.

Lowell, Amy. *What's O'clock*. Boston and New York: Houghton Mifflin Company, 1925.

Marrot, H.V. *The Life and Letters of John Galsworth*. New York: Charles Scribner's Sons, 1936.

Mikell, I. Jenkins. *Rumbling of the Chariot Wheels*. Columbia, S.C.: The R. L. Bryan Company, 1990.

Murray, Chalmers S. *Here Come Joe Mungin, A Novel*. New York: G. P. Putnam's and Sons, 1942.

Naipaul, V. S. "Charleston: The Religion of the Past." In *A Turn in the South*. New York: Vintage International, 1970.

O'Brien, Michael and David Moltke-Hansen, eds. *Intellectual Life in Antebellum Charleston*. Knoxville: University of Tennessee Press, 1986.

O'Brien, Michael. "The South Considers Her Most Peculiar: Charleston and Modern Southern Thought." *The South Carolina Historical Magazine 94, no. 2 (!DATE!)*: 119-133.

Oliphant, Mary C. Simms, A.T. Odell, T.C.D. Eaves, T.C.D., eds. *The Letters of William Gilmore Simms*. Columbia: University of South Carolina Press, 1954.

O'Neill, Frank Q. "Light on the Water: The Golden Age of Charleston's Art." *Kiawah Island Legends* 2 no. 1 (1991): 31-36.

Percy, Walker. *The Last Gentleman.* New York: Avon Books, 1978.

Peterkin, Julia. *Bright Skin.* Indianapolis: Bobbs-Merrill Company, 1932.

Peterkin, Julia. *Black April.* Dunwoody, Ga.: Norma S. Berg, 1972.

Peterkin, Julia. *Scarlett Sister Mary.* Indianapolis: Bobbs-Merrill, 1925.

Pinckney, Josephine. *Great Mischief.* New York: The Viking Press, 1948.

Pinckney, Josephine. *Sea-Drinking Cities.* New York and London: Harper & Brothers Publishers, 1927.

Pinckney, Josephine. *Three O'clock Dinner.* New York: The Viking Press, 1945.

Poe, Edgar Allan. *The Unabridged Edgar Allan Poe.* Philadelphia: Running Press Book Publishers, 1983.

Powell, Padgett. *Edisto.* New York: Farrar, Straus, Giroux and Company, 1984.

Pringle, Elizabeth Allston (Patience Pennington). *A Woman Rice Planter.* Introduction by Charles Joyner. Columbia: University of South Carolina Press, 1992.

Ravenel, Beatrice. *The Yemassee Lands.* Edited by Louis D. Rubin, Jr. Chapel Hill: University of North Carolina Press, 1969.

Ravenel, Mrs. St. Julien. *Charleston: The Place and the People.* New York: Macmillan, 1906.

Ripley, Alexandra. *Scarlett.* New York: Warner Books, 1991.

Rosengarten, Theodore. "History Alley, Memory Lane." in *Places With a Past: New Site-Specific Art at Charleston's Spoleto Festival*. New York: Rizzoli International Publications, 1991.

Rosengarten, Theodore. *Tombee: Portrait of a Cotton Planter*. New York: William Morrow and Company, 1986.

Rubin, Louis D., Jr. *The Boll Weevil and the Triple Play*. Charleston: The Tradd Street Press, 1979.

Rubin, Louis D., Jr. *The Edge of the Swamp: A Study in the Literature and Society of the Old South*. Baton Rouge and London: Louisiana State University Press, 1989.

Rubin, Louis D., Jr. "Finisterre." *The Southern Review* 14 (1978): 813-836.

Rubin, Louis D., Jr. *The Heat of the Sun*. Atlanta: Longstreet Press, 1995.

Sabatini, Rafael. *The Carolinian*. New York: Grossett & Dunlap, 1924.

Salinger, Wendy. *Folly River*. New York: Dutton Signet, a division of Penguin Books USA, 1980.

Sass, Herbert Ravenel. "Carolina Marshes." *Country Life*. January (1930): 35-38, 78-79.

Sass, Herbert Ravenel. *The Emperor Brims*. New York: Doubleday, Doran, and Company, 1941.

Sass, Herbert Ravenel. *Look Back to Glory*. Indianapolis: Bobbs-Merrill Company, 1933.

Saunders, Boyd and Ann McAden. *Alfred Hutty and the Charleston Renaissance*. Orangeburg, S.C.: Sandlapper Publishing Company, 1990.

Sayers, Valerie. *The Distance Between Us*. New York: Doubleday, 1994.

Simms, William Gilmore, ed. *The Charleston Book: A Miscellany in Prose and Verse*. Introduction by David Moltke-Hansen. Spartanburg: The Reprint Company, 1983.

Simms, William Gilmore. *Charleston: The Palmetto City*. Columbia: University of South Carolina Press, 1976.

Simms, William Gilmore. *The Life of Francis Marion*. Freeport, New York: Books for Libraries Press, 1971.

Simms, William Gilmore. *The Writings of William Gilmore Simms: Centennial Edition*. Columbia: University of South Carolina Press, 1974.

Smythe, Augustine T., Herbert Ravenel Sass, Alfred Huger, Beatrice Ravenel, Thomas R. Waring, Archibald Rutledge, Josephine Pinckney, Caroline Pinckney Rutledge, DuBose Heyward, Katherine C. Hutson, and Robert W. Gordon. *The Carolina Low-Country*. New York: The Macmillan Company, 1931.

Stoney, Samuel Gaillard. *Charleston: Azaleas and Old Bricks*. New York: Houghton Mifflin Company, 1939.

Stoney, Samuel Gaillard. *This is Charleston*. Charleston: The Carolina Art Association, 1944.

Stoney, Samuel Gaillard. *Plantations of the South Carolina Lowcountry*. Charleston: The Carolina Art Association, 1938.

Timrod, Henry. *The Collected Poems*. Edited by Edd Winfield Parks and Aileen Wells Parks. Athens: The University of Georgia Press, 1965.

Styron, William. *Set This House on Fire*. New York: Random House, 1960.

Timrod, Henry. *The Essays of Henry Timrod*. Edited by Edd Winfield Parks, Athens: The University of Georgia Press, 1942.

Timrod, Henry. *Poems of Henry Timrod*. Boston and New York: Houghton, Mifflin and Company, 1899.

Trowbridge, John Townsend. *The Desolate South 1865-1866*. Edited by Gordon Carroll. Boston and Toronto: Little, Brown and Company, 1956.

Warhol, Andy. *The Philosophy of Andy Warhol: (From A to B and Back Again)*. New York and London: Harcourt Brace Jovanovich, 1975.

Wister, Owen. *Lady Baltimore*. New York: The Macmillan Company, 1906.

Wolfe, Thomas. *Look Homeward, Angel: A Story of the Buried Life*. New York: Charles Scribner's Sons, 1957.

Worthington, Curtis. "Legends, Lyrics, and Letters: The Literary Renaissance in 1920's Charleston." *Charleston Place* 1 (1995): 88-98.

Yearbook of the Poetry Society of South Carolina. Charleston: Poetry Society of South Carolina, 1921.

INDEX OF TITLES AND AUTHOR'S NAMES

Al Aaraaf, xxviii

Alchemy, xxx, 105-106

Allen, Hervey, xxix, xxx, 105-106

Ambassadors, The, xxxvi

American Scene, The, xxxvi, 85-91

Anthony Adverse, xxx

Arrow of Lightning, The, xxxii

Aspects of the Pines, xxiii, 7

Aspern Papers, The, xxxvi

Audubon, John James, xliii, xliv

Bartram's Travels, xxi, xxii, 3-4

Bartram, William, xxi, xxii, 3-4

Battle of Charleston Harbor, The, xxiii

Benet, Stephen Vincent, xxii

Bennett, John, xxix, xxx, xxxi, xxxiii, xlv, 106, 125-141

Bostonians, The, xxxvi

Brawley, Benjamin, xliii

Bresee, Clyde, xliii

Brown, Bubberson, The Life and Times of, xl, 313-314

Bryant, William Cullen, xliii

Buzzard Island, 107

Captain Blood, xxxix

Carolina Chansons, xxx

Carolina Marshes, 191-199

Carolina Sports by Land and Water; Including Incidents of Devil-fishing, Wild-cat, Deer, and Bear Hunting, Etc, xxviii.

Carolinian, The, xxxix, 175-190

Case of Mr. Crump, The, xxxix, 166-174

Cassique of the Kiawah, The, xxv

Charleston, xxiii, xxvii, 27-28

Charleston: Azaleas and Old Bricks, xxxviii

Charleston Book, The, xxiv

Charleston, SC, 7 P.M., 216-217

Charleston, South Carolina, 92

Charleston: The Place and the People, xxxii

Chestnut, Mary Boykin, xliii

Civil War: A Narrative, The, xliii, 239-250

Coley Moke, xlii, 251-259

Conrad, Joseph, xxxix

Conroy, Pat, xxxix, xli, 221-238

Cotton Boll, The, xxvii, 28-32

Daisy Miller, xxxvi

Davidson, Donald, xliii

Day at Chee-ha, A, 37-43

Deliverance, xl

Doctor Golf, xlii

Doctor to the Dead, xxix

Dickey, James, xxxix, 203-209

Dixiana Moon, xlii

Dreams of Sleep, xlii

Dusk, 107-108

Earthquake Weather, xl

Edge of the Swamp, The, 9-11

Edisto, xlii, 323-329

Elliott, William, xxvii, 37-43

Emerson, Ralph Waldo, xliii

Emperor Brims, The, xxxviii

Ephraim Bartlett, the Edisto Raftsman, 12-26

Epitaph In A Church-yard In Charleston, South Carolina, 94

European, The, xxxvi

Farquhar, George, xx

Finisterre, 330-360

Fireman's Fair, The, xlii

Folly River, xl

Foote, Shelby, xli, xlii, xliii, 239-250

Fox, William Price, xlii, 251-261

Frost, Robert, xliii

Gadsden, Sam, Tells the Story, xl, 293-312

Galsworthy, John, xxxviii, 142-149

Gershwin, George, xxxiv, xxxv

Gold Bug, The, xxviii, 142-149

Ginsberg, Allen, xliii

Great Mischief, xxxi

Greene, Harlan, xxi, xlii, xlv, 262-275

Griswold, Francis, xliii

Hag, 110

Hayne, Paul Hamilton, xxiii, xxiv, xxxi, 7-9

Hedonist, A, xxxviii, 142-149

Heyward, Dorothy, xxxiv

Heyward, DuBose, xxix, xxx, xxxii, xxxiii, xxxiv, xxxv, xxxvii, 107-108

Home Sketches or Life Along the Highways and Byways of South Carolina, xxv

Humphreys, Josephine, xxxix, xli, 276-292

Israfel, xxx

James, Henry, xxxvi, xxxvii, 85-91

Joyce, James, xli

Kerouac, Jack, xl

King, Edward, xliii

King, Susan Pettigru, xliii

Kleinzahler, August, xl, 210

Kuhn, Dorothy, xxxiii

Lady Baltimore, xxxvi, xxxviii, 95-101

Laocoon, xviii, 8

Last Gentleman, The, xliii, 315-322

Legare, Hugh Swinton, xliii

Legare, James Matthewes, xliii

Lewis, Sinclair, xliv

Lewisohn, Ludwig, xxxviii, 166-174

Light Moonshine Bright, xlii

Lindsay, Nick, xl, 211-213, 293-314

Lindsay, Vachel, xl

Literature In The South, xxvii

Longitude Lane, 210

Look Back to Glory, xxxviii

Look Homeward, Angel, xliv

Love (Prime), 363-367

Love In The Ruins, xliii

Lowell, Amy, xxxiii, xxxvi, xxxvii, 92-94

Lowell, James Russell, xxxvii

Lowell, Robert, xxxvii

Madame Margot, xxx, 125-141

Magnolia Gardens, xxiii, 8

Main Street, xliv

Mamba's Daughters, xxxiv, xxxvi

Mamoulian, Rouben, xxix

Master Skylark, xxix

McCullers, Carson, xliii

Message in the Bottle, xliii

Middleton Place, The, 93

Mikell, Isaac Jenkins, xliii

Millay, Edna St. Vincent, xliii

Miller, Arthur, xliii

Monck's Corner, xlii, 259-261

Monroe, Harriet, xxix

Moviegoer, The, xliii

Murray, Chalmers, xliv

Nabokov, Vladimir, xliv

Naipaul, V.S., xliv

Oblong Box, The, xxviii

Ode. Sung on the Occasion of Decorating the Graves of the Confederate Dead at Magnolia Cemetery, Charleston, S.C., 1867, xxvii, 33

Oral History of Edisto Island: Sam Gadsden Tells the Story, An, xl, 293-312

Oral History of Edisto Island: The Life and Times of Bubberson Brown, An, xl, 313-314

Partisan, The, xxv

Percy, Walker, xliii, 315-322

Peter Ashley, xxxii

Peterkin, Julia, xliv

Pilot Boat, 211

Pinckney, Josephine, xxix, xxx, xxxi, 109-110

Pirates, The, 113-119

Plantations of the Lowcountry, xxxviii

Poe, Edgar Allan, xxvi, xxviii, xxx, 44-82

Poem, 212-213

Porgy, xxix, xxxiii, xxxiv, xxxvi, 150-165

Porgy and Bess, xxix, xxxiii, xxxiv, xxxvi

Portrait of a Lady, xxxvi

Pound, Ezra, xxxvii

Powell, Padgett, xlii, 323-329

Prince of Tides, The, xli, 221-238

Pringle, Elizabeth Allston, xliv

Quincy, Josiah, xliv

Ransom, John Crowe, xxix

Ravenel, Beatrice Witte, xxix, xxx, xxxi, xxxii, xxxiii, xxxvii, 111-122

Ravenel, Harriott Horry, xxxii

Recruiting Officer, The, xx

Rich in Love, xlii, 276-292

Rosengarten, Theodore, xliv

Rubin, Louis D., Jr., xxv, xxvi, xxxii, xxxix, xliii, 330-360

Ruby Red, xlii

Sabatini, Rafael, xxxix, 175-190

Salinger, Wendy, xl, 214-217

Salt Marsh, The, 203-204

Sandburg, Carl, xliv

Sass, George Herbert, xliv

Sass, Herbert Ravenel, xxxviii, 191-199

Sayers, Valerie, xliv

Scaramouche, xxxix

Sea-Drinking Cities, xxxi, 109

Seasmoke, 214-215

Shiloh, xliii

Simms, William Gilmore, xxiii, xxiv, xxv, xxvi, xxvii, 9-26

Slave Quarters, 204-209

South Considers Her Most Peculiar: Charleston and Modern Southern Thought, The, xxxi

Southern Fried Plus Six, xlii

Stein, Gertrude, xliv

Stoney, Samuel Gaillard, xxxviii

Styron, William, xliv

Tate, Allen, xxix

Thackeray, William Makepeace, xliv

Three O'Clock Dinner, xxxi

Tidewater, 111-113

Timrod, Henry, xxiii, xxvi, xxvii, xl, 27-33

To Science, xxviii

Treasure of Peyre Gaillard, The, xxix

Trowbridge, John Townsend, xliv

Turn of the Screw, The, xxxvi

Virginian, The, xxxviii

Wandering Minstrel's Song, The, 106

Warhol, Andy, xxii, 363-367

Warren, Robert Penn, xxix

Washington Square, xxxvi

Why We Never Danced the Charleston, xlii, 262-275

Wilde, Oscar, xliv

Williams, Tennessee, xliv

Williams, William Carlos, xl

Wister, Owen, xxxvi, xxxvii, 95-101

Wolfe, Thomas, xliv

World Unsuspected: Portraits of Southern Childhood, A, xlii

Woman Named Drown, A, xlii

Yemassee, The, xxv

Yemassee Lands, The, 120-122

ABOUT THE EDITOR

Curtis Worthington was brought up in Charleston, South Carolina and is descended from Calhoun, Pickens, and other notable South Carolina families.

Educated in Montreal, South Florida, and Oxford, he is the author of occasional critical writing and literary history. He is a member of the Board of Governors of the South Carolina Academy of Authors. In 1967, he received the "Skylark Prize" from the Poetry Society of South Carolina.

He has traveled extensively in Europe, the Pacific and South-east Asia and is a practicing neurosurgeon in Charleston.